Crystals

Also by Ann Zavala

Mormon Wives
San Francisco Gold

Crystals

A Fiona Kendrick Mystery

Ann Zavala

A Tom Doherty Associates Book
New York

CRYSTALS

Copyright © 1996 by Ann Zavala

This book is printed on acid-free paper.

A Forge Book
Published by Tom Doherty Associates, Inc.
175 Fifth Avenue
New York, NY 10010

Forge® is a registered trademark of Tom Doherty Associates, Inc.

Library of Congress Cataloging-in-Publication Data

Zavala, Ann.
    Crystals : a Fiona Kendrick mystery / [Ann Zavala].
        p.   cm.
    "A Tom Doherty Associates book."
    ISBN 0-312-85440-4
    I. Title.
PS3576.A88C79   1996
813'.54—dc20   95-39743
                                                             CIP

First Edition: April 1996

Printed in the United States of America

0 9 8 7 6 5 4 3 2 1

To Megan-mouse, who is still
    happily alive.
And to Princess, who is waiting for
    us in Summer Land.

Crystals

I

"Toilet paper! Damn, how did I forget it three times in a row?" Fiona wailed as she coasted to a stop at the YIELD RIGHT OF WAY sign. She looked to the left, watching traffic, before she moved forward. "I'll pay the extra ten cents at the Stop and Rob."

It served her right for having missed the last sale at Safeway, when she should have bought several cases of stuff to store in the garage until they needed it. She had just about decided it was safe to pull out in front of an old green pickup when her head snapped forward and hit the steering wheel and light changed to darkness. Someone had smashed into the back of her van.

She awoke spitting teeth and blood. Her ears were ringing from the sound of the impact of metal on metal. She'd been rear-ended, and it felt as if the person who'd hit her hadn't even tried to stop.

"Oh shit, I don't have time for this," she thought groggily, as she tried to lift her head and focus her eyes. Everything was red. She thought she was looking through blood until she reached up and pushed her hair out of her eyes. A

blaring horn and the sound of swearing pulled her further
back toward consciousness.

Fiona reached for the door handle and was surprised to
discover that she was reclining at a ridiculous angle; the van
seat seemed to have broken.

"Megan, are you all right?"

"I think so, but it hurts to open my eyes," her daughter
said, slightly slurring her words.

"Hold on, kid, I think it's hospital time, just as soon as
I've sorted things out with the idiot who hit us."

Fiona pulled herself upright, wincing as she saw the
long gouge on her arm. Blood had spattered the wheel and
dripped on her new size sixteen jeans, bought because she
was, despite her best efforts, expanding at the hips again.

It was not going to be a good day.

Fiona realized there was a mounting furor of angry
horns honking behind her. She looked out the window as
the driver of the Malibu assault car got out and began to
survey the damage. She was a cute size-three blond girl who
didn't look old enough to have a driver's license and about
three years older than Megan. She smiled pertly at Fiona
and waved, an offhand flip that was meant to show that
there were no hard feelings about the accident and that
nothing much had been damaged.

Fiona considered murdering her.

"I'm a good woman, God. I take care of my kid, I feed
hungry animals, I don't use plastic unless it's absolutely
necessary—why me, God?"

The girl minced up to Fiona's window.

"No damage, so I guess we don't have to exchange
names and all that junk, do we?" the blonde said, peering
into the van. She studiously ignored the blood on Fiona's
face. She didn't even acknowledge Megan.

"Don't even try to leave without giving me every bit of
information I need to sue you. Do you realize you could
have killed my daughter in this accident?"

"Don't be silly, it was just a little fender bender!" The blonde was beginning to perceive, although dimly, that things might not go as easily as she'd expected.

"I mean my kid has a brain tumor and any blow to the head is dangerous to her. Your 'little fender bender' knocked her head into the metal side of the door. This is going to mean a major medical claim on your car insurance and your rates are going to be so high it'll be a couple of years before you're going to drive again. Now does that get your attention, you little twit?"

Fiona was clenching her teeth together so hard that her jaw ached.

"Well, gee, you can file if you want, but I don't think I have insurance," the girl said, pouting. "It's such a bore, having to spend all that money on the car instead of clothes."

"It's going to be even more of a bore to have everything you own sold because I want to be paid for the damage you did," Fiona pointed out. "Pull over into the schoolyard so we're out of the way. I'm going to call an ambulance for my daughter, and once she's on her way you can talk to the police. Don't try any funny stuff or I swear to God I'll run right up your tailpipe and over that pea-size little brain of yours."

The ambulance arrived in a matter of minutes. By then, Fiona had all the information she was going to get from the girl.

"I'm coming with you," she announced to the paramedics as they loaded Megan into the ambulance.

"I'm afraid you'll have to drive over to the hospital on your own, ma'am, we're not allowed to carry passengers."

Fiona was about to blast the man into the next county, then decided on a different tack. "All right, then, you'll have to take care of this yourself because she's a complicated case and even the slightest delay could cost her life. Be sure and call whoever is on duty from Alta neurosurgery even before you get to the hospital. They're the ones who have treated her before and know her case. It's important that she be seen by them right away. Do not under any circumstances leave this decision up to your emergency-room doctor, because by the time he decides there's a problem, she could be dead. She has a tectal glioma, with possible metastasis to the meninges." Fiona watched the paramedic writing frantically and held back a smile. It served him right for saying she couldn't go with her daughter.

"Oh, I almost forgot, and this is important. She has a shunt that blocks and she'll have to have another MRI almost immediately. She's immune-suppressed from radiation and there is a good chance that she's going to have a crack in her skull from the knock on the window frame because the radiation weakens the bone anyway."

The paramedic stared at Fiona, snapped his book shut and waved her into the emergency vehicle. He knew he'd been outmaneuvered.

It took four hours for the hospital staff to determine that neither of them had suffered anything more than cuts and bruises.

"You can both go home, but tell your husband that if either of you gets sleepy or has a bad headache, you're supposed to come back in," the neurosurgeon said. "I gave Megan some IM morphine. It should hold until she can get back to her medication at home."

"So, kid, we'll have a taxi ride, and then you can lie down while I have a good cry," Fiona said. The shock was beginning to kick in. Her head was a thousand miles from her body and the whole world buzzed when she talked.

Fiona opened the front door of the house and noted absently that the weatherstripping was still loose enough to trip the unwary visitor. She'd have to remind Harper to bash the nails back in place when he had a few seconds free during the weekend.

She sniffed. The smell of freshly brewed coffee and hot

rich cake suffused the air. She stopped in the hallway. Had
the blow on the head been bad enough to cause hallucina-
tions? Especially warm, chocolate-cake-scented olfactory
ones?

No one ought to be home now. Her husband, Harper,
should be at work. The only ones in the house would be all
twenty-seven of her cats, and Fiona didn't know a feline in
the world who would put on coffee and cake to heat.

"So you finally decided to show up!" Gia, Fiona's best
friend, greeted her. "Sally and I've been sitting in the
kitchen, talking about our sex lives and waiting for you to
come home. Sally has one, by the way, and I don't, sex life
that is." Gia was dressed in her usual swirl of red and blue
scarves and a blue skirt that reached almost to her ankles.
As usual she talked with the speed and precision of a buzz
saw. With her black hair and dark eyes, Gia could easily
have passed for a Gypsy.

"I hope you don't mind but Sally and I evicted at least
ten cats to the garage to keep them from trying to eat everything. Did you know that Princess likes white frosting?"

Her voice petered out as she looked at Fiona and
Megan. "Good God, there's blood all over you—what happened?" She reached out and took Fiona's arm, shocked by
the pallor that made her friend's red hair and freckles stand
out in stark relief against her white skin. The blood had
dried to dark brown stains on Fiona's shirt and her discol-
ored lips looked as if someone had hit her with a crowbar
and then had forgotten to stitch up the damage.

Gia reached out and hauled Megan along behind them.
"Come on, let's get you kids into the family room and settled on the sofa."

"Oh darlin', what happened this time?" Sally's Texas
drawl was almost thick enough to make her unintelligible.
As usual, Fiona thought, Sally looked disgustingly gorgeous. She was tall and rangy and had what had once been
brown hair, except that it had bleached in the California sun

to a beautiful shade of strawberry blond. She was also the kind of woman who could manage to wear ten thousand dollars' worth of diamonds and gold with jeans and make it all look perfect.

It took a few moments for Gia to fluff the pillows and for Sally to move four cats and make Fiona comfortable.

"Megan, honey, sit here beside your mother so we can keep an eye on you," Gia ordered.

"I think I'd rather go upstairs to my own bed. This couch isn't comfortable and my head aches." Megan looked over to her mother for confirmation that it was all right for her to go.

"Just keep the intercom open from your room. But the instant it shuts off, you'll have to come back down here."

Megan didn't even have the energy for her usual whine, which was something along the lines of "you always treat me like a baby." Instead, she just trudged upstairs, turned on the intercom and fell face down in the bed. Her head hurt too much to do anything else.

Gia and Sally bustled around their friend's kitchen and family room, setting up one of the wooden television tables to hold coffee and a piece of cake.

"Oh Lord, that feels good," Fiona said gratefully as she leaned back against the sofa cushions. "I'm beginning to ache in places I didn't know I had and I can't stop shaking."

"So tell us, what happened?" Gia asked.

"And don't leave out any of the gory details," Sally said. "Look at you, with blood all over the place!"

"Someone rear-ended me." Fiona was racked with chills.

"Here." Gia leaned over the table and lifted up the sea-foam-green afghan made from the best mohair she'd been able to afford when she knitted it for her friend, and wrapped it around Fiona's shoulders. "This should help you warm up."

Princess, the top Siamese in the twenty-seven-cat pack,

instantly settled in Fiona's lap, and another cat climbed to the back of the sofa and began to purr in her ear.

"What are you and Sally doing here? Did I forget something?" Fiona asked when the shaking and chills subsided a little.

"Don't you remember?" Gia frowned. "You invited us over for coffee and a good gossip session. That bump on your head must have done real damage if it wiped that out of your brain."

Fiona closed her eyes and put her head back on the couch, resting it mostly on the cat. "Oh God, I did forget. Megan was up last night with problems and I had a weird nightmare and then I got in the accident and everything else just got bumped straight out of my mind."

Fiona moved her head gently, trying to ease the ache that started at the back of her neck and ran upward to the crown of her head. She hoped the cute little blonde was beginning to hurt, too.

"On top of everything else that is going wrong in my life, I think I'm going into early Alzheimer's. I can't remember anything for more than a couple of minutes. How could I have forgotten that you guys were coming over when I've been looking forward to it for days? That was one of the reasons I was out shopping. I couldn't have guests over who might need to use the bathroom if I didn't have toilet paper and then I forgot the stupid stuff anyway."

"That's not Alzheimer's, that's middle-aged memory crisis, two different things entirely," Gia said. "I should know, I just got blasted by Larry this morning for forgetting to pick up his suits at the dry cleaners when I knew he needed them. He didn't want to hear me say I'd forgotten again. He's absolutely certain there's some malign reason that I don't want to do wifely things for him. But it's just that I always have so much on my mind."

"Knowing Larry and the way he acts, maybe you really

don't want to do something for him. No one in their right mind wants to do a favor for a snake. He doesn't hit you, does he? I saw a report on family abuse last night and some of the things I've seen Larry do came awful close to what these people were talking about."

"Nope. No abuse, except for his normal shitty moods. The first time he touches me, he's going to be so severely sorry that it will take him weeks to recover," Gia said.

"I've seen him in action. You don't need him, you know. No woman as nice as you needs trash like that."

If it had been anyone other than Gia, Fiona would never have said such a thing about Larry. But she had shared too much of Gia's frustration and anger to be anything other than brutally honest about her friend's husband. Even Sally knew all about the terrible times Gia had been through with the man they called Larry the Louse.

"I keep thinking that this year, it'll get better. We've been through twenty years of a lousy marriage and wouldn't you think he'd like a better home life? I know I'm getting tired of sticking around with a man who is never satisfied and never happy, especially since it's taken a real turn for the worse these last couple of months," Gia said as she poured a cup of coffee, liberally lacing it with sugar. "Here, drink this. A toast to my rotten husband and your terrible memory!"

Sally lifted her cup in a salute, and they all sipped the hot brew in silence. Outside a cat meowed and scratched at the garage door, demanding entry to the kitchen.

"Would you go let the cats in? They can tell something is wrong and they want to come in to see what it is."

"Yes, oh Cat Mother of the Western World. We wouldn't want the poor felines to get some kind of complex," Gia kidded her as she opened the door.

"This whole thing is beginning to wear me down," Fiona said as the cats dashed in to inspect everything in the kitchen. "I'm always too busy and too tired, there's never enough money and then something like this accident happens." Incautiously, she took a large swig of the coffee and almost burned out the roof of her mouth. She'd forgotten that Gia considered coffee drinkable only when it approached the temperature of hot lava. Her memory was definitely going.

Gia nodded. "Same thing with me and I don't have a kid and a thousand cats, like you do. But I still can't get ahead, either. Even that killer budget we worked out only lasted until the car needed a new computer to make the fuel injection work. Wham, six hundred dollars onto the Visa." Gia shook her head at the memory.

"Budget. That's a laugh," Fiona said. "There's a two-hundred-and-fifty-dollar deductible and I don't have the money to put into getting the car fixed right now no matter how hard I squeeze. And I still need toilet paper and cat litter."

"I'm positive someone's out to get us," Gia said. "That's the only explanation. Somewhere someone is just standing there at the sidelines of life, waiting for a chance to throw shit on us."

Sally interrupted her, waiving away Gia's comment.

"Oh, that's just an exaggeration, you girls. I know my life runs pretty smooth. We have our little crises, but you two always seem to be constantly in a state of trouble that you cause yourself."

Sally had been her friend for over twenty-five years, ever since their first day in college, but at the moment Fiona wondered what she'd ever seen in a woman who had never had any serious problems in her entire life. Of course it helped for Sally to have inherited mega-millions from her parents when she turned twenty-one. In fact, Fiona had wondered more than once why Sally and her husband, Carl, even bothered to live next door to her in this middle-class neighborhood. Surely they would have been more at home somewhere on Nob Hill or over in Marin.

"Believe me, Sally, trouble is real," Fiona said. She snuggled farther down into the comfort of the mohair afghan.

Gia looked thoughtfully at the cake she had been eating as if it might hold the answers for her life. "You know, maybe there's something to this 'bad luck' we're always having."

"What do you mean?" Fiona asked.

Gia shrugged. "I'm beginning to have a funny feeling about the way our lives are going. All except Sally, of course, whose life is perfect." Gia didn't like Sally nearly as much as Fiona did.

"Something is wrong and I can feel it deep in my bones," Gia went on. "My grandmother used to talk about these kinds of feelings when I'd visit her. She was certain bad luck happened because someone sent it. I always thought she was not only uneducated, but also nuts. Now I wonder if she might have been right. For instance, how long has it been since you've sold a painting, other than at craft fairs?"

Fiona had to stop and think. "Over a year, except for the calendar pictures and those are at slave's wages. I keep sending out the photos and contacting people and hanging paintings in dentists' offices and at the bank and nothing happens, except that the paintings usually get ripped off."

"Right!" Gia said triumphantly. "And look at me. I've written books that get nominated for big prizes, books that sell well and stay in print. But I've gone years without a contract. Perfectly good submissions come back with 'We liked the writing and the ideas were good, but it doesn't quite fit our line right now.' I sit there and scream at the letters because if the editors like the ideas and the writing, why the hell don't they buy it! The screaming makes me feel better, which is good because it doesn't make a bit of difference to the editors."

"Maybe it's because your kind of writing doesn't have a

market anymore," Sally said. "And as for Fiona, maybe she hasn't quite made the right connections for people to appreciate her art."

Gia paused to take another bite of cake in lieu of stabbing Sally with the knife she'd used to cut it, and then continued. "Nope, it's not anything we're doing. The only answer that really makes sense is that someone actually is out to get us."

Fiona looked around the cozy family room, which should have been at least ten feet wider and twenty feet longer for all the stuff she'd managed to find a place for. She had a couch that needed to be recovered, a hutch stuffed with various antique glass containers, and a few rocking chairs. Books crammed any spare spaces, from which they tumbled to the floor with each earthquake above five on the Richter scale. It was a perfectly normal house in a perfectly normal community. Could someone actually be out to get her with bad luck?

"It sounds like Harper just drove up and the car still sounds like hell. That's just what we need: I wreck one car and his car develops trouble. Of course someone is throwing bad luck at us; this kind of thing can't happen naturally."

Gia stopped for a moment, her head cocked to one side. "I didn't hear anything. Probably just your imagination after that knock on your head. At least I hope so. You don't need the bad luck associated with another car bill when you don't have the money to pay it."

"You two are just being silly," Sally said. "Of course there's no conspiracy. You just don't know how to organize your life so that the unexpected simply doesn't happen. I've done it for years and it works."

Fiona, her body aching from the impact of an accident that she hadn't caused, snorted. There were times when Sally really got on her nerves.

"Of course we're being silly," she said. "There's no real

conspiracy, it only feels like it. No one cares that much about Gia and me. After all, we're hardly interesting material, three middle-aged women with drooping boobs, spreading seats and gray in our hair. We aren't *worth* sending bad luck to, it would take more energy than most people have."

"Speak for yourself, Fiona, old girl, I haven't a bit of gray," Gia said as she smoothed her bun of coal-black hair and resettled a royal-purple scarf that threatened to drop from her shoulders. "I still say we're getting dumped on. Even the Tarot told me that yesterday. I read the cards just for fun and they said something drastic was going to happen."

"You believed what a pack of paper cards supposedly told you?" Sally lifted her tilted nose even farther into the air.

"What's wrong with asking for a little guidance?" Gia demanded. She reached over to her purse and extracted the richly colored deck. The silver and garnet rings she wore on four fingers flashed in the reflected light from the pottery lamp. Larry hated those rings and bitched at her every time he saw her wearing them. Looks like a damned fortune-teller, he complained. Not good for his image as a top-flight lawyer, he'd sniff. Tear them off your fingers so you can't wear them anymore, he'd threaten, and Gia would answer that she'd rip his nose off his face if he tried. Now she wore them when he wasn't around to complain.

"Here, let's try just one card each to see what the future holds for us." She began to shuffle the deck and then handed them to Fiona.

"Shuffle them again, cut them from left to right and pick a card out of the middle," she instructed. "Ask a question about the future."

Fiona hesitated. "You know, this makes me kind of uncomfortable. I have enough trouble dealing with the present without worrying about the future." She picked up one card and turned it over.

Gia whistled as she looked at the gold tower outlined against the background of dark blue. Figures of people spilled from the upper stories toward the jagged, evil-looking rocks below.

"I don't even have to look that one up. It's the Tower. Cataclysmic change." Gia shuddered delicately.

Fiona handed the cards back to Gia. "No thank you, no more change. Hasn't life been uncertain enough lately without asking for more?"

Gia shuffled again and tried to hand the cards to Sally.

"Not a chance. I don't trust anything that has to do with the supernatural. Don't you remember, Fiona, when we were in college, I was the one who had to drag you out of the all-night Ouija board marathon because you were getting so upset over the answers? I'd have thought you'd learned."

Sally stood up and dusted cat hair off her pants. "I'm going to be going now. It's been nice, girls. Let's do it again when a catastrophe doesn't interfere." She waved as she opened the back door and went across the porch to the gate that connected Fiona's yard to her own.

As Gia and Fiona waved goodbye the front door opened and Harper walked into the house. His usual whistle was silent and Fiona could tell, just from the way he dragged his feet on the worn wood floor, that her husband was tired. As usual, Fiona had heard the car fifteen minutes before he actually drove into the driveway. It was a peculiar form of precognition she'd never mentioned to anyone.

Harper stopped just inside the swinging door and stared at Gia and Fiona. His strong, craggy face was lined with fatigue and his shoulders slumped under the weight of his old raincoat. He stared at the two women in surprise. He hadn't expected anyone else to be home.

"What happened? I've been trying to call for the last four hours because I knew something went wrong. Where's the van?" he asked. "And why do you have a bandage on your forehead?"

"I'll be going now." Gia picked up her purse and slung it over her shoulder. She patted Harper on the arm as she passed, knowing that the accident was going to be almost as much of a blow to him as it had been to his wife.

She envied Harper and Fiona their marriage. It was filled with the kind of sharing two people are supposed to have when they promise to love each other forever. It was the kind of marriage she'd never have with Larry.

"I'll come back to check on you tomorrow morning and I'll remind Sally that there's no way in hell we're going shopping tomorrow afternoon. You'll be too sore."

"Why will she be too sore?" Harper asked Gia's retreating figure. He flipped on the kitchen lights so that he could see what was going on. The pottery lamp had never given off enough light for him. The bright glare of the 200-watt bulb revealed the bruised and battered state of Fiona's face as she began to cry.

"What happened? I knew you were hurt, I just didn't know what happened to you." His tanned face was an open book. Like an ancient Celtic warrior, he worked and fought for love of his family. He couldn't stand it when something went wrong. He always felt, Fiona knew, that he should have been able to stop whatever disaster threatened and to push aside all the bad luck so that his family was safe. Too often, though, he could only help pick up the pieces and comfort everyone.

Fiona was used to Harper's always being tuned in to her. She did the same thing with him, most of the time. It wasn't really mind reading as much as it was a connection that came with years of deep love.

"Was Megan with you?"

Fiona nodded again. "She was hurt, but not badly, at

least that's what the doctor said. Just a bump to the head, like me. He said to watch and make sure that we don't have headaches or get tired suddenly. But Megan's always tired and her head always hurts. How can I tell if something is happening to her?"

"It'll be all right, love. But I'm going to go kill the bastard who did it," Harper said with absolute finality. "I'm going to tear him limb from limb and then I'm going to shove him right on through my brand-new, bright red leaf-shredder and use him for mulch. How dare someone hurt my family!"

Fiona giggled. She had no doubt that he was capable of carrying out the threat, but she still laughed at the image of him shredding the flippant teenager who had hit her.

Everything else in the world could go wrong, but even in the worst of times she could rely on Harper to take care of her. They had managed to hold on through twenty-one years of a marriage that was supposed to have failed within the first three months, and he was still her strength when everything else went awry.

"Actually, it's a her."

"What?"

"It's a her that did it to the car and me."

"Damn her, I'll still use her for mulch. Tell me what happened," Harper demanded, as he gathered her carefully into his arms to make certain there were no bones broken.

Harper's face was a study in baffled rage by the time Fiona reached the end of her tale. "She saw that you and Megan were bleeding and she knew she'd bashed the back of the van and she still didn't give a damn? And she doesn't have insurance? I'll go over to her house and show her what insurance is for, because she's going to need it after I dismantle her and her damned car, too."

Sally interrupted his furious blast as she rapped on the back door and walked in carrying a very expensive white casserole dish and several smaller white pots.

"I couldn't let you cook tonight; you're in no condition, so here is quiche lorraine and escarole salad stretched with some extra shrimp sprinkled on the greens," she said as she handed the delicate china to Harper. "There's some chocolate mousse in the container on top. It's hell on the calories, but I figured both of you could use some comfort food tonight."

She turned toward the couch and grinned as she gave Fiona one four-pack of toilet paper.

"This should save your Sears catalog from a fate worse than death, but the animals will have to make do with shredded paper. I don't have any cat litter."

Harper reached over and hugged Sally with his free arm. Friends like her were hard to come by, even if she was occasionally very strange.

"There's nothing like a good neighbor to help out in trouble. Toilet paper and food, the essentials of life!"

"Enjoy." Sally waved and hurried back out the door. "I've got to get back before Carl decides the filling for the bacon quiche is up for grabs and eats it all."

Harper was quiet for a few moments. He stood in the middle of the kitchen, ignoring the weight of the dishes Sally had handed him.

For the moment the house was quiet. Normally Harper would have made a lascivious comment and tried to pull Fiona up the stairs and into the bed. Most of the time it seemed as if their sex lives had gotten lost somewhere in the shuffle of jobs and kid and the house, so Harper took every chance he had to make some kind of romantic love to Fiona. Unfortunately, the chances were few and far between, averaging a lot less than the three times a week the statistics claimed most married couples managed. Harper always had the sneaking suspicion that everyone lied when pollsters asked them about their sex lives.

"You okay?" Fiona finally asked, when he didn't make a move toward the sideboard to set Sally's dishes down.

"I'm not sure," he said slowly.

"What do you mean you're not sure? Do you hurt someplace? Do you have any pain down your left arm or a heaviness in your chest?" Fiona sat upright, ignoring the ache in her back and head. "Any ache in your jaw?"

Harper shook his head. "Nothing like that. It's just that I'm beginning to think the vortex is back, like it was in college." He finally set the dishes down and reached for the dinner plates, noting that the baby latch wasn't working again and that if an earthquake hit now, they'd lose all their old china.

He began to serve out a healthy helping of the bacon-and-cheese-laden pie for himself, an equal one for the cats who circled his legs and a smaller one for Fiona. He put the rest of the dish in the microwave for Megan when she felt like eating, and came back to sit next to Fiona on the couch.

"What do you mean, vortex, and back in college?"

"Don't you remember? We used to laugh about how everything that could happen did happen to us. We called it the vortex, because it seemed to keep sucking shit in and dumping it on us. Other people could have nice calm quiet lives, but we lived like there was a constant hurricane around us."

Fiona's eyes widened. "Now I remember! Whatever went wrong never happened to Sally, it always happened to us. She used to kid us about it."

"It hasn't changed, has it?" Harper said. "I'd give anything to be able to stop it, but we seem to attract bad luck like some people attract money. But I don't like it when the bad luck begins to hurt you." He put out a finger and touched her tenderly on the cheek, right at the point where a large bruise was beginning to swell and blacken.

"The vortex. I think you could be right." How could she have forgotten? "This time, though, we've got to do something to stop it. I'm tired of being fate's punching bag."

"How? Who are you going to tell to leave us alone? The IRS? The kid who hit you? The neighbor's dog? Who do we tell that we've had enough and we want the trouble to stop?"

Fiona shook her head. "I don't know."

She hesitated, looking around the room they'd never had the time to really decorate. It was comfortable and it served their purposes, since they rarely entertained anyone except good friends who came for the company and not a fancy house. But the couch was almost twenty years old and the decorating scheme could charitably be called comfortably worn.

"Harper, I'm scared. When we first got married the troubles were small ones, like getting term papers stolen, remember?" She paused. "Then the calamities started multiplying and now we're up to the real big time. Do you realize that in the last ten years we've had more of a soap-opera life than the people on *Days of Our Lives* and *Santa Barbara* combined?"

"Isn't that stretching it a little?" Harper asked.

"No, it's not!" Fiona insisted. "You slipped on those stairs and broke your back. You could have been crippled for life and you're still in pain every day. We've had four cars totaled in various accidents and not one of the drivers who hit us had insurance. Our daughter has a brain tumor that is under control but could flare up at any time. The only thing that hasn't happened yet is someone getting killed. It's too much. I'm not going to take that chance, not to my family, not to the people I love. It simply has to stop."

"You tell me how we're going to escape and I'll be with you one hundred percent," Harper said. But both of them knew there was nothing that could be done other than following behind whatever happened, trying to pick up the pieces and put their lives back together once again.

It was much later that night when Fiona finally gave up

on waiting for the pain pill to take effect and began to prowl around the various bookshelves in the house, looking for something to read. She had expected to drop right off to sleep, but she was still shaken by the accident. She'd lain beside Harper, the lights out, the soft sounds of the house soothing her, until she'd snapped awake again as the memory of the accident and a whiff of smoke on the night air jolted her out of her almost-sleep. The sudden start had made her bones ache agonizingly where she had bruised them.

She had finally turned on the light, hoping that it wouldn't disturb Harper, and slipped out of bed. She didn't think there was a book that would tell them what to do, but maybe she was wrong. She'd bought every self-help paperback that had come along in the past ten years. Somewhere in the bookcases that lined every inch of spare space there had to be an answer.

She looked past *How to Live on Nothing,* which had been out of print for almost twenty years but still had great ideas for living cheaply. She picked up the book about cleaning up the house and getting control of her life, and then set it down again. The house was clean; it was just that there was too much stuff and not enough house. The budget book had been a real bomb; no use trying to read that again.

"Why doesn't one of you just jump out at me and give me the answer? I'd be forever grateful," she said, shoving the budget book back in where there really wasn't space for it. There wasn't space anywhere in the bookshelf; she'd long ago reached the point of triple-shelving everything and then laying the books in sideways in the spaces at the top. She took another step to the left and a red book fell to the floor with a thump, pushed out by the budget book.

The Beginning Witch's Book of Amulets and Talismans. She picked it up and looked inside at the table of contents and the pictures. She had bought the book at a library sale years ago but had never managed to find the time to read it. Perhaps the time had finally come.

Thoughtfully she tucked it under her arm, grabbed a soda from the refrigerator and went back to bed. Harper never stirred. She opened the paperback to the first chapter: "How a Grimoire Can Help You."

Fiona laughed out loud as she saw the definition of a Grimoire. "An ancient book of knowledge," the small print said right under the name. She flipped back to the copyright page and saw that the publication date was 1976. Not all that ancient, my friends. Who are we kidding?

Fiona had never done well with pretension and this book held out every promise of being not only pretentious but worthless. It was a shame, because she was ready to use anything that came her way to help her fight back whatever the vortex of bad luck had in store for the family.

Witchcraft, an ancient Celtic religion, uses talismans and amulets for protection and to obtain heart's desires. The purpose of the talismans is to invoke the power of the God and Goddess for blessings, including money, happiness and protection in everyday life.

She read the statement and grimaced. Witchcraft was a religion? She'd had enough of religions. She had something more practical in mind, like a way to make something good happen immediately.

But the book had said money. She couldn't sneer at the idea of money. And protection.

Hadn't one of her neighbors back in Idaho, a Mrs. Riley, clutched a medal of St. Christopher in her hands every time she got in a car? She'd never been in a car wreck. In fact, the old lady had died when she was eighty-nine from eating some home-canned beans that had developed a lovely strain of botulism. But she hadn't died in an accident and maybe that little talisman of silver and blue had done some good. And if it had, then Fiona could figure out her own talismans to use to protect everyone in the house. Or she could if this book didn't go all soft on her and forget to give instructions on how to make these amulets that the authors claimed were so good.

Lord, it would be nice to have money and not scrape by from paycheck to paycheck. She picked up the book and continued reading.

The sixth chapter had the answer, or at least the glimmer of one.

> Money is one of the easiest of problems to solve. A talisman to bring money can be made following the directions in Chapter Eleven. Are you having trouble with more than your share of bad luck? Maybe you need a protection amulet in your car and a warding talisman around your house to keep the forces of darkness at bay. Here, in shortened version, is what you'll be doing to make the Goddess's protection your own. First, invoke the Goddess and ask her for help with the drawing of the spirits to your talisman, and then make the actual talisman.

Fiona nodded. Right on the button. That was what she needed, money and protection. Maybe the book wasn't so dumb after all. She sat cross-legged and hunched as she kept on reading, saying the invocations that should have brought the powers of the Goddess to her, testing the taste of the chants in her mouth. They fit better than anything she'd been taught in her family church. There was even a flicker of power, she was certain.

At three in the morning she finally stretched, felt the muscles in her back protest the unnatural position they'd been in, and closed the red book. She had it planned, right down to the silly little chant she was going to use, to test

just how well all of this worked against whoever or whatever was trying to control her life with accidents and unexpected problems. "It can't hurt," she said aloud. Harper
muttered an answer in his sleep.

She looked down at Harper, his face tanned, his red-
dish-brown hair in wild disarray around his face. He was
from Wales. If she needed backup power, his background
should help some. She seemed to remember something
about how people back in that part of the world accepted
the old beliefs. Maybe one of these days she'd ask Harper
about it.

"It's going to work," Fiona said firmly. The toilet
grumbled a reply as it ran more water into the tank, filling
up again as the ball cock let gallons run unused down the
drain. Harper was going to have to fix that, she thought
drowsily. And the weatherstripping. She'd forgotten to tell
him about that. Maybe if she got really good at this magic
or witchcraft, or whatever it was called, she could witch the
plumbing fixed and the refrigerator back into working effi-
ciently and then her back could stop aching from tension
and worry about what terrible thing was going to happen
next.

She knew she should go to sleep. If she didn't, she was
going to feel wasted in the morning and then she'd lose a
whole day. But what she really wanted to do was get up and
go into her studio and try to make an amulet. The whole
idea of doing something positive to influence their life gave
her energy.

Just as she slid her legs over the edge of the bed, the bedside lamp flickered once and then went off. She waited a few
minutes and then sighed and took a matchbook from the
nightstand drawer and lit the candle in the copper holder.
They'd started keeping a candle by the bed ever since the
new section of houses had gone in up the street and the
power grid had stretched too far. Every time someone
turned on their microwave or table saw, the power went off

for the whole area. Fiona had discovered long ago that she couldn't paint by candlelight.

"I'll do the chant then. No use just lying here waiting for the lights to come back on." She picked up the book again and peered at the letters, reading the chant. The darkness calmed her and the shadows closed in. The pain pill she had taken when they first went to bed finally kicked in and she nodded off as she whispered the words. Her hand relaxed and tipped the book onto the table by the small candle flame. The curtains lifted as an errant wind entered the bedroom and shifted the pages of the book, bringing them nearer to the flame. The heavy cream paper began to darken as smoke rose in a tiny spiral above the candle.

2

W hat do you mean, you're leaving?" Gia asked. She watched Larry transferring his custom-made Egyptian-cotton shirts out of the closet and into the suitcase. It was too early in the morning for her to think straight, but something was definitely wrong here. She sat up in bed. Her hip-length black hair, freed from the daytime bun Larry insisted on, covered her shoulders and breasts. "You aren't scheduled for a trip until the end of the month, right? For the Eagles case, isn't it?"

Larry grimaced, something he'd started doing every time she talked to him. He grabbed a handful of Italian silk ties.

"It's not company business."

Gia blinked. "Not company business? Then why are you packing?"

Larry snorted in disgust. "Because I'm leaving you, you idiot. Do I have to announce it in big bold letters before you twig to the fact that I don't want to be in the same house with you anymore?" He zipped the suitcase shut, ruthlessly pushing the sleeves, underwear and stray socks out of the way of the enameled pull tab.

Gia couldn't think of a single thing to say. She just stared at him, numb with the shock of his pronouncement. He was leaving? They'd been married all this time and he was packing his bags and walking out of the house as if he were doing nothing more important than taking off for another business trip with the law firm? The sudden memory of their lovemaking the night before stung her, waking her from the hypnosis of shock.

"So what was last night, you son of a bitch? A goodbye fuck, just for old times' sake? Who the hell are you leaving me for?" Gia was so furious that her voice broke in the middle of the demand. She held her stomach, almost doubled over with the pain and disbelief. He couldn't be abandoning her. That happened to other people, not to her. "What is so special that you're going to give up me and the house and everything we've worked for?" Her voice rose to a scream as she bounced out of the bed to confront him before he made his escape down the staircase and out to his red Mercedes.

"Don't push, bitch. This may be the time I finally hit you. God, it'd feel good." Larry raised his right hand, palm toward her.

Gia faced him without flinching.

"Don't even think about it, Larry. Don't you feel like an absolute fool, letting your prick do the thinking for you again? You never could keep from dipping it in whatever happened to smell good, could you? I've stayed with you all these years because I kept hoping you'd mellow with age and we'd end up with a reasonable marriage. Instead you've just putrefied. Something's happened in the last couple of months. What's wrong, middle-age crisis? Or is it what my grandmother used to say about men who went off the deep end—you've just got a wild hair up your ass and it's driving you nuts?"

"Don't be crude, Gia," Larry said, his look unutterably pained.

"Crude? You screw me and leave me and there isn't even a hundred-dollar bill on the table? Don't you call *me* crude! What is it this time, the pressure from the office now that you're a partner? All those trips back east made being single again look good? Or is it time for your 'trophy wife,' like the one Harry Evans got when he was promoted to senior partner and vice-president? Remember what happened to him? She took him for everything he was worth when she decided she didn't want to be married to a sixty-year-old man who kept talking about retirement, no matter how much money he had. Is that what you're looking for?"

"Leave it, Gia," Larry said. "Yelling at me isn't going to change a damned thing. I'm still walking out that door and the only place you're going to see me again is going to be in court when we divvy up the goodies."

He turned around, blocking the door. Over the years, he had tried his best to keep his figure, but it was beginning to show the effects of age and too many hours spent on the tanning table. Gia kept expecting the dark spots on his skin to turn into malignant melanoma. In her darker moments she had thought that maybe cancer would solve the problem of her loveless marriage for her.

"You know, Harry Evans isn't the only one to show his age lately. Have you looked in the mirror recently? Your blond hair isn't blond anymore, it's gray and white. I don't care how many times a week you play racquetball, you're still developing a paunch. You are not my idea of the perfect hero anymore, I can promise you that."

She'd stopped using him as the basis for her novels' romantic heroes a long time ago. The packaging didn't live up to the contents anymore, if it ever had. Maybe having to use someone else as a hero should have given her a clue that something was seriously wrong with the marriage. A lot more wrong than she'd thought, but she hadn't wanted to admit it. It was easier to be married to Larry than it would have been to divorce him and start over, or at least it had been until the last few months.

"You're not my idea of the perfect heroine either. Look at you, you haven't changed since college. You still wear your hair long and your skin looks like you haven't been out in the sun in twenty years. It's time for a change."

"So," Gia said, her voice calm, as she stood at the top of the stairs and looked down at him. "Who are you leaving me for? Because there has to be someone else. You aren't even up to delivering your shirts to the cleaners, you're so damned busy all the time. You aren't dumb enough to get stuck without someone to do the pickup and cleanup and cooking for you."

Larry shrugged.

"Tell me, Larry. And while you're at it, tell me something else, like what you're going to do when it comes time to perform?" She felt a rush of satisfaction when she saw him wince. "What are you going to do when your girl wants something more than the expensive gifts I've watched being charged on the American Express? Silly me, I wondered when you were going to give them to me because you realized what an absolute bastard you've been to live with since January."

The gifts bothered her more than she would ever let him know. She had honestly thought he was getting ready for a special occasion like their anniversary to tell her how sorry he was for being so selfish. It would have been the perfect romantic reconciliation.

The betrayal hurt.

"What's she going to say when you tell her you're too tired? We both know you can't get it up more than once a month even under the best of circumstances. And honey, last night was it for about three months if the past couple of years have been any indication."

Larry's face reddened. His hands flexed against the strap

of the suitcase. "She's got you beat all to hell there, Gia. Kelly and I make it every chance that we get and there's never any problem. If anything, the one who caused the marriage to go into deep freeze is you."

"Bullshit! How many times did you come home with one drink too many and then couldn't perform, even when I asked?" Gia demanded. "It's never been great, but this last year has been a complete sexual drought. You can't get it up most of the time."

"Not as many times as you think."

Gia blinked. "What's that supposed to mean?"

"It means that most of the time I'd just come home after making it with Kelly. She's a hell of a lot more exciting than your once-every-couple-of-months screwing on the one night when you aren't too tired or having your period or cramps or whatever else is wrong."

"You bastard!" Gia was outraged. "Kelly? You're leaving me for that nothing little slut with bleached-blond hair and an IQ that might go up on a warm day to seventy to match the temperature? What do you see in her?"

"She thinks I'm something special," Larry said quietly.

"I think you're something special too. A specially nasty specimen of bastard. I'll take you for everything, you miserable excuse for a man!"

"Take me? I'm the one in the family with the legal connections. You don't stand a chance."

He turned and stalked out the front door, leaving it open behind him.

Gia raced down the stairs, reaching the doorway just in time to see him slam the door of the car, gun the motor and back out of the driveway.

Gia stood in the arch of the two-story entranceway and listened to the sound of the Mercedes's motor diminish with the distance.

Never coming back.

Larry was never coming back.

He was going to Kelly.

He'd been screwing Kelly all this time and then coming home to her and lying about being tired.

The marriage she'd decided to stay with because it was easier than leaving and living alone had crashed down around her head and she'd still end up alone.

He was a bastard.

She should have known this was coming.

Another car started on the court. Someone's husband drove by in a sedate black Lincoln. He glanced over toward her house, slowed abruptly and stared at her. Suddenly Gia realized that she was standing in the doorway of her house in a completely see-through pink cotton nightgown.

"Oh hell," she said and stepped back, slamming the door shut. She was trembling with anger and frustration.

How the hell had this happened, this complete disintegration of a life within the first two hours of the morning?

How did he think they were going to keep up with the bills if he moved out? How did he think he could pay for everything it cost to keep the house running and have another house, too?

The image of Larry in bed with Kelly superimposed itself on the vision of the bills and Gia threw her head back and screamed in wordless outrage as she pounded on the wall, her knuckles leaving bloody streaks on the yellow paint.

Gia turned and walked up the stairs, nursing her bruised fists. She was still in a state of shock. She'd stayed in a so-so marriage, just to have it end like this? Why hadn't she gotten out before? Why had she lived for years with an empty shell of a relationship, thinking things would improve?

"Because I'm stupid, that's the only answer. I always thought if things got too bad, I'd be the one to leave him. I never expected him to leave me. I thought we'd simply stay together because it was easier."

She stomped up two more steps.

"It's not even that I want him," Gia said to the house, the anger still burning in her gut. "I just want to be the one to tell him to get lost. I don't want him walking out on me!"

She strode into the bedroom and stared at the bed. She wanted to throw up. He'd used her for one last fling because he was certain she'd bring him to a satisfactory climax and then he'd walked out. She couldn't stand to look at the bed. She had to keep going, keep moving.

She sniffed, smelling the scent of him in the bedroom.

"I'm going to take a bath. I'm going to strip the bed. Then I'm going to throw every last single piece of your clothing out on the front lawn for the neighborhood dogs to piss on," she said. She grabbed the black and red comforter and the black sheets, the ones Larry had insisted they buy to jazz up their sex life, and pulled them off the bed. She laughed as she heard them rip under the assault. She flung open the windows and threw the bedding out into the backyard, where the red and black drifted to the ground, landing in a mud puddle.

Gia slammed open the wall-to-wall closet that was filled with Larry's stuff and began to grab anything she could reach. Fine Italian silk suits for summer, a couple of English woolen suits for winter and every damned Aran sweater he owned went sailing out the window. She didn't stop until the closet was empty. Even the cashmere overcoat he'd brought from back east and his Gucci shoes were summarily dispatched to the mud.

She still seethed with rage.

"You bastard! You leave me for a girl who isn't even smart enough to be a full-fledged bimbo and you think she's the answer to your prayers? You fucking well deserve each other!" she screamed at the top of her lungs, the sound reverberating off the walls. She caught a glimpse of herself in the bathroom mirror and ripped off the nightgown, shredding the expensive pink cotton that had been lovingly hand-embroidered by some lady in the Middle East and brought back for her after one of Larry's many trips.

Maybe the nightgown wasn't for her, either. She had helped him unpack his bags and the gown had been in the bottom of the suitcase, carefully wrapped in tissue paper. She had thought at the time that it was a lovely present to make up for his absence over her birthday.

How could she have been so naive?

Why did it hurt so much when she didn't care about him?

How could he be mean enough to hurt her?

She looked at herself in the mirror and saw nothing that should have repulsed her husband. Her figure was full and her breasts had begun to sag, but for a forty-three-year-old woman, she was in remarkably good shape. She'd never tanned because Larry didn't like the way she looked with black hair and a tan.

"What a laugh, you telling me I'm too pale and my hair is too long. You'd never let me step outside without a hat."

"Too foreign," Larry had said when he convinced her that she looked better with pale skin. "Can't afford to have a wife who doesn't look one hundred percent American, especially with that weird Italian name your mother gave you. Firm doesn't like anything except WASPs, you know."

Because of him, her skin had remained pristine and her ears unpierced. "No holes that God didn't put in your skin," he'd decreed, and she'd given in to another of his fetishes. She'd gone along with everything he wanted and he'd still left her for someone else.

Her hair tumbled around her shoulders and breasts, giving her the look of a naked Fury. Black hair that her husband had always loved to wind around his hands while they were making love. He'd begged her never to have it cut.

Gia opened the drawer and reached inside, her fingers searching for the scissors.

She stood for a moment, the cold steel gleaming in her hand before she lifted one long tress and brought the scissors up to the hair. She began to hack through more than twenty years of growth. A three-foot strand of hair fell to the floor.

She lifted and cut until it was done and she stood in front of the mirror, her hair spiked into one- and two-inch lengths all over her head.

She stared at herself for a few more seconds and began to sob. The hair changed her. It made her look different. Part of her identity, along with her husband, had just vanished.

The tears rolled down her face as she stepped into the bath, washing the remaining hair from her body. The salt mixed with the fresh water and she stood there until the water began to run cold and she had no more tears to cry for herself, for Larry or for what she might have done with her life if she'd left him earlier.

Slowly the anger began to build again. There was nothing wrong with her, no matter what Larry had done to her. She knew what she was going to do now. She'd decided on a fitting retribution for her shattered marriage.

She dressed quickly in a long red skirt and white blouse and wrapped a purple sash around her waist. She knew exactly where to start with the revenge she had planned.

"You want two holes in each ear?" The jeweler she had always dealt with looked at her in surprise. The gems Gia had bought before, the tennis bracelets and the daytime diamonds, had always been in impeccably good taste. Two earrings in each ear and spiked hair definitely did not fit that image.

"I'm certain. And I want the one-carat emeralds to go in the lower hole and the one-carat diamonds in the upper hole."

"That will be almost twenty thousand dollars, with the ring you purchased." The jeweler looked at her worriedly. His fat little Swiss face pinched at the thought of losing such a fine profit because her credit wouldn't cover the purchase.

"I'd appreciate it if you'd make certain that the Visa card has enough room. If it will, we'll get on with this," Gia said. As far as she knew, the credit card had been saved for emergencies and $30,000 of credit had languished unused until just this moment.

She crossed her fingers, her breath coming in short spurts as the anxiety built. The jeweler dialed the phone and then they waited. He punched in the numbers. She could tell he had been transferred from the normal immediate electronic acceptance to a human questioner.

"Yes. Yes, I know what the total is. Yes, I am certain . . ." The man began to sound a bit testy.

"Mrs. Michaels, the woman would like to speak with you," he said finally. He handed her the phone.

Her heart sank. It wasn't going to work. She wasn't going to be able to screw Larry over this last time. She accepted the heavy black receiver and held it to her ear.

"Mrs. Michaels?" the voice asked briskly.

"Yes."

"Could you give me your birthdate, mother's maiden name and your social security number, just for verification, before I okay the purchase? We have to be careful on such a large amount."

Gia felt the bands of tension loosen. It was going to go through! Happily she gave the woman what she asked for, confirming her identity. Within twenty minutes she walked out of the jewelry store, her ears aching from the pain of the piercing and the weight of the earrings. She waited until she slid behind the steering wheel of her Mercedes before she removed her wedding band and replaced it with the heavy emerald and diamond ring she had just bought.

She felt a rush of delight. She'd done it. She'd managed to run the bill on the card almost to the limit. Kelly dearest wasn't going to get so much as a ten-dollar lunch out of it by the time she got through with her purchases. The glow in her stomach was warm, curling with satisfaction.

"I'm on a roll. Let's keep going until Larry pulls the plug," she murmured. She sat back in the warmth of the leather seat and thought about what she would need. She had a computer and printer, but she needed backup on both if she was going to be on her own and responsible for earning her own keep. And clothes. What if she had to go out and actually look for a job? She'd never be able to go to work in an office in the slightly bohemian clothing she favored. She'd need office suits.

Four hours later she was faint with hunger and dizzy with exhilaration at what she had done. She stepped outside the last boutique and juggled the packages, managing to wedge them inside the trunk on top of everything else she'd bought. She slammed the trunk lid down and looked around. She had to get something to eat.

There was a little combination cafe and bookstore to the right of the boutique. She could hear baroque flute and drum music wafting from the entrance. The smells of fresh croissants and melted cheese drew her toward the front of the shop.

THE MAJOR ARCANA BOOK, HERB AND COFFEE SHOP, the handcarved sign declared. Inside, she was overwhelmed by the sheer pleasure of being in the shop. Herbs and flowers hung from the rafters and a whole selection of incense perfumed the air, adding to the exotic mélange of smells that wafted out to greet her.

Gia was amazed at the selection of Tarot cards, Rune stones and crystals, and the hundreds of books on how to interpret the various devices for telling the future. Her own Tarot deck she had used since she was barely in her teens. She'd heard of the Runes, but never seen a set before. She picked up a pouch that had been laid to the side of the display, presumably for people to look at. She reached in and took out one stone and turned to the blue book to see what it meant.

"Eihwaz," a deep voice beside her said.

Startled, Gia turned to see what appeared to be a Norse god standing next to her. He was well over six feet tall, with massive arms and legs, and a muscular torso that only got better the longer she looked at it. He should by all rights have been wearing a Viking helmet, a wolf pelt and shaggy lace-up boots. Unfortunately for her fantasy, he was dressed in running shoes, cotton shorts and a tightly stretched knit shirt.

"It means take your time, wait, see what needs to be done next, instead of forging ahead wildly, where you could do yourself harm," the man added helpfully. "Going through a rough time, are you?"

"Yes," Gia said, then looked him up and down again and grinned. "Of course you'd know the Runes. It's typecasting."

"I've been using them for a hundred lifetimes," the man said, and it didn't look as if he was kidding.

"Right," Gia answered, moving away. He was a nut. A handsome one, but definitely a lunatic.

"Let's see what Rune comes up for my relation to you," he said.

He hesitated as he rummaged in the bag. "Odd," he said, and withdrew two stones. "They seem to be sending me two messages this time. Ansuz and Wunjo, the god Loki, the trickster. This is a warning to be especially alert when I meet new people. And Wunjo tells me that through you, there will be change and light."

The man replaced the stones in the bag and reached into his pocket as Gia tried to carry out a dignified retreat.

He saw her backward movement and smiled. He pulled a business card out of his pocket and handed it to her.

"Here, please take this. You are going to need me. And the stones are definitely warning you to be wary of strange men. I suppose I'm included in that."

"Right," she said. She grabbed the card and scuttled toward the counter, where she could order some lunch and get away from the man.

She considered tossing the card in the wastebasket, then reconsidered. Eihwaz—time to sit back instead of acting on impulse? It was like a psychic window to what she'd been doing all morning long.

GUNNERSON
ATTORNEY-AT-LAW
990 BOALT HALL #3, SAN FRANCISCO
(415) 555-1567
DIVORCE AND SETTLEMENT SPECIALTY

She might need him? Indeed she might.

She slipped the card into her purse and ordered lunch.

"Your number is forty-three and it'll be about fifteen minutes for the next batch of ham-and-Swiss-cheese croissants to finish baking," the waitress said. "Why don't you have another look around the shop? As soon as there's counter space open, I'll call your number."

Gia asked her aching feet if they could take another couple of minutes of standing up. The answer was an emphatic "No!"

The waitress looked at Gia's face and leaned closer. "Take your shoes off and go to the back of the shop. There's a section back there with a Persian rug and some old cushions where you can relax. You might find the books interesting."

Gia nodded gratefully. She reached down and slipped off her shoes and walked toward the cushions. She didn't see the Norseman again, but there were plenty of other good-looking men around. More, she thought, than she'd seen in a long time. She'd have to remember to come back here once she was ready to start dating.

A slightly older, handsome man, his brown hair touched with gray, smiled at her, frankly appraising her figure. He obviously liked what he saw.

Normally Gia would have blushed or looked away or found some other way to indicate that she wasn't free, but this time she smiled back. He was clearly prosperous. She noted his thin gold watch, the fine weave of the cashmere slacks and the casual elegance of the English sweater he wore. It was a look that Larry had aspired to but never quite managed, for all the money he spent on himself.

Part of this man's style had to do with the aristocratic tilt of the head, the fine, yet still masculine bones of the face and his apparent breeding.

The man nodded toward her, acknowledging her existence, but didn't follow her. She sighed. No harm in looking.

The books lining the shelves were interesting. As a writer, she was always on the lookout for something intriguing to add to her research library. The well-handled old volumes called out for her to discover the secrets inside. Interspersed with the leather-bound books were vials of oils, all neatly labeled with blue and red and lavender Spencerian writing. Gia would have sworn that the bottles themselves were antique. Her aunt had collected tiny crystal containers when she finally came into a little money late in her life and had willed several of the most valuable to Gia.

Gia reached out and picked up one square-faceted bottle labeled "Mixed Oil of Comfort." Feeling a little bit like Alice, she lifted the stopper and sniffed. A scent like cedar smoke, lavender and roses, with just a hint of chocolate cookies baking, swirled around her. Comfort indeed. She inhaled again and looked down at the bottle, hoping to find a price. She had to have this. Spread around her bed and sprinkled over the new white eyelet sheets and comforter she had bought, the oil would erase all memory of Larry.

"Nice, isn't it?" The tall graying man had followed her to the back of the store. "Selene makes the best herbal oils I've ever come across. I put them in my car, a drop here and there to keep the air fresh."

He turned toward one of the other shelves and picked up a squat round bottle filled with an amber oil.

"Try this one." He held out the bottle and lifted the stopper, waving it under her nose. Gia tried to read the name on the bottle, but his fingers obscured the label.

"Oh . . ." she said, her eyes widening in surprise. The oil in the bottle had caused an immediate and completely unexpected reaction. The man's eyes seemed to grow larger, the green and brown color melding and becoming a reflection of gold. She was intimately aware of his hands. She wanted those hands to caress her, touch her breasts, warm her inner thighs. She felt her nipples crinkle with the force of the sudden assault of sheer sensuality.

"Oh damn . . ." She recoiled, closing her eyes. He couldn't possibly have known what the oil would do to her. No man would have loosed that sensual explosion on any woman except someone he was absolutely certain of.

Gia felt the bottle of Comfort in her hand and raised it to her nose, clearing her head. She took a deep breath and forced herself to relax the muscles that had clenched in fierce desire at the assault of the other scent. The roses and lavender brought her back to a reality untinged with the haze of sex.

"I take it you like Comfort more than Selene's special mix?" The man was laughing at her, the light in his eyes merry, as if he'd played a great trick on her.

Could he really have known what happened? Gia saw his gaze move to her breasts. Her nipples showed against the gauzy white blouse, which was just tight enough. He had seen her reaction.

"I like Comfort better," Gia said frostily. She looked around, hoping there was someone else near her. For all his elegance, there was the look of a predator about this man. She had no intention of becoming anyone else's prey at the moment.

"Number forty-three," the waitress called out.

"That's me," Gia said. She pushed by the man and hurried to the front of the shop, where she could sit in the sunshine and enjoy all her new jewelry. She ignored the low, silky, dangerous laugh that followed her.

3

Fiona woke with a start as the power came back on. The light blinded her and she groped for the lamp's switch to turn off the glare. Her hand connected with the soda she had left on the nightstand. The glass tipped and liquid cascaded over the red book she had been reading, dousing the flames that had already burned a corner of the book and greedily reached for the curtains. Fiona heard the sizzle, but was too sleepy to respond. As the light went out, she turned over and burrowed into the pillow again. A strange, eerie sound echoed through the night as the balance of power began to shift, ever so slightly, in Fiona's favor.

The next morning she cleaned up the mess of spilled soda and charred pages. She ran water over the paper in a valiant attempt to unstick the pages of the book. She didn't comment on the near-disaster to Harper, figuring that he had probably had enough trouble without adding to his worries about the vortex and weird accidents. Still, it made her

stomach knot with anxiety when she thought about what
could have happened if the fire had really caught. She had
the oddest feeling that the only thing that could possibly
have made a difference was the chanting she had done
before she went to sleep.

"Megan, how's the headache this morning?"

"The headache is fine, but I'm feeling icky. I think I'll
miss school today and just stay in bed."

"Anything the neurosurgeons should know about?"

"No. I know where I live and what day it is and where I
am. I also know that I'm going to shove this cat off the bed
if she doesn't quit digging her claws into my stomach and
pushing," she said as she moved Theadorble Cat out of the
way so that she could sit up.

Fiona could see the pain hit as Megan moved. The same
futile wish that she had every day came back again. If only
she could do something to help her daughter, to heal her so
that she never felt pain again. The doctors were certain it
would never happen for Megan. No chemotherapy actually
helped Megan's particular tumor. It might slow it down and
it certainly would make her terribly sick, but nothing
would cure what ailed her. Surgery? The doctors had already said they couldn't get to the places that might hide
the dark seeds of cancer. Megan was in remission now but
no one could tell what the future held for her. And the damage from the treatment would always remain.

Fiona was ready to give the spells and amulets and
charms a try, no matter how ridiculous she felt, because
they seemed to work. If the little fire had turned into a normal catastrophe, she and Harper would probably have been
burned out of their room and possibly their house.

Fiona waited until Megan had taken her morning morphine and gone back to bed to wait for the painkiller to
work and Harper had left for work. She didn't want any
interruptions when she tried her hand at this new witchcraft
stuff. She picked up Sally's carefully washed dishes and

hurried out the front door toward her friend's house. Normally she would have used the back door and the gate that connected directly with Sally and Carl's backyard, but the ground was uneven and the way her body was aching she wasn't sure she'd be able to keep from dropping the dishes before she returned them.

Fiona rang the front-door bell and waited. She amused herself by looking in through Sally's shiny-clean window, past the freshly cleaned damask draperies to the curio cabinets that lined the walls of Sally's formal living room, right between the mounted heads of all kinds of innocent African wildlife. She'd never seen anyone who had more collectibles than Sally or more dead animals than Carl. Of course Sally could afford to buy objects d'art like the tiny green and gold glass box that caught the light and reflected it outward toward Fiona. Next to the box was something that looked suspiciously like an ancient Egyptian game board, and Fiona remembered that Sally had said something about her father having known someone who was with Carnarvon at Tutankhamen's tomb and had taken just a few trinkets as mementos.

"You didn't have to bring that back this morning!" Sally opened the door and took the dishes from Fiona's hand. "Would you like to come in for a few minutes? Carl's just on his way out but we could share a cup of coffee."

"No, thanks, I think I'll go back and work this morning. Tell Carl hello for me," Fiona said. She avoided Carl whenever she could. She thought Sally had made a mistake when she married the man straight out of college, and nothing over the intervening years had changed her mind.

"I know you don't like Carl's trophies, but a man has to have his hobbies," Sally said.

"Including slaughtering innocent deer and mounting their heads on the wall? It's hardly the height of fashion to decorate with carcasses."

There was an unintelligible sound from the back of the

house and Sally began to close the door. "I'll talk to you later, then."

Fiona turned and walked down the steps. It was funny, she thought, how many times she'd stood on that doorstep and either Carl or the dead animals had kept her from going inside. The few times she had actually steeled herself to withstand the gaze of the deer and antelope, she'd felt uncomfortable the whole time and had been desperate to escape the oppressive rooms. Not even Sally's wonderful collection of crystal and gold trinkets could make it worth her while to stay in that house.

Fiona sighed in relief as she looked around her cluttered kitchen tabletop with the books stacked everywhere and cats all over the place and smiled. She liked her own home a lot better than Sally's palace. She also liked her own husband a lot better than Carl. She'd known the instant she met him that Harper was special and it had taken her only two weeks to convince him that it made sense to get married right away. Up until now they'd shared everything, but she wasn't sure she was ready to share magic with him quite yet. She didn't like the idea of anyone laughing at her.

Fiona called the cats into the kitchen. The book had been very explicit. It had to be psychically and physically quiet for her to attempt any kind of magic. She knew from experience that twenty-seven cats waiting for breakfast would give out the most awful psychic vibrations known to mankind. Quieting them with food was necessary. Chopped chicken in oatmeal sauce also would keep her three Siamese from climbing the legs of her jeans while she was trying to meditate and call the Goddesses of the North, South, East and West to help her with the first experience of bringing the powers to her.

Fiona finished dishing out the disgusting-looking food and retreated while the cats were eating. She went upstairs and closed the door to the studio behind her with a heartfelt sigh of relief. It was time to get to work. The first thing she

was going to do to test the power of witchcraft was to ask
for some money.

She opened up the book to the dog-eared pages she had
marked for her first foray into the bizarre realm of attempt-
ing to work magic. She had already searched for and found
plain white cardboard inside the one good shirt Harper had
stashed in the bedroom in case of an emergency. The shirt
was specifically restricted for use only when the ironing
wasn't done and there was no clean shirt that could be
popped into the dryer for a quick heating that would make
it office-presentable for an assistant comptroller.

Her work area already had all the paints and the pens
she would need to make the round shape with designs spec-
ified by the book. She had been adding to the chant she'd
started using the night before. She'd changed and strengthened the words all morning as she helped Harper pack
lunch and remember important papers. She thought she had
it just about right for the first time around.

Fiona went to the desk and gathered up the most profes-
sional photographs of her recent paintings. The one she
liked best was a portrait of Princess as a tiny Siamese kitten
in the geraniums. If that kitten didn't charm everyone,
nothing would. She set the photos on the desk. Two years
ago she'd sent five photographs out to the biggest greeting
card maker in the United States and received the pictures
back almost by return mail with a form rejection of her
work.

Maybe this time, with what these people called the Old
Religion's help, it would be different. She lined the snap-
shots up neatly on the wooden surface and opened the
book. It took a few moments to find the exact pages that
would lead her through the maze of ritual information she
needed to sell the pictures by using spells.

It's a good thing Harper doesn't know anything about
this, she chided herself as she picked out the base color she
wanted for the small round piece of cardboard that would

become her money-calling amulet. He'd laugh her out of the house if he found out. At least she thought he would.

"This is really dumb," she muttered as she looked up "wealth" in the color index and then quickly painted the circle a bright warm orange. She added an outer ring of dark blue for luck. She'd need luck. Even though she knew her paintings were easily as good as any of the others bought by the card company, she'd never hit exactly the right art editor at the right time to sell them. She was always either too early or too late, just behind or ahead of the trends. If witchcraft worked she wouldn't have to worry about that anymore.

Her mind wandered for a few minutes as she thought of what she could do with the $5,000 she'd get if Big Skies bought the kitten paintings. Fixing the plumbing came to mind immediately, along with enough other desperately needed house repairs that she realized she needed a contract for $10,000.

"Sufficient for your needs . . ."

The phrase popped into her mind from nowhere at all. She was certain she hadn't read it the night before. But there was a clear voice telling her to ask for what was sufficient for her needs, not just the $5,000 the paintings might bring.

"All right, then, as I'm painting this thing, I'm going to concentrate on asking for enough money for our needs instead of limiting myself to some arbitrary dollar amount."

She colored in the circle carefully until her artist's sensibilities were satisfied with the way the deep blue and orange worked together. The acrylics dried quickly and she looked in the book for the next set of designs she'd have to paint on the circle, both front and back.

"Ancient symbols control your mind," she read and almost called the whole session off again. She felt so damned foolish doing this and the book wasn't helping. Every sentence she read made her feel as if she was taking a trip into some kind of silliness that probably should have been left

behind in the sixties. No one had said she should be doing
drugs while working with magic, but she had the feeling
that smoking something wouldn't have hurt.

She closed the book decisively, determined to look for
some other answer; the small wind created by her slamming
the book made the letter from the IRS drift lazily to the
floor. She didn't even remember bringing it into the studio,
yet there it was, taunting her. "Your painting is a hobby,
not a business. Prove that you are entitled to the business
deductions you've taken as an artist." She still had to answer that damned demand, and the only way she could
prove she was a real working painter and not a hobbyist
was to show them work she had actually sold. Somehow
she had the gut feeling that twelve calendar pictures each
year wouldn't be enough to sway their judgment. Especially since the calendars were given away by a local savings
and loan company to anyone who asked for one.

"All right," she said. She'd give magic a chance to help
her defeat the IRS and whoever else was dumping on her.

The sign of the pyramid, with the eye in the middle,
has gained so much power from being on every dollar bill in circulation that you can tap into this power
and release it for yourself almost without effort.

That's one ancient symbol. I'll put the dollar sign around it
for good measure. She thumbed through the book until she
found the drawing she had decided to copy. On the back
we'll have an apple tree with lots of fruit, so that the jobs
will keep falling in my lap like apples.

She heard the persistent skritching of one of the cats at
the door. She tried to ignore it and failed. Obviously someone wanted in very badly.

She opened the door and looked down at Princess.

"I should have known it was you. I've never seen a Siamese with quite the curiosity quotient that you have. Not a closed door in the house, right?" she said as she picked up the cat and brought her into the room. She did a quick dance step designed to keep Derf and several of the other cats out—all they would do would be try to find a spot to spray and then they'd start fighting.

She could count on Princess not to bother anything. As official office kitty, she was the only one allowed free access to the studio. The cat positioned herself underneath the lamp on the desk and surveyed the whole proceedings as if she understood everything that was going on. She studied the pictures and reached over to gently pat the painting of her as a baby. She didn't make any other moves toward the objects on the desk.

Fiona decided it was all right for the cat to be in there with her. After all, the book had said something about animals sometimes helping the witch work spells. She didn't qualify as a witch and she supposed that cats and other animals that worked with spells were specially trained, but if any cat could help without any further instruction in the art of magic, it would be Princess.

She managed the chanting right up until the final line of the incantations and decided she had to make at least one more change. " 'So mote it be'? Oh come on, I can't say that and keep from laughing!" she argued with the book. "If it ruins the spell, then I'm sorry. But it's going to be changed to 'So cause it to be' or even 'So cause this to happen.' It's better English, anyway."

Fiona touched each of the pictures with the orange and dark blue disk, said her spell again and then quickly put the pictures in an envelope with a cover letter to Madge Lorenz, art director for Big Skies Greeting Cards, the biggest greeting card company in the nation. She had the whole package out for the postman before ten.

She walked back into the studio and looked at the book.

She was torn between the idea of creating a talisman to keep her family safe and the need to do some painting on the calendar that was nearing deadline.

I'll work, she finally decided. She would put the whole idea of doing anything else with witchcraft out of her mind until she found out how the picture whammy worked. No reason to use up energy, which she didn't have very much of to begin with. Besides, she hurt too much to paint for more than another twenty minutes. Her back ached and her leg felt numb. Her hands hurt and she had already noticed that she was having double vision. The doctor had warned her about that, but she hoped he was wrong about its being a sign of a more serious head trauma. She didn't have time for a head trauma at the moment.

She'd just have to do her best.

"Okay, Princess, we've had our fun for the morning, but it's getting late. Time to get to work," Fiona declared. She selected an environmental tape from the pile beside her tape deck and popped it into the player. Soon the sounds of a blizzard surrounded her, almost to the point where she smelled the sharpness of the snow-laden air.

She began working on November, hoping the people at the calendar company wouldn't mind that there was no Thanksgiving turkey in sight. She was sick of turkeys. She'd never liked painting them because they were intrinsically ugly, despite Benjamin Franklin's love of the bird. Instead, she'd given November a basket of leaves almost covered with snow, and a trail of animal tracks through a yard in front of a house, to show that there was life in winter, even if you couldn't quite see it. For the people who really looked at her paintings, she had hidden two tiny mice at the base of a tree and a kitten peering out from behind one of the balustrades on the porch of the old house as the wind whipped snow around the yard.

That was another "want" she could add to the list to be "magicked" into reality for her. She wanted a house with a huge yard and a real live porch that went around at least three sides. She wanted the yard filled with hollyhocks and geraniums, and Johnny-jump-ups growing in grand profusion in the garden at the base of the porch, and apple, peach and pear trees out back. A house with gingerbread woodwork and solid wood floors and high ceilings. And an efficient heating system, she added, reality exerting its pull on the wish. She'd had enough of three- and four-hundred-dollar heating bills in the house they lived in now. It leaked like a sieve and she was never warm, no matter how much money they spent. Yes, she definitely required a nice insulated building. No use trading a real house for a dream house with the same faults.

As she painted, she fantasized about the perfect place. A basement for all her canned stuff would be nice. Space enough to put the spinning wheel and loom she'd taken classes to learn how to use and then never had time to work with. A place that was dry and cool in the summer so that she could paint in the basement to get away from the heat. The perfect basement. Fiona painted in a small, almost hidden window for the basement with the merest hint of rows of jars and a spinning wheel in the shadows.

Playing make-believe was one of the reasons she liked painting. She could put herself so thoroughly into the pictures that coming back to real life was sometimes very difficult. At the moment, the house in November's canvas was so real to her that she could have pushed back the snow that had piled against the window and crawled into the basement. She'd climb up the stairs and go into the kitchen, where there would be a shiny old cast-iron stove and pine-plank floors and the smell of freshly baked brownies. She'd have curtains of her favorite feed sacks, the ones with the Jersey cows on a blue background, and there'd be plenty of heavy, expensive copper pans to cook in. None of that fancy don't-use-it copper, but the real thing, really meant for cooking. The snow would swirl around the house, making it feel cozy and comforting. She pulled the feeling of the house around her like a fluffy blanket.

Outside, the warmth of the sun had dimmed as fog moved in over the Berkeley hills, heading for Fiona's house.

The phone rang, breaking the spell, and the fingers of fog began to retreat as the sun burned into the mist.

"Hey, how long have you been painting? Are you about ready for a break? I really need to talk to you. The strangest things have been happening today . . ." Gia sighed dramatically. "Wait till you hear the latest about Larry the Louse. And you'll die when you see my hair."

"Hair? Gia, what did you do now?" Fiona asked. "Come on over and I'll take a break. I deserve one because November is finally finished. Even the last bit of cloud in the sky is done, complete with a silver lining."

Fiona hesitated and then decided to ask Gia for a favor. She ached enough that she deserved something chocolate, and the smell of the brownies from the kitchen in a house that existed only as a painting still lingered. "Stop by the store and pick up something chocolate, will you? I'll pay you back. I can't move well enough to even think about cooking something and I'm about to go into withdrawal. Damn the budget, anyway, I need double-fudge cookies."

Twenty minutes later the two women were eating still-hot chocolate squares from the bakery and talking about the day's happenings.

"Do you suppose we should invite Sally over?" Fiona asked. "She's usually home now."

"Nope. I want to talk to you alone. I always have the feeling that she's sitting there waiting for me to say something she can use against me. And believe me, with this change, she'd almost certainly say something I wouldn't want to hear."

"Well, it's different." Fiona hadn't believed that the woman who came in the back door was actually Gia until she'd had a good look at her friend's face. Short spiky hair and glittering jewels had a way of changing people's looks.

"But it's great. I'd never have thought that short hair suited you, but it does!" Fiona could see that Gia was beginning to have second thoughts about the impromptu hairdo. "And to go on a diet and get rid of two hundred pounds all in one nasty lump—I'm proud of you, Gia."

"Don't forget the man at the shop. I guess that was a pickup attempt. It made me feel good, too. I wish I knew who he was." Gia's voice was dreamy. "He was good-looking and wore clothes that Larry would have killed for. Of course the man couldn't have had any idea how I would react to that incense oil he had me sniff. Can you imagine putting that oil on and then going to bed with a complete stranger? If it made me feel like throwing myself down on the cushions and telling him to ravish me, imagine what it would have done if I'd actually accepted a date with him. What if he spilled some of it on me in the car and I'd had that reaction? It makes me shiver to just think about it. And I could have an affair, you know. Now that Larry is gone, there's no reason at all to stay monogamous, is there?"

Gia fiddled with her ears. The jewels were beautiful, but, like the place where her attachment to Larry had been, there were sore spots that didn't bear too much poking.

"You mean to tell me that your husband leaves you in the morning and by afternoon you've practically fallen in bed with another man? Harlot!" Fiona laughed.

"Not exactly," Gia admitted. "It's just that I was so angry with Larry that when that man made a pass at me, well, I was ready to take a tumble."

"Tell me more about this store. What do they do, serve witchcraft with the luncheon specials?" Fiona asked.

"Not exactly, but the reading selection is a little bit eclectic. I picked up a newspaper, thinking it was one of those free trade and barter things, and it was all about Pagan Circles, and who was joining what coven. Oh, and there was a section of ads thanking the Goddess for her help with wishes—kind of like a pagan St. Jude message. Strange!"

"Do you think the man you met had anything to do with witchcraft? Could he have used that oil to pull you into some kind of spell with him?"

"No, all he wanted to do was pull me into bed. I'm sure of that. But I wouldn't mind at all if there was some spell work going on between me and that beautiful hunk of a blond with the Rune stones. Oh Fiona, he was beautiful!"

"Sounds pretty good to me, too, if it weren't for Harper."

"I looked over some of those books and I might go back and buy one just to set such a voodoo on Larry that his penis shrivels up so small it'll take a magnifying glass to find it. Then he and Kelly can enjoy each other as much as they want. Bet you his tongue wouldn't hold out long enough to do any good," Gia said with a wicked smile.

Fiona giggled. "What a wonderful image. That sounds just like the old Gia I knew a couple of years ago. Do you know, it's been months since you've let yourself have a good attack of anger? You've been damping it all down trying to please Larry, and it's got you nothing but heartache."

"No more! He can have that two-bit bimbette if he wants, but I'm not going to let him control me any longer. And I just may give this Wicca idea a try, too. It couldn't hurt, could it?"

Fiona was just about to tell Gia her own day's adventures when the phone rang. Her stomach tightened into the familiar knot of worry that the call would be from a creditor or would mean a hassle with the school over Megan's continued absence. It could even be from Harper about his job. They were the same worries that hit her every time she answered the phone.

"May I speak with Fiona Kendrick?" It sounded like long distance.

"This is Fiona Kendrick," she admitted, wondering why she felt as if she had been pinned to the wall and was about to be eviscerated, long distance, by a bill collector.

"Oh, I am so glad that I finally managed to track you down," the woman said. "The people at Primarily Calendars simply did not want to tell me anything about you, including how to reach you."

The woman paused for a second to catch her breath. "This is Madge Lorenz from Big Skies card company." Her voice ended with an upward questioning lilt. "We've been looking at some of the work you did this year for the Country Calendar series. We're interested in knowing if you've ever considered submitting some of your work to us? We're about to start a new country line and think you'd be a great addition to our team."

Fiona sagged against the counter. Big Skies? *The* Big Skies? And Madge Lorenz was the art director she had sent her sample photographs to when she made up the package this morning! Of course she recognized the name; she'd been chanting it for almost twenty minutes trying to put a whammy on the woman to make her look at the paintings. And Madge Lorenz was calling her because she wanted Fiona Kendrick herself to paint for their new line? Incredible!

"Hello, are you still there? Darn, I hate this, the lines keep going dead on me," Madge said.

"Yes, yes, I'm here, I was just surprised, that's all. You won't believe this, but at ten o'clock this morning I sent a package to you. It has photographs of some of my latest work and should be on your desk within two days."

Madge was silent for a moment. "I like people who are prompt, but I think you've outdone just about everyone else I've ever known in the punctual department. Tell me, do any of the paintings you've sent have pictures of cats or kittens in them? We're looking for people who can really do cats well and you have a talent for it. Tell me, do you own any cats?"

Fiona bit back a laugh. Any? The woman wouldn't believe her if Fiona told her the truth about the twenty-seven-cat household.

"Yes, I do. There are four different paintings that will interest you in the group." She remembered Princess daintily touching the portrait of her as a baby, all blue eyes and fuzz and cuteness in the geraniums. There was a second painting of her trying to bury a mouse in the flowers. "I think there are two of a Siamese that will catch your eye." Strange, she thought. The cats had never been anything but an expense, yet here they were, playing an active part in her getting a new plum of a job. Maybe there was something to this "familiar" business for witches who had pets.

Not that she thought of herself as a witch, of course. Not after just one spell that seemed to have worked.

"Well, that's fine then. I'll be getting back to you. If these are what we want, and I can almost promise you that they will be, we'll be sending out a standard contract for you. I know you have other jobs, but since the line is new and we're going to need a great deal of material, we'd like it very much if you could count on us as your primary customer for the rest of the year. We promise to make it worth your time."

"I think that could be arranged," Fiona said, proud that she could manage to say anything at all.

She hung up the phone and grabbed Gia, dancing her around the room in a mad gallop.

"I did it, I did it, I finally made the big contact and I think I'll really get a contract from it. Come on, Gia, we're going out for the biggest, stickiest double chocolate fudge sundae in existence and I'm paying!"

"Oh my God, you mean you've really got a contract? A real one that will bring you in money?"

"Enough to fix the plumbing, I'll bet. And all because of the cats and that calendar last year."

"You call Harper and then we're going out for lunch. Ask Megan if she wants to come along, because this is going to be one whale of a celebration!"

"Oh." Fiona skidded to a sudden stop. "How about we order in Chinese food and I check the freezer for whatever we have in the way of ice cream?"

"Bad day for Megan?"

"Very. I'm keeping my fingers and toes and eyes crossed for good luck, because otherwise she's going in for more surgery. The pain's a lot worse than usual. If it's just the accident, we're all right. If not—" Fiona left the rest unsaid. Gia had stood by her through months of surgeries with Megan. She knew what was at stake if the headaches got worse. "So how about a celebration dinner here tonight?"

For right now, though, if Megan recovered even a little bit, Fiona knew what to thank for the shift in fortune. Someday soon she'd have to tell both Gia and Harper what had really happened to make the luck change.

4

"To the ready-to-be-most-famous artist in the country, may you be as popular as Laurel Burch and as rich as Norman Rockwell!" Gia lifted the glass containing the best red wine she could find in Larry's small wine cellar. Harper raised his own glass in a salute to his wife.

"To my best friends," Fiona answered, raising her own glass.

"May you enjoy the wine, at eight hundred dollars a bottle the last time Larry bought it," Gia said as they all sipped.

It was the perfect topper for the celebration dinner that took the place of the lunch they couldn't have. Fiona choked and Harper set the goblet firmly down on the table as he regarded the bottle with the quaint French label. French was the one language he'd always failed back home and the only word he could decipher was "Mouton," written in gold on the black background. "Maybe we'd better cork it back up. A celebration dinner is one thing, but drinking almost one-tenth of the profits in one gulp might be overkill, don't you think?"

"Don't worry about it, it's not your profits that are being spent. It's ill-gotten gains from people he swindled on every legal case he ever handled," Gia said. "Larry deserves to lose every cent he ever made. Not once did I hear him talk about exerting himself or putting forth his best effort for a client unless he was going to have a major financial gain himself."

"So why did you stay with him all this time?"

"Because it was easier to stay than to leave. I wanted to be comfortably married more than I wanted to be divorced and on my own, is the best explanation I can give."

The three of them talked late into the evening about the ways their lives had changed just in the past week. Fiona and Harper did the dishes while they chatted with Gia. Twenty minutes after the dishes were done, Gia left for home.

"I'll sleep with a gun under my pillow. Just think, if Larry decides to come calling in the middle of the night, I could shoot him and legitimately claim that I thought he was a burglar. What a nice thought."

Harper and Fiona closed the door behind Gia and climbed the stairs to their bedroom.

"Anything good on?" Fiona asked as she settled down beside her husband. She didn't particularly like television, but she used the chance to just be next to him, enjoying the comfort of his arm around her shoulder.

"There's *MacGyver* on forty-one, something in Spanish on thirty-six and wrestling." As he talked, he flipped the channels back and forth between wrestling and all the other channels available. He knew channel surfing drove Fiona nuts, but he did it anyway.

Fiona reached for the channel changer, but he moved it smoothly out of range. "We could talk, you know," she said. "There are a couple of things we need to discuss and we never have the time."

Harper groaned. "Not now, please? I'm dead tired." He

flipped the channel to the twenty-four-hour sales network, stopping just long enough for Fiona to get a glimpse of a silver cat ring with a garnet.

"Stop! Go back, I want that ring," she ordered. "I'm getting a good contract, I should be able to spend twenty-five dollars frivolously, right?" For the first time in ages, she set aside the thought of all the unpaid bills and considered something she wanted just for fun.

"Honey, you deserve anything you want," he said. He even found a pen and paper to write down the number and the price for her, then fumbled with his wallet and handed over the one credit card that wasn't maxed out.

"Go for it, love," he said.

Fiona barely finished hanging up the phone when she heard a bone-chilling thunk and a yowl of agony from the backyard. The sound rose to a screech that made the hairs on the back of her neck stand up.

"It's a cat," she cried, grabbing the flashlight and heading down the stairs and outside.

"What's going on?" Megan asked, roused from a sound sleep.

"I don't know, but someone's hurt bad," Fiona yelled as she stood on the back deck, trying to analyze where the agonized screaming was coming from. Above her, she heard her neighbor laughing.

"You son of a bitch," she snarled and raced up the back hill toward the man's backyard. She crashed through the bramble she had planted to keep the skunks and raccoons safe and hidden, ignoring the thorns that ripped into her skin. It took almost a minute to make it to the top fence. There was a small area where the posts met that she could squeeze through.

"Got another one of them little bastards. Should be dead by the morning," she heard the neighbor say almost in her ear. She whirled, ready to push the man down the hill to pay him back for the agony he was causing an animal.

"Skunk, raccoon, cat, who the hell knows as long as that trap kills it and it don't bother me no more."

She opened her mouth and then shut it when she realized he wasn't talking to her. She could see him through the window, his grizzled head looking out toward the darkness. He was in his kitchen talking to someone on the phone.

The cat continued to scream.

She doused the flashlight and walked forward, using the light from the kitchen to guide her. Ten feet from the man's back porch, an embankment cut down to the drainage ditch that dead-ended above her yard. Below her she could see a cat writhing in pain, its black and white markings bleached in the moonlight. A trap glinted, the ugly steel teeth closed through the cat's left hind leg.

"Loner cat," she breathed. It was the cat she'd been feeding for months, hoping to get close enough to catch him and take him in to the vet for shots and a checkup. Despite her best efforts, the cat had always eluded her. Tonight he hadn't eluded the steel fangs of the trap.

Fiona raced down the slope and grabbed the cat, supporting his hindquarters and the trap. She ignored the cat's hissing and the occasional fang sinking into her arm as she turned and ran back home. She couldn't negotiate the slope behind her house with an injured animal in her arms, so she raced to the steps leading out of the drainage ditch and then down through the court and back to her own house. By the time she reached the house, the cat had stopped fighting. Fiona didn't know whether it was from the pain and shock or because the cat was beginning to trust her.

"Hurry, get the keys to the car, we've got to get this cat to the emergency clinic," she ordered Harper.

"No, wait." She ran over to the intercom. "Megan, honey, I need Dr. Thomyer's home phone number. It's in the Rolodex under 'vets,' and make it fast."

Megan raced down the stairs, bringing the whole Rolodex with her. "I figured this was faster. Want me to dial?" She carefully avoided looking at the bleeding cat in her mother's arms. The scrawny animal had gone silent and the yellow eyes that had always glared defiance at the world were slowly glazing over. Loner's paws twitched once in a while, but the pool of blood on the floor beneath Fiona's feet showed that there wasn't much time left.

"Dr. Thomyer? I need your help. Cat caught in a steel trap, dying in my arms. You've got to help me save him. He either dies here or he gets treated by you because I won't go to the emergency clinic. The last time I took a cat there it died because they took in a dog with a foxtail up its nose first while my little kitten was dying." Her eyes stung with tears.

"You'll meet me at the clinic? Thank you," Fiona said. "Megan, clean up the blood and keep the other cats away from it. We don't know if this old guy has leukemia or not, so I don't want the others exposed to anything. We'll be back when you see us."

She and Harper rushed out of the house with the cat.

"Come on, baby, you can't give up now. I've just managed to get you in my arms and now you're trying to die on me?"

She stroked the rounded black and white head. The cat moved under her touch, but didn't open his eyes. She could feel the battle scars of the years spent on the outside when she touched him. He was fading. His breathing was shallow and rapid and when she pressed her fingers into the space beside his ribs, she could feel his heart beginning to miss beats.

"Don't die," she pleaded with the animal. She couldn't stand to have that last breath wheeze out of the cat's lungs and feel the body go completely limp. She'd held other cats as they died and it always hurt, even when it was better for the cat to die than to live in pain.

"I hate you, you son of a bitch." Fiona leveled a blast of

loathing at her neighbor. How dare he hurt living animals and think it was fun when they screamed. "If I had a way of hurting you where they'd never find out I did it, I'd take care of you in an instant."

It made her sick with fury and disgust to think that someone could actually enjoy the sound of an animal being hurt.

The doctor was waiting inside the clinic with all the lights on and all the machines ready to help save the cat.

Fiona lowered the cat and the steel trap to the shining stainless-steel surface of the surgical table. The doctor took one look, winced and set to work.

Within a few moments she had a blood sample to test for leukemia. If that was negative, they could proceed with surgery. If it was positive, there was no use continuing, since they all knew that a leukemia-positive cat couldn't come into Fiona's house, and with this type of injury he'd never be anything except a house cat again.

"IV first, intubate him, and then we'll get an X ray and see what's going on in there."

The vet worked smoothly, slipping the plastic needle into the vein and establishing a line for lactated Ringer's solution that dripped into the cat's body. She slid the tube down his throat without bothering with lidocaine to deaden the area. The cat was so far gone that he didn't even fight.

"Here, Harper, you stand here, count to ten and squeeze this bag shut when you reach ten. You're going to be breathing for him. I'll tell you if you need to slow down or speed things up." The vet handed Harper the black vinyl bag that was attached to the cat's breathing tube and showed him how to begin the count, squeeze the bag shut and let it fill up again.

The machine pinged and Dr. Thomyer read the numbers from the blood test.

The cat was negative.

She eased a thermometer up the cat's hind end, and waited.

"One hundred. Not the best, but it'll do. Any lower and we'd have to put him on a heating pad while we work. I'll set up the X ray, and then at the last moment, I'll tell you to move out of the way. Go around the corner while I take the pictures, then run back in to keep up the bagging."

Harper was barely out of the way the required ten seconds before he rushed back in to start breathing for the cat again. He reached for the bag and stopped.

"Look, I think he's breathing on his own."

Dr. Thomyer gave him a thumbs-up sign. "You're right. But stick around in case the next part gets hairy and he needs a little more help." She shoved the X rays she'd been carrying into the lighted panel that illuminated the pictures.

"Look how the trap shattered the leg when it hit. The poor kid is a mess. We're going to have to amputate, no question about it." She waved at the various lines that meant something to her and nothing at all to either Harper or Fiona.

"First we get that trap off him. Help me pull these damned steel teeth back and jam that pin into the spring to keep it open," she instructed Fiona.

Working together, they loosened the metal from the cat's hind leg. Fiona's stomach did a strange little dance when she saw the shards of bone jutting through the muscles and skin.

The doctor looked up and saw Fiona start to turn green. "Don't you dare pass out or throw up on me, I don't have anyone else to be an assistant and the cat will die without help," she said. She did something with some of the cat's blood, setting a machine and timer.

"Yes ma'am." Fiona grinned weakly.

The vet opened the cat's mouth and pushed down on the gum above the left canine tooth, leaving a white mark that almost immediately turned back to a nice healthy pink.

The cat gave a weak heave and settled back down. Fiona peered at the little chest, hoping the movement hadn't been the cat's dying breath. No, the chest was still moving up and down.

The machine pinged and the vet leaned over to read the numbers. "I know you said he lost a lot of blood, but right now his platelet count is all right. We can amputate and then check again to see if he needs a transfusion from our little donor kitty. And I think he's going to be okay enough to tolerate anesthetic, too."

The vet began to cut into the leg, suturing as she went, cleaning up the mess the steel teeth had left. It took almost half an hour before the last flap of skin was pulled over the gaping wound.

Fiona wished death to the old man for causing this kind of damage in another living being. No, she amended her thoughts, death was too good for him. She wished a slow agonizing decline that ended in a painful death.

"Loner cat's going to have to stay with us for a week or so," Dr. Thomyer said. "He's going to be getting medication and we'd like to make sure he starts to eat and has all the other functions intact. It's going to be rough without that leg for an old tom, but I think he's going to survive. He's a fighter. Why don't you go home and go to bed and just rest now? Both of you look completely bushed."

"That's because you wouldn't believe the day we've had," Fiona said, rubbing the cat's ears. She was shaking with tension and elation.

The cat opened his eyes and stared at her; the yellow eyes gleamed with life. He managed one hiss before going back to sleep.

Fiona smiled. "That's okay, old boy, we'll work on your personality later."

5

Gia heard the familiar roar of the Mercedes while she was standing in front of the refrigerator, trying to decide between eating the last piece of cheesecake before it could go bad, shaving the fur off some ancient cheddar, or going shopping to replenish her badly depleted stores of food. She picked up the cheese and a knife, thinking she'd at least try to be healthy, when she heard the car and all thoughts of food vanished.

It couldn't be.

He couldn't be coming back. He wouldn't be stupid enough to do that. Well, he wouldn't have been so stupid if he'd been acting normal. Who knew what he'd do now?

She heard the car doors slam and frowned. Two doors. Why would he bring someone with him to the house? Surely he couldn't think he was going to squeeze so much stuff into his red Mercedes that he needed help carrying it out of the house.

"Come on in. Gia's always out shopping in the morning, finding places to spend money." Larry's voice echoed in the hallway. He wasn't even making an effort to keep quiet.

"Ohhh, Larry, is this where we'll live when you finally dump the bitch?" The thin, shrill voice cut through the hushed interior of the house like a saw blade.

"Yes, of course, sweetie, this is exactly where we'll set up our love nest, if you like it. I'll have Gia out of here in no time at all. With the lawyers I've got on my side she won't get the house, the money or the cars out of me. In fact, she'll have a hard time finding an apartment she can afford, much less a house." Larry's voice was rich with satisfaction.

Gia listened, her hand closing quietly on the handle of the knife she had been holding to slice the cheese. Should she call the police? No, he'd just pull his credentials as an attorney and the policemen would creep away and she'd be left looking like a fool. Worse, she might be in danger.

Larry could decide to attack her.

She lifted the cheese knife. If he tried anything, anything at all in her house, she was going to use the knife on parts of him that were rarely exposed to light.

"We'll go upstairs and get my stuff and . . ." he whispered something to the woman.

"Oh Larry, that would be positively decadent! Let's do it!" she giggled.

Gia was so angry that she almost stopped thinking. Then her natural instinct for self-preservation took hold. She could use this. When it came time to meet Larry in court, this would make a juicy, nasty tidbit that would sway the jury toward her side. She had to think of the best way to turn Larry's indiscretion against him. If she wanted to make a real mess in a courtroom, what would she need?

Damn, she wished she had time to call E. T. Gunnerson. He'd have known what she needed to do to protect herself and her home.

Witnesses—she had to get witnesses. She lifted the phone in the kitchen quietly, certain from the chatter on the stairs that Larry wouldn't hear her. She hit the memory button and Fiona answered almost immediately.

"Fiona, don't ask questions, just get over here and watch what Larry is doing. Come in the front door, but be quiet. Don't make a sound. I'll be upstairs."

Gia's mind raced. What more could she do? What more damage could she cause that would backfire against Larry? It would look great in court if she had something concrete showing just how stupid he was acting.

She really wanted to stab him. She wanted to catch him naked and cut off his balls and stuff them down his throat as an appetizer to his skinny little prick. But if she physically attacked him, she'd end up in jail and that wouldn't help her case. All she wanted was a way to make certain he didn't get anything out of the marriage except trouble. She deserved all the money and goods just for putting up with him. She didn't want to lose her freedom while she figured out how to take everything.

The videocam.

She sent up a quick prayer of thanks that she had never managed to find any other place to stash the bulky silver case other than in the pantry. The camera was available, ready to go. She was going to make the damnedest home movie any judge had ever seen.

She kicked off her shoes and walked silently to the door that separated the kitchen from the pantry. She eased it open and reached in for the camera case. She took out the camera, plugged in the battery and set things up without making a bit of noise. The tape of Larry's last birthday was still in the camera. There was plenty of space for a movie of his latest little peccadillo.

Larry's voice faded as he and Kelly slowly worked their way up the stairs, certain that they didn't need to be in any kind of hurry.

"Now, you bastard, I'll take care of you."

Gia stepped out of the kitchen just far enough to be able to see the stairs. She looked up and saw Larry kissing the woman, his hands groping her buttocks, pushing her body close to his. If they'd been on the street, they'd have been arrested for public lewdness as Larry bumped his obvious erection against her.

Gia focused the camera, wishing she had more light. Still, she knew she'd get a good picture. She'd filmed in worse circumstances and the camera had adjusted just fine. She pressed the button that would date and time the pictures and began taping. The green light blinked as the tape wound slowly, recording every squishy kiss and bump and grind. Gia grinned. Larry was costing himself thousands of dollars and she was going to enjoy spending every little cent. Her husband stood there, fondling Kelly as if he had every right to bring his whore into the house. Outrage almost overcame reason as Gia watched them slowly move up the stairs toward the bedroom.

Gia took a deep breath. She couldn't afford to let her emotions get in the way. Anger and hurt pride weren't good enough reasons to blow a shot at having a judge give her even more than the community property she was entitled to. With this video to back up her claims, she had instant dreams of Larry folding and not fighting her as she took everything. No, she couldn't give in to emotions. Instead, she focused on Kelly. Larry had lousy taste in concubines. His playpal had obviously bleached-blond hair, thick lips that looked as if a doctor had gone wild with collagen injections, a figure that was skinny to the point of emaciation and a high whiny voice that would drive him crazy inside of a year.

The bastard deserved everything he got, including the clap.

Gia followed them up the stairs, walking so softly that they couldn't possibly hear her. She had it all planned out. She'd give Larry the scare of a lifetime, if she could keep her temper under control.

She stood in the hall outside the bedroom. She wanted to see if Larry would actually be crude enough to take this woman into the bedroom and try to seduce her on their marriage bed.

"Ah Christ," she heard Larry whine. "Look what she did, replacing everything with this ruffled shit. And I paid a fortune for the black and red set." The sounds of his footsteps faded as he went to the closet. "Where did all my clothes go?" He slammed one door open and then the second one. "What did she do, give it all away? I knew I should have come back here and taken it before she could do anything. My Italian suits, my sweaters, my Guccis, everything's gone!"

"So we'll buy you more. Stop yelling. I thought we were going to have a good time, not talk about your ex-wife," Kelly pouted.

Larry was silent for a few moments; then Gia heard him moving toward the bed. He was actually going to make love to Kelly on her bed, on her new sheets and comforters. For a moment, Gia's resolve not to interfere wavered; then she decided she wanted the video more than she wanted pristine sheets.

She kept recording, the lens focused toward the door, so that there would be no question in the jurors' minds when they watched and heard the video.

Gia padded over to the open door and walked into the room. She stood in the shadows of the darkened bedroom, watching. She was surprised to discover that she felt no emotion as she watched her husband caressing another woman in the middle of their bed. Instead, she focused on the mechanics of making the most of the spectacle in front of her. She pushed the button that would take an automatic close-up of Larry's naked behind, which was a little flabby and pocked with cellulite. He had his pants down around his knees and was trying to hold them up while he fought to raise his legs high enough to get onto the bed with Kelly.

As he crawled onto the bed, she panned over to Kelly.

The woman hadn't even bothered to get undressed. Instead, she had simply pulled up the skirt of her dress, bunching the bright yellow material around her hips. Since she wasn't wearing any underwear, Larry was presented with a sight of open legs that apparently drove him wild. He growled and launched himself at her as his wife got a full frontal view first of Kelly's wanton display and then of Larry's erection.

He had almost entered her when Kelly moaned in fake pleasure, turned her head and focused on the shadows near the door.

She gave a heart-stopping scream.

"What happened? Did I hurt you?" Larry jumped back and almost fell off the side of the bed, where he was precariously perched amid the pillows.

"Larry . . . look!" She pushed him off the bed, her arms amazingly strong for a skinny woman.

"What the hell's wrong with you?" He stumbled and then turned around to see what had upset Kelly so much.

"Surprise!" Gia said, taping the look of blank shock and then the one of indignation that crossed Larry's face.

"You bitch, what the hell do you think you're doing!" He lunged for her, then lurched as his pants fell around his ankles. He snatched them back up and reached for the camera. "I'll kill you, I swear to God I will. How dare you intrude on our privacy—"

"Your privacy? This is my bedroom," Gia said. The tape was still running.

Larry grabbed for the camera again, connecting with Gia's shoulder and knocking her off balance. The camera swung wildly, but she maintained her grip on the strap as she fell and the green light kept blinking as the recording continued.

Grimly she went on filming as Larry punched her. He tried to wrest the camera from her. He couldn't break her grip on the camera, so he kicked her in the face. One-quarter of an inch to the right and he'd have blacked her eye. Instead, he bruised his toes on her cheekbones. He screamed in pain and hopped backward, cradling his foot.

"You bitch! I think it's broken." One toe stuck out at an odd angle. Larry had gone white with the shock of the pain. He pulled back his arm and prepared to deliver a roundhouse punch that would have knocked Gia unconscious.

"Larry, what are you doing? Larry, don't." Kelly's voice was a high frenzied wail.

"What the hell is going on here?" Fiona's voice cut through the confusion as she ran up the stairs and into the room. "I heard screams and I thought you'd kill each other before I got here."

Larry leaned against the bed and moaned. He held his foot and tried to zip his pants at the same time.

Gia managed to sit up against the wall, the camera still held in a death grip in her right hand. Kelly's mouth snapped shut as Fiona surveyed the room.

"Are you all right?" Fiona asked Gia, glaring at Larry as he finally managed to close his pants. He sat on the bed and cradled his injured foot. "What's the matter with you, Larry? And what the hell is that woman doing here? No wonder Gia called me to come over!"

Fiona narrowed her eyes as she pointed at Kelly. "Pull your dress down, you floozy, no one wants to see your smelly old parts around here except Larry, and he'll have to do that someplace else!"

"Shit," Larry said. He reached down and grabbed his shoes and socks in one hand and Kelly's arm in the other. He pulled her off the bed and hobbled out of the room and down the stairs. Gia followed him every step of the way, the camera still relentlessly recording.

At the door Larry turned around and confronted his wife. "That's all right, Gia, you keep this recording, lot of good may it do you. When I'm through with you, you won't have even a penny of my money. I promise you, as a lawyer I have the people on my side. I've got the power, I've got the money and I've got the name. And *you* are going to get the shaft. I'll die and go to hell before you win."

"Yeah! He'll do it, too!" Kelly said, peering out from behind Larry, where she had retreated as Gia advanced on her.

He grabbed the front door and slammed it shut, effectively cutting off any reason to continue taping. The car motor ground to life and the Mercedes raced away from the house.

Gia and Fiona looked at each other and breathed a sigh of relief as their hearts began to return to a more normal rhythm.

"What a hell of a scene! I didn't know what was going on when you called, and then I saw Larry's car outside and didn't know what I'd find. I've got to tell you, I was afraid I'd discover blood and bodies when I came through that back door."

Gia walked ahead of Fiona into the pantry. She set the camera on the counter and extracted the tape. She reached over to her purse and slipped it inside, where it would be safe. She took out the battery, plugged it in to recharge and put the camera safely away in the silver case.

"First thing we're going to do is get a copy of this tape. I'll keep one, and you keep one at your house. Then we're going to figure out a way to fight Larry, and I don't mean legally, either. I need more help than the law can give me right now."

"How do you intend to get this help?"

Gia took down a couple of cups and opened the tin of coffee she had ground that morning. She was debating whether to go ahead and tell Fiona and risk having her best friend in the whole world consider her crazed enough for an institution, or worse, weird enough that Fiona would just walk out of the house, never to return. Finally Gia decided to risk revelation.

"Remember I told you that my grandmother used to say that people could put hexes on you and cause trouble?"

"Sure. But what has that got to do with you and Larry?"

"I didn't tell you everything my grandmother used to say or do. You have to understand, she was kind of a strange person. She kept to herself, like a lot of our family, because no one quite trusted her. They used to say she had powers. I believe she did."

Gia fixed a couple of cups' worth of ground coffee and popped them into the coffeemaker to brew. She pressed the buttons and continued. "One thing Larry doesn't know is that I have an old book full of what she used to call her recipes. She used them to remember incantations and potions. I'm going to see if any of Grandma's talents came down to me."

"What are you talking about?"

Gia hesitated. She could lose Fiona as a friend forever, if she'd misread her. It had happened before when she'd confided to a friend in college about her grandmother. But there was no going back now.

"Witchcraft," Gia said softly.

6

W itchcraft?" Fiona repeated. She couldn't believe this. Something weird was at work here. There was no reason in the world for Gia to have come up with witchraft as a way to solve problems at the same time as she had.

"Yes, that's probably the right name. Does that shock you?"

Fiona shook her head. "However, it strikes me as a very odd coincidence, considering that I took my first baby steps with witchcraft a couple of nights ago."

"You? Nah!"

"Believe it. I'm tired of trouble, and witchcraft promises protection. You should see the fire that almost happened. Then there's the matter of Loner cat. I saved that trap and brought it home and I've been trying to think of a way to use it against my neighbor. The best I can do right now is to plan on setting the trap outside his front door and hoping he steps out to get the morning paper without looking. The only drawback is that if he sidesteps the trap, he'll be able to use it to hurt animals again. So it's time to try witchcraft against him to get even for the damage he caused."

Fiona paused and then continued, "The other thing that brought me to Wicca is some reading I've been doing. It seems that I've been using the Craft naturally for years. I just didn't have a name for it. You know, like my being able to tell when Harper's having a bad day or hearing the car coming up the road before he actually arrives. It's always been there, I just didn't realize what it was called."

"Well, I'll be damned," Gia breathed. "From opposite ends of the universe, for opposite reasons, we've both reached the same conclusion. I think it's time for a visit to that quaint little bookstore, restaurant and witch's supply house I found the other day."

"Sounds like a great idea to me. Megan's down for a while. I hate to leave her alone, but it should be all right. I'll call a couple of times, in case her headache gets bad."

Gia raised her hand as her friend began to stand up. "Maybe we'd better read Grandma's book and find what I need to buy. Then we'll go shopping. I wish I lived back in the hills, I wouldn't have had to spend a dime. Grandma made everything herself and used what she collected from the area around her cabin. It sure made doing spells a lot cheaper."

They studied the pages of the little book, the spidery writing faded to brown. As they read, Gia made a list of the bare essentials.

"Grandma always had a cast-iron pot, a copper kettle and rock salt. Did you notice she used rock salt in every spell? I wonder what it did, other than raise blood pressure."

"Maybe that was the whole secret. She could knock someone off by making them have a stroke and die," Fiona suggested.

"In a love potion?"

"It made getting an erection easier?"

"I don't know. Anyway, we'll find out soon enough. I've got the list, so let's go," Gia said.

Within ten minutes they were on the street where Major Arcana stood.

"What are you going to try first, protection or revenge?" Fiona asked and then laughed at the weirdness of the question. It was strange to be discussing such things, as if it made perfect sense to be sitting in the sunshine in the middle of an ordinary day, waiting for another car to back out so that they could park, while talking about spells and protection.

"Maybe both," Gia said. She led the way down the street toward the shop. "First thing I want to do is to bind him so completely that he can't harm me. Then I think I want to go to work on Kelly. She deserves every nasty zit I can send her way."

Fiona whistled quietly as she entered the store. It looked exactly the way a shop catering to the more outré aspects of New Age philosophy should look. She was fascinated by the shelves that lined the walls, the staircase and most of the second floor, and were filled with oils, essences, crystals and a number of objects that defied classification. Dried herbs hung from every post on the curving staircase that lead to the second floor and from overhead racks that lined the ceiling of the first floor. She could identify some of them but certainly not all. There were books everywhere and a warm comforting scent of bread being baked somewhere in the back. The yeast and scent of hundreds of herbs mixing into a pungent, satisfying odor. The lunch counter had a sign on it that said Closed, but coffee was still being served from a steaming pot. As she entered the store, a large gray and white tabby cat greeted her and began to wind himself around her legs.

"The place can't be too bad if it's got a cat," Fiona said, picking up the animal. He began to purr and settled into her arms so that she could carry him around the store. His paws kneaded her skin and she winced as the claws drew blood by digging in a fraction of an inch too far.

A woman moved out from the shadows. "Hello, my name is Selene. Can I help you?" She stared hard at Fiona and passed her hand over her face, as if clearing her vision. "What an odd sensation. I could swear you've been important in one of my lives before."

"Hate to say it, but this is the only life I'm aware of and I don't think we've met," Fiona said. Past-life regression had obviously done a lot for this woman.

Selene was dressed in iridescent shades of deep blue. She didn't have any shoes on and Fiona wondered for a moment what the health department would say about a place that served food and had cats and barefoot people on the premises.

The woman shook her head and focused on Gia and the list she was holding.

Gia nodded. "Yes, you can definitely help me. I'm looking for whatever I'll need to work a hex on my almost-ex-husband. Death would be nice, but I'll settle for making him have to give me everything in the divorce. Oh, and I'd like his nuts to become lodged somewhere around his upper intestinal tract and stay there for a couple of years."

"I sense a little anger there," Selene said dryly. "Have you done this kind of work before?"

"Never. But I think now's the time to start. I've got a list of some items I need. Feel free to tell me what else I should add to the list. Let's start with dried tansy and mugwort, and a piece of willow root. Oh, and do you have any mallow?"

"We do," Selene said.

She motioned for them to follow her up the stairs. "Once we've got those herbs you'll need a couple of manuals and things to set up your altar. I'll show you some oil, an athame and the proper herbs for the altar. Don't forget candles, they're essential." She handed Gia several squat candles marked at five dollars each.

Fiona didn't say anything about the candles. Gia could

spend her money any way she wanted, but any candle that came into Fiona's house for a ceremony would be Pic N Save forty-nine-cent specials that were exactly like the five-dollar candles from the Major Arcana. The only thing they'd done to make these candles special was wrap them in multicolored plastic and tie them with a ribbon.

"I need to know if your husband has always mistreated you, or if this is something new."

"It's new. Well, relatively new. We never had a great marriage, but over the past year he's really hit a midlife crisis and changed."

"You could be dealing with bad influences causing the change; let's be sure and cover that with a different spell and this special oil."

Fiona let the tide of conversation flow around her as she studied Selene. The woman had the most intriguing face she'd seen in a long time. The artist in Fiona was busy analyzing the play of light and shadow on the high cheekbones. She examined Selene's flowing movements as she went about her business.

For the first time in years of people-watching, Fiona realized that she couldn't put an age to the woman. Selene might have been anywhere from thirty to sixty. There were fine lines around her eyes and mouth, but none of the deeply etched crow's-feet that usually came with age. Her light blue eyes looked ancient and there was a slight hesitation when she climbed the stairs that might have been the movement of an older person. Even the clothing was meant to obscure rather than delineate the body beneath. The blues flowed into one another and there were no belts or definite lines hugging any contours.

Fiona tried to focus on the woman as a person, but the image blurred until she seemed to see five or six people.

She shook her head. Fantasy of course, or a side effect of that knock on the head from the accident. There was only one woman in front of her.

Selene's hair was silver. Not blond, not gold, but silver. There was no way to tell whether it was artificial or natural. Her makeup had been so skillfully done, the light brown eyebrows and eyelashes blended so carefully, that she could even have been albino underneath all the cosmetics.

"You're going to want to set up an altar. I'll find you a couple of books for the incantations to help you get started. You've got some candles. You'll need a blue glass for the water and a dish for the salt." She piled the things into a wicker basket. "And don't forget the crystal to focus the power. I've got a wonderful pink one back here that should do fine."

They meandered through the store filling the basket. Selene handed Gia a silver knife called an athame. "Use only for ceremonies and rituals, never for mundane work," she instructed.

They added black candles and some cornhusks and straw to be woven into a representation of Larry. "These are the best oils for mixing and burning when you want a powerful spell to work." Selene pointed to a selection of dark amber oils.

"You'll want to bind him and keep him from harming you in any way, so burn a red candle in front of the figure and bind the straw with a gold chain. If both of you are just starting out, you might want to take a series of our classes. Here's a complete listing of everything we offer, from your first rites right up through initiation into our coven. Have you ever thought of joining a coven? You'd find that being around other witches not only increases your own effectiveness, but it makes you feel a little less alone. It's nice to find others who have the same interests you do." Selene glanced at Fiona, including her in the invitation.

"A coven?" Gia said blankly. Somehow she hadn't quite thought of her little attempts at protection and destruction as anything real. "The thought has never entered my mind."

"And you?" Selene asked Fiona.

"I don't think so." Fiona stopped short of telling Selene this was an experiment. She didn't want to make the woman feel bad by telling her she thought most of the stuff in the store was pure hokum.

"Let me give both of you a card with some numbers on it and a few dates. We're holding a full-moon work ceremony this Saturday in the backyard. There'll be a barbecue afterward. Everything's provided except the meat, if you're still a carnivore. Come if you feel like it. It's one of the few ceremonies open to the public. If you're interested, we'll find someone who will be willing to take both of you on as students."

Fiona stifled a laugh. Incantations and barbecues were a little much! From the looks of it, Selene really meant what she was saying.

It all sounded so real and so sane and so sensible. Fiona had a momentary sense of having been displaced in time and the cosmos. When had it become normal to talk about summoning up the Goddess to help with the heart's desires?

Fiona drifted back toward the book section and selected a few of the most interesting paperbacks. She even picked up a book specifically because the cat in her arms reached out for it and pulled it down from the shelf.

Two hundred dollars later, Gia was pronounced ready to weave a spell against Larry that should stop him cold.

"Now, my dear, what about you?" Selene turned her attention to Fiona.

"Oh, I was just looking around. I'm not going to buy anything except these books." Fiona held out her small stack of paperbacks.

"You don't need anything else? Oh, I must have been mistaken, I thought you came here to get started, but with your powers you probably aren't a beginner, are you?"

Fiona had the uncomfortable feeling that Selene somehow knew about the call from Madge Lorenz and that a spell had caused the forthcoming contract. And she still had the sensation that Selene split into several people every time she looked at her.

"Never mind, we'll work it out later," Selene said, thoroughly confusing Fiona. She took the books and rang them up on the register.

"That'll be forty-two dollars and fifteen cents and lucky you, you've won a prize!" Selene pulled out the register receipt and pointed to a star printed on the side. "You've won a black tourmaline ring."

She pushed a basket toward Fiona and let her select a ring that fit her finger.

Fiona wouldn't ever have said anything, but she'd much rather have had a ring with color in it. The tourmaline felt heavy and cold, not at all like the rose quartz circle she'd tried on earlier.

"Here, now that we have you protected with the ring, you must take this witch's bottle. It's filled with a wine that will help protect your house. Place it on the rafters where no one will discover it," Selene instructed Fiona. She handed another one to Gia, who was beginning to fume because she was being ignored after spending so much money. "For you too, my dear."

"Thank you, what a nice surprise to win something. I'm not usually lucky," Fiona said.

"That's only because you haven't begun to use any of your talents," Selene answered.

"Right." Fiona patted the cat one last time and hurried out of the shop with Gia trailing behind her.

They stuffed the things in the back of the car, stopped at the grocery store and went back to Fiona's house to talk. Fiona slipped the ring off her hand and let it fall into her purse. She didn't like the feel of it at all.

"If you don't mind, I'd rather not go back home right yet. I didn't think that scene with Larry had affected me, but I get the shakes when I think of going back in there before I've settled down. Let's look over the books and stuff we bought while we eat something."

"I'll fix lunch," Fiona offered. The first thing she made was a quick batch of brownies; she stuck them in the oven with the French fries while she fixed hamburgers. She took up a tray to Megan and checked on how her daughter was doing. The headache, as usual, was bad, with no relief in sight.

"Let's see, what do we have to do to set up this altar and get going?" Gia said, reaching for one of the books she had bought. She was about to read Fiona a passage from the first book she picked up when Sally knocked on the back door and then breezed into the kitchen. As usual she looked fantastic. This time she was wearing a huge emerald and diamond ring Fiona had never seen before. The colors exactly matched the main color in her muted plaid shirt. Also as usual, her jeans were a perfect fit on her perfect size-six body. Fiona was uncomfortably aware of her own spreading girth and was beginning to deeply resent Sally's absolute blond perfection.

"I saw your car in the driveway. I thought you two weren't going out anywhere because Fiona didn't feel well after the accident."

Fiona and Gia looked guiltily at each other.

"I decided that maybe walking around might help my back," Fiona said, not quite lying.

"Well, since I wasn't included, tell me what you all have been up to." Sally helped herself to one of the fresh brownies and poured a cup of coffee.

Fiona motioned desperately for Gia to hide the books they had set on the table. She knew Sally would never understand witchcraft. She was a good Southern Baptist, and through the years she'd put forth a lot of effort steering Fiona away from anything that smacked of the occult.

Gia moved the books, but didn't want to be obvious about it by taking them all the way up to Fiona's studio.

"So, what's been going on? I hear that you and Larry have split and that Fiona got a great contract. Anything I've missed?"

The women gossiped for almost forty-five minutes, going over the events of the past few days before Sally idly picked up one of the books Gia had transferred onto a chair and partially covered with a shopping bag.

Sally looked at the covers and recoiled in horror: *Power of the Witch. The Magical Household. Magical Herbalism.* She shuddered. "Where did you get these? What on earth are you doing? Don't you know that's straight from the devil? You'll go to hell if you fool around with this!"

"Oh come on, Sally. I know you don't like the New Age stuff, but that's ridiculous. I won't go to hell, I'm not consorting with the devil, I'm just learning how to use natural forces against Larry. Besides, this is witchcraft, not devil worship. Don't you know the difference?"

"Don't try to weasel out of what you're doing by playing around with words. This is bad stuff. You don't get involved with witchcraft and come out of it all right!" Sally set down the brownie she had been munching on, her pretty face clouded with worry. "Please, girls, don't do this. The trouble it's going to cause isn't going to be worth the gain. No money or revenge could possibly be worth the price you're going to pay."

"The problem with you is that you're still Southern Baptist and you've never looked any further," Gia said. Her dislike of Sally had just taken a huge jump upwards.

"Not that it's bad to be Baptist," Fiona interrupted. "But it is interesting that you've never moved away from your childhood church and beliefs. Remember when we were in college and I tried out the Ouija board and contacting the spirits?"

"I sure do. I wanted you to come back to Christ's path

and you just laughed at me. And you still need to come back, girl, before you cause real trouble."

"If this works, it's not going to cause trouble. And according to Selene, the Old Religion doesn't cause problems, it sets them right," Gia said. "I appreciate your concern and I'm glad that your church works for you. But I'm tired of waiting for God or whoever else is supposed to be in charge to decide I need help. I watched this craft, religion, whatever you want to call it, work with my grandmother and it's going to be my own particular salvation now. I want revenge, Sally. Nothing is going to stop me. Larry deserves every bit of bad luck I can throw at him."

Sally slumped in the chair. "You're really going through with this?"

Gia and Fiona nodded.

Sally stood up. "I'll pray for your souls and your salvation." She walked out, closing the door quietly behind her.

Gia stuck out her tongue at the door and picked up the book Sally had been looking at. "Shall we give all this a try? I'd hate to spend two hundred dollars just to have it languish because we never take the time to cast a real spell."

"Let's go up to the studio. That's about the only place there's room for anything," Fiona said, grabbing a shopping bag and heading for the stairs.

"Okay, the altar . . . where can we set it up?" Gia asked, evicting Princess and dumping the candles, straw and other paraphernalia into a convenient overstuffed chair. Princess walked away stiff-legged, outraged that Gia would actually move her off the place she had claimed as her own.

Fiona looked around the room. There wasn't a clear surface anywhere. She had all kinds of painting equipment on the bookshelf, taking up the few inches that were left in front of the books, already double-shelved to save space. Projects in progress occupied the table and easel. Even if she cleared everything off, the chance of ruining the new supplies with paint smudges was more than she'd care to risk.

Gia had spent a fortune on the proper witchly trappings and she deserved better than half-dried paint drips on her crystal and silver.

Gia was busy studying one of the books. "Here's a lay-out for the altar."

Fiona took the book from her friend and started to read the instructions for setting up the various things they'd bought. "Look, he says the altar can be as simple as a box. I've got a box—remember when I cadged about a hundred of the really good wooden wine crates from the store?"

"Great. You get that and I'll find out what else we need." It wasn't exactly what Fiona had thought an altar should be, but she couldn't be picky. She reached under the bench and extracted the empty box and set it on a part of the table that was relatively clean. She spread a tiny white tablecloth that her grandmother had used once for a bridge party on top of the crate. They began to set out the knife, candles, salt and other essential items.

"I love this little cauldron, it's the cutest thing."

Gia admired the cast-iron pot as she set it down on the middle part of the altar. "What's next?" She checked the layout again.

"Bolline," Fiona said.

"Bolline?"

"Yep."

"What's a bolline?" Gia asked.

"I don't know. If you didn't buy one, maybe we don't really need it. How about we wing it and find out what the bolline is later?" Fiona suggested.

"Right. Now for the pages we're supposed to read out loud to call the power to us. I'm glad they're real specific, I don't think I have a good enough imagination to come up with it all on my own."

Gia flipped the book back a few pages and started to read. Then she began to giggle.

"Um, Fiona, I think we may have just hit the next snag in an otherwise perfect plan."

"What?"

"It says we're supposed to be sky-clad to do this rite correctly."

Fiona didn't like the sound of that.

"What the hell is sky-clad?"

"It means standing around buck naked. It's supposed to be the proper way to approach the Goddess so that there's no interference between her and you. Clothing does something to the waves of power we're trying to tap into."

Fiona was already shaking her head. "Naked in front of you? Not in this lifetime. Don't you remember? I wouldn't even undress in gym in high school. I'm a prude, didn't you know? Nothing is going to get me out of my jeans and work shirt."

"Come on, it says here it works better."

"Then it'll have to be a little less effective, won't it?"

Gia saw the mutinous set to Fiona's chin. She knew from bitter experience that argument wouldn't do any good.

"Okay, I don't care what you do, but I'm going to do it right. I want this to work and if I'm embarrassed for a couple of minutes, I honestly don't care," Gia said.

"Gia! Don't you dare! Stop it this minute!" Fiona was horrified when her friend stripped down within seconds to nothing whatsoever and stood there, naked, in the middle of her studio. Fiona was so embarrassed that she was certain her whole face was on fire from the blushing. Nudity had never been her strong suit.

"I can't look," she said, hiding her eyes.

"Come on. It's not so bad. I promise not to sneak a peek, if that's what's bothering you about shedding your clothes. Please, Fiona, I want this to work," Gia pleaded. "It's my only real chance at getting even with Larry. The truth is that with his connections with other lawyers, I stand to have everything in the world taken away from me if I'm not careful. I want fate to lean a little on my side."

"Look, friend, I haven't walked around unclothed since I tried to work my way through my repressions by doing my housework naked. All I got then was an iron burn on my stomach and a really surprised meter man."

"Please?" her friend asked again.

Fiona wavered. She reached for the first button of her shirt.

"Do you think the spells will work as well if I leave on my bra and pants?"

"No, naked."

"It's not going to happen." Fiona couldn't even look at her naked friend. She looked up at the ceiling and counted the cobwebs that needed sweeping. Her gaze slid sideways to the corners of the room and discovered another bunch of cobwebs and a couple of daddy-long-leg spiders raising families there. Her eyes never intersected with Gia's figure.

"I can't."

"Fiona . . ."

"No, listen to me. It's all right to do a ceremony or invocation or whatever it's called. I'm happy with that and I hope it works. But there are some things that I just can't manage and getting naked in front of you or anyone else is one of them. So if you don't want me to participate while I'm dressed then we're going to have to stop right now and you'll have to go back to Selene's to find a coven you can work with, because I'm not going to change." Fiona rebuttoned the shirt. She stared at her friend defiantly, careful not to let her gaze go below the collarbone.

Gia finally sighed. "Okay, then we'd better get on with the ceremony before someone comes home and finds me like this."

"I sincerely hope that won't happen." Fiona probed outward, trying to find Harper. Most of the time she could

Crystals 95

get some kind of mental image of where he was and what he was doing. At the moment all she could get was a blur of action. They were in no danger of discovery, because she hadn't heard the car pull up front, as she always did fifteen minutes before he arrived.

Fiona relaxed. "What do we do first?"

Following the instructions, they cleaned the area with a new broom. Fiona laid out a circle on the bare wooden floor, using most of a ball of white yarn left over from a sweater she had knitted for Harper. They were ready to invoke the Goddess.

"We'll call the power now," Gia said as she lit the candles and the incense that rested on the charcoal briquette, which Selene had assured her was necessary to make the little cone burn all the way through the dedication. Fiona coughed as the smoke reached her. She wanted to laugh as she watched the sky-clad Gia raise the knife and implore the entities of the North, South, East and West to come to them and help them win their heart's desires.

Gia began to chant over the salt, water and cauldron.

"Watch out for the incense. It'd hurt like hell to have some of your skin hit that hot cone."

Gia walked in a circle, careful to go clockwise as she sprinkled the salt around the edge to contain the energies they needed to bring this whole ceremony off. Princess sniffed at the yarn, giving it a few experimental bashes before she decided no one was going to play with her. She settled for licking the salt.

Fiona read the same words as Gia. Her desire to laugh at everything faded as the energy they summoned actually began to fill the circle. She was almost becoming comfortable with her friend's nudity when the focus turned to the actual ritual.

"Goddess, I ask for help in stopping Larry from harming me in any way. I ask that he be punished for hurting me and that his powers be taken from him as completely as he has tried to take my power from me," Gia said. It wasn't exactly what she had expected to ask for, but it was what she needed to say. She formed a small figure of a man with the cornhusks and the wheat and tied it with a gold chain. "Keep him chained so that he cannot harm me until I take the shackles from this figure and let him loose again. Even then, keep him from bothering me in any way," she added, just to be on the safe side.

She poured a little of the amber oil marked "Control" on the briquette and the remnants of the cone of incense. The glowing charcoal burst into flames as the oil sizzled on the surface. A pungent smell of cedar and snow rose from the fire and surrounded them.

Gia would have sworn that the smoke was contained within the circle of power they had drawn, leaving clear air beyond the area marked with the yarn. But that was crazy.

Once Gia had finished with her invocation and prayers for help, Fiona moved forward.

"I ask that my family be kept safe and that no harm come to any of us. Help me make amulets and talismans for their safety."

They took a few moments to thank the Goddess and the spirits and dismiss them before Fiona began to cut the circle to end the ceremony.

She was just reaching down with the athame when Harper slammed the studio door back against the wall and roared into the room.

"What the hell are you doing?"

7

Oh shit," Gia said as she recovered enough to race for her clothes. She scooped them out of the chair and headed downstairs past Harper. She only paused long enough on the landing to pull on the minimum amount needed to exit to the street with some sort of decency. She was about to bolt toward her car when she heard something from upstairs that she hadn't heard in all the years she had known Harper. He had actually raised his voice and was yelling at Fiona. She closed the door quietly behind her, glad to be out of the middle of the maelstrom.

"Witchcraft, that's what you're doing, isn't it? You were playing with witchcraft!"

"No, it isn't what you think," Fiona said, even though that was exactly what it was. She tried to talk over Harper's tirade, but she didn't make any headway.

"What are you doing here?" She tried to deflect him by asking about his sudden arrival. And why hadn't she heard him coming? What had made her fail this time when she'd always been able to anticipate his return?

"It's dinnertime, in case you haven't noticed. You were

all wrapped up in your ceremony and didn't notice the time."

That explained the blur, Fiona thought. He'd been driving home and the blur was the other traffic.

"How dare you do this? How dare you bring this murderous worship into my home? I never want to see anything like this around me again, do you hear me? Do you understand me? Never!"

Fiona stood in the circle and stared at Harper. Harper believed in witchcraft and he was frightened by it.

Harper's anger stunned her. Harper never yelled. He never lost his temper except when something threatened his family. What was it about a knife and a couple of candles and a circle of yarn on the floor that sent him into such a rage?

"It isn't that important, honey, I was only playing around."

"Get out of that circle and we'll talk about how important this is!"

Fiona wanted to disappear, sink into the floor, anything to get away from the look on Harper's face and the sound of his voice. If Gia had asked her what Harper would think about the ceremony before they'd started it, Fiona would have said he'd probably think it was funny. She would have been wrong.

She made a surreptitious gesture cutting the circle before she stepped over the yarn and confronted Harper. She hadn't felt this bad since that horrible time before they got married, when her parents had come home early and found her on the floor in front of the fire with Harper and had told them they'd have to elope because they wouldn't pay for a whore to have a proper wedding. It had taken Harper fifteen years before he'd spoken to her parents again.

"So you've brought the Old Religion into my home?" he said when Fiona didn't say anything, his voice like death.

"I thought it might help us against the vortex. It was like a game . . ."

"Oh God, a game, just playing around." Harper passed a shaking hand over his face. "I don't care what you thought. I don't care what you hoped. I don't even want to know anything more about it. Just understand me, Fiona. I do not want anything like that in my house. Remove that altar and the athame and everything else."

Fiona was beginning to seethe at the high-handed way he was ordering her around. It could have been the starting point for one hell of a good fight. But there was something about the way Harper was talking, the dead seriousness in his eyes, the stark anger and terror that had been on his face when he'd first walked into the room, that kept her quiet. There was something more going on here, and trying to force him to accept her point of view wouldn't help any. But she'd sure like to know how he knew enough to call the knife an athame and why he hated witchcraft with such a passion.

The evening passed in tense silence. They didn't touch before they went to bed, and Fiona finally dropped off to sleep after hoping that the fight wouldn't start a nightmare, the way it usually did.

She didn't get her wish.

Her nightmare started as it always did, without warning. Screams in the night. The peaceful suburban darkness was shattered by howls of terror, the despair ringing though the halls and bedrooms and out into the smoke-tinged darkness.

Fiona shrieked with panic as she swept forward toward the fire. She shook with cold and wondered what had happened to the thick sweatshirt she had worn to bed to keep her warm. She could feel the people of the shadows near her, hidden behind veils of haze and mind-numbing cold. Her eyes teared as the smoke from the small wood fire carried toward her on the icy wind, engulfing her.

"Burn the cat. That is the only way we will ever control her and her power," a deep voice behind her said.

She screamed again and whirled to face the man. He wore nothing but a silver emblem that seemed to waver and flash in the light. His eyes gleamed in the dark, their hazel lightness startling against the shadows. He was tall and perfect in every detail and he was tightly erect, his penis thrusting upward toward her.

Even though his brown hair was tinged with gray and the curling hair around his genitals had already been frost-tinged with white, he radiated sensual promise.

A cat howled in fear. Fiona's barely born lust turned to panic as she realized that one of her beloved cats was in danger.

The mists parted and a naked woman, her drooping breasts bobbling obscenely in the light, raised a bamboo cage above her head. The door swung open. The cat scrabbled to the back of the cage, crying in a frenzy of terror as the smoke rose and engulfed the trap. It was trying to keep out of harm's way, but its fate had already been decided and there was nothing the cat could do to stop its own death. Taken in a cage, kept confined until its part in the ritual, the cat had never had a chance to save itself.

"Into the fire, take my plea, soul of the cat, bring the power to me!" the woman chanted. "The power is waning, make it strong, heart of cat, now be gone. Strengthen the lines, keep control, never let loose the reins of the soul."

A man stepped forward into the light and she recognized her neighbor up the hill. She wished with all her might that she had set the trap and chopped off his foot so that he'd never move freely again.

Fiona saw the cat clearly for the first time as the Siamese tried to hang on to the slick bamboo of the cage. The brown and cream cat drove her claws into the wood in a desperate effort to gain a purchase that would save her from the flames below.

"No!" Fiona lunged forward. "Not my cat, not Princess!" She stretched out her arms, praying that she could catch the animal before she fell and burned. She had to save Princess. The cat would never understand dying in pain, with her mistress's voice ringing in her ears as the fire consumed her.

Fiona stumbled forward, wrenching herself free of the invisible bonds that had held her. Her feet landed on the hot coals and pain fried her ankles and shins and knees until she screamed in agony. The cat's lament melded with her own, a wail of terror and grief and pain as Princess fell toward the fire. Fiona's fingers barely brushed the soft silken fur. It was all over. There was no way she could save Princess, and Fiona's heart-rending sobs filled the air with her anguish.

"Fiona, Megan, wake up! What the hell is going on?" Harper's voice cut through the dream, bring Fiona solidly back to the reality of her daughter's messy room. Megan sat up in bed, her eyes staring into nothingness. Her thin high shriek filled the room.

Fiona suddenly realized that she had been matching her daughter's screams as she had somehow sleepwalked from her own bed into Megan's room. The terror of the strange circle of fire and the pain receded as she felt the worn carpet beneath her feet instead of the flames and heat of glowing coals.

"We've got trouble," Fiona said. She looked at Megan. She knew that sound—a dead, flat panic-driven ululation that went on and on. Three times before, the same frantic crying had preceded months in the hospital while the various neurosurgeons tried to patch her daughter's brain back together. Neurosurgery was wonderful; it had kept Megan alive for seven years since the tumor had been discovered; but there were times when Fiona wondered if her daughter thought the daily agony was worth it. She'd never dared to ask, for fear that Megan would tell her she'd rather die and only kept on with the struggle to please her mother.

"Megan, you have to wake up. Come back to us, do you hear me?" Fiona grabbed her daughter's shoulders and began to shake her gently. She had been through it before, been through the night terrors and all the trouble that was coming if Megan could not awaken from the dark places she slipped into as the pressure and pain built up again within her brain.

Megan didn't respond. Her face was dead white. She had dark circles underneath her eyes and her lips looked blue.

Fiona reached over and felt her daughter's head. The thumbnail-sized dome set into the skull was tight with pressure from within the brain. Somehow the shunt that took the fluid from the brain and transferred it down to her belly, where it was reabsorbed, had closed off again. Megan had begun to lose consciousness as the brain stopped being able to cope with the extra fluid that was building up.

Quickly Fiona began to press down on the reservoir. It took a lot of pressure to force a tiny amount of cerebral spinal fluid down the tube. Gradually the dome started to fill more slowly and the pressure eased enough that Megan began to come back from wherever she went when the pressure overwhelmed her.

"Honey, come back to your room. Come back to the cats and Daddy and me," Fiona coaxed her daughter, holding on to Megan and hoping for some reaction. Harper switched on the light, illuminating the tangle of books, catalogs, cat toys and clothes that Megan piled on her bed and never quite cleaned up.

A shudder racked the girl, and finally her eyelids fluttered downward. She sighed deeply as her mother finally stopped pressing the shunt.

When Megan opened her eyes again, she focused on her mother and father. She blinked and shook her head. "What happened?"

"You had a little trouble," Harper said.

Megan looked around her, still dazed.

"Okay, let's get on with this," Fiona said briskly. "Tell me where you are."

Fiona started the neurological testing that had to be done before she called the doctor to report a problem that would need surgery to correct. Once she'd asked all the questions, she could give Anders the vitals and classification for Megan's responses. If it was bad, he'd prepare an emergency admission to the neurosurgical critical care and have an operating room standing ready.

"Where am I?" Megan echoed Fiona's question.

Harper and Fiona exchanged worried glances. The last time this had happened, Megan had insisted that she was in the hospital and demanded that they find out why the doctors were refusing to help her when she hurt so badly.

"Can you tell me where you are? Are you in the hospital or at home?"

"I'm at home. In my room," Megan said slowly, looking around her to make certain it was true.

"What's our address?"

"1108 North Twenty-third," Megan said, beginning to snap out of the dream state. Her cheeks had taken on a pink color in the last few minutes, another good sign.

"What city, what state?"

"Mom . . ." Megan whined, and then capitulated. She'd been through this before. She knew the routine.

"Walnut Creek, California, and my telephone is 555-4068, all right? And you look really bad, Mom. Your hair is sticking up all over the place. I'm glad I didn't inherit that red mess. Can you imagine having curly hair grow back in after surgery? I'd look like a walking Brillo pad!"

"Thank you, darling," Fiona said, grimacing. Megan might be all right after all.

Fiona began to relax. She felt the ache of her fear-stiffened back all the way down to her knees. Her back always hurt when something bad happened.

"She's making sense. Maybe this time we won't have a desperate ride over the bridge, eighty miles an hour, to get her into surgery. Follow my finger," Fiona commanded. She moved her hand up, down and sideways as she watched Megan's gaze.

"Everything looks pretty good. You haven't lost the ability to look upward, and your eyes are tracking pretty much together. I really worry when the eyes start going in opposite directions and she can't bring them back together," Fiona told Harper.

Her husband nodded.

"Neck," Fiona ordered and Megan obediently bent her head to both sides and then touched her chin to her chest.

"No pain," she reported. "It's not meningitis this time."

"Any pain anywhere, belly? Head? Behind the eyes?"

"None. Bet you it was only a bad dream. I felt something pop and then I woke up and saw you standing there . . ." Megan said, yawning.

"I guess you can go back to sleep. I'll be checking on you every couple of minutes for the next few hours. You know the drill."

Fiona didn't tell her that in addition to the normal neurological tests, she'd also been scanning Megan's aura. The bright lights pulsing around her daughter's body were gold, with a slight blue tinge. She wasn't completely well, but at least she wasn't surrounded by the dark deadly black Fiona had seen a couple of times when Megan was in real trouble.

She'd be safe for tonight.

Megan nodded and slid down under the covers, pushing aside the magazines to make space for herself.

"Tomorrow, if you're well, we'll muck out this room. I don't know how you can stand it," Harper said, relaxing.

Fiona and Harper trudged back to their own bed, pushing cats out of the way as they lay back down. Fiona remembered a fragment of the nightmare that had tormented her and grabbed Princess. The cat tolerated Fiona's holding her for a few seconds, then squirmed away.

"I'll stay awake. You have to go to work tomorrow," Fiona said.

"Sounds fine," Harper said. The fight about witchcraft forgotten, he gathered her into his arms as she sagged against the bed.

"Don't worry. It actually will be all right this time."

"Maybe," Fiona said. She couldn't shake the images of the nightmare. Had it been a dream or had there really been a man telling her he was going to take back the power she had started to use? Were Princess and the rest of her family in danger or was it just a figment of her overworked and too-tired brain?

Something had changed, though. She had been given a contract for her art. She had felt the power built within that circle, even if she hadn't been sky-clad. Something had changed with their little ritual and she was almost certain that someone other than Harper didn't like it.

She could feel the threat in the air all around her. She couldn't stop now. If she set aside the witchcraft as Harper asked, she had a gut feeling that the vortex would sweep them away and leave nothing behind except broken wishes and one hell of a mess.

Fiona turned sideways in the bed and looked at the man sleeping beside her. She had loved him with all her heart and soul for more than twenty years. They'd always managed to survive even the hardest times. But the marriage had worked because they agreed on things like how to raise Megan and spend money. They were united in every way that was important.

What would happen if she defied him and continued with the Old Religion? They were so close that she was certain Harper would know, even if she didn't tell him.

If he found out, he'd be furious. She hoped he wouldn't

be angry enough to push for a divorce. Wouldn't he understand that she did it for the benefit of the family, just as he
went off to work every day, whether he felt like it or not?

No, she didn't think she wanted to risk throwing out
those hand-painted talismans. She wanted to go ahead and
make up more stanzas for her own personal spells. She definitely did not want to retreat.

Still, by the next morning she hadn't figured out what to
do about her newly budding beliefs.

8

The mockingbird sat on the top of the century plant, decorating the single stalk of creamy white flowers. The trills and loops of song invaded the silence of the night. Gia smiled as the bird shifted his position to sing toward the pyracantha, where other intruders might establish a nest in the mocker's own territory. There was a flash of white in the moonlit night as he spread his wings and began another theme and variations.

"Welcome home, friend. At least I can count on you each year, unlike my miserable bastard of a husband," Gia said. She had no idea whether the same mockingbird came back to grace the cactus every year, but she always looked forward to the round-the-clock serenades from whichever bird was the dominant male for the spring.

She had been sitting in the darkness with a lone candle. She could have switched on the lights, but the glare of electricity was an intrusion. She'd worked to lose herself in the music of the bird and the flickering of the flame, to take herself away so that she could ask questions of the cards and actually get answers that made sense. She'd long ago

discovered that if she tried to work with her Tarot cards
without taking the time to clear her mind of extraneous details the cards wouldn't tell her anything. In fact, some of
the time they told her absolute tripe. She had gone from the
high of catching Larry with the video camera to a low a
couple of weeks later that even Fiona's best efforts couldn't
raise her out of.

Gia shuffled the Tarot cards idly, her hands following
the familiar feeling of the cardboard between her fingers.
She had been talking to the images as she prepared the familiar routine of letting the cards pick an answer to her
problem.

"Let's not think of Larry. He's sealed his fate. The only
answers I want about that man are how badly he can screw
me up, okay?" She cut the cards again. "And I'd like to
know if I'm ever going to have a happy love life."

The Tarot had guided her for years, through her teens,
when no one had time for her, right into her adult life.
Larry had never known anything about her reliance on the
cards. She had understood instinctively that it would have
been too "foreign." He never did approve of anything that
wasn't one hundred percent white-bread middle-class. The
Tarot had warned her over twenty years ago about her
soon-to-be-ex-husband, but she'd chosen not to listen.
After all, what did printed cards know about true love? It
had turned out they knew quite a bit, but Gia's inability to
hear what they had to say had defeated her. She wouldn't
make that mistake again.

"So, old friends, what should I do? How about if I sell
the house and run away to live in the wilds of Mexico? Or I
could find a way to cause irreparable sexual dysfunction for
that stupid woman Larry is screwing. Any ideas, clues?
How about recommendations?" she asked the cards. She
was ready to hear an answer. She'd spent the last days sift-
ing through her life and the possibilities that lay ahead now
that her marriage was irrevocably over.

The only positive step she'd taken was getting in touch with the gorgeous Norse-god lawyer who had given her his card in the Major Arcana. She'd interviewed several other lawyers and all of them were afraid to tangle with her husband. It was the old boys' network all over again. She kept waiting for one of them to tell her he was on her side and that she'd be taken care of, but it never happened. She had almost despaired of finding someone who could help her until she remembered the tall blond who had said the Runes promised she would need him.

He was right.

Two days ago she'd finally given in and called him. It was seven in the evening and there was no reason for her to think he'd actually be in his office, but he picked up the phone on the first ring.

"You might not remember me," Gia started to say, but he interrupted her.

"The woman in the shop. Yes, I've been waiting for you," he said. "Why don't you tell me what's happening with your divorce?"

Gia was surprised that she was memorable to a man like Gunnerson.

Briefly Gia outlined the situation. Larry had abandoned her, he'd tried to beat her up when she took a videotape of him and no one knew what his next little nasty surprise would be.

"That man is just Mister Personality, isn't he? I don't know what it is about some attorneys and physicians—they all develop God complexes that make them above any ordinary accounting for their actions. But we're not going to let him do that, are we?" E.G. chortled, a nice warm sound. He had a slight Nordic accent and a deep voice that practically insisted that she believe in him.

"How do you feel about playing hardball?"

"For instance?"

"You've got a tape of him hitting you, right? There

can't be any mistake, now. Tell me the truth, are you certain that if a jury or judge looked at that tape they'd find that he physically attacked you?"

Swiftly Gia reviewed what she had seen through the eyepiece of the camera. "I'm absolutely certain that they'd see that he hit and kicked me."

"Then you come on down here Friday and sign all the necessary papers. First thing we'll do is send your husband notice that we're filing assault and battery charges. And then we'll go for a civil suit for damages caused by his assault. Then there's the girlfriend and her money. There's a possibility we can add the girlfriend's salary on to his own when we figure maintenance and alimony."

"Oh come on, we can't do that!"

"Hey, it's been done before. The men are always furious to find out that we can do it. If he's a good lawyer, he'll know about that law, but I'll bet you he doesn't think you'll find someone to represent you who is half as nasty and sneaky as he is. I think he'll have a surprise when he finds out about old E.G.'s brand of divorce law."

The attorney and Gia chatted for a few moments longer and made an appointment for late in the afternoon Friday.

Now, in the candlelight, she fanned the cards one more time. "Okay, guys, what is the choice I should make right now to make myself happy?" She pulled a card from the middle of the deck.

"The three of swords—" She looked at the two people, back to back, swords crossed in front of them and their expressions forbidding. "Come on, guys, I know Larry and I are in trouble. I want to know what I'm going to do about it that will make me happy."

Just like the cards to throw a sword at her. They always ended up being prickly and unhappy messages.

She opened the divination book. " 'Disappointment, strife, opposition, separation—' Oh good, all the things I wanted to hear."

She snapped the pack back together and picked another card. The nine of swords. She knew the meaning of that one, too. Something about a man all dressed up with nowhere to go, alone with the worries and problems that are taking over his life. She remembered thinking about that card sometime in the past, wondering why the man hadn't walked away from his troubles. Couldn't he have found some fun instead of brooding about what was going wrong?

She looked out at the moonlit nightscape in front of her and realized that the cards had indeed helped her. Sitting alone in the dark wasn't going to solve anything. She needed to get away from the house, from Larry and from all the other problems of the last few weeks.

Gia felt a rising excitement. She was ready for something new and different. She stood up abruptly and blew out the candle.

"Something exciting. But what? A ride in the car? Hell, it's better than nothing. Maybe all I'll do is drive around for a couple of hours, but it'll still be a change."

Gia shucked the jeans and huge T-shirt she'd been wearing and dressed in one of her more outrageous outfits. The skirt was tie-dyed cotton gauze that in certain lights was almost transparent. She had long, well-shaped legs and the skirt was as close as she could get to going out naked while actually being dressed. She wrapped her waist with a long blue band of silk shot through with real gold, whose ends reached to the hem of her skirt. Now something that will make me look bright and exotic, she thought, standing in front of the blouses in her closet. "Purple, that should do it." She reached for the deep purple East Indian blouse edged with mirrors.

"On my way," she said as she finished dressing and ran down the stairs and out the front door. The mockingbird trilled again as she opened the car door and slid behind the wheel. The lighted clock on the dashboard, the only car clock she had ever had that really worked, read 12:30 A.M.

She drove aimlessly for almost half an hour before she ended up in front of the Major Arcana bookstore and restaurant.

"Of course my subconscious would lead me here. This is where the change started. The Tarot must love this place, it fulfills all the requirements for helping me go in a new direction."

Soft yellow lights glowed in the back of the store. Several candles had been lit and placed in bowls of water on a table beside the front windows. Someone was obviously in residence far past normal store hours.

She debated for a few moments about trying to interrupt whatever was going on in the store, and then shrugged. "What the hell, I was going to come down here in the morning anyway. The worst they can do is tell me to get lost."

Gia looked through the front windows, but couldn't see a soul inside the store. She marched around to the back of the shop. The sounds of laughter and chanting and some vaguely Renaissance music came from inside. The beat was moving faster, rising toward a crescendo with every measure. The air smelled different here, sweeter and heavy with a scent that was maddeningly familiar. Screwing up her courage, because she had begun to wonder about whether this was even reasonable, she knocked on the thick wooden door that opened onto the alleyway.

Suddenly the music died at the peak of the intensity and the chanting stopped in mid-word. There was the sound of scuffling and a sibilant whisper behind the door. The doorknob began to turn.

Gia watched the door inch open and considered running away. What if she'd interrupted something she didn't want to know about? She started to turn away from the entrance, but there was no time to retreat. The door swung open and a man stood in the portal, his head cocked to one side. He looked at her quizzically.

"Can I help you?"

Gia gasped and then almost stopped breathing. Under the circumstances, the man's question was almost ludicrous. She couldn't believe what she was seeing. Never mind that she liked what she saw; she had never expected a totally naked man to open the door.

Well, she amended, not completely nude. He was wearing a necklace.

"Um, that's a beautiful pendant. What are the stones in it?"

She couldn't believe the stupidity of what came out of her mouth.

She tried to keep her eyes on his face. He looked vaguely familiar, but she couldn't quite place him. Wherever they had met, the incident had been slightly unpleasant, but no other images came to mind.

"They're all magickal stones, meant to help me concentrate and work my spells," he said, as if it were the most normal question in the world.

Gia was agonizingly aware that she felt responsible for not embarrassing him by drawing attention to his nudity. Stupid, she chided herself. He certainly knew he didn't have clothes on when he answered the door. After all, most men didn't run around naked in the back of a shop without quite intending to, so why should she be embarrassed for him?

"You know, this was a really dumb idea. I just drove past and saw the light in the store and I'd been here before so I stopped—" She was babbling.

Suddenly Gia understood why women who had been approached by flashers couldn't describe the men's faces but could give minute and detailed descriptions of other body parts.

"I'm glad you did stop. We can always use some company." He smiled at her. "I think you might like to see what we're doing in here."

"With you dressed—I mean, undressed like that?" she stammered.

"It's perfectly acceptable. Please, we promise we won't harm you."

She caught a glimpse of something bobbing below his waist.

She couldn't help herself; she had to look.

Her eyes followed his tight stomach muscles downward, past the curl of dark hair. He definitely was naked and while he wasn't erect, he wasn't completely flaccid either. Whatever the condition of the interesting organ, he was huge. Hung like a horse was the way she'd heard it described—now she knew what all those slavering women had meant. The speculation swept over her, as hard to hold back as the water over a breaking dam. What would it be like to make love to him? Was it true that men with bigger penises were better lovers? She'd written enough love scenes in her romances that she could just picture what it would be like. Her vivid imagination made her squirm with sudden passion. This would be a whole chapter in the next historical romance.

She gulped and tried to bring her mental processes back into some semblance of order, banishing the outright lust.

He wasn't a character in her books. He was real. Any man who would answer the door, flaunt his naked body and not even look concerned about the effect he had on her could be dangerous.

Gia began to back away from the door. "I'm sorry, I'll come back in the morning."

"No, please step inside," he said. His voice was a low purr, dangerous and wild. He moved toward the candlelight that cast half his face into darkness.

Gia finally managed to tear her gaze from his not-so-private parts and looked back at his face. He was peering down the alleyway, as if he expected her to be accompanied by someone else.

"I'm in trouble," she said to herself as the memory of where she'd met him before finally flashed into being. This was the same man who had opened the bottle of oil that had had such an amazing effect on her the first time she'd come into the bookstore.

A blush suffused her face when she remembered how she had reacted to that one inhalation of scent. She had wanted to throw herself down on the couches and wait for him to ravish her. She had run away from him, and he had laughed at her.

The oil—that was the basis of much of the sweet heavy scent in the shop.

"I don't think I want—" she started to say as she turned away from the door.

Selene reached out to her, her voice soothing and calm. "My darling, how nice to see you here. Please come in, you might find something interesting. You've met Asron and I'll be happy to introduce you to the rest of us."

To Asron she whispered, "She is one of the two we need. The other one is more powerful, but we can use her."

"Hey, what do you mean you can use me?" Gia felt the first flutter of real fear.

Asron reached out, grabbed Gia by the hand and pulled her into the room. When she tried to break the grip, she found herself pressed against his bare warm flesh. She blushed as she felt the length of his legs against her. His— what should she call it, she thought wildly, his manhood?— nudged her through the thin layer of cotton. She was terribly conscious that she hadn't put on underwear. Could he tell that there was nothing between her skin and his body except that skirt?

"Gia, what a pleasure to be able to include you in our little gathering." Selene turned to the naked man. "Asron dear, you can release her hand. She looks like she's about ready to bolt and I don't want her to be afraid of us."

Selene moved closer to Asron, passing her hand between Gia and him and just incidentally caressing his lower body with her hand.

Gia looked at Selene and then around the room, which was lit only with candles. There were four or five other people in the room and all of them were naked. There were candles on the floor at five different points. A beautiful polished burl table stood in the middle of the floor. On the top of the table were a knife, an ancient-looking pewter goblet and several dishes, along with even more candles. Everyone smiled at her, totally unconcerned about their appearance, even though Gia squirmed in the presence of so many undressed adults. For the first time, she understood just how Fiona had felt when asked to do a ceremony sky-clad.

Sky-clad.

That's what they were doing. It wasn't some kind of orgy, it was only a worship circle. They were just praying in the way all the books said was perfectly respectable for witches. She could relax.

"Here, have a drink of this. It's relatively good wine, though not the best of the year's production. I'm saving the best for another ceremony," Asron said, handing her a pewter cup, a mate to the one on the altar.

Selene nodded and smiled, but Gia noticed that her hand was still softly caressing Asron, as if she and she alone wanted to be responsible for his excitement.

He was getting excited. There was no mistaking that. Gia couldn't have missed it even if he hadn't been naked. Something that size wasn't easy to hide.

She stared down at the cup of red wine, glad to have something to concentrate on.

Her embarrassment changed to arousal. The scent of the oil and the sight of the naked man had disturbed Gia more than she wanted to admit. She wanted this man. She wanted to have him spread her legs and give her the loving she craved and had never found with Larry. She felt as if she were in heat. There was no way to control the feeling of urgency and need, no way to get her mind off it, at least as long as she stood and stared at the naked man, and no way to escape gracefully.

"Grab a cushion, and sit back. We're doing casting with crystals to unlock our personal chakras," Selene said, pointing to a thick blue cushion. "We'll do one for you, if you want. There's a strange color to your aura, a pulsing red and a dark blue that doesn't bode well for your future unless they're cleared."

Gia took another sip of the wine and let the talk flow over her. The wine was making her sleepy. The smell of the incense cone that burned in a beautiful jade-green holder relaxed her, lulling her into a state of suspended animation. Drowsily she wondered if the incense had something other than good-smelling ingredients. She was caught between sleeping and waking, with the pewter cup dangling from her fingers, almost spilling the rest of the wine. She breathed deeply, unable to move a muscle to free herself from the wonderfully comfortable cushion.

Gia watched, bemused, as the others began to chant and hold crystals in front of them, moving their hands from the center of the forehead to the throat, the heart, the belly. She was almost ready to close her eyes and drift off into a deliciously relaxed sleep when they moved the stones again. The women held the stones between their legs while Asron moved a silky crystal slowly, sensuously over his penis until he was completely erect. Selene licked her lips and reached for him, but Asron waved her aside.

"No, tonight we have a new one, someone who really should give us her powers freely." He walked toward Gia and extended a hand, lifting her effortlessly toward him.

"Do you come to this circle of your own free will?" he asked her.

Gia nodded.

"And do you agree that you wish to join with me in the

ceremony that brings the God and Goddess's energies to this circle?"

What the hell, I guess so, Gia thought and then nodded again.

Asron removed the pewter cup from her hand and gently placed her fingers on his penis. "Let us begin the ceremony."

"Throbbing manhood," Gia murmured, pushing the palm of her hand against him and enjoying the feeling of the bristling hair against her fingers. "I've been writing romances too long when I begin to think about descriptions at a time like this." She pressed her fingers down on the head, running them gently over the swollen tip. Asron moaned involuntarily.

"Yes, I want this," Gia finally answered.

Asron pulled up her cotton skirt and began to caress her. His hands reached between her thighs to tickle and tease her until she could not wait another moment to feel him inside her.

"Please," she begged, pulling him down on the cushion, where he loomed over her, his manhood dangling tantalizingly just out of reach. She arched her hips upward, but he withdrew so that he barely touched her.

"Are you certain you want to join in the worship of the God and Goddess in this manner?" he asked.

"Please," she asked again and he took a small bottle of oil and began to anoint her. He started with her hair and then moved to swift featherlike movements between her legs while she silently screamed for him to stop fooling around and get on with it.

Then, with stunning swiftness, he entered her. There was a concerted sigh from the onlookers as the bodies met. The susurrus of a chant began again as he pushed even farther into her.

"Power, her power to me, my power to the Goddess of the North, South, East and West," Asron said as he moved in and out, slowly, teasing Gia with every inch of his flesh. He knew the pitch he wanted, the excitement that would build slowly toward the deliriously satisfying climax he was going to wait for. Gia had to be with him every moment for the prayers and the request for forces they called to work.

Gia bucked against him, still convinced she was dreaming and not wanting to awaken from the most sensuously satisfying vision she'd ever had. This was what she'd waited all her life for. She opened herself to Asron, urging him faster and deeper into her, accepting the drag of his skin against her, the meshing of the hair when pubic bone met pubic bone. There was a gentle tickling of his balls against her body, telling her that she had every inch of him inside her.

She began to feel the power the group was chanting about, but it was a different strength than Asron thought it was. He brought her forward toward the climax, urging her on as he rubbed her body against his own. She knew Asron was wrong about the power because he couldn't take it from her. It was hers and would stay with her and she could use it any way she wanted.

The energy grew between them. There was a subtle shift, and she knew that for the first time she was in control. The ultimate force worked for her and with her, not with him.

"Now," she said, exercising that power and taking him with her. Her body began to convulse as he followed her, unable to keep the measured slowness any longer.

"Now, now, now," she pleaded and finally it came, the huge crushing orgasm she had waited for all her life. It didn't matter that it was a stranger's body she was using to give her the pleasure. She had never felt anything like the orgasm that curled upward from her toes, spread out and went deep into her body and made her nipples stand at attention.

Gia screamed in ecstasy and dug her hands into his buttocks, urging him to keep moving within her until he'd done everything he could and the last spasm of pleasure had quieted.

"We have satisfied the Goddess. Thank you, Gia."

Asron moved aside, and then stood up in one graceful motion. "Thank you for serving the Goddess and me, dear. You'll never know what you've done. Next time, with the two of you, it will be even better," Asron said, patting Gia familiarly on the thigh.

"Selene?" he asked.

Selene had her face turned away from Gia and Asron. Gia had the oddest feeling that she had deliberately turned away so that she wouldn't see the coupling.

"Selene!" Asron's voice was harsh. The woman moved forward and handed him something that glinted in the dark.

"Here is something to bind you to us and to deflect some of the troubles headed your way. We accept your gift of your primal force and we know that you will bring the other one to us."

Asron slipped a silver cord around her neck. Gia tried to focus on the small pewter wizard holding a globe of pure black stone that dangled from the chain.

The silverwork was absolutely beautiful, but she got the strangest jangle when she took the wizard and looked closely at the eyes. They were staring at her. The expression was almost baleful, as if she were to blame for something and he was trying to right the balance again. The globe reflected the misshapen images of Asron and herself and it almost looked as if there was a third person in the background. When she turned to look, there was no one else in the room. All the other people in the circle had disappeared.

"The stone is a'a, a special form of lava from the inner crater of Kilauea, where the goddess Pele lives, and said to be protective of the person who wears it," Asron said. "I picked it up and had it fashioned into a globe the last time we went to Hawaii for vacation and ceremonies."

"We?" Fiona wondered who had that kind of money.

"The coven. I usually pay for everyone to go. We'll be leaving again in about two months and I'm looking forward to having both of you with us."

"Right," Gia said and put her head back against the soft cushion. She was too tired and too satisfied to ask him what the hell he was talking about. She closed her eyes and drifted off to sleep, lulled by the incense and warmth. She touched the figure again and felt a jolt of power from the magician, almost as if by touching it, she'd connected with something she didn't quite understand.

Asron left her, limp and satisfied, to sleep off the effects of the wine and the incense while he went home to try to use the power of the ceremony to deal with the upstarts who were trying to bend the world to their own will.

9

The trees whipped and bent with the night wind that swept inland from the ocean, bringing the smell of the salt and sea with the gusts. Pressure changes, Fiona had thought before she went to bed. Megan was already having trouble with headaches and wind or storms always made it worse. The family had a running joke that Megan could have been a great television meteorologist because she always knew when the storms were coming from the pain in her head. For the very worst storms, she could have given the broadcast from her bed, with her eyes shut and her face pasty white with pain.

Fiona went to sleep thinking about her daughter and the pain she was in and woke with a start as Megan materialized at the side of her bed. Fiona fumbled for the light and turned it on, wincing in the sudden glare. She was glad that Harper slept through most of the nightly ordeals with Megan.

"Mom, my head hurts," Megan said. "Is it time for more medicine?"

Fiona picked up the spiral-bound pad where she listed

medications and time. Megan wasn't due for more morphine yet. "Can you wait two hours more or do you need something now?"

Megan shrugged, which meant she was in more pain than she wanted to talk about.

"Okay, kid, let's run you through the neuro tests and if everything is all right, I'm going to fudge on your morphine and give you an extra dose. It can't hurt."

Some of Megan's responses were slow, but nothing that would alarm the doctor sufficiently to put her in the hospital. "Thank heaven it's just pain tonight," Fiona whispered. She'd had enough of absolute terror over the past few years when Megan suddenly lapsed into a coma. "No crisis that I can see, so here's the medicine." Fiona mixed the bitter liquid with Dr. Pepper and handed it to her daughter. While Megan drank, Fiona piled a couple of pillows behind her so that she could lean back comfortably and put three more pillows down on her lap, creating a soft place for Megan to rest. She reached into the bedside table and took out the old green glass canning jar that held the homemade whipped rose cream.

Fiona loved the smell of the ointment, which she used to soothe away at least part of the pain when her daughter's headaches became unbearable. The mixture was made from her grandmother's directions, compounding the white rose petals and beeswax with just enough honey to give it a sweet scent without making it sticky. Fiona had added a modern touch by melting the beeswax in the microwave and whipping the liquid and rose petals in the Cuisinart.

She still used the roses grown from cuttings of bushes that were easily two hundred years old. Her grandmother had been adamant that she take at least twelve cuttings from the old bushes so that some of them would survive, no matter what disaster befell Fiona in California. The old woman had been so worried about losing the special roses that she'd even potted one in an old worn-out copper tub and made Fiona promise that if there was ever a fire, earthquake or other disaster, she'd grab the rose and put it in the car to take with her.

Her grandmother had taught her every step of the process, including a special song to be sung with the mixing and use of the cream. The words and melody had always intrigued Fiona. One day she'd taken the time to look up the words in the *O.E.D.* and found they were a combination of Old English and Gaelic. The song had obviously been around a long time.

Megan crawled onto the bed and put her head back against the mound of pillows her mother arranged for her.

Fiona started to hum while she rubbed Megan's head. It usually took fifteen to twenty minutes before there was some kind of relief. Sometimes the relief never came. Fiona hoped this wasn't one of those nights.

"I'm sorry about waking you up, but this is a real bad one."

"Don't worry, I've got a good book to read." Fiona slipped the hidden volume out of her nightstand. She'd bought five books on witchcraft and devoured four of them in the past few days. She had only one book to go and she wasn't about to allow Harper's decree of no witchcraft make her set the book aside unread. She'd already looked into the introduction and was fascinated by how many things her family did as a matter of course that this woman said were part of the Old Religion.

"How interesting. It's nice to know we're not the only ones," she murmured as she read about the ability to read other people's thoughts. Fiona had always believed that their family was the only family in the world where everyone always knew what everyone else was thinking. They'd long ago developed a joke that no one in the house had ever had an original idea in his or her life. The images were floating around as part of the general consciousness and merely picked up by the person who finally gave them voice. Fiona had used this psychic closeness for purely mundane things, like thinking really hard when she needed to have Harper pick up a loaf of bread or milk from the store and she couldn't reach him by phone. Ninety percent of the time it worked.

Then there was the matter of the childish paintings Fiona had done when she was six years old. She remembered being lectured on how bad it was to draw anything except pure reality. She'd never understood what bothered everyone so much about her simple figures. After the third or fourth talk about reality, her mother and teacher asked her why she insisted on putting colored lines all around her figures, instead of just drawing them on a blue background for sky or green for lawn. No other kids drew bright colored areas around their figures, she was informed severely.

Fiona had been puzzled as she tried to explain that everyone had different colored lines around them. Her teacher's lines, she said, were red with jagged edges and her mother's were usually blue but right now they were pinkish orange. The teacher had reacted with horror, calling her a little pagan who needed a good whipping to get those ideas out of her mind. Fiona needed church learning, the teacher told her mother. Fiona's mother could wait outside while the teacher talked to Fiona and let her know what was expected of her in a nonheathen classroom.

Her mother stormed out of the room and Fiona was left with the teacher. The teacher stared down at Fiona.

"You know that no one else sees those lights, don't you? And you know that you'll never see them again, right? Because if you draw that again, you'll go straight to hell."

"But you see them. I know you do. Why don't people yell at you?"

Slowly the teacher smiled a wicked smile. "Because I lied," she said in a voice filled with laughter. "I lied and I never got caught. All these years I've seen what the devil wanted me to, but I've never let anyone else know. You were stupid."

Fiona's mother waited for her outside the school. Her face was white with anger as she looked down at her daughter. "I'll spank you within an inch of your life if you ever draw something that wicked again."

Fiona had solemnly promised not to draw what was reality for her. She's always wondered where the idea that it was bad to see colors around people's bodies had come from.

And here she was, thirty-five years later, reading a book that told her all these things made her a witch with special powers that were good, not evil. Again and again the book emphasized that this was not the devil's work; the powers were the gifts of a religion that had been old long before Christianity invented the devil and labeled any woman's powers as evil.

Fiona rubbed her daughter's head and read until she began to drift off to sleep. Half awake, she dreamed of reading minds and spells and the ability to make her life better using nothing more than powers she already had.

What would it have been like, she wondered, still dreaming, if she'd been allowed to go ahead and develop each of these possible talents during her life?

She was still humming the salve-making tune when it dawned on her that the author of the book would have classified the making of the beeswax-rose cream and the incantation that went with it as witchcraft. For some reason the things she did naturally hadn't clicked into the Old Religion framework she was beginning to build for herself.

"Well, I'll be damned," Fiona said wonderingly. The song, the precise measurements, the rosebushes she had tended for years just to be able to gather the flowers with the heavy, old-fashioned scent—it was all part of a tradition that she hadn't even realized existed. "Nothing more than a bit of the really old-time religion that made it into the New Age." She laughed softly at the thought.

Her musings were interrupted by a rush of cats racing up the stairs, through the hallway, into the bedroom, across the bed and back out of the room again.

Megan moaned, but didn't wake up.

"Damn!" Fiona swore. Blood started to ooze from the puncture marks the cats had left on her hand. She grabbed some of the cream and rubbed it on her wounds.

Downstairs, she could hear several cats begin to screech, and the pack of running cats thumped around and then started back up the stairs for another pass over the bed with all claws out. She could hear Loner wailing in the garage, where she'd had to put him in a cage until he could heal properly.

"What the hell is going on?" she asked, grabbing a tissue to mop up the blood that ran from one deep gouge.

"Numph," Megan said, responding from a drugged almost-sleep.

"Honey, you just stay here on the pillows while I go check." Fiona slipped out of bed and hurried downstairs. She noticed in passing that each windowsill held at least two cats and most of them had their tails fluffed. Several of them growled as she walked by. Something outside was upsetting the cats.

A paragraph in the book had said that familiars, particularly cats, could guard a house. If multiples meant more protection, no one could ever hurt her in this house, she thought.

She heard the scrabbling sound of skidding felines cornering on pine floors and stepped aside just in time to save her feet from being lacerated as another four cats raced up the stairs and through the rooms.

"Earthquake?" she asked. Several of the cats could pre-

dict seismic events, but usually they simply went to the
highest point in the house and screamed until the shaking
started and then bitched when it ended.

Princess was standing in front of the French doors that
led to the backyard. She cried in a rising wail that ended in a
hiss and then started over. Her entire body was fluffed and
her claws flashed in the moonlight as she snatched at ghosts.
The other cats added their voices to her howl.

"What's the matter, baby?" Fiona said, trying to pick
up the cat. Princess danced out of range.

"What the hell is out there, a wolf?" Fiona asked and
flipped on the back light. She saw the flash of a black cat,
barely visible in the surrounding darkness. To one side she
saw that dirt at the base of the hill had been dug up by some
animal.

"Sillies, it's only another cat. He was probably waiting
for the mole that was making that hole," she soothed the
assembled animals. The explanation didn't satisfy the cats.
They continued to prowl and scream while Fiona climbed
the stairs and went back to bed.

She sat with Megan's head on her lap for most of the
night, only moving when her leg cramped unbearably.

Harper was the enigma that kept her awake. She kept
returning to him and the way he'd looked and acted when
he'd seen that poor little makeshift altar and circle. What
was wrong with Harper? What made him hate the very idea
of practicing a few innocent rituals? Why didn't he want
her to protect the family as best she could?

Things keep happening to us, like we're meant to be vic-
tims and Harper's just allowed it to happen. Why doesn't
he want to fight back so our life can be easier? Fiona fretted
as she went back over the battle that had started when he
found her in the circle with Gia.

They'd always had to fight for everything, even for the
right to get married. Their courtship had been a grand passion, a force that swept them both toward marriage because

they couldn't stand to be apart another second. Her father and mother had thrown her out of the house, called her a whore and then told her she was stupid for thinking that lust was love. Her brother had tried to tell her not to lose her head over a piece of tail. She'd ignored them all. When her parents refused to participate in any wedding plans, Fiona eloped. She had never regretted her decision. She and Harper had always worked together despite terrible adversity that threatened to rip their little family apart time after time.

So why would Harper object to her plan to help out the family? It didn't make sense. Harper had always wanted to protect his family. If a little chanting and candle-burning helped, where was the harm? But his reaction said there was something about witchcraft that was desperately important to Harper, even if he wouldn't tell her why.

She let her mind drift, hoping she could go far enough into him to discover what the secret was. She'd always been able to pick up snatches of Harper's thoughts, mostly, she decided, because they were close and thought about the same things. There had been a couple of times, though, like when she discovered that her big Christmas present was a set of Le Creuset pans that she'd lusted after, that she regretted being on the same wavelength. Sometimes she'd inadvertently picked up more than she was supposed to know about something, but this was the first time she'd actually tried to pry loose information that he wanted hidden.

It was like a trip through a strange land. She hadn't realized that Harper dreamed in some foreign language. It was an odd mixture of Welsh and something else, a language she'd never heard before. The images were dark and gloomy, straight out of *Macbeth*. There was some kind of tragedy involving a huge mountain and death that invaded his refuge of home and family. He was crying, until he stumbled back into the light of the cozy warm home, making her sigh with relief. Their home, their family were safe and secure against the tumbling mountain of worry that threatened to engulf him.

She pulled back, leaving Harper to his dreams, warmed by the way he saw their small clan. Surely he couldn't begrudge that clan whatever protection she could give it.

The cats began to quiet down; there were only occasional yowls from downstairs and Loner had stopped screaming from the garage.

Princess still patrolled from room to room, uttering small wails as if something was hurting her. When Fiona tried to call her up on the bed, the cat wouldn't respond. It looked almost as if she were checking to be sure there were cats in all the windows for protection.

Fiona shrugged and picked up her book again, then laughed when she realized what she'd been reading before the great cat avalanche.

> Witches are generally able to read people's thoughts. This is usually accomplished by a keen observation of other people and good guesswork, but occasionally actual thoughts are transferred. This accounts for picking up a phone before it begins to ring, or answering a question before it is asked.

Further on, Fiona let out a small gasp as she came upon another chapter that explained even more why she felt different from most other people.

> Witches realize that there are souls in everything, including trees, flowers, spiders and cats. We also understand that none of these are meant to be subjugated by man. We are equal to, not better than the animals.

"Of course!" Fiona said, delighted that someone finally understood. She had always been able to see living souls in everything from the maple trees to the fox who came and stole pieces of fat from the bird feeder to take back to the kits in her den. For years Fiona had been cultivating families of wild animals around her. There were forty acres of undeveloped land behind her house and as the drought had worsened, she'd started putting out water and food to tide over the raccoons, skunks, possums and other wildlings until there was enough natural forage to allow them to survive on their own.

For her efforts, she'd been rewarded with being able to watch baby skunks on their first venture out of the burrow under the pyracantha bush. She'd been amazed to see that their bodies were tiny, but their tails bushed out to spectacular breadths. They had ferocious teeth and occasionally they'd stamp to warn a sister or brother away from an especially tasty tidbit, but for the most part they were the best of neighbors. For one whole year she'd never had any slugs or snails in the garden because the skunks thought they were better than popcorn and ate any that dared venture toward the tomatoes.

The raccoons had also given her hours of pleasure as she watched the babies skinny-dipping in the children's pool she kept filled with water and rocks. She'd seen the most aggressive raccoon play king of the mountain on top of the plastic box she used as a feeder and witnessed firsthand the truth that skunks and raccoons could coexist.

She heard a scratching sound outside her open window and turned around to look down on the patio. She switched off her light for a few moments and then peered into the moonlit darkness.

Standing in the shadows was a huge raccoon, closely followed by a small skunk.

"Hello Ray, hi Fred. Sorry we didn't make any corn for you today," she said in a low voice to the raccoon, who was now foraging in the pan of cat food she had left there for the nightly visitors. The skunk just stared at her as if she couldn't believe there wouldn't be immediate handouts from the person inside the house.

"I know corn's everyone's favorite; you were the kids who came up to the door and begged until I cooled off some of the corn I was cooking and gave it to you. But at ninety-nine cents an ear, Harper won't let me buy corn for you unless the humans get some too."

The raccoon probably couldn't hear her; she never talked loudly to them or even turned on the back light to really take a good look at them. She lived in daily fear that her little patch of wilderness would be discovered and destroyed someday by people who didn't understand that she loved the animals.

Instead, she watched for a few more moments until they decided they would be satisfied with the cat food and fresh water that were already outside.

Fiona finally managed to drift off to sleep at six in the morning, just moments before Harper's alarm went off to wake him for work. He burrowed deeper into the blankets and moaned about getting up. He finally focused on the real world after ten minutes of early-morning radio news and pulled the covers off his face.

"I had the weirdest dream last night," he said as he swung his legs over the edge of the bed and sat upright.

"What was it about?" Fiona asked, dread settling near her heart. She didn't want to hear this, she was almost certain. Harper had a nasty habit of dreaming about the future in terms of absolute reality. He'd foretold real tragedies with his visions, even though he denied the prescience when it was pointed out to him. "Was it about the family?" Fiona demanded as she slid out from behind the mound of pillows, leaving Megan asleep on the bed.

"I'm not certain. It was all jumbled up with the old song that you sing when you make the rose pomander and cats screaming. You were just starting to stir in the rose petals when I looked up and saw a silent dark mountain sliding toward me."

He shuddered at the memory. "It rolled over everything, the schools, the houses, the stores. It was huge; the path was as wide as the whole town and there was nothing I could do to stop it. I remember screaming at you to stop singing and for the cats to shut up because that was bringing the mountain down on us. When you turned to me, you were blind and deaf and the mud was going to swallow you up and with it, everything I love," Harper said, shivering. He hopped on one foot and then on the other; the morning air was cold and his thin cotton sleep shirt did little to warm him.

"Fiona, you have to listen to me. I know you don't understand why I'm so afraid of what you were doing with Gia, but believe me, it's nothing to mess around with. If you're thinking of fooling around with spells and stuff again, don't, okay?" He looked at her, his expression solemn. "Please, just this once don't argue. Do me a favor and don't even think of messing around with the supernatural. That mountain moving toward me could be a warning—fool around with an immutable force and it's going to destroy us."

"You already told me not to," Fiona said, hedging. She felt like a kid with her crossed fingers held behind her back. Kings Cross and he wouldn't guess that she wasn't telling the complete unvarnished truth. She knew better than to give him a real promise. If she swore she'd never work with whatever it was that was helping, then she'd really have to stop or she'd be guilty of lying to Harper. She had never lied to him and she didn't want to start now, but how was she going to stop something that seemed to be an intrinsic part of what she really was?

Harper studied her face thoughtfully. "Telling you not

to do something usually doesn't work. It just makes you do it twice as fast as you usually would."

"That's not true!" Fiona objected. She was hurt by his reluctance to believe her. "I listen to you."

"Right. And then you do what you want," Harper said. "Remember when we decided you should stop saving cats when we finally counted fifteen felines in residence? Now we're up to twenty-something. You really listened on that one, didn't you?"

"That's different. They would have died," Fiona objected. "I'll promise not to do anything more with spells and such if you'll tell me why you're so worried about this. It's just a silly little ritual."

"Nothing having to do with that stuff is silly," Harper said, his voice strained.

"But why are you afraid of something that's helping us?" Fiona asked again, hoping to pry loose an answer. She started to blurt out that she'd used a spell to bring her the contract for the paintings, then decided she'd better keep her mouth shut. There were some things Harper could guess at, but he didn't need to know for certain.

"I was asking for protection for the family when you barged into the studio and scared Gia and me. What could be wrong with protection?"

"Everything, if it comes through those sources. You don't know what will happen. It kicks back on you. First someone will report us for the number of cats we have and then we'll lose them. Or someone will come along and harm the outside animals, like the raccoons or skunks or even that family of opossums under the back deck. Or Megan will get worse and we won't be able to get help for her. Hell, it could be that I'll have to commute more than the three hours a day that I already spend on the road, because they'll move the headquarters. It could be anything. I know how it goes when this starts kicking back, and you don't want to be around when it does!"

He broke her grip on his arm and retreated to the bath, closing the door behind him. He rarely shut her out and that made Fiona even more worried. Normally Harper left the bathroom door open, since the bathroom tended to be communal anyway. All he really wanted to do was luxuriate in his hot shower, the water blasting across his weary and aching back. He didn't sing in the shower, he didn't talk, he just let the water roll over him and wash away the worries. This morning, however, Fiona heard him repeating something while he bathed. She eased open the bathroom door, but the words still weren't clear.

"Damn, he's either gargling or talking in Welsh again," she muttered. She'd tried to learn Welsh, but it had been a lost cause. Nothing sounded the way it was written. The language had developed with an absolute disregard for a human tongue trying to form the words. Worse, everyone who spoke Welsh seemed to take a perverse pride in making their language completely unintelligible to the novice.

Fiona listened for a few more moments until the low, serious tone gave her goose bumps. She would have sworn when she looked into the fog-filled bathroom that there was something swirling around in the gray clouds of steam that issued from the bath. Fingers of steam crept out the door, caressing her toes with an almost human touch.

She screamed as quietly as she could, jumped back and shut the door.

"Imagination, that's all it is. It's just that I'm so tired," she said.

10

Fiona had to push several dozen cats out of the way before she could fill the old copper teakettle with filtered water and set it to heat on the back of the stove. Heating the tea water in the microwave would have been faster, but there was something solid and down-to-earth about the feel of the wooden handle and the heavy metal.

She heard a peculiar sizzle as she turned her back on the kettle and began to retrieve the bread from the drawer, where the cats couldn't steal the center out of the loaf or kick the hard crust to death. She ignored the popping sound, thinking it meant that she'd splashed some water on the bottom of the kettle. It took a few more moments before she realized that there was a god-awful stink in the air.

Fiona wrinkled her nose. "Skunk? Did Fred somehow get into the house?" Nothing else in the world smelled like a skunk who was really pissed off. She looked around, but there was no telltale black kitty with a white stripe mixing with her bunch. All the cats were just the normal felines.

She turned back to the stove and followed the smell to the cheery blue flames that were bending to one side on the burner.

"Ick!" she said as the smell got even stronger. She looked underneath the kettle and saw the source of the stink. A yellow puddle had spread from the burner to the stainless-steel pan and into the holes where the gas came out from the main line. She reached over and turned off the gas.

"Oh thank you!" she said to the cats. "Which one of you guys decided to make a rotten day even worse?" She opened the windows and let the frost-tinged air into the room. Even with the cold wind, it wasn't enough fresh air, so she flipped on the fan over the stove. Nothing did much good, not even using Citra-Solv to clean the stove, though the concentrated orange scent did cover the smell a little.

Thoughtfully she watched the animals while she cooked breakfast, making certain to make enough steak and potatoes to feed the cats as well as Harper and her. It had been a long time since anyone had made a mess like that.

"So whatever happened last night bothered you enough that you had to make a statement right on the burners," she said.

She wished the cats would choose another way of giving her a warning that something was about to happen or that there was danger nearby. It wasn't something like Old Jezebel batting at her face when she was asleep because Megan was in a coma and couldn't call her for help. No earthquake had shaken the house.

"I sure wish you could talk," Fiona sighed.

"My God, what's that smell?" Harper demanded as he walked down the stairs.

"Someone left us a message by peeing in the burner," she informed him.

"Well, watch and make certain no one has a urinary tract problem. I'd hate to lose one of these kids." Harper picked up two twin cats and nuzzled them. The animals spat at each other when he put them back down; they were jealous of each other.

Fiona waited for Harper to say something more, but he was unnaturally quiet about the morning's upsets.

Fiona thought seriously about going back to bed when Harper left. Megan would sleep all day, and Fiona was so tired that her bones ached. But there was the underlying electricity, the excitement of what she'd learned and what she wanted to do, that made it impossible for her to sleep.

Finally, desperate to talk to someone, she called Gia. "Can you come over if I promise to bake some brownies and give you a cup of cappuccino?"

"When have I ever been able to resist a good gossip session, especially with food involved? I want to hear all about what happened with you and Harper after I left the other day and then I've got to tell you about the wildest night I've ever spent! You'll never believe it."

Gia took only fifteen minutes to make it to Fiona's back door.

"What is that awful smell?" she asked.

"Nothing important. Just cats."

"Is that all?" Gia said, laughing. "I thought you might have been trying out a new incense that didn't work out too well. If I were you, I'd leave out essence of cat from anything you're going to burn." Then she moaned dramatically, threw herself down in the comfortable old recliner and began to relate her experiences with Asron and Selene.

"Oh, God, I don't know what happened, but I feel like someone's turned me inside out and done tattoos on the parts that shouldn't be mentioned in polite society," Gia moaned as she accepted a cup of cappuccino from Fiona. "And look at this." She took off the wizard pendant and handed it over to her friend.

Fiona looked at the figure. She didn't like the expression

of malice on the magician's face and she didn't like the feel of the stone against her hand. It felt slick and almost oily to the touch.

"Interesting," she said as she handed it back. "You do get into the most peculiar situations, but I guess you can use it in a book."

"Oh, have I got some great attributes to give to my next hero. Now if only I could think up a story to go with it I'd be in hog heaven. I miss writing, you know. Maybe the next thing I should do is a spell to bring back my ability to write one hell of a good romance."

"Somehow I don't think that a man answering the door with an erection and an invitation to come in and get screwed would be something romance editors would want. And for the life of me I can't understand why getting yourself into this situation doesn't bother you. You just accept what happened. I mean, there's AIDS and venereal diseases and all kinds of problems that you could have picked up."

"Maybe it's the divorce and the need to really break loose from Larry. You know when Asron asked me if I wanted it, I said yes, because I couldn't think of anything else except that magnificent penis. The truth is, I've never had such a good time in my life."

She reached for the magician.

"Would you worry if someone gave you something this expensive, just to make you happy?"

"I don't like it. The expression gives me the willies."

Gia slipped it back underneath the top button of her blouse. "It made me feel funny at first, too, but it's supposed to be protection and I need that right now."

Princess came into the room and made a beeline for Gia. She hopped up into Gia's lap and clawed at the front of her shirt until the top button opened, showing the wizard nestled between Gia's breasts. The cat took one look at the magician and hissed and swatted at it.

"What do you think you're doing, you little monster?" Gia said, protecting herself against the claws. "This is a good silk shirt, don't you dare shred it, fish breath!"

Fiona grabbed the cat, who set up a wail of anger at being deprived of her objective. "I'll just stick her in the bedroom until you leave. The cats were in a weird mood all night, anyway."

"I love the cats, but this is ridiculous," Gia said, smoothing her blouse and checking to make certain the cat hadn't damaged the heavy silver chain that held the wizard.

"Princess isn't usually downright destructive. I wonder what's gotten into her." Fiona looked at Gia. The only thing that was different about her was the pendant with its malign aura.

Gia was quiet for a moment. "I understand what you're worried about. In the glaring daylight, yes, I'm thinking that maybe it wasn't the smartest thing I've ever done to just lie down and let this man screw me. But Fiona, you have to understand that it also helps to know that I appeal to someone like Asron Burke. Imagine, I can just be myself and still have someone like that make love to me. I don't make men want to run away when they look at me."

Fiona added more freshly ground beans to the espresso maker for another cup of cappuccino. The sound of the machine made conversation impossible until the last bit of steam had escaped.

"Toward the end, Larry would look at me and his erection would deflate. Do you have any idea what that did to my self-esteem? The mere sight of me naked was enough to make a man's erection wilt?" Her finger curled over in a most expressive gesture.

"Pretty devastating," Fiona said.

"That doesn't even begin to describe it. And now this handsome man who is hung like the guys in the centerfolds is making it with me? He thinks I'm the sexiest thing to cross his path in ages? All I have to do is make sure that I don't lose Asron and don't catch something horrible and I'll be on the road to recovery."

Gia eyed Fiona speculatively.

"What are you thinking?" Fiona asked.

"Harper didn't completely ban you from going out with me, did he?" Gia asked.

"No."

"He didn't say you couldn't meet new people, right?"

"No."

"Fine!" Gia lit up. "First I'm going to meet with my divorce attorney and then I'm going to the Major Arcana. Come with me and meet Asron. It'd be fun to have you along!"

They were interrupted by another earsplitting scream from Princess; the cat seemed to be throwing her voice under the bedroom door and directly out into the family room.

"Your attorney? You finally hired someone?"

"Yes. One of these days I'm going to have to tell you all about the Norse god and his Runes, but right now I have to run. Can you come with me? You can meet E.G. and Asron all in the same day. Asron's teaching a class on sensuality and spiritualism. It might even help your sex life with Harper. I'm telling you, a few drops of that oil and you'd really soar!"

Fiona laughed. "Darling, I hate to disillusion you but I haven't had to wait until I was forty to find out just how good sex can be. I'm only sorry it took you so long. We do fine without the oil or the biggest prick in captivity."

"Then you don't want to come with me?"

Fiona hesitated. She really did want to go, if only to make sure Gia was safe with this new man. But there was the nagging feeling that Harper wouldn't have asked her to stay away from people like Asron and places like the Major Arcana if he didn't have a good reason.

Megan was the perfect excuse.

"I do want to meet both of them, but I can't go with you today. Maybe in a couple of weeks, when Harper has calmed down and I can talk to him about it."

"In other words, Harper is still going to run your life. I did that with Larry and look what it got me."

"It's not the same," Fiona said. "Besides, I can't leave Megan after a bad night. Today just won't work out."

"Then I'll be back tomorrow," Gia said as she ran out the back door.

Fiona let Princess out of the room, went up to check on Megan and headed for the studio across the hallway.

A small spell, she promised herself. Nothing fancy. Protection for everyone and an end to some of the things that were making her life miserable. Surely she could ask for that without incurring Harper's wrath?

The second time around she was more comfortable with the drawing of the circle and the setting up of the altar. She took care to arrange the box and implements like a still life, so that if Harper came home and barged in, it would look as if she'd created something she would use in one of her calendar paintings. She lit the candles, which she could blow out in an instant if anyone intruded.

Fiona followed the ritual meticulously, doing it slowly to make sure she didn't forget anything. She was halfway through the ceremony when she began to feel the presence of the force the books talked about. It was a feeling of being able to do anything if she set her mind to it. She began her petitions and the weaving of a powerful spell to keep her family safe. She listed the problems in her life that she wanted solved.

"I want Megan to be healthy. I want Harper to not commute so long or work so hard and to enjoy life more. I want more money. And I want that damned IRS off my back with their idiotic proclamations that I'm not a working artist!"

Money. That reminded her. She'd sent back the contracts and she'd been looking for a check in the mail ever since. If it didn't come today, she'd have to call the company and ask when she could expect payment.

The doorbell interrupted her. Hastily she sketched an opening in the circle, closing it behind her, and hurried down to answer the summons.

"Certified letter for you," the mail carrier said. "Sign here."

Fiona scrawled her signature, hoping the letter was the long-awaited check. She took the envelope and her heart dropped to the vicinity of her toes. The yellowish envelope was marked "U.S. Department of the Treasury." Her stomach clenched. IRS again, damn them. What were they doing this time? Putting a lien on the house when they didn't have any right to do any such thing? Attaching Harper's wages?

She ripped open the envelope. Inside there was a short letter and what looked like a check. She stared at it unbelievingly and then read the note.

"It has been determined that you were assessed taxes and penalties in error and that your income tax refund was withheld in error. Enclosed is a check for $4,587.00 including the refund and interest."

She looked at the check.

$4,587.00. All the right numbers and in all the right places.

Slowly it penetrated. After all the fighting and the certified letters and the desperate attempts to give the IRS more and more documentation to prove her case as a working artist, they'd actually won. The IRS had given in.

"You lousy miserable sons of bitches, may you all rot in hell for what you put me through," Fiona said as she looked again at the letter and check. With the help of the Old Religion, she had defeated the IRS!

II

Gia stared at the fat yellow envelope from her husband's divorce attorney. It boldly proclaimed Ron Anderson's specialty just in case someone at the post office wanted a divorce attorney fast and saw this come through the mails. She'd known Ron for years socially. He was a good friend of Larry's. She and Ron's wife, Sarah, went outlet shopping when they had time. The men had sent business back and forth for years as their law firms grew and prospered.

Gia felt a sting of anger and hurt. She had thought that Ron and Sarah were her friends. But if Ron was representing Larry in the divorce, it meant he'd picked sides in the marital battle and she'd been on the losing side. Larry the Louse meant business and social opportunities for Ron, while she, being only a divorced wife, was a liability for most attorneys.

"You son of a bitch," Gia said conversationally, picking up the letter with two fingers as if it were a dead rat and carrying it over to the kitchen table. The envelope had been packed so tightly that it split open as it hit the oak surface.

Papers slid out onto wood, all of them with thick black type and legal-looking forms, with Larry's name down the left side and numbers for every line.

"It's going to come back to haunt you, darling. All that time I spent as your secretary when you couldn't afford anyone else and all those underhanded tricks I saw you play, they're going to cost you now," she whispered as she riffled through the documents. She unfolded the heavy paper and scanned the court headings and the titles of the actions. She saw immediately that Larry's attorney was asking for an order to make her begin to pay half the cost of the mortgage, insurance and taxes. The second set of papers advised her that Larry had terminated her health insurance. The third filing was an order to produce any and all evidence of abuse, including but not limited to any videotapes.

"So you *are* worried, you slime monster," she said. Let him sweat this out for a while. It would do him good to have his blood pressure up in the 200s for a while. With any luck, he'd have a heart attack and die.

She opened the fourth set of papers and saw orders blocking her from using more than half of the money in the banking account. She looked at the amount listed for the account, which was impossibly small. If she read it right, she had less than $300 at her disposal to get her through the next twenty-three days of the month.

Gia stared in disbelief at the papers. "Oh yes, Ron, you did choose sides, didn't you?" If she paid what they were asking, she'd have to shell out over $2,000 a month out of an income of precisely zero.

She was glad she had E.G. beside her. Once he looked at these papers, she was certain he'd have all kinds of neat tricks up his sleeve to stop Larry from taking everything he could get his hands on. She was willing to bet that Larry thought she'd never be able to afford anyone. Surprise, Larry.

Gia picked up the papers, realized that her hand was

shaking and set the documents back down. "I don't just want him unmanned, I want him dead," she said quietly. Never in her life had she wanted to kill someone as much as she wanted to kill Larry.

She picked up the expensive boning knife she'd bought for one of her cooking classes and began to play with it, flicking the thin carbon-steel blade, which could just as easily slice through her finger as through the carcass of a chicken. She could feel the power of her wishes flowing down through her fingertips to the knife. She could have carved Larry up like a trussed turkey if he'd walked through the door at that moment. She balanced the surgical steel in her fingers, enjoying the lightness of the blade and the peculiar thrum of expectancy that came from a well-sharpened, often-used knife that had seen more than its share of blood. The long blade would work wonders on Larry's ribs. The thin steel would bend and snap back as each piece of rib bone was sliced clean through and the muscles parted company with each other. The thin tip that slipped in between bone and cartilage would tickle his heart. She'd circle the muscle and make certain all the connections to the lungs were severed.

It was so real that she could almost smell the blood and feel the slight resistance from the thickness of the muscles and veins, the hot liquid gushing over her hands as she made sure everything vital was destroyed.

Gia smiled beatifically as she worked her way downward, slicing the liver neatly into sections. It would look like the meat she got from the butcher shop, red and fresh enough to serve on a plate, all fried and brown with onions. If she were in a cooking mood, she could make another dish from the pancreas, sweetbreads to be served to other women who hated their husbands as much as she hated Larry.

Once his internal organs had been sliced and diced and his heart pierced, she'd withdraw the knife and make one clean cut from sternum to pubis, eviscerating him for easy dissection by the coroner.

She was entranced by the imagined sight of Larry, his steaming guts coiled on the floor. She could have called in fortune-tellers who read the entrails of pigs and cows to tell her fortune as a widow by reading her ex-husband's intestines.

Widow. She liked that word. It was so much better than divorce. It was also more profitable. If Larry died, she'd inherit everything, instead of having to settle for half of what E.G. could find.

She focused on the dream-image of Larry's eyes staring at her, in shock that she could do such a thing. The whole idea was so pleasing that she almost didn't hear the doorbell.

The bells pealing finally penetrated her gory daydreams as whoever was on the front porch leaned on the bell and didn't release it.

Gia let the knife clatter to the tabletop as she hurried toward the door.

She looked into the peephole, ready to retreat if it was someone she didn't want to see. Asron stood on the doorstep. She was reaching for the knob when he started beating on the door in desperation.

She flung the door open and stood there in shock as he loomed over her.

"Who's trying to kill you? Death, death all around, that's what I got from you! Where's the blood—I thought someone had stabbed you in the heart! What the hell were you just doing?"

Gia stared at him, dumbfounded. "What do you mean, death? How did you know what I was thinking about doing?"

Asron was apoplectic. "I was practically dragged here by the force of the images from this house. There I was, working on a deal to buy a bunch of restaurants that would

bring a great tax write-off and suddenly all I could see and
smell was blood and destruction, all of it circling around
you. I want to know what happened! You have no idea
what it's been like, trying to drive with gore dripping in
front of my eyeballs for ten miles while I raced here! I
thought I'd find you dead in the kitchen with a crazed mur-
derer standing over your hacked-up body.''

He was sweating and his face had gone from red to
deathly white as he sagged against the door. He ran his hand
over her arm and face as if making certain she was really still
there and alive.

Gia smiled uncertainly. "What a vivid picture, but I
promise you, no murder has taken place yet.''

She shivered, though the day was hot.

"I'll have to be careful who I slice up from now on," she
murmured.

"No murder? Goddess, it was so clear. I could have
sworn—''

Gia didn't want him to follow those thoughts any further than he already had. It was bad enough that he could
hear her and react when she was doing nothing more than
fantasizing. What was she going to have to do to keep her
thoughts private?

I'll just have to find a way to block him out, she
thought.

Asron saw her shiver and pushed her back inside the
house.

"Don't lie to me. Something's happening here, something that smells of blood and hate. I can feel it. Tell me
about it and I'll see if I can help you.'' He led her into the
kitchen.

Gia didn't even stop to wonder how he knew the layout
of the house and how he'd gone to the precise spot where
she'd daydreamed about disemboweling Larry.

Asron saw the packet of legal papers and swooped
down on them before Gia could stop him.

"This couldn't be the source, could it?"

"No, those are personal." She pulled them from his grasp.

"Certainly." Asron smiled, and it was obvious that she didn't have to tell him anything at all about the papers. He already knew. "What an interesting problem. Your husband is a fool. Here you are, with your powers beginning to come into focus. You're working with the strongest coven on the West Coast and he thinks he's strong enough to win? He doesn't know what he's tackling, does he?"

Gia lifted one shoulder. "This witchcraft stuff isn't something I'd share with him, particularly as we haven't talked since he moved in with his bimbette."

"Good. That way it will be a surprise when we help you make his world come crashing down. I understand from Selene that you're already working on the sexual side of the problem. Perhaps I could cause a sudden decrease in his business or declining health. Or maybe your idea of killing him is the best. Simply removing the problem works in many cases."

This was definitely getting out of hand. Asron was talking as if killing Larry really were an option. "How about if I just try this on my own for a while. I'm not sure that anyone else's help is necessary, though I really appreciate the offer."

"Don't make any hasty decisions. Help is very useful."

"I understand. But there are complications. For instance, if you make his business slack off, then I won't get as much money when it comes to trial. If he has bad health, Kelly could throw him out and he could land right back here on my doorstep. So I thank you for the offer, but right now I'm just going to let things happen naturally."

No, Gia thought, she wasn't sure she did want to involve Asron and the people in the shop. There were an awful lot of similarities in what she'd seen in the store to things she'd been told about as a child, things that good

Christian people didn't traffic with. Like the devil, for instance.

"Oh, you think it's satanism, do you?" Asron asked, catching her thoughts perfectly. "You think we'd use black magic or something like that to gather the power of the Goddess to us? You know us better than that, my dear. The Goddess comes on her own terms and only to those who harm no one else."

Gia wanted to believe him. He was handsome, rich, virile, everything she liked in a man. But there was an underlying sense that he was lying. She couldn't tell just how, but that link he had forged between them seemed to work two ways and this time it wasn't to his benefit.

He reached out and picked up the phone. "Before we go any further, let me show you the kind of help I'm talking about. You need a lawyer and I'm going to get you the best one in town." He punched in a number.

"No!" She pressed down the cutoff switch. "I found an attorney a couple of days ago. I'm doing fine."

"Who? Where did you meet him?"

"I don't believe that's any of your business."

Asron backed off. "I apologize. I know I do a good executive ogre imitation, it's one of the things that Selene likes least about me, but it's for your own good. You're still new at this. You don't understand that there are people out there who will harm you as soon as they find out about the witchcraft in your life. It isn't safe for any of us, so we have our own closed societies. That's why I would have found you an attorney who is sympathetic and who would also understand the kind of power that we can wield, if necessary."

"It just happens that I picked an attorney I met in the Major Arcana, so I would suppose that he's safe. I went to his office a couple of days ago and it looks like everything is going to work out fine."

"Except that you got these papers today!"

Gia shrugged. "He hasn't had time to file."

"Let me get you someone who will go down to the courthouse first thing in the morning and take immediate action."

"Let's give E.G. the benefit of a little time. And please stop pushing. I don't like to have someone try to force me into doing something."

"Would you have any objection to calling the power to help E.G. on your behalf and to protect you against Larry?" He gave her a slow seductive smile as his gaze caressed her body. "You know how effective the last sexual ritual was."

He began to trace the swell of her breast underneath her T-shirt. She wasn't wearing a bra and her nipples were instantly, tightly erect against the material.

She wanted him. Her thighs were ready to open and welcome him, her body eager to enjoy his thrusting. She wanted to feel him inside her again, the gentle bounce of his testicles against her inner thighs just as she had felt it a few days before.

She pushed upward, against him.

"Yes, that's right, let yourself feel the passion. Let the softness between your legs begin to pulse and swell. Think of what I'm going to do to you and the strength we will have when we finish the ritual," Asron said. He leaned over and kissed her gently on the neck, his teeth nibbling at her fine skin.

She was sweating with need. Back, far back in her mind, she wondered how much of her desperate response to him was engineered by his mind's feeding her the right impulses instead of her own body's responses. If he could pick up on her thoughts, could he overlay her own thoughts with his desires?

The thought vanished as he pulled her against him and

she felt his heavy flesh against the fabric of his pants. If the solidity of his erection was any indication, he wanted her as much as she desired him.

"Wait," he said. His voice cracked with the word. "If we're going to do this right and use the ritual to take your husband's hatred and turn it back on him, we have to employ the right invocations and tools."

Gia ran her hand along the front of his trousers. "I think we've got all the tools necessary."

He moaned as he pushed her hand away. "Wait here."

He went to his car and came back carrying a wickedly sharp knife. The polished wooden handle was etched with arcane symbols, and the steel itself had been marked with more writing. He also carried a bag containing two bottles of oil and a silken rope.

"Do you have any roses growing outside?"

"Roses? I've got a few bushes that are blooming beside the back fence."

"I'll gather them while you find some cinnamon sticks to burn, something to burn them in, and some salt for the circle."

There it was again, Gia thought. He ordered her around as if it was for her own good.

She lifted down one of the wicker baskets from the decorations around the kitchen and placed the small granite metate in the bottom. She'd brought back the heavy flat three-legged dish from Mexico, fully intending to grind her own corn for tortillas. It had sat on the corner of the counter for three years and not one ounce of corn had ever been sacrificed on its rough surface.

But it would make a great incense burner, she thought. I've never seen stone that would burn and it would stay upright even in an earthquake. She set the sea salt crystals in the basket and rummaged through her spices to find one lone piece of cinnamon. It would have to do.

Gia watched through the window as Asron murmured a

swift invocation, complete with hand gestures, then cut the flowers and brought them inside. As he passed the table, he lifted an orange from the bowl of fruit and motioned her up the stairs toward the bedroom.

She picked up the basket and preceded him.

Through all the activity, she noticed that he had managed to keep a tight erection going. That was good, because the fire between her legs was still burning as strongly as it had been when he touched her breasts.

He stopped in front of the bed and began to pull off all the covers, dumping them in front of the closet. The blanket, sheets, even the wool pad followed the comforter, until the only thing left was the blue mattress.

"Making love totally naked in front of each other and the Goddess is the best way to worship," Asron said. He reached over and pulled up the edge of Gia's T-shirt. She lifted her arms and he slid the shirt up, kissing her breasts as the cloth opened. His tongue was everywhere on Gia's firm flesh, licking her nipples and tasting the small indentation in the middle of her neck. His teeth bit at the skin, not enough to hurt, but enough to make her want to grab him by the balls and pull him down on the bed and take him with a force that would split them both with pleasure.

Gia couldn't wait. She tried to grab his hand to let him feel how indecently ready she was, but he held back.

She unzipped his pants and began to pull them down until he pushed her hands away so that he could step out of his trousers. He hesitated for a moment before touching the red bikini underpants.

"No, don't stop. I can't wait," Gia said as she reached out and lowered the elastic waistband. She drew her breath in as his penis bobbed into sight. He was every bit as magnificent as she'd remembered. Her response was instantly, excruciatingly the same—she could hardly wait to get him into bed.

She reached for him, massaging the swollen flesh, urging

him to forget anything else other than the pleasure that awaited him. She lowered her face and was within inches of him when he stopped her.

"Not yet. We have sacred work to do first."

Asron picked up the roses, athame and salt and began to walk an unsteady circle around the bed. "God and Goddess, bind our work with the passions of our bodies. As we fulfill each other, please fill us with the power to do what we need to do." He scattered a few drops of oil, roses and salt and lit the cinnamon.

Gia noticed that the very tip of his penis glistened with moisture and she licked her lips. He was so ready, so full, that she ached to taste him.

He poured more oil over the cinnamon and lit the match, setting it to the reddish brown stick. There was a moment of silence; then flames blossomed from the cinnamon and sweet-scented smoke filled the room. The hiss of burning wood broke the quiet.

"Now," Asron said.

Gia didn't need another invitation. This time he lay on the bed and allowed her to play with him. She rubbed at his nipples, making the hard brown buds warm and swell with her touch. She kissed the hair on his belly and circled the palm of her hand down his shaft, enjoying the sensation of his skin against her fingers. She pushed back the coarse hair and tickled him on the scrotum where the flesh was tight from his erection. He pushed upward and with a swoop she engulfed him, her tongue licking. The suction of her mouth was hot against him.

She expected him to let go and come to orgasm immediately so that they could take the time to return to another frenzy of need as they worked their way through the afternoon. Asron moaned, but didn't come, prolonging the ecstasy as long as he could. When it was obvious that he couldn't stand another moment of stimulation, he withdrew and turned Gia onto her back.

She lay with her legs apart, ready for him, thinking that it would only be a moment or two and then she'd have all of him inside her. The explosion she'd felt building since he'd touched her breasts would burst.

Instead he dipped his head, and his tongue licked her and she gasped, trying to push him away. She'd never had a man touch her with his mouth, not down there. Larry had always said the idea disgusted him. Then the sensation of the firm but gentle probing and delicate kisses erased any thought other than the sheer pleasure of having Asron make love to her. She'd never felt the kind of response that washed over her as he played with her, enjoying her eager response as he flicked his tongue along the most sensitive parts of her body. The lovemaking took on a soft rhythm that built as she squirmed against him. When she thought she couldn't stand anything more, he pushed his tongue deep into her and she screamed as she began to feel wave after wave of delight wash over her.

"Magnificent," she finally managed to say as her body relaxed and she retreated into a haze of satisfied numbness.

"Ah, but that isn't all," Asron said. "We want to make sure we've done everything we could to worship the Goddess, and that was only a start."

He pulled on the cord that held the wizard around her neck, loosening it until it slipped over her head. He began to rub her with the rounded black stone the magician held in his hands. The dark mineral was cool against her flesh. "The work is more powerful if it lasts until everyone is so satisfied that they can't move."

This time as he touched her he probed spots she didn't even know she had. With each torturous new delight, he told her that with his help she had the power to defeat Larry completely. She could subjugate men with the force of her body and passions. She had the strength to call down the moon and take it inside her and give back pleasure to men who wanted to taste her succulent, wonderfully erotic flesh.

As he talked, she felt the fires rekindling where she had thought the pleasure had left only ashes.

Asron moved against her. His flesh was still taut. She'd had her satisfaction, but he was still waiting.

"Now, I can't wait any longer. We'd better get on with this and do our part to serve the Goddess before I explode," Gia purred. Asron lay on his back as Gia slid her legs over him and impaled herself on him, bucking as he reached deep within her.

The climax was almost too fast. He imprisoned her breasts with his hands and forced himself even deeper into her and let the stream spill.

Gia screamed as they finished. It was torture and ecstasy, everything she expected from an orgasm. It was even better than the first time.

"I bind you to me with this pleasure," Asron said as soon as he could speak again. "You will help me against the forces that threaten to disrupt everything."

Bind her to him? After Larry, she wasn't certain she wanted to be tied to anyone, even Asron Burke. Maybe especially not Asron Burke, with his strange ability to listen in on her thoughts. But she couldn't have turned down his offer of sensual pleasures if her life had depended on it.

She expected him to stay longer, but he picked up the athame, cut the circle and slipped on his clothes. "I hate to serve the Goddess and run, but I've got a dinner appointment on a very important deal. Can't keep the man waiting. He's from Japan and gets very upset if all the courtesies aren't observed."

"Right," Gia said. If it hadn't been a religious ceremony, she'd have said that, like Larry, he'd just come over to the house to get laid.

She slipped into her T-shirt and shorts, and put the magician back around her neck. It was getting so she felt naked without the little guy to watch over her.

She opened the door to let Asron out and was surprised

to find E.G. standing on the front porch. He had just raised his finger to ring the front-door bell.

Gia stared at him, thinking that if he'd had a good operatic voice, he could have had a permanent job singing in Wagner's Ring cycle.

And if she'd been able to sing, she wouldn't have minded playing his Brunhilde.

"What a surprise," Gia said, and blushed. "E.G., this is—"

"I know who this is," Asron said curtly. He pushed by Gia, nodded at the other man and headed for his car.

"I'm sorry, he doesn't usually act that way," she said, then realized that she was apologizing for a man she hardly knew, except in the carnal sense.

"Don't worry about Asron. We've met before and he didn't like me then, either," E.G. said. "I know I should have called in advance, but I had to come out this way and thought I'd drop by some copies of papers that will be served on your husband in the next twenty-four hours."

"Come on in, I'll fix you some coffee, and you can tell me all about them. This is good timing because I got a whole bunch of stuff today from Larry's attorney. You can see if there's anything that needs to be taken care of immediately, like telling that louse to give back the ten thousand dollars that was in the account right up until he cleared it out."

E.G. sat down at the kitchen table, his long legs spread out almost to the other side. He was even taller than Gia had remembered. That blond hair and those blue eyes were really something.

He was much more attractive than Asron Burke, and she couldn't help wondering how he was in bed.

He handed Gia the papers he'd brought over while he looked at the pleadings Larry's attorney had filed. She looked down at his hands, and blushed. He had a big, thick, perfectly formed thumb. What was the formula? Add four inches in length and a couple more inches in circumference and you'd know a man's penis size?

God, she had to stop thinking about sex! She forced herself to look at the papers. She was happy to see that he'd already moved to tie up Larry's business account and asked for complete information on Kelly's checking and savings accounts. E.G. had served notice on Larry that he was to keep his business at the same level or higher until the case was settled. If Larry cut down on the number of clients, as some attorneys had been known to do to avoid having a good income that could be used as a basis for alimony, E.G. would ask for review of the past ten years of business and extrapolate his future earnings from that information.

E.G. saw her reading the document and smiled. "That's a great one. The court decision just came down that we can ask for judicial review of income each year in setting alimony for the next ten years. It means that if he's thinking of dropping clients until the divorce is final and then picking them back up, it won't work. He'd have to impoverish himself for ten years and no sane attorney would do that."

"No one ever said Larry was sane," Gia said.

E.G. grinned. "He left a wonderful woman like you, didn't he? You're gorgeous and smart, even if your hair is a little short. That man definitely hasn't got a full load of bricks. So we'll pass on the question of sanity and work on screwing him out of every cent he's ever made and expects to make."

"Sounds great!"

He leaned closer and looked at the magician.

"Curious figure. I've never seen one like it before."

"Asron gave it to me," she said. The magician seemed to grow warmer when she said Asron's name, but of course that was only illusion. She was probably hot from being so close to E.G.

She took off the necklace and handed it to him. He examined it carefully, delicately touching the shiny black ball held by the wizard. "This looks like polished lava."

"I think that's what he said it was. Something about it being from Hawaii, and he and the coven go there at least once a year for rituals. Why?"

He handed the figure back. "You might consider sending this back to the tourist department at Mount Kilauea and Pele's home inside the crater."

"Why?"

"Because unless this stone was removed with all the proper offerings and incantations, you've got the Pele on your ass. She gets really mad when someone steals lava and has a real penchant for causing trouble until she gets it back. We're going to have enough trouble with this divorce. Why give a goddess a chance to make life difficult for us?"

Gia looked with new respect at the tiny globe. "I hope that's not the problem. I'd hate to destroy this by tearing out the rock."

"Think about it," E.G. said. He looked up just in time to see Gia yawn.

She blushed, embarrassed at being caught. "I'm sorry, it's not that you're boring me. But I am so tired that I could just lie right down here in the middle of the kitchen and go to sleep. Maybe it's the flu coming on."

He stood up and reached across the table to touch her forehead with his huge hand. She felt rough skin against her face and wondered what kind of physical work an attorney did to work up that kind of roughness on his fingers. There was a shock of energy at the contact. He left his hand on her face just slightly longer than necessary and his fingers trailed across her cheeks in a lover's touch.

Suddenly she had a vivid vision of E.G. as a pure romantic hero, riding to her rescue on a white charger. Her mind had the oddest ability to step outside reality and cast the people around her in her books, and E.G. was definitely hero material. The only problem was, she didn't need rescue.

"No temperature," he said. "But I think you need to go to bed and rest. Don't try to write or think or do anything other than regain your energies. You look absolutely drained."

His obvious concern made her feel good. Someone cared about her.

E.G. walked to the door and then looked back at Gia. "You might also consider not seeing Asron again. He's not good for you."

"What—" Gia began, meaning to ask him just what he meant by that remark, but E.G. was already halfway to his car, leaving her to ponder his enigmatic parting shot.

12

The studio felt different, Fiona decided. It felt stripped bare, as if something vital were missing from the composite smell of oil paints, cleaners and the props she worked with. And she knew exactly what was missing. She'd dismantled the small altar. She'd returned the salt to the kitchen. The fluffy cream-colored yarn was neatly wound around the yarn ball, and she'd put away the dishes and candles and her grandmother's embroidered bridge cloth.

The old pine table with the huge crack down the middle now held only the props she was using for the snow scene with Princess for the Big Skies calendar. She'd set out a toy sled and part of a tree branch so that she could get the shading of bare wood exactly right, along with a piece of barbed wire and lots of photographs of Princess in the snow. It was a fine display, but it didn't have the force of the altar that had drawn her to the spell-making almost every morning.

Fiona looked longingly at the sheaves of wheat and blue flax that she'd planned to weave into wreaths. She'd intended to hang the wheat weavings over the house to protect the family from danger and evil. Last week she'd played around with a few pieces of wheat after soaking them in a pan of water to soften them. She'd learned very rapidly how to stop the stems from splitting beyond repair and what to do when the wheat seemed to be losing all the grain from the head. She'd practiced just long enough to be able to make the protective wreaths. It wouldn't have been outwardly witchy, she decided; it would have blended in with her country decorating scheme. Harper wouldn't notice the wreaths. He laughed about her propensity for hanging odd things on the walls. She usually brought in flowers and pretty weeds during the spring and summer and cornstalks and pumpkin vines in fall. Even dead leaves and straw had flourished in decorations from time to time.

He'd never know they were for protection, but I would. And I promised him no more witchcraft. Fiona sighed. Harper had never asked her to do anything half as difficult as give up her sudden dependence on even the small amount of witchcraft she'd been working with. He wouldn't even talk to her about how right it felt, and why she thought that maybe, without even knowing it, she'd been born into the Old Religion and was only now discovering that fact.

It was maddening. What made him so opposed to a little simple spell-making? If only I could make him tell me what frightens him so much about the whole idea. There's something in his past, but I don't know how to get to it, she thought.

When they were first married, she had pestered him unmercifully about his past. She'd been intrigued by his accent and wanted to know more about where he came from. The most she'd ever been able to elicit was that he was from Wales and his family were all dead.

She hadn't let it go at that. She'd read books on Wales and found pictures of the dark hills and misty countryside. She'd asked him incessant questions about what it had been like to live there. He'd never answered her.

One time she'd pushed too hard and told him that if he didn't stop the mystery-man pose, she was going to go look through immigration records to find out more about him. He'd disappeared for ten days. She'd been heartsick, knowing that for her own foolish curiosity, she had lost the love of her lifetime. She had promised herself that when he came back, if he came back, she'd never ask him another question.

When Harper did come back, because he was desperately in love with her, she kept her promise and never raised the subject again. If he wanted to be a mystery man, that was fine, as long as he was *her* mystery man.

Now her mystery man wanted her to give up Wicca rites because something in his background, the background he wouldn't talk about, made him afraid of witchcraft.

Fiona didn't want to give it up. She relied on the feeling of control and power the workings of the circle gave her. She'd psychically held her breath the whole time, waiting for the world to fall in when she stopped the rituals. So far nothing horrendous had happened, but it felt as she were standing naked out in the middle of a storm just waiting for the lightning to strike.

If it did, she might break a promise for the first time in their entire married life.

"Damn, damn, damn! I'll work on my paintings and get my mind off this whole mess," she said. She started the blizzard tape and picked up her painting of a Siamese playing in the winter snow and set it on the easel. The work had been going well. She'd cast about for a pose for the cat in the snow and finally discovered the perfect idea of using a picture of Princess as a tiny kitten on her back, rolling from side to side as she did when she was delighted with life. The shadows in the snow showed little cat angels. It was the perfect idea, not sticky sweet, but cute enough to elicit *ahh*'s from everyone who saw it. She was prouder of that little portrait than of anything else she'd ever done.

She looked at the picture critically. Maybe Harper was right. She didn't need magic to make her painting come out right. She'd learned from years of hard work how to put everything together and come out with a salable item.

"But the picture sold because of magic," an inner voice nagged at her. "The IRS went away because you asked for help and received it. Nothing short of witchcraft would have made them back off. And you're going to just walk away from it all?"

"Yes, I am," Fiona answered the voice firmly. She had promised.

She went over to the bed where Loner reclined. He'd finally been allowed out of the cage once the stump had started to really heal, and now he was in the process of learning to hop around on three legs. It hadn't done his disposition any good. She offered him a can of wet cat food, something he'd always loved when he was still outside. He turned his nose up.

"Come on, cat, you've gone through so much, you can't let the loss of a leg do you in. You can't let that miserable old bastard at the top of the hill win. Come on, eat, and live to be a hundred years old just to spite him."

She put a swipe of the food on her fingertip and rubbed it against his gums, hoping he wouldn't take off the finger while she was coaxing him to taste the stuff.

Loner began to eat, just a few licks at first, but when she looked back, he'd finished the whole can of food.

"Good boy, you'll make it."

Fiona was finishing the portrait and thinking about what she could do to make December really spectacular when she heard Harper's car pull up outside the house. The old Volvo made a distinctive sound, more like a two-cylinder lawn mower than any car that had ever lived, and the hill taxed the poor motor almost beyond redemption.

She looked up, startled. Nothing ready for dinner—had she actually worked that long without stopping? It was dark outside, but that was only because clouds seemed to have drifted in over the Berkeley hills, carrying fog and a surprisingly chilly wind with them. She stared at the clock. Two in the afternoon—not anywhere near dinnertime.

What was Harper doing home this early in the day?

Flu, she thought. He said there was a bug going around the office and I'll bet he caught it. I'll make chicken soup and dumplings for tonight. The soft meal should make him feel better, if he can eat anything at all.

Fiona met Harper at the door and the first sight of his face confirmed her worst fears. His face was pasty white and his hands were trembling as he placed his canvas briefcase on the living room table.

"Harper?" Fiona asked, but he just shook his head.

He walked into the kitchen and for the first time Fiona could remember, he opened the cupboard above the stove, took down a bottle of Scotch and poured himself a glass. He started to gulp it and then thought better of it and took the rest of the glass of liquor over to the couch in the family room.

"What is going on? If you've got the flu, booze isn't going to help your stomach any," Fiona said, her voice tight with anxiety. She was struck by the colors that surrounded him. They were dark orange and a dark yellow that was almost a muddy brown. For the first time she could remember, Harper's aura was not the healthy thick yellow band that had always surrounded him. Something bad had happened.

"Work," Harper said, one word. His hands were still trembling.

"What about work?" What had happened at work to push Harper into one of those dark deep Welsh depressions?

"They've sold the company. They're closing down ten restaurants and consolidating everything in a new home office. They're cutting costs."

Fiona sat down fast. Cutting costs was usually double-speak for firing everyone who happened to walk down the corridor at the wrong time.

"What exactly does that mean?" she asked. She didn't want to let her mind run wild. Given the chance, she'd imagine planting For Sale signs in the front yard, being turned out in the street and losing everything they'd managed to painfully scrape together.

"It means that unless things change or I have an incredible stroke of luck, I won't have a job by next Monday. They've already said there's too much duplication in personnel between the two companies. They're going to be cutting back at least half of the people. I'm certain I'm on the hit list. The other company has a better-qualified comptroller, CEO and assistant comptroller. They don't need another financial wizard."

Fiona could barely breathe. Sometimes, late at night, she'd thought about what they'd do if Harper lost his job. She'd long since decided there wasn't any way they'd be able to survive without his paycheck. All those terrors that had crept up on her at three in the morning came back to rush over her—images of starvation, of the family broken up. All their belongings in storage and no promise that they'd ever have a place of their own again. Megan without medical insurance.

"What will we do?" she asked, trying desperately to keep her voice from quavering.

"I don't know. I've been thinking about how much we've got in the bank—"

Fiona snorted. What good would $147 do them? That was the sum total of what they had available.

"I know we're broke. But I can draw my pension fund now and that will get us through a couple of months. Something will come up, I'm certain of it." Harper didn't look certain of anything at the moment. His face had a little more color in it, but that was only because of the liquor.

He took another swig of his drink. "God damn it, how could this happen? How could I do everything right and still lose? I save money for the company and make profits for them, and then end up tossed out like I was worth nothing? How can they do this to my family?"

"I don't know." Fiona reached out and tried to soothe him, but he drew back, enmeshed in the agony of the moment. "Maybe we'd better sit down and see if we have any options."

"I think I'd rather get drunk," Harper said, but he put the glass down.

"You make dinner. Hot dogs and sauerkraut will do. I'll take care of Megan; then we can plan," Fiona said. It was actually a little early for Megan's medication, but she wanted to have Megan sedated when they talked so that there wouldn't be any interruptions.

After dinner, Fiona and Harper discussed the disaster. It was late in the evening before they finished making plans. They'd checked the deep freeze, decided what jewelry could be pawned or sold and called the woman who held the mortgage on the house and offered her half payments until Harper could find another job. They might just make it if they didn't breathe for fear of spending an extra cent.

Finally Harper fell into a deep exhausted sleep. He had to get up early to go in and find out about his fate with the company.

Fiona, however, still wasn't ready to settle down. She was in crisis mode, awake until three or four in the morning planning and replanning, until she was certain she'd taken all the steps she could to make life work out right for her family.

Finally, around 5 A.M., she flipped off the light and stared out into the darkness. In the distance she could hear the rumble of early summer thunder and see flashes of sheet lightning against the hills. The storm that had blown up while she worked on Princess's painting had grown over the hours. The smell of rain was carried into the room on the air current that belled the curtains. She thought about the singed magic book and the spilled soft drink and the fire that hadn't started the last time she'd left the windows wide to catch a breeze. She had just started reading about the Goddess then and had done one small chant, but the Old Religion's power had still worked to avert a catastrophe.

Fiona pulled her knees up to her chest and watched the storm moving toward her. Power. That was what it was all about, whether Harper wanted to believe it or not. He'd made her stop her work with the Goddess and look what had happened. Her entire life had just been torn apart and she wasn't certain there was going to be a way to pick up the pieces, and it was all because she'd stopped working witchcraft.

"If only I'd done those protection wreaths. If only I'd made the amulet and slipped it into Harper's wallet. If only I'd put the oil on the windowsills and in the car, none of this would have happened."

Silently she slid out of bed, grabbed the package of wheat, oil and blue flax from the studio and hurried down the stairs. She stopped long enough in the kitchen to pick up salt and her heavy glass dish for the ceremony.

"The books say I should have a sacred knife to cut flowers and herbs and wands with. The bolline should have a dark handle." She thought for a moment and then reached into the lowest drawer beside the stove. Peeling away the plastic on the new knife, she laughed quietly. How many other witches were armed with a sacred Ginsu knife?

She took her hoard and stepped into the backyard. The smell of rain was even sharper here, overlaid with the metallic scent of lightning. The storm was moving toward them, and she was going to try to use that power in her own magic. Add a full moon behind the clouds to give her the power to draw down the moon and she was certain she could change at least some of the bad luck headed their way.

She looked around to see if her skunks or raccoons were down for their evening snack and stroll through the yard. She wouldn't mind if they joined her. She'd never had any trouble with even the most active animals. She located one skunk idly scratching his ear and watching her from behind the trunk of the peach tree, and farther up, she could hear the rustle that meant the raccoons were out and about. Soon, she knew, they'd come down looking for water.

She drew the circle in the damp ground, summoned earth, fire, water and air, and asked for the help of the God and Goddess. She set up a makeshift altar on the stone bird-bath, lit a small candle that would never have been seen by anyone else and began to dip the wheat into the skinny-dipping pool the raccoons used.

"Okay, this might not be in perfect ritual form, but I am asking for the power of the elements to come and help me with this ceremony."

Swiftly she plaited the flax and wheat together into a wreath, tying the ends securely with some of the pieces of yarn that had been fluttering in the wind since she'd decorated the trees with string for the birds to use to make their nests. As she worked, a sense of calm settled over her. She finished two more wreaths and then realized that she had only enough wheat left for half of another decoration.

She looked around her, wondering what she could substitute, when her gaze was drawn to a patch of weeds underneath the peach tree.

No one had ever said anything about using weeds for spells. She couldn't see any reason why not, though. They were good clean weeds and should work up fine.

Grabbing her special knife, she cut into the patch of dried grass and carried her prize back to the swimming pool.

The last garland, she decided a few minutes later, looked even better than the others. There was a certain primitive beauty about it that satisfied her.

As the storm neared, she imagined that she felt the energy of the moon and lightning rising through the bottoms of her feet and filling her body. Even when she'd worked in the circle with Gia, she had never felt this much in tune with whatever forces ruled the night.

She cut the circle and stepped out, ready to move on to the second part of the protective ritual she was using. She wandered around the yard, letting herself be guided by a sense of what the magic needed. She had no idea whether her choices were what other witches would have made, because she was gathering on pure instinct. Roses and lavender, geraniums with sweet petals and several green switches from the maple tree that had been filled with so much sap a month before. She felt as if someone else were directing her, telling her what to do, and she followed the directions. If it wasn't hurting either her plants or anyone else, then it should be okay.

"Fiona Kendrick, what are you doing in your backyard?" Sally's voice reverberated through the yard as Fiona squealed in shock. "Witchcraft! You're doing the devil's work again, aren't you?"

"Oh dear Lord, you scared me!" Fiona said, gasping.

"Well, I should hope I did! Look at you cavorting around in nothing but your shift. And I suppose it's more of that pagan devil worship, isn't it? It'll get you in trouble, believe me."

"You're going to get me in more trouble if you don't shut up," Fiona said, exasperated. Here she was, in the middle of a deep and intense spiritual experience, and Sally had to butt in. She hoped Harper didn't hear the voices through the open window by the bed and get up to investigate. What the hell would he say about the very obvious altar on the birdbath?

Sally slammed the gate, drawing out the screech from the rusty hinges. She almost ran into the yard, heading for

Fiona and her ceremonial objects. She scuffed the circle as she came near Fiona.

"I've saved you from the Ouija board and now I'll save you from this. You can't practice if you don't have the devil's implements." She reached past Fiona and smashed the dish and candle against the inside of the birdbath.

Fiona was so astonished she couldn't move.

Sally took advantage of her surprise and made a grab for the wreaths, intent on crushing them.

Fiona gasped and lunged toward her, knocking Sally off balance so that she had to retreat a few steps.

"What do you think you're doing?" Fiona demanded, shocked that her friend thought she had a right to come over and destroy her belongings. "Who died and left you in charge of the universe and what makes you think you can just come charging in here and tell me what to do in my own home?"

Sally was breathing hard and there was a wild look in her eyes. "My pappy said that the way to deal with sinners was to drive the ideas right out of their heads. It was good enough for him and it is good enough for me."

She lunged forward again, but Fiona was ready for her. She grabbed Sally by the arm and pulled her forward and around, so that Sally spun away from the altar and wreaths.

Sally cried out as Fiona's fingers dug into her arm, but Fiona didn't care.

Sally tried again to get to the altar, hunched over and moving like a prizefighter intent on a knockout. "I will stop you. I will drive these ideas out of your mind once and for all."

"You just stay the hell away from me," Fiona said. She'd never seen Sally out of control and it was frightening to watch the wild light flaming in her eyes as she preached damnation at her.

"I don't want to be living next door to any pagan. I

don't want to be best friends with someone who has pacts with the devil. Fiona, I have to save you from yourself. I'm going to use everything I can to drive these ideas out of your mind, even if I have to destroy everything you have to do it." Sally was gasping and, for the first time in all the years Fiona had known her, her beautifully cut blond hair had become mussed.

"Sally, you said you wouldn't interfere if we didn't talk to you about witchcraft."

Sally laughed. "I lied, can't you tell? I'm going to save you no matter what!"

"Stop it, Sally." Fiona's voice was barely above a whisper, but it cut through Sally's rantings. "You don't know what you're talking about. Witchcraft, the Old Religion, doesn't have anything to do with worshiping Satan. Satan is purely a Christian invention. The only thing I'm doing is using the natural power of the earth to help me. I don't sacrifice animals, I don't say the Lord's Prayer backwards, I don't paint my house black inside and out. Come on, Sally, witchcraft is just another religion, like Episcopalian or Mormon."

"Blasphemy! God said not to suffer witches and I will not! You will renounce it now!" Sally tried to break the hold Fiona had on her.

"God said not to suffer liars! Go back and check the translation! God didn't give a tinker's damn about witches!"

Suddenly the storm overhead let loose the first huge drops of rain, splattering the two women; then the water came down in sheets as lightning popped and sizzled almost directly overhead.

"Go home, Sally, before we both get killed. I don't need your help." Fiona caught Sally by surprise as she propelled her friend through the gate, slammed the door and locked it behind her. She panted as she leaned against the rough wood.

"Fiona, you must repent," Sally cried.

When Fiona didn't answer, the other woman went into her own house, slamming the door behind her.

Fiona finally relaxed. She hadn't been sure that Sally wouldn't go around and start banging on the front door to continue her harangue. She picked up the shattered pieces of the glass, the candle, the knife and the flowers. The spilled salt she left as the rain washed down into the bird-bath and began to dissolve the crystals.

She felt like crying. She'd had such a great feeling of control and energy and Sally had killed it all. She needed the spell to work, and because of Sally's Bible-thumping inter-ference she might have lost the only chance she had to save her husband's job and their home.

She stood in the rain and tried to let the fresh water wash away the urge to go over and strangle Sally. She knew she was probably presenting a great place for lightning to hit, but if she went inside now, she'd awaken Harper with her angry thoughts. Instead she imagined sending lightning into Sally's bedroom and hitting her just hard enough to re-arrange the molecules in her mind into a more forgiving and accepting pattern.

There was a slight popping sound and the lights in Sally's house flickered, but that was only because the storm was affecting everything in the city.

Fiona looked at the drenched flowers and wreaths, which Sally hadn't managed to touch. There was one last part of the ritual she could use, one Sally could never inter-fere with.

"I'll give it just one more try," she said and then whis-pered the last request for help into the wind.

She took the flowers upstairs to the bedroom. She had left the wreaths Sally had tried to crush on a nail outside the door.

She walked as far around the bed as she could, stopping only by the window to watch the storm building outside.

The sweet winds from the farmland carried a hay scent that mingled with the heavy perfume of the white roses and the astringent aroma of lavender. She tucked the sprigs and blooms underneath the edge of the mattress, stopping every time Harper snorted or began to awaken at the movement.

Every side of the bed had flowers under it and she'd even managed to garland some of the window with the magically charged blossoms.

Harper sneezed in his sleep. She'd forgotten that he was allergic to a lot of the flowers she grew. He sneezed again, snorted and settled back into a deep slumber, snoring as his nasal passage became more and more congested.

Fiona stripped off her wet cotton gown and climbed into bed. The curtains were open and the storm swept inside the room, bearing with it rain and the smell of a distant fire, and all the promises of magic wrought by the elements.

Fiona looked at the clock. It was almost three. She hoped it was close enough to the midnight hour, which was supposed to be highly charged for spell-making. She had one last bit of sorcery to perform, with Harper's help, even if he didn't know it.

"Goddess, stay with me," she whispered and snuggled up to his back. He jumped and mumbled something nasty and she moved away from him until her cold clammy skin had a chance to warm up. Finally she began to run her hands over his back. He moaned slightly and turned over, still not even approaching awake. He was now wheezing.

Fiona knew his body as well as she knew her own. She was intimately aware of every response that went with all the years of pleasuring each other. She drew her hand over his flat belly muscles, wondering that he managed to keep his almost youthful appearance even after the onset of middle age. He had added some weight, but not too much—not nearly as much as she had.

"More to love," he always said. She nuzzled against his chest. Her hand went with unerring accuracy between his legs and she began to massage him gently. She knew all the right moves, but this time there was no response.

She tried again. He started snoring more loudly.

"Damn that Scotch, anyway," Fiona said in frustration. What good was it to do a sexual energy invocation if your partner slept through the whole ceremony?

She hadn't exactly lied to Gia about how good sex was with Harper. When they managed to both be awake and both be rested enough that sex was a viable option, their lovemaking was wonderful. But lately those times were coming fewer and farther between. Whole months had gone by without more than a kiss and a promise. If Fiona wasn't tired from taking care of Megan all night, then Harper had had a very bad day at the office. Sometimes they even went to bed at nine in the evening, promising themselves that they'd wake up early for a quickie. It almost never happened. The few extra minutes of sleep at five-thirty in the morning were more precious than sex.

Fiona considered trying to awaken Harper again, but a sudden wave of absolute exhaustion swept over her and she was asleep before she could attempt another seduction.

13

"Come over and hold my hand while I wait for the guillotine to fall and chop off our heads," Fiona said when Gia answered the phone, her voice still heavy with sleep.

She wanted to tell her friend about Sally's bizarre behavior during the night, but decided to keep quiet. As far as Gia knew, she was still being a good little girl and not fooling around with the Old Religion.

Instead, she told Gia about what she'd done to keep occupied. "I've already made two kinds of cake, mixed the dough for cookies, cleaned upstairs, and put through three washes, and I've only been up since five-thirty. If you don't come over, I'll have completely renovated our house by the time Harper tells me he's got the final word on losing his job."

Fiona couldn't banish the image of Harper in his car, coming home for the last time from work. She knew the heartache he'd feel and it hurt her so much that she wanted to cry. She didn't want to be alone in the house while she waited for Harper to appear with the remnants of what had been in his desk at work. She'd seen the people who had been fired riding home on the train. They'd carried the cardboard boxes that held the plants and pictures and silly little toys that had made the desk their home for eight or ten hours a day. There was terror on their faces as they contemplated the future without a secure job or a paycheck. They'd sift aimlessly through the box as if hoping to find a clue about their future, but there was nothing left but their own little mementos. Back at work, there would be an empty, clean desk waiting for someone else to fill it when times got better. And now Harper would be coming home with his own box.

Fiona kept right on working. She scrubbed both bathrooms until they sparkled, changed all the cat boxes and hung out two loads of wash before Gia finally straggled over for morning coffee. Even though her friend wasn't going to be ready to talk for another hour or so, Fiona was glad to have Gia's company while she sorted through cupboards and listed what was on hand for the inventory they'd be using to survive through the next couple of months.

"Why are you doing all this?" Gia finally asked, when she could think in coherent sentences after the second cup of double-strength espresso and milk. The brain fuzz seemed to be twice as thick as usual, but she couldn't figure out why.

"Doing what?" Fiona asked blankly.

"Cleaning. What good is it to go into a frenzy like this?"

Fiona shrugged helplessly. "It gives me something to do. I can't tell Megan what's going on, it'd only worry her. She's upstairs with one of her worst headaches. She's taken enough morphine to make a horse drool and it still hurts. So I clean house because if I don't do something I'm going to go nuts. It's a way to keep a grip on what seems to be totally out of control."

"I know what you mean, but I don't think we're in charge of our lives anymore. Larry's inundating me with court orders, all of which are meant to drive me bankrupt. E.G.'s fighting back, but even he can't completely stop an asshole like Larry. Besides, cleaning house would just keep up the value of his property and frankly right now I don't feel like doing that."

"Makes sense. Larry doesn't need to profit from your work any more than he already has. For me, though, it helps to know what is in every drawer and cupboard and shelf, all neatly categorized and cleaned. Besides, if I have to go out to work as a secretary or something, having a clean house makes it easier."

"Why would you have to go out to work as a secretary? You can earn a hell of a lot more money working for Big Skies card company, can't you?" Gia was beginning to feel a little better with the coffee, but her muscles still felt like limp spaghetti. She had been drained of all her energy when she made love to Asron. She'd have to make sure he never kept her at that peak of sexual frenzy again for that long. It was too difficult to recover the next day.

"Once the card company starts paying regularly and once I'm certain they'll keep buying from me, yes, of course. But the money's not coming in that fast."

"Didn't Madge Lorenz tell you she needed every painting you could produce?"

Fiona nodded. "I know, and yes, I probably could make more money and you're probably right. But I'm still worried."

"Damn right I'm right. Okay, you've kept moving for the past two hours. I've had enough coffee and the place is spotless, so why don't you do me a favor?"

Fiona looked up blankly. Gia never asked for favors. "What do you need? As long as it's not money, you've got it."

"First, read the three chapters of a new book that I've written over the past three days. For some reason, after months of a writer's block the size of Mount Rushmore, I got up Sunday morning and had the perfect romance all planned in my mind. No hunting for characters, no wondering what the action was going to be, not even a worry about what each character's fatal flaw was. The complete story was crystal clear in my mind and all I had to do was start writing." She held out a sheaf of pages, which she'd hidden in her purse until the time was right to ask for Fiona's attention.

Fiona grabbed the pages and sat down. "Of course I'll read them. You know how long I've been looking forward to another book from you! I figured this dry spell was your way of announcing that you never wanted to write again."

"No, I think my block was my way of telling myself that my life had to change before I could think about heroes and lovemaking and all those nice twists and turns that go into a romance. Sure as hell Larry wasn't helping any."

Fiona waved vaguely toward the sideboard as she began to read the first page. "There's more cake and coffee. You know where everything is."

She settled in, glad for a chance to get her mind off the impending doom of Harper's job and all the other catastrophes that were poised at the top of the hill, just waiting to crash down on her. Harper's dream of a mountain coming to destroy his family wasn't so far off the mark.

Within a few moments, Fiona was sitting in a stalled car on a dark and stormy mountain, right beside Rebecca Rian. She could feel the fear of the heroine as a strange man approached her in the rain-slick night. Could he be from the school where she would be teaching? He was handsome, but forbidding, and he had an uncanny knack of reading her thoughts, as did the older woman who greeted her and took her up to her room. The house was warm and inviting after the chill October storm that had lashed her with freezing rain, but there was something about the house and the people that made her fear for her safety. She walked through the candlelit hallways with the sounds of the storm booming around her and wondered about the rumors of people coming to this place and disappearing forever. "We never have lights during a storm, hope you don't mind," the older woman said as she escorted Rebecca to her room.

By the end of the second chapter, Fiona had begun to fear for Rebecca's sanity. At the end of the third chapter, she had to believe in psychic abilities and in Rebecca's worries for the people she had come to love. How would she protect the children and Jared from the dangers those abilities could cause in a small mountain community where rifles were just as common as trucks and no one wanted anything to do with people who had a sixth sense?

Fiona put down the last page and sighed in satisfaction. "That was perfect. How soon can you finish it, and does Rebecca believe in Jared and help him survive, and do they actually have a shootout with the locals and does anyone get killed?"

Gia relaxed, satisfied with Fiona's reaction to the book. "So I wasn't sucking bathwater. It is good, isn't it? No one gets killed, that's not what happens in a good romance, but there's a fight and of course Rebecca and Jared come out all right in the end. It has to have a happy ending."

"Absolutely perfect. You should have dumped Larry and found someone to go to bed with long before this if it's going to produce books this good."

"I know I'm not supposed to say anything about this around you, but part of the breakthrough was because I asked for help in the circle with Asron and the others."

"I'm not surprised. This stuff really works. I have a confession to make—I haven't stopped with the witchcraft either. I'm even using sex magic, if I can seduce Harper tonight and it still works on the night after the full moon."

"Perfect! As long as mentioning the coven didn't elicit a

scream, I have a second favor to ask. I need for you to come and be a part of my circle tonight. I'm going to do a power-raising ritual because I need all the help I can get to fight Larry. You are one of the smartest women I know and you're my best friend—it can't hurt to have a circle with only you and me when we ask for the right tools to fight the son of a bitch."

Fiona hesitated. "Haven't you ever thought of doing it alone? I've got some books that tell you how to be a solitary practitioner."

"No, I need someone with me. I'm bringing E.G., too. I don't know if he's ever been involved in something like witchcraft, but it just feels right to have him along."

"And you don't want Asron or Selene? I thought the idea of a coven was to have people to work with you when you needed help."

Gia lifted one shoulder. "Not this time. This is personal, and I want to keep it that way. Working with Asron had definite disadvantages. I've found out that when we do a ritual together and it involves sex, I'm swacked out for the next two days. And right now I don't want to lose two days' worth of writing. Besides, I want my best friend in the circle with me. Come on, I need your help and I don't ask for that very often, do I?"

Fiona debated for a few moments. Her own witchcraft had turned into something intensely private and hidden. It was one thing to work outside at night in the middle of a storm and call down the forces she needed by herself. It was something else entirely to help Gia with the same observance. She had the feeling that Harper might possibly forgive her for last night, if he ever found out, because her work had been prompted by a family crisis. But he would never under any circumstances understand her going back into witchcraft with Gia.

"Please?"

Fiona hesitated a few more moments, then decided that

she could do this just one more time to help out Gia. Her common sense said no, but her sense of friendship said yes. "When and where do you need me?"

"Tonight. I'll pick you up. I decided that having the circle out in the open would probably be better for bringing power to us. We'll just go out to some little park that's deserted at night and set up our altar and no one will bother us."

"No! I'm willing to help in your own home or even up in the studio, even if it's a little dangerous. But a park? How do you figure I'm going to sneak out of here and come back without Harper seeing me?"

"Easy. You just get out of the house, I'll take care of picking you up."

"Look, Gia, I mean it. I'll go to your house because if Harper found out I could always say you were having a bad time with Larry and you needed me. But if something happens while we're prancing around in a circle in the middle of a public park, I'm dead in the water. What the hell would I do if we got caught?"

"Don't worry, it'll never happen. We're not doing anything that's against the law. Wiccan rituals are a form of worship and the police have special orders not to try and do anything to anyone who claims to be worshiping in a public park. The U.S. Army recognizes it as a legitimate religion, so the local folk have to do the same. Besides, I've found a park that has a huge oak tree. Oak has power and that's what we need. There isn't anything on the grounds where I live except a spindly little mulberry Larry planted last year. Mulberry's okay, but it isn't oak."

"Mulberry would be more private."

"I'll tell you what, just to get in the mood, how about we do a little work right here and now? If it works, you'll come with me. If it doesn't, we'll forget the whole idea."

"What, do a circle right here in the family room?"

"Sure. We'll ask that Harper be protected from the upheavals at work. We can ask that he either not be fired or that he get another job on the same day the restaurant chain lets him go." Gia was already up, moving the furniture back so that they could draw the circle.

"Maybe we shouldn't," Fiona protested. "Harper could be home any minute now." The truth was that he didn't feel close. Just to be sure, she checked again, but there was no sense that he was anywhere near the house.

"You really don't want to?" Gia stopped moving the furniture.

Fiona was torn. She wished she could rely on the night's work that she'd done, but Sally might have destroyed any effect. Maybe she should work with Gia, just to make sure she'd done everything she could to help Harper.

"Hell yes, let's do it," Fiona said. Every bit of support was welcome. Besides, Megan was asleep upstairs. There was little chance that she'd come down and ask what was going on.

Fiona drew the curtains and made sure no one could see in. She wouldn't put it past Sally to spy over the top of the six-foot fence and come charging over if she thought anything was going on.

Gia and Fiona did two rituals. The family room smelled of sandalwood and mint and the candles had burned down to a puddle of wax when she cut the circle. They had just thanked the Goddess when the phone rang.

Fiona answered and was silent for a few minutes. She hung up without saying another word. She left her hand on the receiver as if it would keep her in touch with whoever had called.

"Would you care to tell me what that was all about?" Gia asked with some asperity.

"That was Harper. He only had time to tell me that he hasn't lost his job yet. It was kind of a 'more news at eleven' flash. He'll tell me more when he gets home," Fiona said quietly. She sat down and tears of relief began to pour down her face.

"So what are you crying about?" Gia said, mystified.

"Because I have just spent several of the worst hours of my entire life and I deserve a good cry. Besides, I'm not sure I trust the luck that sent this reprieve."

"It wasn't luck, it was power. What more could you want in the way of proof that this stuff works? Once you help me tonight we'll both be safe and happy. Harper will have a job and I'll have power over Larry," Gia exulted.

It took only a few more minutes to set up the time, midnight, and the place, out in front of Fiona's house, where they would meet and then travel on to their destination.

"Now that you've got the good news and we've got it all set up for tonight, I'm going to go home. I have to write another couple of chapters. I know exactly what's coming next, and oh, Fiona, just like when your painting goes right, it's a great feeling!"

"You have to promise to bring me every page that you finish. I don't care about the polish, I want to see how the story comes out," Fiona said, finally beginning to snap out of the shock of hearing that Harper wasn't fired—at least not yet.

Fiona sat back on the couch once Gia had left. Megan was still asleep upstairs, and the house was quiet. She listened to the sounds, the creaks and moans and slight whistles that would tell her everything was fine. The house, though, was silent. Not just kind of quiet, but simply without sound at all.

Fiona suddenly thought of the bottle of spell wine Selene had given her when she first went to the shop. She'd long since lost the tourmaline ring; it was somewhere in the van or Gia's car, but the bottle had made it into the house with the stash of witchcraft fixings.

"Maybe I should protect the house so that trouble

doesn't come visiting here anymore," Fiona said. She'd meant to get around to using the various iron nails, salt and flowers that she'd been told would protect the house, but she'd never had the chance.

She hurried upstairs and found the bottle hidden in the cubbyhole behind the overstuffed chair. No one ever cleaned there; it was a perfectly safe place to hide all sorts of things. She doubted Harper even remembered it was there.

"There you are." Fiona reached in and pulled out the bottle. It was old, very old, she thought, looking at its heaviness and the imperfections in the glass. The wine shone in the light from the window, casting deep red reflections around the room.

On the rafters, Fiona thought and then steeled herself to the task of mingling with spiders and other creatures that lived in dust. They'd installed a ladder several years back so that the attic would be accessible for storage. It was such a pain to take boxes up and down that they'd never really used the area, but Fiona could easily reach the rafters where Selene had told her to put the bottle.

Fiona pulled on the long cord that brought the stairs down and climbed through the opening. The dust sparkled and danced with the movement of the air. Fiona was glad they'd laid down pine planks to walk on. With her luck she would have put her foot through the ceiling within the first few steps. She looked around for the highest rafters and then decided that the junction of ties that made up the main support for the house would just have to do. Carefully she walked over to the beam and reached up to place the bottle on the highest timber she could reach. She began to chant the incantation that was supposed to be said when she sought protection.

Suddenly the house groaned and tilted as a small earthquake rumbled through the area. "Shit!" Fiona screamed as she grabbed for support. She could see the beams moving against each other as the temblor rolled the house from side to side. She tried to keep from screaming again so that Megan didn't wake. The bottle slipped from Fiona's grasp and smashed to the pine flooring, breaking into a thousand pieces. The red wine spread like blood along the floor and began to drip through into the heavy pink insulation.

"Fine, you'll have to do your work from there, then," Fiona said. She looked at the bottle. She'd have to clean up the mess.

Fifteen minutes later, she had finally swept up the rest of the bottle. Megan had slept through everything, including the earthquake. The morphine might not be curing the cause of the pain but at least it allowed her some rest.

Fiona hadn't given up on the idea of house protection, though. It took three trips up and down the attic stairs before she managed to place an iron nail, a small mound of salt and an evergreen bough at the highest point while calling for the spirits to help her drive away evil and protect the house and those inside.

When she finally pushed the stairs up, she was wheezing from the dust and was positive there were spiders in the cobwebs that festooned her hair. Still, she felt good. Today she had done something to make her family safe.

14

Moonlight bathed the front yard when Fiona heard the car coast to a stop in front of her house. Her heart began to thud with excitement and a little worry.

"I hope I'm not making a mistake," she whispered. Harper snored deeply, his form motionless underneath the sheets. Fiona slipped out of bed. She was dressed in shorts and a halter top in deference to the deep heat that had cloaked the inland Bay Area after the storm the night before. Even the normal night winds that came rushing down the hills still breathed leftover heat, and the fog that usually cooled the area had disappeared in the hundred-plus temperatures.

Fiona felt her way down the stairs, carrying the sandals she would wear once she was safely out the front door. There was a delicious sense of wickedness about the mid-night meeting. It reminded her of the times when she had sneaked out of her parents' house as a teenager. She used to stay up most of the night and then climb back through the window just in time to hear her parents' alarm ringing in the morning.

Of course this was different. She was escaping from a husband, not parents, and not just to raise hell.

The almost-full moon cast long shadows as she slipped her feet into her sandals. She could see Gia's car, but not Gia. Silently the door opened and she ran to it, pulling it closed as the motor started and they glided away. Gia's interior light must be broken; it hadn't flashed on when the door opened.

"Gia, you'd never believe what kind of afternoon I've had. I really need to do some work on my everyday life so it isn't a series of catastrophes," Fiona said as she sat back. "The big things are working out—Harper is definitely going to have a job even though they might freeze his salary, which is just barely enough right now. But the little things! I broke Megan's bottle of liquid morphine and then had a two-hour fight with the hospital pharmacist about replacing it. I actually had to bring in the shards of broken glass for him to agree that I might not have sold the medicine to the junkies in town."

"But you got the medicine?" Gia knew Megan couldn't survive without the morphine when the headaches got bad.

"Yes, finally. Then I called about the check that was due from the card company and somehow it had gotten lost and they're having to reissue another one. I couldn't very well get down on my knees in front of the phone and say how badly I needed the money, now could I? So tonight had better work for just you and me and that big oak tree."

Gia squirmed in the seat, rubbing her back against the roughness of the vinyl.

"What on earth is the matter with you?" Fiona asked.

"I don't know. I've had this itch all day long. Would you do me a favor and just scratch the hell out of it to see if I can finally get some relief?"

Fiona turned toward her friend and as she did so, a flash of light reflected from the backseat.

Gia caught Fiona's start of surprise and began chattering nervously. "I hope you don't mind. Things kind of changed when I went back to E.G.'s office this afternoon. We met Asron and Selene outside the building and they wanted to come along, so here we all are."

Fiona turned around and stared at the people in the backseat of the car. Her face was frozen into a smile as she contemplated jumping out of the car and running back up the hill to the safety of her own house.

"Gia, how could you? You know how I feel about this," Fiona said softly, hoping the people in the back couldn't hear her. "You said this was a private ritual."

"It's for Gia's own good," Selene said, a faint reprimand in her voice.

Fiona was silent. She was so furious that she didn't dare open her mouth because she'd start yelling at Gia and it would take quite a while for her to stop.

Gia pulled the car into one of the parking spaces in front of the park and turned off the engine. "Come on, let's get going before the moon sets."

"You can't expect to hold a ritual here!"

Her friend had driven only two blocks from Fiona's home. There was a small park that was frequented by thousands of children in the daytime and by lots of teenage lovers and parents who couldn't sleep at night. It was a family place where everyone knew everyone else. Gia thought they could do a ceremony undisturbed here?

"Damn it, Gia, how could you do this to me?" Fiona asked bitterly. She started to open the door when she felt a soft touch on her arm.

Asron smiled at her, his hand resting gently on her elbow. "Don't worry, I promise there won't be anything happening that will make you uncomfortable. Gia had not originally intended to include us in the ritual, but this is such an important night that she hoped you could both profit from our being here. If you'd rather not participate, we'll take you back to your house right now."

Selene added, "Before you decide, why don't you and E.G. and Gia walk around the park while I find a place to set up the altar. Then if you still want to go home, we'll take you back up the hill."

Fiona was trapped. They were counting on her not having the strength of character to tell them to take her home and the hell with disrupting the ritual.

E.G. finally got out of the car, and Fiona stared at the man in amazement. Gia leaned over to whisper in her ear. "Isn't he the most fantastic person you've ever seen? I couldn't believe it when I met this guy at the store and he's only gotten better as I get to know him. Guess who's going to be the next hero in a romance for me!"

Fiona could only nod. The man was six and a half feet tall and built like a wrestler. He was strikingly handsome, with blond hair and shocking blue eyes that seemed to catch the moonlight and reflect it outward. He was also aware of the impact he had on people and was already laughing at the expression on Fiona's face.

"I'm glad to meet you," he said and stuck out a hand that was twice the size of a normal human appendage. His touch was surprisingly gentle.

Fiona gave a sudden start as she caught a few random thoughts from E.G. Something about being there just for safety's sake and something else about danger for Fiona and Gia.

"I'll be damned," she breathed. Gia had finally found herself a real man, just like Harper. It was about time.

E.G.'s hand lingered just a moment longer than normal and his eyes widened a fraction. So he knew she could hear his thoughts, or at least some of them.

Interesting, Fiona thought.

"So, tell me, what does E.G. stand for?" she asked. "And while you're answering questions, I'd like to know how you got mixed up with the Major Arcana and that bunch—"

"Of heathens?" E.G. interjected, his voice still tinged with laughter.

"Maybe." Actually Fiona had been going to call them nuts.

"That's a long story. Someday you'll hear it, because our lines cross several times. But not tonight."

"Are you going to tell me what E.G. stands for, since you won't answer my other question?" Fiona prodded. The more she talked to this man, the better she liked him. There was something here that she responded to, a feeling of goodness that was totally lacking in Asron and Selene. It might have had something to do with the image she saw, almost as an overlay to the reality of here and now, of a Norse warrior ready to do battle.

"Fiona! Leave him alone. If he wants to tell us, he will in time," Gia said. She knew her friend had a habit of asking outrageous questions, but she hadn't expected her to do it to her attorney.

"Name?" Fiona asked again.

E.G. reached the bench and sat down, folding himself up until he looked as if he were nearly normal height, no mean feat for a giant. Fiona and Gia were still looking at him expectantly. He sighed. "All right, since neither of you is going to leave me alone until I reveal my terrible secret. E.G. stands for Elf Gunnerson."

"Elf?" Gia echoed. Never, even in her wildest dreams, could she have considered the name Elf for this man. "You mean, E-L-F, as in the little people?"

"Exactly."

Fiona's laughter pealed through the grove of trees. Gia couldn't help joining in, even though Elf's face was a study in chagrin.

"I'm sorry," Gia finally said, "But Elf is so—so—incongruous. What on earth possessed your parents to name you that?"

E.G. shrugged. "My mother's Celtic and my father is

from Sweden. They decided long before I was born that any children's names would reflect both cultures. The first boy would be Elf Thorsson Gunnerson; the first girl was Fairy Caitlinnsdotter Gunnerson. And it's bad enough to be called E.G. my whole life, but can you imagine what would happen if I used the initials for Elf Thorsson?"

"E.T.—oh my," Fiona said.

"Exactly. My parents couldn't have known about the movie years before it happened, but they sure as hell knew about what Elf would do to me. Neither my sister nor I has ever forgiven our parents, no matter how wonderful they were otherwise, for their flight of fancy. And both of us are known solely by our initials."

Fiona and Gia managed to nod and fight back the tears of laughter that threatened to well up again.

Asron and Selene interrupted them. "We've found the perfect place up on the hill behind the swings. We were looking for something with a presence of the earth and trees and there is a wonderful circle back there where we can be safe to do our work."

"This is my ceremony, guys. If you have work of your own, why don't you go find another park and do it there?" Gia said. Her voice was thin and tense. It was obvious things were not working out at all as she had envisioned them.

"No, Selene needs some healing work done," Asron said. "Don't worry, we'll get to your stuff, too, but hers is very serious."

"What kind of healing?" Fiona asked.

"Trying to get rid of proliferative cell growth." She turned away, effectively cutting off any more questions. Fiona considered sticking her tongue out at the woman for being obnoxious.

"But my work!" Gia was almost wailing. The evening was definitely out of control.

Asron dismissed her with a wave of his hand. "Shall we

go to the tree circle? The best thing about it is that no one should see us when we are sky-clad."

"I'm not going to be naked," Fiona said, determined to make the man listen to her. She really didn't like him. Asron seemed to think that just by virtue of being himself he could command everyone.

"No nudity," she said again, wanting to make certain he wasn't going to indulge in public pubic exposure.

"Not for you, but certainly for the rest of us."

Fiona squirmed. He might think that was all right, but she wasn't certain she was ready to see his famous penis swinging in the wind. She'd heard so much about the appendage from Gia that she knew she couldn't look at him naked and maintain any kind of equanimity.

"What about my neighbors? All they'd have to do would be to look out their back windows, the ones that overlook the park, and they'd see us plain as day. I mean, dressed in shorts and a top and walking in circles, that's fine, but nude is going to get you arrested!"

"We'll be careful," Selene said. "This is a ceremony that must be correct. I promise you, no one will ever know."

"And if someone does see and object?"

"Then we'll get dressed," Selene said, clearly tired of the subject.

"Why won't you listen to me and save everyone a lot of grief?" Fiona finally had put up with enough from these pushy people. "I'm not some kind of country bumpkin and this is my neighborhood. Now will you listen to me?"

"No," Selene said coldly.

Gia and Elf were already following Asron and Selene to the small wooded area on the hillside, well away from the main part of the park. There was a hidden circle in the middle of ten thick redwoods. Asron was carrying a small cauldron and stand; Selene had some bags of stuff that could have been incense, and other paraphernalia.

Elf called Gia, making her hang back. "Fiona really isn't

comfortable. How about we call this off, and let Asron and Selene go do their own ceremony? We'll go out for pizza and beer and forget this for tonight. I promise you, there's enough power in the legal processes that I'm using to stop Larry. You don't need Asron and Selene mixed up in this, too."

"But I want to have a ceremony," Gia said stubbornly.

"Come on, you guys, quit hanging back, we've got to get started," Asron said.

"Damn!" Elf watched Gia join the circle while Selene was setting up some candles on the makeshift altar.

Fiona looked at the candles and recoiled in horror. "No, absolutely not, you can't light candles out here, either. What do you want to do, start a fire that'll take out every porch on every house on the upwind side?"

"We're going to have candles," Selene said in a bored voice. "Why do you feel you have to object to everything we do?"

"Damn it, *listen* to me instead of pushing to get your own way! We've already had three fires on this hillside that were set by kids, and everyone is real jumpy. You could kill people by being stubborn and insisting on open flames."

Asron cleared a small space, making certain there was nothing but dry clean dust near the candles and the cauldron. Selene helped set up the altar with water, willow branches and salt and lit the candle. He started to cast the circle, calling the earth, air, wind and fire to him using the athame as a focal point.

"That's it, I'm leaving," Fiona said.

She turned on her heel and stalked off toward the street.

"Fiona, come back," Gia cried, and Asron and Selene swore in anger.

"Please, we need your energy," Asron called, his voice still honey-sweet.

Fiona shook her head and kept on walking.

She looked back only once, just in time to see Asron knock over the candle on the altar.

Then with stunning rapidity the danger she had warned them about became real.

The tiny flame, spurred by the wind, touched one long dry pine needle that hadn't been cleared from the dust around the altar. The needle exploded in fire.

"Oh my God," Fiona breathed.

She turned and ran back, stamping on the thin line of flames, managing to put most of them out, when another fire sprang up at the outer edges of the dusty circle. Then with a whoosh and a bang the fire leaped the circle and caught the tall dry grasses that covered the hillside.

Gia shrieked; Asron and Selene swore and Elf ran after the fire, as if he could catch it and bring it back.

Fiona scooped up handfuls of dust and threw it on the blaze, but nothing was going to stop the raging flames as they raced up the hillside toward the houses.

"I've got to warn my family!" she shouted and ran for the street. She zigzagged over toward a path the others would never know about. It went straight up and over the hill, through Sally's yard. Just a few more moments and she would be home, if she'd left the back gate open and unlocked. She didn't remember whether she'd done that during the afternoon or not. She could hear the shriek of the fire engines as they headed toward the park and her heart sank. Someone had been watching. Someone had called the fire department.

Her side ached with the sudden exertion. She wanted to stop and bend over and wait for her breathing to return to normal, but the fire was leaping upward and she didn't have time. She ran on, trying to ignore the knife of pain in her side.

"Stop, you miserable son of a bitch, you're not going to be able to run away from hell's fire this time," a man yelled at her from the house up the hill. She ignored the voice. If he didn't know her and she didn't stop, he couldn't identify her.

She was almost to the top of the ridge when she heard the roar of a rifle being fired and saw shot spray through the tall grass beside her. She gasped in shock and her step faltered, but she couldn't stop. She ducked and kept running. She had to warn Harper. She had to get Megan and the cats out of the house. She had to make up for her terrible lack of judgment in coming out tonight.

"Oh God, don't let me lose Harper over this," she wept as she scrambled through the rocks and dry grass. Suddenly another blast split the air and the world spun and crashed around her. She felt a stab of pain and then numbness in her leg as she fell face first into the tall grasses. The sharp blades cut her skin and threatened to blind her and her hands burned with the impact of her palms against hard rock. A hundred bees stung the calf of her leg, but she couldn't brush them away.

"I've been shot," she thought hazily, as she lay in the dirt and felt the blood seeping from her leg and wetting the ground around her. "How the hell am I going to explain this to Harper?"

She was terribly thirsty. There wasn't a drop of moisture left in her mouth. She couldn't have screamed if her life had depended on it.

She saw the flames jumping up the ravine toward her. She tried to move and realized she couldn't escape from the destruction. She was going to be burned to death and there was nothing she could do about it.

"Hah, got you, you heathen bitch! That's the last time you're going to be starting fires around this area," the man shouted. His footsteps pounded up the slope toward her as he crossed in front of the flames. He threw himself down on top of her, grabbing her arms and wrenching them back, almost dislocating her shoulder. He pushed her face down into the dust, choking her.

"Die, sucker, before you cause anyone any more problems."

Fiona whistled with anguish as she felt the man's knees bash her in the small of her back. Her muscles spasmed at the insult. She tried to breathe in, but the dust filled her nose and mouth and all she could do was gag.

"Get away from my wife!"

Fiona heard the meaty sound of flesh hitting flesh, and the roar of Harper's voice. Suddenly the weight rolled off her and she was able to breathe again.

The fire was almost upon them, the flames singeing her arms and back and lighting patches of Harper's jeans as he ran upward, carrying her as if she didn't weigh anything at all.

"Your back—oh please don't hurt yourself because of me," she whispered and then passed out as the pain of the shot and the burns overwhelmed her.

15

S o, Marilyn, how was last night?" one of the doctors asked the other as they leaned over Fiona's leg. "I heard you and Harry were going to be boning up on that osteomyelitis case that Johnston is so intense about. What was the big attraction, being ready for the case, or were you hot after Harry's adorable bod?"

"The attraction was about equal between medicine and playing doctor, but nothing went on. He's interested in landing a post-doc research position, not a horizontal one. I'll bet he's still a virgin, even with all those obvious and lovely assets." Marilyn sounded distinctly disgruntled and disappointed.

"Wow, will you look at this one—" The emergency-room physician dug deep into Fiona's leg and emerged triumphantly with a piece of shot that had penetrated the muscles and lodged against the bone. "She's really lucky it didn't shatter the bone. Look, there's a little pitting where it hit, but nothing that's going to require any treatment."

Fiona lay face down on an emergency-room gurney that had all the comforting aspects of a torture rack, smelling the mixture of hospital sheets and smoke that hung in the air around her. She had been dozing after the doctors had given her something for the pain. The shot had burned, and then blessed relief had spread through her, knocking her out.

"Hey." She managed to raise her head, despite the awful pain in her back where her neighbor had landed on her spine. "Hey folks!" she repeated.

"Yes ma'am?" the doctor asked as she continued working.

"What do you mean, you were studying?" Fiona demanded groggily. "What the hell are you doing giving me shots and digging stuff out of my leg if you aren't for-real physicians?"

She heard a sigh from one of the women. "Don't worry, we really are doctors. We're residents and this is our turn to work in the emergency room. And if we get into trouble or find something we can't handle, there's always a senior resident or the head of the emergency room close by."

The explanation didn't soothe Fiona. "I've burned down my neighborhood, I may have destroyed my house, I've been shot and now I'm in the hands of residents instead of real doctors. This is definitely not good." She put her head back down on the gurney and felt the hot tears beginning to leak from under her eyelids.

She drifted off again into nightmares of the park and the fire. In the dream, she could see Asron raising his cup and knife to the four corners. Selene stood beside him, her beauty a marked contrast to his heavy masculinity. They finished invoking the circle and slipped out of their long robes, which opened in the front, revealing everything Fiona didn't want to see.

"It's time for you to become one of us, join us with body and soul." Asron and Selene advanced on her.

"No, you want Gia," she said, looking around for her friend.

The two shook their heads and motioned to her to join them. "We need both of you."

Fiona tried to retreat, but the circle held her prisoner. She put her hands up to push her way out into the fresh air of the park, but the circle had become a wall of glass instead of a radius drawn in the dust. She tried to turn away, but her limbs were heavy; she couldn't move them and her arms dropped uselessly at her side.

"Darling, we wouldn't hurt you. We just want to have you help us," Selene purred. She reached out and lifted Fiona's shirt, pulling it loose from her shorts. Asron held her arms up while Selene removed the cotton shirt, revealing that Fiona hadn't worn a bra. The woman touched Fiona's breasts, circling the nipple, then holding the heavy flesh in her hand.

"Such beauty. Why do you hide it?"

Fiona looked at Asron and saw, to her horror, that he was responding to the nakedness of her body. His penis was already swollen.

Asron hooked his finger around the elastic of her prim cotton shorts and began to lower them. As he did so, he ran his finger along her body and explored areas only Harper had ever touched. She could feel him moving inward, tickling her and causing an involuntary reaction to his caresses. She hated the feeling but she could see why Gia had been swept along—her own body was responding to his advances.

"Harper," she whispered, calling the only man she ever wanted to make love to her. If Asron forced her it would be rape. Despite her body's response she fought against the violation.

"Just give yourself over to us. Help us and everything will be fine. The power will be back in balance and you will be tied to us, and none of us will need to worry anymore, will we?" Asron said. "We're getting closer every minute."

Fiona tried to figure out what he was talking about, but

all she could think of was that she wanted to get laid. It wasn't going to be making love, it was just sex. She knew he had bewitched her, though she fought against the entrancement that would take her away from Harper and give her over to these people. His hands burned into her skin and when he touched her with the very tip of his penis against the junction of her legs her body leaped in response. She forgot to think of Harper or of Gia. She responded only to Asron and the need for satisfaction that had grown over the past few minutes into a desperate passion.

The nightmare chanting from an unseen chorus grew louder as Asron moved closer, now completely erect. She knew that if he entered her, she would never get away from him. He'd have her as completely under his control as he had Gia. She fought the temptation to give in.

"No!" she said, but it was only a whisper. Her body was betraying her.

Suddenly she was snatched back into the world of bright lights and astringent smells in the hospital emergency room.

"Fiona—yo, Mrs. Kendrick, wake up!" Someone shook her shoulder roughly.

"Whaaa?" she said.

"Good, you're back with us. That pain killer must have really put you out." The young woman patted her on the shoulder, glad to see any kind of response. "We've finished the leg. The last piece of shot has been removed and we're going to be putting antibiotic cream on the wounds and a dressing. Then we'll start on the burns on your face and hands."

"You've finished my leg?" Fiona said, her mouth barely working around the words. She shook her head to clear it. The nightmare had been so vivid that she could almost taste the dry dusty air of the park before it burned. At the moment, the doctors were less real than Asron's penis sticking up out of that thick thatch of pubic hair.

"Ohhh," Fiona groaned, half from the pain that was beginning to surface in her back and arms and half from sheer frustration. It had been a long time since she'd been that hot and been left unsatisfied.

"Sorry, Fiona, just a few more minutes, okay?" The doctors misinterpreted her moan. "These burns won't take long at all. How about if I give you another shot for the pain?"

Fiona opened her eyes wide at the suggestion. "Please, no more medicine. I'm fine." She was trying very hard to pronounce her words clearly. She didn't want to be unconscious again. She might return to the dream. There was something terribly wrong and disturbing about it, a quality of actuality that made her feel eerily as if it had been real instead of something induced by painkillers.

"All right, if you're sure. But if you need it, just sing out. We don't want any of our patients to be in pain," the doctor said, pulling her hand back from the hypodermic that was already on the tray.

Fiona stayed awake for the rest of the treatment. She felt every bit of the pain on her arms and face when the residents cleaned the burns. The flaming patches of weeds and the chaff had stuck to her like napalm, crisping into her skin and leaving patches of blistered white flesh. Each time they removed a bit of skin, it felt as if something were taking bites out of her.

"This is going to hurt. Are you sure you don't want something for it?"

"It's already hurting. I thought I wasn't supposed to feel burns right away," Fiona said.

"You aren't, not the big ones, but these are just little patches and they sting like sin. You wouldn't feel the pain if you had half of your body burned, but you'd feel it if grease splashed from a hot pan onto your hand. This is like a grease burn."

Fiona nodded and set her teeth against her lip as they set to work cleaning the rest of the dirt out of the burns.

"Doesn't look too good," one doctor said as she inspected the flesh. "I suggest that we put a graft on that burn on her upper thigh. That's a pretty large area to go without something to help it heal."

"What do you mean, graft?" Fiona asked.

"Simple. We take skin from a donor, slice it thin, grow it, and then wash and prepare it so that it's like a bandage we can spread over the burn. It's done all the time. Nothing to worry about."

It took a while to come back to normal as the medications wore off. Fiona had heard about skin transplants and she didn't think the doctor knew what the hell she was talking about. "Nothing to worry about? And where do you get the original donor skin? From cadavers, I'll bet. And what happens to cadavers? They've died, and sometimes they've died of AIDS, only you guys don't know it."

"Never happen," one doctor said quickly.

"Hah, liar. It has already happened," Fiona said as her brain began to work a little more clearly. "Five years down the line you start finding out that the tissue and organ recipients have AIDS and you say, oh whoops, sorry about that. No, thank you, I'll take my chances without the extra help of a skin graft."

"Wow, you've come out of that painkiller just fine if you can put together a coherent thought like that."

"You bet I have. Enough to know I don't want a skin transplant unless you take it from me for myself."

"Okay, how about we put antibiotic and a bandage on you and you'll be out of here within another hour."

They were true to their word; she was released in forty-five minutes. Harper was waiting for her in the reception area when she was wheeled out and pronounced ready to go home, if her husband had paid the $4,000 bill that had been run up in the emergency room.

"The four thousand dollars is only an estimate," the starched and proper lady who handled the billing said. "If the estimate is over, then we will of course refund the money within sixty days."

Fiona watched Harper begin to object to the obvious unfairness of the billing procedures, and then he closed his mouth.

The woman handed him a receipt for the check he wrote and he wheeled Fiona out to the car.

Fiona smiled uncertainly at him, but he remained grim-faced and remote.

"Aren't you at least going to say you're glad I'm alive?" Fiona finally ventured when he'd helped her into the car and started home.

"No."

It was like a slap in the face. Fiona sat back in the seat, careful not to put her arms against the rough plastic because she knew it would hurt. She was on the verge of tears from the pain and the medication and Harper's mood didn't help her at all.

"Who's taking care of Megan?"

"Sally."

"Sally?" Fiona closed her eyes.

"Yes. She was so distraught over Carl's shooting you that she was desperate to help. I told her she could stay with Megan until we got back."

"Carl! That's why the voice sounded so familiar!" Fiona said, stunned. The man who had landed on her with every intention of killing her had been Sally's husband.

"She says they have household insurance to pay us back eventually. Right now the police are questioning Carl. Both of them were almost hysterical."

"You sound more worried about Sally and Carl than you do about me," Fiona said resentfully.

"I'm not feeling exactly happy with you, Fiona. I saw the fire when it had enough of a start to begin glowing through the trees. I saw you running up that hill and I saw you get shot. I had to rescue you, my back is killing me and I've just had to come up with *four thousand dollars* that I don't have and had to borrow. How the hell do you expect me to feel?" Harper's voice had begun rising until he was almost shouting with the last few words.

Fiona and Harper rode the rest of the way in silence. He helped her out of the car and past the neighbors, who stared and whispered comments. Everyone wanted to know about the shooting and the fire, but no one was willing to ask her. Sally was effusive in her protestations about how bad she felt, right up until she carefully hugged Fiona.

"I told you retribution would be taken for your devil worshiping. Only God could have caused a fire and a shooting to bring you back into the fold," she said in a whisper only Fiona could hear.

"God didn't have anything to do with it. Carl's the one who shot me."

Sally disappeared into her house, locking the door and pulling the blinds so that the neighbors wouldn't bother her.

Fiona didn't want to talk to anyone. All she wanted to do was crawl into bed and die.

"I'll die, right after I kill Gia," Fiona muttered as Harper helped her into bed. Gia had cost her pain, $4,000 and possibly a marriage. She wasn't in a forgiving mood.

"What?" Harper demanded.

"Nothing, nothing at all," she said hastily. "It just hurt more than I expected when I sat down on the bed."

"You can have some pain medication. I'll get it for you," Harper finally offered when she tried to turn over and moaned aloud with the ache from the shots and the burns.

Fiona shook her head. "No thanks, I think I'll just let myself hurt for a while."

Harper muttered something that sounded like "Good, you deserve to," but she wasn't certain.

The few remaining hours of night passed slowly. When the alarm rang, Fiona expected Harper to shut it off and stay in bed. It was Saturday; he didn't need to go in to work and he certainly needed the rest after the night before. He rolled over and out of bed and went on with his morning ritual as if there were nothing different about this day.

"Harper, please wait. I want to talk to you," Fiona said. He left the room without saying a word.

Fiona stood the pain of the mattress against her body as long as she could, and then crawled out of bed and into the studio across the hallway.

The smell of smoke and burned trees hung heavy on the air. Outside, Fiona could hear the neighbors talking about the fire and the damage. There were already adjusters from various insurance companies taking pictures of the damage to the row of houses that looked out on the park. The people across the street had been hit hard; some of the houses had actually burned and one family had lost their kitchen and family room before the fire was put out. Other luckier neighbors had only lost every bit of their trees and gardens and decks to the flames.

Fiona had been staring at the mountain of bills that was sitting in the bill box. Four thousand dollars? Where had he found the money? And if the money was from his wages, what was she going to use to pay the bills?

"If only I hadn't—" she started to say and then stopped. She had given in to Gia and met her at midnight and the consequences had been far more serious than any time that she'd slipped out of her parents' home. Then she'd only risked pregnancy. This time she'd risked her entire life with Harper.

"Stupid, stupid, stupid," she chanted.

Downstairs she could hear Megan and Harper talking about the Saturday work and what each of them could do. Neither of them came upstairs or included her in any of the decisions. It was obvious that she was exiled to coldest Siberia.

It had been a long time since Harper had been angry enough to give her the silent treatment. Normally he tried to discuss problems with her, to reason and come to some kind of agreement. He'd tried to do that about the witchcraft, Fiona thought guiltily, and she hadn't listened.

If he wouldn't talk now, then he certainly would sometime in the future. She knew there would be a hell of a fight soon. It was the waiting that was killing her.

Fiona worked on the bills for almost two hours, trying to find a way out of their predicament. Even if she got her check from the card company they weren't going to make it.

The mail came and Harper delivered an envelope from Madge Lorenz at Big Skies Greeting Cards and left, still not speaking to her.

Dear Fiona,

We are delighted with the sketches, and hope that you're ready to just dive in and get these paintings out as fast as possible. The good news is that we want to buy everything we can get from you. The bad news is that due to a contractual problem with the printers, we've got to get your stuff into production two months earlier than anticipated. This means you'll have until July 15 instead of September 30 to produce the paintings. Hope this isn't too much of an inconvenience. Please let me know if this won't work out.

She couldn't mean it! Fiona looked at the calendar and back to the note. She'd have to put out eight paintings in two months instead of the original four and a half?

"I can't do it—" But she knew she'd have to. She couldn't afford to pass up the chance of a lifetime and all that money.

"But how am I going to do the work if I can't stand up and can't sit down for more than a couple of minutes? I guess I'm going to have to tough it out or we're going to be standing in front of a bankruptcy judge," Fiona said to herself grimly.

She rubbed her hand over her leg, carefully avoiding the bandages. She'd already hit one of the open wounds once and almost died from the pain. She looked up at the clock, but it was too soon for another pain pill. She had to admit to having thought longingly about her daughter's morphine several times during the night when the codeine wasn't doing the trick. She wouldn't take the little purple pills or the liquid, though, because she'd never be able to wake up in an emergency and help Megan.

Witchcraft. Look at all the trouble it'd just gotten her into.

Well, not exactly—Fiona began to rationalize her thoughts about the Old Religion. After all, the magic itself hadn't caused any of the troubles. The mess had come mostly from Gia and her bringing those other people to their own private little ceremony.

The charms and amulets and spells she'd done on her own, for her family, had only had beneficial results. She could justify every time she'd used the Old Religion to help them out.

"Damn," Fiona said as she realized what she was doing.

She was hooked. It was like cocaine or something else that could pull her in and never let her go. She could almost visualize the page of the book that told her how to bring luck and money.

Besides, I've already started the spell. I might as well finish it up since we need the money so badly, she thought, justifying herself as she picked up the book and let the page fall open to the information she needed.

Right after the first visit to the Major Arcana she'd mixed up a sludge-like blend of cloves, cinnamon, nutmeg, coriander, ginger and oils and put them all to soak with a little water and gum arabic. She'd felt as if she were playing with mud pies again when she'd patted them into little disks and put them to dry on the windowsill. The book had said the dough should be dried in the sunshine, but she couldn't find a place where some of her outside animals wouldn't nibble on the tasty chips. Several chips had already been destroyed by two of the cats, who thought carrying the hard disks around the house clenched in their sharp little teeth was the best game ever invented.

"It's time to use the money charms," Fiona said. She listened for any sounds from Harper or Megan that would indicate that they were coming up to the studio, but heard nothing. She hobbled over to the windowsill and retrieved the three remaining fragrant dark brown coins. Along the way she grabbed her Swiss army knife, which she used as her second sacred knife, in addition to the long Ginsu. She'd reasoned that Harper would probably notice real witchcraft supplies, but he'd never suspect her new army knife, not after she'd already worn out two of them in the past ten years.

She looked up the instructions just to be certain she had it all right. "Call the Goddess to help me empower these, mark with a pentagram, and ask for my wish, right?" she murmured as she flipped the pages. She read the instructions again.

Damn, I was supposed to have marked the pentagram way back when I made them. Well, it'll have to do it now, because I don't have time for any more of this. She began to draw the knife across the hard surface. The spicy scent drifted up and surrounded her as she worked. She inhaled deeply as she called the Goddess and told her exactly what she wanted. "Sufficient to allow us to live comfortably despite the crisis," she said firmly. Let someone else decide what comfortable meant.

Once she had finished and thanked the Goddess, she put one disk on top of the unpaid bills, following it with five shiny pennies she found in the bottom of her purse. She cast one more tiny spell and closed the bill basket. She placed the other coin in her wallet, hoping the money spell would work there, too.

Finished just in time, she realized as she heard Harper's footsteps on the stairs.

"Fiona, I'd like to talk to you," Harper said, opening the door to the studio. He sniffed suspiciously at the smell of the spices. "What have you been doing, eating gingerbread in here?"

"No," Fiona lied. "I've just been spreading some cinnamon. The ants were making tracks for my bottle of See's candies and I'm not giving those little beggars even a smidge of that chocolate. Where do you want to talk?" she asked. "In the bedroom?"

Here it comes, she thought, The Blowup. Harper wasn't good at keeping his anger in, so eventually he'd have to tell her what was bothering him. The only problem was that The Blowup was usually conducted at a full-throated roar, with a lot of repetition, until he was sure she understood every bit of what he was angry about and what he wanted her to do about it.

"Bedroom is fine. I know you can't make it downstairs." He didn't reach out to steady her as she climbed painfully up out of the chair and walked into the bedroom. He waited while she arranged the pillows to support her back and her leg, and finally lay back on the soft down mountain.

Harper sat facing her, leaning forward with his legs

crossed. It was the only way he could sit on the bed without back pain and even then he was limited to a few minutes in any one position.

"What happened last night?" he asked quietly.

Fiona was on the alert. Where was the yelling? This was a very bad sign. He'd gone straight to the discussion part of the fight.

"I was worried about Megan and the bills and everything else and I couldn't sleep. You know how the three o'clock horribles are. So I decided to go for a walk and ended up down in the park. I saw the fire start and was running up the hill to warn you and then Carl shot me. You know all the rest."

Harper stared at her. His eyes were icy blue, almost the same shade as Elf Gunnerson's eyes, she noted with surprise. It was clear from his expression that he hadn't believed a word she'd said.

He'd never looked at her like that before, with a cold gaze that told her as clearly as words that at the moment he considered her the enemy.

"Come on, Harper, don't you believe me?"

"No."

"It's true!" she insisted.

Harper exhaled heavily. "Eventually you'll get around to backing your way into the truth, you know."

"But I am telling the truth," Fiona insisted again. She shifted uneasily.

"No, you arc not." It was a flat statement. "Here's what I know for certain. You slipped out of bed and went downstairs without turning on the lights. There was a car waiting outside for you and you left in the car. I don't know how you got to the park or what you were doing there, but there were other people with you. It's probable that the other people were the ones who started the fire because even you wouldn't be stupid enough to use a flame in the middle of the worst fire year we've ever had."

"Thanks," Fiona said.

"You're welcome." He stopped and waited for her to say something. "Come on, Fiona, tell me I'm wrong. I lay awake last night and wished that I'd wake up and your leaving would all be a terrible dream. But it didn't happen. Instead there was the fire and the shooting and you were right in the middle of it and my nightmare was real after all."

Fiona heard the pain in his voice, but she wasn't about to say anything. She'd damn herself if she even blinked.

Harper continued. "You might have been running up the hill to warn us, but you sure hadn't walked down to the park because you couldn't sleep. You've never in your entire life walked anywhere in the dead of night, because you're afraid of something happening to you. I know the cops talked to Gia while the fire was still burning. They also gave me the names of two other people I didn't recognize. They think they've found what started the fire—a candle in the middle of a cleared circle. They said there was a drawing in the dust, but declined to tell me what it was."

He stopped again, waiting for Fiona to comment.

Fiona couldn't have said a word if her life had depended on it. She reached down and rubbed her leg. Maybe she could stall, say that she hurt too much to talk right now.

"No, Fiona, don't even try it. I want to get to the bottom of this and you're going to tell me what happened down in that park. Then we're going to decide what to do about it. Telling me that your leg hurts isn't going to influence me in the least."

There was something in Harper's voice she'd never heard before, a hardness and despair she felt responsible for.

"Damn it, can't you understand what I'm going through?" he said. "I thought we had the perfect life together and now you've shattered everything I thought I could believe in. You were everything I'd ever needed in my life. I never wanted anything more than you and our life together and suddenly I find out that I can't even trust you!"

"I may have betrayed you, but don't try and tell me we had the perfect life until last night," Fiona said in amazement. "With all the shit that keeps happening to us, you think our life has been nothing but good?"

"Hasn't it? It never harmed us in any way that broke us up, did it? Nothing was ever so bad that we couldn't face it united. That feeling of us against the world never changed, not when I broke my back, not with Megan's illness, not with bills we would never in a million years get ahead of. I trusted you with all my soul and look what you did."

"What did I do?"

"You and Gia and the others were down there playing with witchcraft again, even after I asked you not to. Do you know, I'd have rather found out that you were sneaking out of the house to see another man than to find that you didn't listen to me when I pleaded with you to stop playing around with the Craft. I could fight a man, but I can't fight the hold magic has on you."

"It wasn't—"

"Yes, it was. I could call the cops and ask if the design in the dust was a circle with a pentagram inside and we both know they'd say yes. And you were there, right in the middle of it."

Fiona gave up. "Harper, you've got to understand, it was Gia, my best friend. I couldn't let her down when she needed my help."

Harper took a deep breath. He looked a thousand years old when he raised his head again.

Finally he whispered, "But what about me? What about our family? What about my asking you not to do this? She's more important to you than our marriage? Breaking your promise to me means nothing to you? If that is true, then our marriage is over."

16

G ia waited three days before she decided it was probably safe to call Fiona and ask how she was doing.

Gia was smart enough to know that her friend would be angry with her. She hadn't bargained on just how furious Fiona really was.

"Hi, Fee, how about coffee and cake? I'll buy. I know you're still pissed off at me, so take it as a peace offering," Gia said.

"You want to come over for coffee?" Fiona asked, narrowing her eyes at the very sound of Gia's voice. "Sure, I guess this would be as good a time as any for us to talk. Let yourself in and come upstairs."

"Upstairs? You don't want to sit on that nice comfortable couch in your family room?"

"I'm working. Besides, I can't make it downstairs quite yet."

Gia was silent for an inordinately long time. "Care to explain what you mean when you say you can't make it downstairs? Did something happen to you in that mess?

The way you split after the fire started, I thought you were back at the house long before things got crazy."

"Why don't you come over and we can talk about it," Fiona said and hung up the phone. "At least I'll get another chocolate cake out of you before we have a complete breakup," she said to herself.

She was ready for a sugar infusion. She had been up and working at five in the morning, trying desperately to figure out a way to paint while she moved from a chair to standing upright and then back to the chair. She'd always painted while she stood, and she found the mechanics of sitting and working almost impossible. Not even the blizzard tape could help her get into the mood to really paint well. She spent most of the time filling in little details and otherwise wasting time while the fog crept in over the hills toward her house.

Drawing was preferable to being around her husband for the time being. He was in a perfectly foul mood after their discussion Saturday. The situation hadn't improved Sunday. He'd put pillows between them when they went to bed, ostensibly because he didn't want to take the chance of hurting her. Fiona knew that the real reason for the wall of feathers was that he was so angry, if there had been another bed available in the house, he'd have slept there.

She'd tried to get up and fix him breakfast, as she always did, but he'd growled at her to stay down. He'd fixed his own food and slammed plates around in the kitchen. Finally, tired of all the noise, Fiona had dragged herself into the studio to try to paint.

While she sketched, erased and revised, looking for a way to make the idea work, she thought about Gia. As she did, the storm clouds outside thickened even further, but she didn't notice the change.

There was a tentative knock on the studio door and Gia entered.

Fiona switched the tape off and greeted her friend.

Within five minutes the storm clouds that had gathered
overhead began to dissipate, leaving behind the sunny
morning that was usual for the season.

"Hey, Fiona, here's the best chocolate cake Safeway
had—What happened to you?" Gia placed the cake on the
table and gently touched the bandages on her friend's arms
and face. "Oh honey, I had no idea!" Then she caught sight
of Fiona's legs.

"More burns?"

"No, gunshot."

"Oh my God!" Gia gasped. "I heard what sounded like
a rifle but I thought it was just the fire popping. Who shot
you? Why would they do that to you?"

"Do you remember when Asron and Selene were setting up the circle and I told them not to use candles because
we'd had fire scares?"

Gia nodded.

"You never said a word in my defense or to back me up
with an order not to do anything dangerous. You just let
Asron and Selene do whatever they wanted and to hell with
me. Yet you knew we'd had three fires already this year and
the neighborhood was really jumpy. As a matter of fact, Elf
came to my defense when he offered to just stop all the nonsense and take us out for pizza. You refused."

Gia had the grace to look uncomfortable. "I'm sorry, I
was wrong. I thought the ritual was important."

"I'm sure you did. What Gia wants usually is most important, isn't it?" Fiona said bitterly. "By deciding that you
didn't want to embarrass yourself by speaking up, you
managed to get me shot."

"How do you figure that?"

"If the fire hadn't happened, Sally's husband wouldn't
have grabbed the gun he had loaded and ready to stop the
hooligans who've been driving them nuts lately. Carl was
just a little more jumpy than usual because the last fire was
started about ten feet away from their bedroom window on

the uphill side. If the hillside catches fire, their house could go up in flames in a matter of seconds. So he used his shotgun against me, because he thought I was the one who started the fire."

"Sally's husband shot you?"

"He saw me running. I guess he thought I was one of the kids in the area and he'd had enough. He picked up the rifle, ran outside and blasted away. Once I was down, he tackled me and damn near broke my back."

"And the burns?"

"That was when Harper had to carry me through the flames you and your friends started. I suppose he could have let me fry, but he thought maybe I'd better be moved so I didn't become a crispy critter in the middle of the fire."

Gia watched Fiona carefully. She'd never seen her like this before and she was damn sure she didn't like it.

"Well, at least you'll get some money from Carl to pay you back for the pain and suffering. I've been around Elf enough lately to know that you have a good case there if you want to take it to court."

"Sure I do. I need to be involved in a suit against a friend who has never hurt me and would never have hurt me if your people hadn't started a fire."

"I said I was sorry," Gia said hotly, then tried to smile, to bring their relationship back to normal.

"How about some cake?" she finally asked, casting around for something to change the subject. "I'll just make us some espresso and then we can talk this through and solve all the problems, okay?"

Fiona nodded. This was going to be harder than she'd thought. Gia obviously believed they could continue as they had before. Fiona knew that would never work.

While Gia brewed the espresso she tried to plan what she was going to say to Fiona to convince her that all this could be patched up. When she finally had a battle plan, she headed back up the stairs to the studio.

She set everything on the table and turned to Fiona. "All I can say is that I was wrong and I'm sorry. Please forgive me."

"You were wrong?" For the first time Fiona's voice rose above a dead whisper.

"Yes, I was. I never thought a silly little ceremony would end like this. I talked about it when I was at the Major Arcana, and Asron and Selene asked to tag along. It never occurred to me that you'd object or that you'd get hurt." The words rushed out, tumbling over each other. "Look, I know you're mad at me, but that evening just got out of hand. It wasn't really my fault."

"The hell it wasn't your fault. You knew I was doing you a favor and that I wouldn't have even considered a ceremony that had anyone else in it or that was in the park at the bottom of the hill, for God's sake. What do you mean it wasn't your fault?" Her voice had risen to a screech.

Gia stepped back and raised her hands. "Look, I said I was sorry. I don't think there's anything more I can do about it."

"Then you didn't think at all. You betrayed me and that means our friendship is over."

Fiona held her breath. There. It was out in the open. She hadn't been sure that she would say it right up until the moment it was out of her mouth.

"No it isn't. It can't be," Gia said.

"You're my friend, but you aren't worth a divorce from Harper or even worth any more heartache. I'm beginning to wonder if you didn't cause this trouble on purpose, just to drive a wedge between Harper and me."

"You can't believe that!"

"Why not? Give me a reasonable explanation for your actions and I'll listen to you. What you did was just as destructive as if I'd called Larry and told him where to come and find that videotape he'd love to get his hands on. Right now, I'm angry enough I might still do that."

"You wouldn't—I don't even have a copy of it. I never had time to set up the machine."

"Now, why don't you hustle your ass out of here and leave me alone for about a year. By that time maybe I'll have cooled down."

Gia gestured toward the cake because she couldn't think of anything else to say or do. "Does this mean you don't want any cake?"

"This means you'd better get out of here before I smash that cake into your devious little face and throw you out the window. Goodbye, Gia, and good riddance."

17

W e're going to talk," Fiona said as she and Harper finished dinner in strained silence. They hadn't really discussed anything in more than two weeks. Harper was still building pillow walls between them, even though Fiona's burns and gunshot wounds had almost completely healed.

"Harper," Fiona said as she put the last dish in the dishwasher and Megan went upstairs to lie down because her head hurt. "Harper, you are eventually going to have to answer me, so you might as well do it now."

He didn't respond. He was making a show of petting a cat instead of listening to her.

"Harper, I'm talking to you," Fiona said, the faint edge of exasperation finally breaking through.

"What?"

"You have to tell me what's bothering you. I'm not going to put up with this lousy temper of yours for too much longer. You mentioned divorce the night after the fire. Well, every day that you keep up this temper tantrum, the closer that comment comes to reality."

Harper stared at her. His expression didn't change much, but for the first time in weeks, he met her eyes instead of letting his gaze slide away as if she were invisible. She'd finally scored a hit.

"What do you want me to say?"

"How about telling me what's making you so angry? Carrying the fight on for weeks after the fire is overkill. I admit I was stupid and I've paid for that, both physically and mentally. I cut Gia out of my life because of what she did. What more do you want?"

"My black mood isn't all about the night of the fire. It has to do with the job and money and all kinds of things that I've been trying to sort out. I wanted to get another job or come up with a plan or do something to make this less of a disaster before I talked to you, but I failed." He reached into his pocket, pulled out his wallet and handed a piece of paper to Fiona.

She looked at the check for his past two weeks of work and blanched. "Boy, someone sure screwed up your paycheck, didn't they? This is almost three hundred dollars short."

"It's not screwed up. The day after the fire, my boss told me they were cutting my pay. Oh, I still have a job and we still have medical coverage, we just don't have the salary that used to barely hold us from week to week. Cost cutting, you know." His voice was bitter. "I've been looking for a job, talking to headhunters, calling in all my markers for all the years I've helped other people out. There's nothing out there and no one can help me get another position."

He shook his head. "It's bad. Even the headhunter I talked to yesterday wanted to know if there was something open in our company that she could apply for."

Fiona collapsed back against the couch and stared at the numbers. They were already flat broke. With this short paycheck they were so far in the hole that she couldn't possibly bail them out without missing payments this month.

There was the promised check from Big Skies, but it still hadn't materialized.

"And that isn't all." Now that Harper had started talking, it was like a dam bursting. He'd had to hold it in, to suffer the terror and worry on his own, and now he wanted to share the burden. "They're increasing my workday by two hours each day, and I may have to go in every Saturday."

"You'll get paid more for these extra hours and overtime?" Fiona asked. "Is that how they're going to make up for what you were already earning?"

"Nope. Extra hours, no pay. I'm management. If I don't like it, I can leave."

"But you can't work more hours! Your back is bad enough now that you don't have any physical reserves left. You're constantly tired. They'll kill you."

"Sometimes I think that's the point," Harper said. "They're going to find a way to push me out without having to pay any benefits. If I quit, they don't have to pay unemployment and other coverage that they'd have to give me if they fire me. And I think it's all your fault."

Fiona opened her mouth and then closed it because she couldn't think of anything to say to answer his ridiculous statement.

"I've been thinking about what you did with Gia. You brought this bad luck to us by fooling around with the Old Religion. I've been watching things go sour for the past couple of months. Our fortunes have taken a sudden nosedive."

"I didn't do this!" Fiona said, and then shut up.

Harper continued, "I've never known witchcraft to help anything. Not here, not in Wales. I've known it to kill and to cause disasters and illness, but no one ever survived and prospered because of it."

"What do you mean?" Fiona waited for him to say

more. It was a peek into the hidden man, a link to his past she'd never seen before.

He shook his head and started to stand up when the phone rang.

"It's for you," he said, handing her the receiver. While she was talking, he poured himself a glass of sun tea from the old mayonnaise bottle Fiona kept on the windowsill. He stared out into the night, watching for the pinpoints of light that were fireflies. He never saw any. As far as he could tell California didn't have fireflies.

His attention was snapped back as Fiona's voice rose with excitement.

"Could you repeat that, please?" She hesitated, listening. "Sigils for power, an aura, and your cat Baast. Yes, I think I could do that if you'll give me a drawing of whatever kind of symbols you want included." She was silent for another few seconds. "Of course you can come over tonight. I'll make sure the camera has film in it. We can get to work right away."

She hung up the phone and clapped her hands and did a little dance. "Money money money! Guess what that was about!"

Harper shook his head.

Fiona knew she'd have to be careful what she told Harper. She could never let it slip that Selene had been at the park the night of the fire. It was obvious that the older woman was feeling guilty about what had happened and this was her way of making up for the disaster she had caused. Fiona was glad that her "I'm sorries" included cold cash at a time when they desperately needed it.

"That was Selene, a woman I met a few weeks ago. She asked Gia if she knew anyone who could do a charcoal and pen drawing for her shop, the Major Arcana. Gia recommended me. If I understood her correctly, I think I've got a portrait job that will pay me four thousand dollars tonight, right this evening. Oh Harper, we'll be able to pay all the bills and still have enough left over to carry us a month or two, even if they cut your salary by three hundred dollars. We can pay the taxes."

"The Major Arcana? That's a store that deals in magic supplies."

"No, it's a New Age store. It has a lot more than just herbs and oils and stuff like that. Very interesting and damned expensive." She stopped for a moment. "Why aren't you happy for me? I've got a great chance to earn some money!"

"You shouldn't do it," Harper said decisively. "This isn't good for you. I can see by the expression on your face that you really don't want to do a portrait of the high priestess."

"Oh, come on, she's no such thing!" Fiona shot back.

"How would you know? People talk and I listen, and I've heard Selene and Asron Burke mentioned several times in discussions about witchcraft."

Fiona's heart sank. The elation of knowing they would have money coming in was being smothered by Harper's refusal to see what a stroke of luck $4,000 would be. It wasn't fair. He should be happy for her! Besides, it was going to save his ass too by bringing in that extra money just when they needed it.

"Fiona, I mean it. No. You really don't want to, anyway."

"The hell you say!" Fiona spat out. She spun and ran out of the room. She raced up the stairs, slammed open the door to her studio and rooted around behind the overstuffed chair where she'd hidden the bill box that morning when Alta Hospital had called and insisted that she pay something on Megan's account or they were going to turn it over to a collection agency. She grabbed the handles of the heavy oak split basket and ran back downstairs. Skidding to a stop in front of Harper, she upended the basket, letting all the bills drop to the floor. They made a huge pile of paper that consumed money as voraciously as any monster in any fairy tale.

"There," she yelled. "These are all the bills that have to be paid and that doesn't count the house payment!" She ran her hands through them, showering them down again so that he could see just how many there were. Then she grabbed the paycheck she had thrown on the counter and waved it under his nose. "This won't even pay the house, much less anything else. We're going to go bankrupt if we don't get any more money. And you want me to turn down a commission on a painting? You're fucking nuts!"

Princess was pawing through the pile looking for a cinnamon disk, aided by at least eight other cats who had come over to investigate the mess in their normally tidy home.

Harper sat back, stunned at her fury.

"What about your other painting? Madge Lorenz and Big Skies? Isn't she supposed to pay you for the sketches you sent to her last month?"

"Sure, she'll pay as soon as she approves them. But we don't have five or six weeks' worth of leeway to wait for the next check. I was standing up there in front of the easel today wondering if I could manage a temp job and still come home and paint. We don't have any money, we're going to have the electricity turned off, and the damned people we owe keep calling me up wanting their money and I don't have anything to give them. That's how bad it is."

She was angry and disappointed and afraid that Harper still wouldn't see what she meant.

Harper sat back down, defeated. He looked at the bills and then at Fiona, and put his head in his hands.

"Go ahead, then," he said, his voice muffled. "There's nothing more I can do."

Fiona scrabbled to put the bills back in the box and take it upstairs. She wanted to comfort Harper, but there was little enough time to make a run through the house, scoop the cat boxes, put all the cats away in bedrooms and make certain no one had left anything embarrassing in plain sight before Selene came over. For the first time in a long while, she had to ask for help from Megan to clean up the papers and other detritus that accumulated during the week. She could hear Harper upstairs. It was obvious he wasn't going to hinder her but he wasn't going to help, either.

Another wedge, Fiona thought. Another piece of the marriage chipped away.

Harper closed the bedroom door behind him, locking out Fiona and Megan. Fiona tried to enter once, but he rebuffed her. She listened unashamedly at the door, but heard only Welsh mumbles and sometimes words that sounded like "penis" and "age."

The doorbell rang as she lobbed the last kitchen towel out into the garage in the general direction of the dirty clothes pile. She heard the cats beginning to yowl from the bedrooms.

"Please come in," Fiona greeted Selene and stepped back so that the older woman could walk into the hallway.

Selene hung back, as if she wasn't sure she wanted to step across the threshold into the house. For a moment Fiona thought she might bring up the subject of the fire and her still visible wounds. Fiona had to wear shorts because she couldn't tolerate skirts or jeans yet, and the red marks were clearly visible on her pale skin.

Selene muttered something as she came into the hallway and looked around. She was carrying her black cat, Baast, who growled as Selene carried him inside.

Fiona felt a cold breeze from outside, surprising since the day had been very warm and the forecaster was saying they'd set a record tomorrow.

"Is there someone else at home?" Selene asked, frowning.

"My husband and my daughter."

"Your husband. How fascinating. The whole family is interested in the occult."

"Oh, he's not!" Fiona objected.

"That's what you think," Selene said, fixing her with a cold stare.

Fiona shrugged aside the cryptic remarks.

She pointed to a small portrait of her daughter at age three that graced the wall beside the stairs. "Here's a portrait of my daughter that I did a few years ago. It will give you a feel for the kind of work that I do."

Selene nodded. Baast looked around as if he were gazing at the portrait, too. Selene had him on a leash, but kept him in her arms.

Fiona reached out to pet the cat, but drew back her hand when Baast bared his teeth at her. None of her own cats had ever done that, even when they were hurt. She was surprised and perplexed at the response.

Megan walked into the kitchen to get a soft drink and said a polite hello to Selene and the cat.

"She is quite ill, isn't she?" Selene said, as Megan disappeared back upstairs.

"Brain tumor," Fiona said. She refused to be impressed by Selene's popping off about her personal life as if she'd read her mind or "intuited" the information. God only knew what Gia had been telling her.

She led Selene farther into the house, showing her the paintings that decorated every wall. Fiona even gritted her teeth and took the woman into the family room, even though all the furniture looked distinctly fuzzy with cat hair. Some people had an absolute fit about cat hair.

"I see that you really like animals. There are an inordinate number of paintings with them," Selene said. She put her hand down on the couch to steady herself as she leaned toward a portrait of Princess. "That's good; I wanted someone who was comfortable with cats."

Fiona's heart gave a leap. Did this mean she had the contract? No, it would probably be better to move cautiously and not get her hopes up.

"How many other artists are you interviewing?" she asked, wanting to see how long she'd have before she knew whether she had money coming in or not. She was interrupted by the howling and hissing of cats racing around the downstairs bedroom that was used as a storage area and throwing books and cups off the tables. There was a crash and more screams, which she tried to ignore.

"My cats," she said in explanation. She tried to get a feeling for this woman. Her aura was a curious mix of all kinds of colors. It wasn't a pleasant effect. Though Fiona could usually get at least a sense of a person if she tried, there was nothing to grab on to with Selene. It was like trying to grasp a hundred ghosts and having them all slip through her fingers.

"I understand how cats are," Selene said, her smile tight-lipped. "As for other artists, I'm not interviewing anyone else. Now, let me be specific about what I want in this portrait. You can block it out and bring in the beginning sketches within the week." She sat down on the couch, flicking aside some of the cat hair, settled Baast on the couch cushion and proceeded to tell Fiona exactly how she wanted the picture done.

"I expect to have a full figure done, with Baast at my feet. I want flowers around me to emphasize the aura you are going to give me. These magical signs are to be included at various points around the portrait and in the corner."

She handed Fiona a paper with symbols carefully printed on it. "I'm only sorry it can't be an oil painting. Gia says you are very good. However, there isn't time for that."

Fiona wished it were an oil painting too. The commission would easily have been double the payment for pen and charcoal work.

Gia looked at Baast, who glared back and then hissed.

She distinctly remembered that the shop cat had been a gray and white tabby, not an all-black bruiser with an attitude problem. However, if Selene wanted this animal in the picture instead of the mellow feline in the Major Arcana, who was she to argue?

Baast had been sniffing around, going to the very end of his leash to smell the scent of the other cats in the area. Fiona was glad no one had chosen to spray lately; she was sure Baast would have marked the territory, too.

What a strange animal, she thought. She'd finally met up with a feline she didn't like.

"If you don't mind, I'll take my leave now," Selene said, standing up and reeling Baast back to her side, pulling on the leash so that he skidded across the floor. The cat glowered at her and then leaped up on the couch, ready for Selene to pick him up.

"Oh, but you can't go! I need to take photos of you. It's a shame you didn't come in the daytime; the light would have given me much better pictures. Then we have to discuss what kind of dress you want and how you'd like to have your hair styled. And that's just the start."

"You may take the photographs. Everything else I leave up to you."

Within twenty minutes Fiona had shot three rolls, which she would have developed in the morning. Selene, still standing, wrote out a check for $4,000 and handed it to Fiona.

"Shall we make an appointment for, say, Friday at three? You can come to the shop, can't you? Please, bring your daughter. Perhaps we have something there that could be of benefit to her." With that pronouncement, Selene hurried toward the front door. "I'm sorry I can't take more time to talk to you, but things to do, things to do!" she said as she disappeared into the evening gloom.

Fiona closed the door behind Selene and Baast. There was another crash and the tinkle of something breaking from the room where she had sequestered the cats. She ran to let them out. Princess screamed at her and lashed her tail as she advanced into the family room. Fiona watched in fascination as four cats made a beeline for the couch where Baast had been sitting. Roddy, the largest male cat, instantly backed up and sprayed, marking the couch with his own scent to get rid of the intruder.

She grabbed paper towels and began to mop the vinyl. "Social comment, huh? Well, don't tell Harper what you think of the people I'm working for, all right?" She cleaned up the mess and put the flannel cover out to be washed.

18

"Good-bye, Gia and good riddance."
Those words had rung in Gia's ears for two weeks. Every time she reached for the phone, she drew back her hand because she knew Fiona didn't even want to hear her voice. The friendship was over and it was like having half of her cut off. The joking, the involvement with each other, the sharing of troubles and joys were all gone. In their place was a terrible void that none of her new friends could fill.

She'd done some long hard thinking since that awful fight, and she'd come to the conclusion that Fiona had been right. She had acted selfishly, and if she'd been any kind of friend, she'd have kept her word and made sure the ritual was just for the two of them. Unfortunately, it was too late to do anything about the trouble between her and Fiona.

Finally, since she couldn't change what had happened, Gia decided to concentrate on her newest novel. It had been hard to get back into the rhythm of writing after so many months away from the computer. She'd started with just a few hours the first day, picking up the story at the end of the pages Fiona had read. Each day she'd increased her writing time until she was back at her desk for ten or twelve hours a day. Within two weeks she had written about half the story and was positive it was the best work she'd ever done.

Then the writing had stopped. Yesterday had been barren. Today was like a desert. On top of it all, her back itched. She'd taken off all her clothes and tried to see if there was a welt or something that could be the cause of the itch, but her skin was pristine. She'd almost rubbed herself raw trying to scratch her backbone and nothing helped. All it did was make it worse and interrupt her writing more.

Gia stared at the screen. She was stuck—not quite writer's block, but close to it. If it had been a normal morning, she would have called Fiona and asked if she'd like to come over and talk for a while. But this wasn't a normal morning.

"I'll just have to break this writer's block myself."

She lit a small candle for concentration, put on her earphones and pressed the button that would start the sea sounds on the tape recorder. She turned back to the monitor. This time the flame of the candle and the soft ocean swells worked their magic and the words began to flow. As she wrote, she went deep into the trance that allowed her to watch her characters as they moved around in their own world. She was almost to the middle of a chase scene down a mountainside, with Rebecca and Jared in grave danger, when she became aware of a strange sound.

There was a regular thumping coming from somewhere around her. Neighbors playing their music too loud, she thought. The teenagers next door had been known to keep the sound up for several hours at a time, until someone called the cops and made them stop. This time someone else was going to have to take care of them, because she was too busy. She went back to the chase scene.

Gia had just gotten Rebecca and Jared safely down the

mountain and into an old abandoned mineshaft where they could hide until the people who were trying to kill them gave up the chase, when she heard a crash from the kitchen.

"What the hell was that?"

She removed her earphones so that she could hear more clearly. There was another loud bang and then the sound of glass breaking.

"That's not the neighbors." Suddenly her heart was beating in an uneven tattoo of terror. She'd had all kinds of daydreams about murder, she'd written about it and imagined all the various ways she could kill off her characters, but she'd never been threatened by a stranger in real life. The sounds coming from her lower floor definitely spelled danger. She picked up the knife she used as a letter opener and considered going downstairs after whoever was in her house. If she surprised them, she might be able to chase them back outside without hurting anyone.

She heard her copper pots and pans crash to the floor as someone knocked them off the rack over the entrance to the kitchen. Someone banged open a cupboard and swept out whole shelves of glassware.

"Maybe going after them isn't such a good idea," she whispered. Why hadn't she bought a gun and learned to use it?

Another blow against the wall of the kitchen startled her. It sounded as if they were bashing in the wallboard over the stove with a baseball bat.

"Shit," Gia whispered. She was in deep trouble this time.

Another crash and the sound of more copper being dropped to the floor let her know that whoever had been in the house hadn't left.

"Take whatever you want, buddy, just leave me alone!" she whispered. She was paralyzed with fright, afraid to move, but knew she had to take some action before the marauder made his way upstairs and found her in the office.

She forced herself to move toward the phone. Reaching out a shaking hand, she dialed 911.

"Someone has just broken in downstairs in my home," she said, trying to keep her voice calm. She was proud of herself for not screaming the way she wanted to. She could feel the shrieks bubbling up in her throat.

"Are you alone?" the 911 operator asked.

"Yes."

"Can you get out of the house without endangering yourself?"

"No," Gia said. "I could go out and down the ledge from the second story, but I'd be an open target. And if I just dropped to the concrete, I'd break every bone in my body and whoever is banging things around downstairs would be able to catch me." She stopped for a moment, listening.

"They've moved into the living room." She heard the sound of her television being smashed. There were a few moments of silence after that boom, and she hoped against hope that the person was dead or badly injured. The sounds resumed. No such luck.

"Can you get to a room where you can lock yourself in?"

"I'm in one," Gia said and ran over to the door to flip the lock shut. She was grateful for the time she'd taken to have the lock installed. The original purpose had been to stop Larry from coming into the office. It had been almost two years since he'd decided to start interrupting her every ten or fifteen minutes, just to make certain she didn't get any work done. Until the deadbolt had been placed, he'd been very effective.

"I've locked myself in."

"Fine, I've already dispatched a squad car. They should arrive in—seven minutes," the woman said, checking with the officers again.

Seven minutes. That was long enough for the person to

come upstairs, find her and try to kill her. Maybe jumping off the second-story ledge wasn't such a bad idea after all. She might be able to grab on to the branches of the almond tree to break her fall.

"Where are you exactly in the building?"

"Second floor at the back of the house in a bedroom that's been converted into an office."

"We'll stay on the phone with you until the officers get there. Can you still hear the person?"

"Goodbye Lenox," Gia sighed. "He's in the dining room breaking my Autumn plates."

"Don't worry about it," the operator said sharply. "Homeowner's insurance will pay for it. Don't even think of letting yourself out and going down to stop him." The operator's voice took on an urgency that told Gia the woman had been on the line before with people who did incredibly stupid things in the face of danger.

"The Lenox isn't that important," Gia said. "Wait—"

"Is something wrong?"

Gia hesitated. "The sounds have stopped. I can't tell where he is." Her voice rose as she fought the urge to cry, and she began breathing harder. Her fingernails were gouging bloody crescents in the palm of her left hand as she tried to control the urge to run, scream, anything to break the terror of being in a house with an unknown madman.

She still had the knife in her right hand, but it wouldn't do her much good in a close fight. Her hand was so sweaty that if she'd had to use the knife, it would have slipped out of her grasp.

"Do not open the door. Do not go out. The officers are on their way. They are only about two or three minutes away right now. Let them take care of it."

"I'm afraid," Gia said, her voice breaking.

"Afraid is natural. It's all right. Just don't do anything foolish!"

There was a faint footfall outside the door and Gia stopped breathing completely.

"He's outside," she whispered into the phone. "Please help me, he's outside my door!"

"The officers will be there. Don't do anything foolish," the woman said.

"He's turning the knob," Gia whispered. "He knows someone's in here. Oh God, he's going to kill me, I know he's going to kill me—" She screamed as something thumped hard against the door.

"He's trying to break in," she shrieked. "Tell them to hurry, oh please, tell them to hurry!" She screamed again as whoever was outside rammed against the door with a shoulder. The door bowed in and the molding cracked and splintered. The lock, which had never been meant to withstand an assault, screeched and then gave way as the figure thrust his way into the room. For just a moment his back was to her and then he turned around.

"The officers are only a couple of streets away," the woman was saying as Gia dropped the phone and backed away.

"It's my husband!" Gia shrieked, her voice thin and high. "No, Larry, please!"

Larry advanced on her, his hands up, ready to strike her. He had a murderous look in his eyes. His pupils were completely dilated. Whatever was happening, he was completely out of touch with reality.

"Where's the tape, Gia? I know you have it and I'm going to get it," Larry crooned. He was so far gone that nothing would stop him.

"I'm going to kill you and rid all of us of a plague on the earth, do you hear me?" He spit at her with each word.

"Help me," Gia shouted, hoping the operator was still on the other end of the line.

"Damn right, bitch." Larry came at her. "I'm going to

murder you and then I'm going after that two-bit son of a bitch you hired as your lawyer."

"No, get away from me!" She held the knife in her left hand and felt blindly behind her for her chair. She didn't want to be knocked off balance and fall where he could kick her.

"Don't even think about it, bitch." Larry grabbed the hand that held the knife and began to squeeze her wrist until she could hear the bones snapping with the pressure.

"Stop, you're going to break my arm!" She tried to push against him and at least use the knife to scare him, but he was too strong for her.

The knife dropped to the floor.

"There, that's the way I like you, all scared and ready to cry. My girl," Larry said, still using the crooning voice that made the hairs on the back of her neck rise. "Good baby, you're going to learn not to fight Larry, aren't you?" He grabbed her chin and shook her head slowly from side to side, bruising the delicate skin on her cheeks.

"You're going to like having Larry back and everything is going to be the way that it was. I'm not going to pay you any money and Kelly isn't going to have to pay any money and little Gia will go back to being a good girl."

Larry leaned over her. "Now, let's take care of that pretty face that's a dirty Indian brown. You know how I hate you when you've got a tan," Larry said. "Let's make your cheeks all pink and pretty." He began hitting her face with his open palms. Perfectly aimed slaps, one after the other, rang across her ears and cheeks. She tried to back away, lifting her arms to protect herself, but he was stronger than she was. He forced her arms down and pinned them behind her back as he held her against the wall.

"Now, you whore, you're going to find out what happens when you try and fight back." Larry began to punch her. She felt the impact of his fist against her right eye and suddenly she was looking at the world through red as the blood began to drip from her face.

The pain and the blood broke through the fear that had held her hostage. "You asshole, I told you if you ever touched me you'd be dead," she screamed. She heard Asron's voice say with absolute clarity, "You can hurt him."

She managed to free one hand and hit Larry, striking him on the nose.

He slapped her again and she lifted her right leg in an instinctive gesture, cringing away from him and trying to cover herself as he aimed for her stomach with the next blow.

Her shoes! Heavy wooden Swedish clogs that she always wore while she was writing. They were the perfect weapon.

She raised her right leg again, as if she were trying to knee him. Larry moved back out of range, just as she had hoped he would. She called up strength from places she didn't even know existed and brought the heavy shoe down onto the top of his foot, smashing the bones with the wood. She could feel his foot collapse under the weight, bones breaking in the soft expensive Italian leather loafer, which offered no protection at all.

Larry bellowed and stepped back. He tried to take a breath to howl again, but he couldn't get the air into his lungs, which had spasmed with the onslaught of pain.

Gia gasped as she tried to catch her breath. What was happening? Larry had never acted like this in his life—it was like watching some stranger take over the body of a man she had once loved. A horrible thought crept into her mind, teasing her with the possibility that this was all a result of her witchcraft. She had bound him so that he couldn't hurt her. Even though he'd landed a couple of punches, he'd ended up hurt a lot worse than her. And what would have happened to her if she hadn't done that spell against him?

Larry swung again, but this time it was to find something to support him as he began to black out.

"Hold it right there!" A policeman stepped through the broken door, his hand on his gun.

Larry's lips were blue and his eyes bugged out as he tried to force the oxygen into his lungs. "Help me," he managed to croak.

The officer looked at Gia's battered and bloody face, her eye, which was already swelling, and the black-and-blue marks on her puffed skin and grabbed Larry. They swung him around and brought his hands behind his back. One officer took out a thin plastic tie and snapped it around his wrists.

"I'll call an ambulance," one of the officers said. He noticed the phone hanging from the desk and picked it up.

"911," Gia said, trying to explain as best she could who was on the other line.

"Laura, that you?" the officer said. He waited for confirmation. "Yeah, we're bringing him in. And send an ambulance for the woman, she's in pretty bad shape, but at least she's alive."

"No!" Gia tried to say. Her lips were so swollen that she could barely talk.

"No?" the cop asked, surprised.

"Please, I'll be all right."

She could see the look of contempt in the cop's eyes. He'd seen it all before, she was sure, the battered wives who let the men do it and then when help was offered, backed away as if it were their fault it had happened.

"I'll press charges, but I don't want to go to the hospital. I hate hospitals." She didn't feel like explaining that Larry had canceled her medical insurance and she didn't have the money to pay for her own care.

The officer shook his head in resignation. "Okay, we can't force you."

Larry finally managed to take a deep breath. He looked at Gia with real hatred in his eyes. He pulled against the plastic strap but only succeeded in making it tighter around his wrist.

"You wouldn't dare charge me with anything," he rasped.

"This time there are a few more witnesses," Gia said. Every movement sent fresh pain through her. Her lips were so swollen that each time she spoke she tasted fresh blood.

"I should have killed you."

"But you didn't."

"Damn lawyer of yours. He wants my money and Kelly's too, just to pay you. He's not getting it. I'll kill you first."

The officer had heard enough. He yanked Larry forward and propelled him down the stairs.

"Are you sure about that ambulance, ma'am?" he asked at the bottom of the stairs.

Gia nodded.

"Will you actually press charges against him?" The policeman looked at her hopefully.

Gia nodded. It was easier than trying to talk.

"Thank you," the officer said, grinning. "Take care of yourself, then. We'll talk to you tomorrow." He turned back one last time. "Are you sure you don't want to go to the hospital? You still look like you're in pretty bad shape."

"I know I am. But I don't have any insurance. I can't afford to pay the hospital."

The cop looked truly shocked.

"Don't you know that you can go to the hospital and charge this bozo for everything it costs you? You could wipe him out with medical bills alone."

Gia began to smile, even though she thought she'd die

of the pain. "Call an ambulance, I'm going to the hospital," she said happily.

She was surprised when the hospital decided to keep her overnight to make sure there were no internal injuries. She'd have loved to call Fiona and tell her all about it, once the pain medications took effect. But they weren't talking anymore. They might never talk again. She had never felt so alone in her entire life.

It was funny, she thought, she missed Fiona more than she did Larry, or at least the new Larry who had taken the place of the man she'd been married to for all those years.

If only he'd acted like such a shit early in their marriage, it would have been better. She could have walked away from the marriage the first time he hit her, and gotten on with her life without him cluttering up all those years.

When she opened the front door of her house, she deliberately didn't look into the family room or the dining room to see what kind of mess Larry had made before the cops hauled him away. Instead, she headed upstairs to the bathroom to take a shower. Nothing could ever convince her that hospital bathrooms were as clean or as safe and cozy as her own. She stood in the shower for what seemed like hours as the cold water cascaded across her battered face and body. She whimpered as she touched her stomach, where he'd landed a heavy punch, and her face felt as if someone were pouring acid in the wounds when the fine spray hit the open cuts. After a few minutes, the pain began to abate and she turned up the heat.

When the hot water finally gave out, she climbed out of the shower, changed into fresh clothes and began to work on cleaning up the house.

The surprise came when she looked in the pantry that connected to the back door. Larry had opened the back door, brought in the two suitcases he'd left home with, set them down in the pantry and proceeded to smash up the house. So that was what he'd been talking about. Larry had thought she would allow him to move back into the house and live with her.

"So what happened with Kelly dearest? Did she leave you when it looked like it might cost her some money? Oh poor baby," she murmured. "You always were a spoiled brat who wanted his own way, but never like this."

She made a quick call to a locksmith, who promised to come right out and change every lock in the house.

She had just started picking up the pieces of her good china and the locksmith had replaced the locks on every outside door when Asron opened the front door and walked into the disaster. He sneezed as he came into the hallway.

"Asron, what a surprise." Gia looked behind him to see the front door standing wide open. "I thought I told the locksmith to close everything behind him, but he obviously didn't listen."

"He listened. But locks don't bother me too much," Asron said.

Gia smiled, but a little frisson of discomfort raced through her.

Asron moved closer and took her face gently in his hands, turning her to the sunlight so that he could see the damage. "What happened to you? I heard the crying and then the incredible rush of anger. I knew hurt; then you were out of the house and I didn't know where to find you, only that you were being taken care of. I came as soon as you were home. I take it Larry came back?"

Gia nodded and gave him a rundown on the previous day's horror and the stay in the hospital. While they talked, both of them picked and sorted through the broken and bashed kitchenware. Gia was putting everything away in boxes and trash cans until the insurance adjuster could come out and examine the damage.

Halfway through the cleaning, Asron and Gia sat down

for coffee. Gia's face was hurting so badly that she knew she had to put ice against the bruises to numb them or she'd never be able to survive the rest of the day and evening. She was glad for the emergency packs she always kept in the freezer.

She dug the packs out and sat in the recliner in the family room with her cheeks against the ice. She appreciated Asron's quiet acceptance of her battered face and bruised ego.

"You know, I've been worrying about you because the forces are gathering around you. You've changed the balance a little by joining the coven with Selene and me and the others, but you could still be in danger. This attack from Larry could be a manifestation of that disturbance. That's why I wanted to come with you when you had the ritual with Fiona. I hoped we could iron out those ripples that are happening." He finished with a sneeze.

"So what do you suggest I do so that these things don't keep happening? I need to be able to work and earn money, not be stopped all the time by troubles that I can't even anticipate." Gia was almost crying.

"What do you really want from us? Remember, I told you weeks ago that we could help, if you'd ask us. You are a part of the coven now, you are one of our own; we'll do anything we can to make your life better now that you are tied to us."

Gia hesitated for a minute. If Larry hadn't beaten her, she never would have given voice to what she felt. Before this, she would have simply said that she wanted Larry to leave her alone and for his prick to shrivel up and fall off. But now everything had changed.

"Don't ask me questions like that right now, because I might answer that I want him dead, and then think how I'd feel if he actually turned up in a morgue."

Asron nodded. "You'd feel guilty, wouldn't you? But that's so silly. Anything can be arranged. And you know, there's something else we can do that builds protective powers around you," he said softly. He came over to stand beside the recliner and his thumb began to massage the areola of her breast through the material of her blouse. The caress was rewarded by her nipples standing out against the fabric of her shirt. It was, however, a completely automatic reaction.

She shrugged his hand away. "I don't want to go to bed with you right now."

"It will make the pain feel better. I promise you. And this time you'll help me with every part of this," he said, his voice husky. "I have some special candles and oils in the car and a few other odds and ends that should help you call the Goddess into you. We'll have a wonderful time."

"I don't think so," Gia said through swollen lips. She kept waiting for some indication that he realized that what he was asking was impossible, but it never came. Instead, the impossible happened to Asron. One instant he was fully erect, and the next he was soft and flaccid. Even with him fully dressed, it was impossible to miss the change.

Gia was shocked. She'd never seen Asron have any trouble maintaining an erection.

"What—oh, this has never happened before!" He was obviously horrified, but neither horror nor embarrassment brought back any fullness to him.

Only the ringing of the front-door bell saved him further mortification.

Elf stood in the entrance when she answered it. "Wow," Elf said as he looked at Gia's face, which had swollen like a melon and taken on a rich blue and yellow coloring as the bruises spread. "You did need help. I would have come last night, but I knew you were at the hospital."

Gia rolled her eyes. "What is this? Does everyone in the world have a link to my private psyche, like I'm broadcasting on PSYK 100 FM?"

"Not exactly, but close enough." Elf followed her into

the kitchen. "What happened here? It looks like a war broke out."

"It did. Her husband tried to kill her. I thought you were supposed to stop things like that from happening," Asron said as he walked into the room to confront Elf. Gia was glad to see that Asron's erection hadn't reappeared as he entered the room.

She watched as Elf's eyes narrowed by a fraction. He straightened and she noticed that his hands clenched at the sight of the other man. "I can only help when I'm told what's going on. No one warned me that Larry would react this way."

"So how did you get here today then? Ride your broom over after you 'sensed' there'd be trouble yesterday? A little late, aren't you?"

"Don't be obnoxious. I didn't 'sense' there'd be trouble. One of the arresting officers on the case is my brother-in-law, and he knew I was representing Gia," Elf said, his teeth clenched so hard that his jaw stood out in rock-like relief.

"You'd better moderate your tone of voice with me, Elf. Remember, I know a lot of your clients and I could cause you real problems," Asron warned him.

"Don't bother threatening. If your acquaintances who are my clients want to leave, then let them go. But I don't think Gia is going to allow you to use her again, particularly not when it's only her pain you want to use."

"What the hell are you talking about?" Gia interrupted them.

"He wanted to have sex with you, didn't he?"

Gia turned bright red. "Yes, but I turned him down."

"Good, because all he wanted was to use the power that would come out of your pain. That's what he and Selene do, they use people up and throw them away and then go looking for the next victim. You just happen to be vulnerable right now."

"You don't know what you're getting into." Asron

turned on his heel and stalked down the hallway toward the front door. He didn't look back at Gia as he slammed the door behind him.

"What the hell was that about?" she demanded.

"Asron doesn't want you for yourself. You know that. Why are you having such trouble accepting that this man isn't good for you?"

"Come on, you just don't like Asron."

"Can't stand him or Selene," Elf said.

"So why did you come with me that night when the fire started?"

"Because I knew you would need help. Haven't you figured out yet that Asron and Selene are dangerous for you? They're offering nothing in return for your devotion. They probably caused the scene with Larry, staged it by using their influence to give him the idea to come over here and beat you up. They thrive on pain and disaster in other people. Somehow it gives them strength." He leaned over and pulled gently on the magician's figure that hung around her neck. "And you'd be far better off not wearing this anymore. It ties you to them."

Gia reached up and touched the figure. It was uncomfortably warm. "I've grown very attached to the little guy."

"I bet you have," Elf said.

She played with the figure for a few moments, but did not lift it from her neck.

"Okay, if you don't want to remove the amulet, would you consider wearing an iron ring as protection?"

"Against what?"

"How about goblins and trolls?" Elf fished something out of his pocket and handed it to her.

Gia looked at the ring and almost wrinkled her nose in distaste. "It's nothing but a plain old iron nail bent into the shape of a ring. This is the kind of jewelry you expect me to wear? At least the magician is pretty."

"Please?"

She slipped the ring onto her finger.

"Good girl," Elf said as he moved into the living room to survey the damage.

"Larry did all this?" Elf asked.

"He decided to come after me. He didn't like the papers you served him with."

"Tough tits. I don't like him either. And this is going to cost him a lot of money. I know you have a video camera, so let's go to work. I need shots of you, shots of the house and the mess that he left, and then we'll go upstairs and you can show me your office. I'll stay the night and tomorrow I'll get a restraining order from a judge to keep Larry away from here."

He looked over just in time to see Gia sag against the wall. He grabbed her just before she slid down to the floor. He carried her upstairs, not even puffing as he pushed open the door and walked into her bedroom.

"Okay, we'll do the videotaping later. For right now, rest," he said as he laid her on the bed. "I'll stand guard. We may yet need help, though. Sometimes Thor's hammer isn't enough against the others." He touched the stylized penis and testicle pendant.

"You're being melodramatic. Nothing is going to happen to us." Gia yawned. "The only thing that's wrong is I'm tired from the beating and hospitals aren't restful. This is the real world and Thor's hammer is just a pendant same as that silly little wizard and the ring made out of bent nail."

"You don't know what you're talking about, but you're too tired for me to reason with you," Elf said. He held her as she closed her eyes and dropped into a deep dream-filled sleep. While she slept he did what he could to neutralize the power of the magician.

19

Fiona looked at the finished sketch. Baast was very good, one of the best cat portraits she'd ever done. Every inch of menace and disdain showed in the way he held himself and the look he gave the world in general. Selene, however, was more difficult to catch. It was strange. Fiona had all those pictures to work from, yet capturing the look of the woman had proved more of a challenge than she'd thought possible.

Even the new charcoals and pencils Harper had picked up at an art store in the city as a peace offering couldn't make the portrait work the way Fiona wanted. The new pencils were wonderful, though, smoother and less prone to smudge that anything else she'd ever had. She'd been lavish in her thanks, just to make certain Harper knew how happy she was with his present.

There was something strange about Selene's head. It wasn't misshapen or out of proportion, but when she went to draw it, she found herself instinctively adding dark spots that had no relation to anything she could see in the photographs.

She'd started the same portrait four times and each time, when she came back to the mundane world from wherever she went to when she painted, the spots had been there. She'd tried erasing them, but she could not lighten the pigment enough.

"Mom?" Megan knocked on the door and came into the studio. "The headache is worse and nothing's stopping it."

Fiona sighed. She laid down the new pencil and closed the large notebook in which she'd been sketching the various images she wanted to put together into the portrait. It seemed that more and more lately, she'd just start work on a project, only to find that Megan needed still more help, time and comfort.

It wasn't that she begrudged her daughter the time she spent with her, but once in a while she heard her work calling forlornly in the background and knew she wasn't going to be able to take care of it until Megan was better.

Or dead, the thought popped into her mind, but she pushed it firmly aside. Megan wasn't going to die.

"What the hell do you think is happening to make this headache worse?"

"It started when that woman was here and it just won't stop," Megan answered. "It doesn't matter how much morphine you give me, the pain just stays there banging away inside my head like some nasty little gremlin is trying to hack his way out."

"Honey, I'm sure Selene's visit had nothing to do with your headache. It's just coincidence."

Fiona looked at her daughter and knew she had to do something to help her.

"I know what I'm going to do. If everything is all right, we'll go on to the Major Arcana after we've seen the doctors. Dr. Anders isn't in this week, but one of the other physicians there is going to have to see you as an emergency case. I don't know what's going on and I don't want to give you more and more medicine without someone knowing how high the dosage has become."

It had been over a year since anyone had even ventured an idea for a solution to the headaches. Mostly the doctors looked at Megan, shook their heads and upped the medication again.

Dr. Kamchatka was the newest, brightest and best neurosurgeon on the staff. He'd only seen Megan once before and then only for ten minutes. Still, he was better than no physician at all.

"Come on, kid, we'll give him a try."

Dr. Kamchatka checked Megan. He took tests and ran her through an MRI just to make sure they weren't missing anything. He ran a blood test and had it analyzed stat to see what the blood levels of her medicine were and if there were any other anomalies.

Finally, he sat on the side of the uncomfortably hard examination table and patted Megan on the hand. "I don't know what's going on. A couple of the tests came back a little questionable, but nothing that I can tell you right now is causing the pain. The shunt is functioning. Everything is fine there. I'm beginning to wonder if we shouldn't start looking at the psychological ramifications. Maybe there's a payback going on here that we haven't looked at. Maybe Megan likes being sick and no one has ever talked to her about that. She should be well for whatever time she has, or at least she shouldn't be allowed to act like a sick child."

"Damn it, she *is* a sick child!"

Fiona could see the tears start to form before her daughter closed her eyes in despair. She'd heard it all before. Psychological, the doctors had said, and then they'd found out that there was something physically wrong. The most the doctors had ever done was apologize for doubting Megan.

Fiona gritted her teeth as she talked to the doctor. "The pain is real. It shows all the signs of being caused by extra pressure somewhere within her skull. The pain is as physical as it would be if I kicked you in the knees and made everything bend new and wonderful ways. Of course, as you lay on the floor screaming and writhing in pain, I could tell you it's all psychological and we'd both know that was a bunch of hooey, wouldn't we?" She'd stopped herself from saying "shit" just in time.

"There'd be an explanation for my pain," Dr. Kamchatka said reasonably.

"There's an explanation for her pain, too. Brain tumors and shunts have a way of causing pain. Do you know that over the years, we've been told at least five times that everything that happened to her was psychological? And for every one of those five times the agony that she endured needlessly was caused by something physical that endangered her life. But not one time was the pain caused by a psychological problem."

She advanced on Dr. Kamchatka until he was flat against the wall, with her leaning toward him. "Now, I want to know if you can come up with an answer. Can you help, or can you tell us where to go to get more relief for her? I'm telling you, this is a pressure problem. Whether it's from the shunt or from the tumor, it still has to be taken care of. Somewhere, sometime, there has to be someone who can deal with this by doing something more than recommending medication to cover it all up."

"We have no proof of that yet. As I said, there are a couple of tests that are equivocal and a couple that I'm not prepared to talk to you about. Dr. Anders will have to do that when he comes back, because Megan is his patient and I'm just filling in."

"Then fill in by helping her. Give me names of people to take her to, give me medications that will help instead of just cover it up. But don't just abandon us and try to say that it's all psychological."

The physician shook his head and slid away from Fiona. "I will do what I can. I'll research it to see if there's any treatment that will help. But for now, just keep giving her the drugs."

Megan was crying by the time they left the hospital, and Fiona didn't feel much better.

"I don't want more medicine," Megan said as she climbed into the car and put her head back against the rest. "It's making me sick and the doctors aren't going to do anything else for me."

Fiona looked at her daughter and saw something that startled her so badly that she swerved the car to the side of the road and sat there shaking.

She looked again, hoping she was wrong. But there it was, just as she'd seen it moments before—Megan's aura was dark, almost black, shot through with pulsating blue and green. Even if she'd never studied a thing about the colors of the soul, she would have known that her daughter was nearing the end of her existence if something wasn't done.

"Goddess, if you are there, help me!" Fiona asked, voicing her plea. Megan looked at her, startled, but didn't say anything.

"Come on, whoever is supposed to be up there, I need a blinding insight, I need something to tell me what to do. There has to be help for this kid!"

She pulled out into traffic again and made her way to the Major Arcana.

"Damn it, there has to be help for you, Megan. I just don't know where to find it. Sometimes I think I'm going to have to come up with the cure for the pain, because no one else is willing to try."

"Try what? Cut me open and see what they can find? They've done that. All it does is make the headache go away until the anesthetic wears off. Face it, Mom, nothing is going to cure me."

Fiona pulled over and parked and held her daughter while she wept.

Megan sniffed and wiped away her tears. "I can't even cry, it hurts too much."

"Would getting out of the car help? We're right by the Major Arcana. You'd like the cats they have inside."

Megan nodded and followed her mother into the shop.

Selene hurried forward when Fiona entered, as if she'd been waiting for her. She took the notebook out of Fiona's hand before she could begin showing the woman the sketches she had done.

"Yes, this one, with me turned slightly to the side. And how perfect, you've caught Baast's good side, too. As if he really had one," she added, looking down at the cat, who was rubbing against her legs. She shook him off. "Bad cat, you broke eighty dollars' worth of glass this morning and you did a naughty on the front carpet. I don't want you around me right now."

"You shouldn't scold him," Fiona said. Even though she didn't like the cat, she knew that Baast was only reacting to the emotional turmoil around him.

Selene nodded, though it was obvious she didn't agree. Her smile was definitely forced. "This has been an especially bad day," she explained. "First Baast acts up and then the health inspectors come by. They've shut us down and I've got several hundred dollars' worth of stuff in the refrigerator going bad because we won't be open for lunch for a week at least."

"Shut you down?" Fiona was suddenly glad she'd never eaten at the small sandwich bar.

"Yes, and for the most bizarre reasons. Like our waitresses sometimes work barefoot—apparently that's illegal. And we don't have everyone wear hairnets because they look so tacky and they've said that no one can be in the kitchen area without them. Stupid things, as if my luck has turned to shit."

Selene clapped her hand over her mouth as if she'd said something she shouldn't have. Hastily she turned her attention back to the sketches. "Everything you've done is fine. It will be ready for next week?"

Fiona nodded. "On time."

"And you'll be sure and come to our little get-together to show off your work, won't you? We'll be expecting you around eight Saturday night."

Fiona nodded, since she didn't know how to turn down the invitation gracefully. But it was a cinch she couldn't be appearing at any party if Harper had anything to say about it.

Selene moved toward the sunlight to study the pictures again and Fiona looked at her as she stood in the light. She closed her eyes, shook her head and looked again. In the pictures at home, she could have sworn that Selene didn't look much more than forty-five at the most. But today in the sunlight, she looked at least ten, possibly fifteen years older. If Fiona hadn't known better, she would have said that the skin around Selene's neck had begun to sag in the few days since she'd last seen her. There were more prominent wrinkles around her eyes, and her hair was beginning to show the wispy white of an old lady instead of the healthy luxuriant hair of someone who had gone prematurely silver. Suddenly Selene looked old and sick. Even her aura was a dark greenish brown, like sewage that had been left to rot in the sun.

"I suppose I have to give these back," Selene said, as she laughingly held on to the sketches for just a few more moments.

"I'm afraid so. I definitely need them," Fiona said, recovering the book.

"Mom?" Megan called her mother from the front door. When Fiona didn't respond immediately, she came and grabbed her mother by the hand and pulled like a little kid.

"Oh, just a moment," Selene said. She hurried toward the back of the store. She returned with a tiny green box that looked as if it could have been dug out of some Egyptian tomb. The green glass was encased in a filigree of gold set with several stones that might have been precious.

Fiona had the distinct feeling that somewhere she'd seen another green box just like it. But that was impossible, she decided. There couldn't be two of these in the world.

"Here," Selene said, handing it to her. "It's filled with a recipe that might help the headaches. I distilled the flowers and herbs into a very strong tincture and then dried it. Be careful that you use no more than about an eighth of a teaspoonful at a time. I'll ask you how it worked next time you visit." She smiled at Megan.

"Thank you," Fiona said, taking the tiny container and tucking it into her purse. "I hope it works."

Megan, however, turned and abruptly left the store without even bothering to say thank you to the older woman.

"Sorry, she's difficult sometimes when the pain and morphine get to her."

Megan was waiting by the car, and almost fell into the seat when her mother opened the door for her.

"It's really bad, Mom," she panted, trying hard not to cry because tears made the pain worse. "Can we go back to the hospital? Because I think something is wrong."

Fiona didn't even argue. She simply circled back to the hospital, had Dr. Kamchatka paged and told him to do something for Megan.

"But I already did everything," he objected.

"Then admit her to the hospital until you get a brainstorm, because she can't go on in this kind of pain," Fiona insisted. "I'm not going to deal with this at home. Can't you see the child is not going to make it too much longer?" Even as she looked, she could see the darker blue of the aura beginning to fade to black as Megan put her head back against the chair.

"Look at her, she's almost in a coma. Megan, can you still hear me?"

Megan muttered something unintelligible and slowly began to slide toward the floor. Fiona grabbed her before she fell. "Look at this! You can't just ignore it!"

"I can't put her in the hospital when there's nothing to treat. Look, Mrs. Kendrick, I did all the tests this morning. There just isn't anything more I can do. She's not even my patient, and I can't accept responsibility for any new treatment without Dr. Anders having a say in it. If you want, we can change her to a different pain medication, but that's all we can offer you. Otherwise I'll have to ask you to leave."

"But she's dying!" Fiona said, her voice betraying all the agony she tried to conceal from Megan.

"That may be true, but that doesn't mean I can do anything about it. You have to accept that sometimes things happen that none of us can help."

Fiona glared at the man. "Not to my daughter. You are going to find a cure for her."

"I would if I could, but there are some miracles I just can't pull off. I'll leave a triplicate for a stronger pain med at the pharmacy," he said and walked out of the room, leaving both Fiona and Megan stunned and in tears at his betrayal.

Fiona closed her eyes and pounded the bed in frustration, until her hand hit the chart Dr. Kamchatka had left behind on the examination table.

Desperate for some kind of answer, Fiona began to flip through the results that had been phoned in from the various departments where Megan had gone for tests. She stopped at the MRI study, but couldn't quite make out what the physician who had interpreted the test was saying. She looked up at the film that was still clipped into the light board in the room and then back at the report. "Sagittal TR 0.5 seconds, TE 11 msec" and "linear area of higher T2, signal areas of high T2 intensity in right frontoparietal region."

Yes, she could see that there were small areas that

looked like bright spots on the film. Maybe that was what the physician had been talking about.

She turned the page to Dr. Kamchatka's summary of the earlier visit.

"Possible metastasis throughout the brain. Further testing will determine if the glioma has spread. There is little help that can be afforded by treatment at this time. Palliative measures should be increased as necessary."

Fiona's legs began to buckle as she read the writing again and again to make certain she hadn't made a mistake. She couldn't think, couldn't hear, couldn't see anything except that death sentence for her daughter. No help. No help anywhere for Megan. Her beautiful, special daughter was going to die and there was no way to stop it. She turned to Megan and saw that her eyes were still closed. She was glad, because she was sure Megan would have read the terrible news from the anguish on her face.

"It's a good thing you're not in the room, you bastard," Fiona muttered. "Psychological problems? You call dying just a little difficulty that a psychiatrist can help with? And you lie to me and say that nothing is showing up on the MRI that should cause concern? Fuck you, you bastard!"

Fiona managed to get Megan out to the car and start home. She wasn't going to tell her daughter. Maybe if she didn't say anything, Megan wouldn't know what the diagnosis was and would live in spite of the malignancies that were even now growing out of control, draining her life from her.

Fiona helped Megan into the house. Already she could see the weakness that was consuming her daughter.

"Do you want to use some of this potion, just to see if it will work? Maybe it's got something illegal in it, like cocaine or marijuana, and that's how it eases the pain," Fiona said, only half joking. Anything would be welcome at this point.

"No," Megan said. "Just give me some of the stuff that Dr. Kamchatka ordered. I need it right now."

Fiona shrugged and placed the fancy box on the mantel, where it would be safe from the depredations of the cats. She wasn't going to fight Megan to have her take the tincture. Maybe later she'd be able to accept it. The gold and gems sparkled as they caught the late-afternoon light and she thought again how strange it was that Selene would give her something so obviously old and valuable. It was almost like the bottle of wine that she'd given her. Fiona started guiltily as she remembered that she had never told Selene she'd broken the old glass bottle.

"I wonder where I've seen that box before?"

Fiona prepared a huge glass of iced tea and went upstairs with Megan. She positioned the pillows on the back of the bed so that she had a comfortable place to lean back against. She turned the radio to soft music and put the three down pillows that Megan liked best across her lap. Then she sat with her daughter's head in her lap. Several of the cats took up positions around them on the bed and waited, holding vigil for their mistress. Even old Loner came into the room and lay down on the worn braided rug at the side of the bed. He was learning to make his way around on only three legs with only a few mishaps on the stairs, but he was still tired and frail after his run-in with the steel trap.

As Fiona rubbed her daughter's head with the rose cream and waited for the new medicines to at least ease the torture, she sang the old songs, hoping something would bring relief.

It took almost an hour before Megan finally dropped off to sleep. Fiona watched her for several minutes and then went into her studio. She didn't shut her door as she usually did. She needed to be able to hear Megan if she began to stir.

She tried to work on the drawing for Selene, knowing that she had a deadline, but nothing came out right. All she could see was the thick file with Dr. Kamchatka's notes. She turned on the storm sounds again, hoping they would put her into the mood and take her mind off Megan.

She began to sketch, letting her mind run free. It was her way of communicating with forces other than those of the everyday world. Sometimes answers came to her through her drawings, and that was what she was hoping for this time.

Outside, the first signs of clouds began to form in the sky. Weather forecasters on the television stations began to mention a new storm front developing that no one had seen before. It was unusual for this time of year, but they could get rain.

Fiona sketched without even looking at what she was drawing. Instead, she concentrated on the storm, on the power of the lightning, to bring her the answer she needed. The first drops of rain hit the window, but she didn't look up or even hear them as she let her mind roam, seeking an answer.

Finally, in the middle of a drenching downpour, she heard a car laboring up the hill. She looked at the time. It wouldn't be Harper; he'd said he would be late.

Now, in addition to everything else, she was going to have to tell Harper that they were losing the fight with Megan.

She wondered who was in the truck that had gone up the hill, then turned back to her sketch.

She was astonished to see what she had drawn while letting her mind roam. There was Selene, but a changed Selene. Instead of the ageless forty-plus woman Fiona had known for a few weeks, she was old, haggard, almost a crone. The drawing in the background showed her young and pretty, as she had been the first time Fiona saw her. "How interesting. Shades of Dorian Gray," Fiona murmured.

Behind Selene there was another figure, shadowy, bent with age. Asron? She wasn't sure. Fiona herself was there, standing in the middle, sheltering Megan, with her cats beside her. There were heavy lines drawn to the various figures from the center, connections sideways and through the middle. Evidently Fiona's mind was convinced that she was still tied to Gia, because her friend was in the picture, as were Elf Gunnerson and Harper, the three of them standing with their arms linked. It was like a spiderweb connecting everyone.

Maybe Harper was right, maybe there is something to his worrying about Selene, she thought. She was surprised that the woman had shown up in her drawing about Megan.

Fiona was willing to listen to any idea her subconscious came up with, but the only thing that kept bobbing to the surface was simply too ludicrous to give any attention to.

There's no way Selene could cause the cancer to metastasize, she thought. It's growing again because the treatments Megan had before didn't work. We were told there was only a twenty percent cure rate, and damn it, she's going to be in the eighty percent.

Her ruminations were shattered by a popping sound from up the hill.

"Damn, gunshots again," she said, running for the back door. The neighborhood kids had gotten rifles over the spring break and they'd been shooting at everything that moved. She was going to have to call the cops if it didn't stop.

She opened the back door and stepped out into the darkening evening. There was another pop; then someone started to walk along the path between the top of her hill and the house above her.

"Hey, you, what's going on up there!" she yelled. "What the hell are you shooting at!"

"Animal Control," a male voice boomed at her.

"What do you mean, Animal Control? What are you shooting at and who gave you permission, anyway?" She hated Animal Control. As far as she could see, their only reason for living was to make sure that if a human and an animal came in contact with each other, the animal died.

"We've shot eight skunks. Six in a litter and the two adults. That male was a big bruiser, ten years old and twenty pounds if I don't miss my bet. You might want to close up your windows until the smell goes away." The man sounded jovial, as if there were nothing in the world wrong with killing animals. Just a job, of course.

"Why did you do that? Who told you to come out here and kill them!" Fiona screamed at him. Her skunks. Her babies, no more than the size of two-week-old kittens, animals she'd watched from their first venture to the cat food she set out each night. She'd laughed when they stamped at each other and threatened in mock battles long before their scent glands were ready to work. Her skunks. The animals she'd carefully nurtured and kept around her yard to eat the slugs and snails that decimated everyone else's garden.

Damn it, he'd killed her mama skunk, the one she'd nursed through a bite that had laid the skunk's rear leg open from the hip to the toes. Fiona had put out antibiotic and extra vitamins on the food and the mama had lived, even though she'd always limped after that. The dad had been around, waddling up and down the hill patrolling his area, a patriarch who had learned to survive around humans until someone played dirty and trapped and murdered him.

Gone. She'd never see them again, with their delicate muzzles and tiny feet and enchanting wildness.

Dead.

"Who told you to kill them?" she screamed again.

"The man up here didn't want them under his deck. That's why we trap and kill them." The officer was clearly aware that she was about as angry as it was humanly possible to be. "Look, lady, they carry rabies. We kill them if we find them and there's nothing you can do about it." He turned and strode off to his truck.

"That old fart didn't want him under his deck? Couldn't

he have waited until they grew up and left? Couldn't he have waited until natural predators took them? No, he had to have them killed because in the fight between human and animal the animal loses until it becomes an endangered species, and then it's too late to do anything about it."

She was crying now, the tears washing down her face and making it impossible to see. She looked over at the feeder, knowing she'd never see her favorites there again. She could put out the old oatmeal cookies, but they'd never come to pick them up in their delicate claws and nibble at the edges. No more stale popcorn snacks, no more sliding into the water and splashing out again in baby skunk games.

She didn't want to think of the terror the skunks must have felt when they crouched in the back of the cage, trying to get away from their captors, but with no way out of the prison. They wouldn't have understood. Their only contacts with humans had been good ones until the bitter, nasty old man up the hill decided he couldn't stand to have something living around him.

"Why the hell didn't you die, you miserable excuse for a human, instead of killing them?" Fiona said. She could imagine the bullet striking them in the head, blasting away until there was nothing left but blood and scraps of flesh where once there had been a wonderful animal that deserved to live a lot more than most of the humans she knew.

She remembered the warning Harper had given her. When witchcraft backfires, it hurts everyone around. He'd foretold the future with frightening accuracy when he'd said Megan would get worse and someone would harm their animals.

He'd predicted the murders that had just happened. What he hadn't counted on was Fiona's fury at the events of the day.

"Bastards! I've got news for whoever is pushing me with bad luck. I've just had the last of your shit. A good witch harms none? Well, then I've just turned into the blackest worst-case witch you ever met. You don't know reality if you think I'm going to walk away from this and not fight back.''

20

R evenge!"
Revenge for Loner and all the other animals the
neighbor had hurt or destroyed.

Fiona whirled into action, gathering everything she'd
ever used in making magic. Salt and wine, water and crystal
to hold the candles, all went onto the table in the middle of
the living room. There wasn't going to be any more hiding.
Hiding hadn't ever done her any good. She'd finally decided, once and for all, that if Harper didn't like her new
religion, that was just too bad. She'd supported him when
he went through the Eastern mysticism and Nehru jacket
phase when they were still in college. Now he could take
her as she came, and that meant witchcraft and all.

She grabbed her sacred Ginsu from the bottom drawer
in the kitchen. She'd been fairly certain it wouldn't be disturbed because no one ever did serious cooking except her.
She hurried out into the dark of her garden. She could feel
the souls of the skunks, like sad little remnants of the animals she had known.

"I will kill the people who did this to you," she said, and

began to gather the rue, foxglove, nightshade and hemlock to use in the spells she was about to craft. She knew none of her books would help her; they all said a witch must never do anything to harm anyone else. Well, they'd never been faced with the disasters she had. The assaults on Megan and the animals were the last straw.

She'd always been able to cause things to happen when she thought hard enough about them. She'd never told anyone, even Harper, about the talent. Her mother had whipped her for being "different" the same way she'd whipped her for drawing auras. Now she knew that her mother and father had been wrong when they punished her. Her talent wasn't something from the devil. It was meant to take care of her and her family, and that was exactly how she was going to use her gift.

Fiona began to cast the spell with the doors wide open so that she could see and hear the storm outside. The lights had gone out when the storm started; the only illumination came from the candles on the altar. As she spoke, she focused on the power of the tempest pounding the house.

"I am powerful and I demand revenge on the man in the house at the top of the hill," she said, concentrating as hard as she could to place the image clearly before her.

She mentally walked through the man's house and finally found him in his kitchen.

"That's all for you, you son of a bitch."

She thought of the man's heart. She looked at it closely as it pulsed. Then with all her might she wished the potency of the foxglove and nightshade into the heart. The heart began to slow with the medicines.

She visualized the thick yellow fat breaking loose and making its way toward the heart, until it caught and plugged up the arteries, completely stopping the flow of blood. The muscle tried to compensate by beating faster as the heart began to die from lack of oxygen, but the fibrillation couldn't overcome the damage. The rhythm stuttered and jumped, nothing like the normal regular beating of a healthy muscle. The veins on the surface stood out in relief as the blood tried to move forward, pushing against the fatty barriers. Next she imagined the foxglove and nightshade entering the system, paralyzing whatever parts of the heart the fat hadn't already killed. The muscle began to change color from healthy pink to a deep blue as it struggled to push through the lifegiving blood. Finally the fight ceased. The tissues gave one last feeble quiver and lay still. The sounds of the lungs ceased. The blood began to pool in the buttocks and legs as the man sank to the floor and lay there, his eyes wide and unseeing. His hand was still clamped to his chest.

"Die, you evil old bastard." She gave the heart one last squeeze to make certain he would never hurt anyone again. "That's payback for the skunk and Loner," she said with satisfaction.

With one enemy dead and out of the way, she switched her anger to the Animal Control man. She reached out and found the white truck he'd been driving. She could see every part of it, including the closed white compartments where he'd casually thrown the bodies, as if they were nothing more than cooling meat. His name was Barney, she'd caught that much the instant she found him. "Well Barney, you are about to die," she said grimly. She thought about the truck. What was there about that truck that had lodged in her subconscious as he drove away?

She played back the horrific view of the Animal Control officer, his hands sheathed with gloves as he carried the dead animals by their tails, blood dripping, to the truck. The smell had been awful, but it hadn't affected the man. He'd climbed into the cab of the truck, started the motor and driven away. The truck clunked as the man put it into gear. She remembered watching the front wheels vibrate slightly as he headed down the hill.

Where had she felt that kind of vibration before?

It took a few moments before she was able to remember the incident. She and Harper had gone out to the movies, one of their rare treats. She'd been driving her van because the Volvo needed a new rear brake light and they'd both agreed that it was best not to drive the car until Harper installed the new light. As he had pointed out, with their luck they'd be stopped and cited, and who needed the grief of taking the car down to the police station to get the citation cleared after the light was fixed?

Fiona had been complaining of a strange clunking sound in her van, but it had never acted up while Harper was with her. But this time, Harper had heard the sound and warned her to drive slowly.

"U joint," he said with the gloom of someone who knows how serious the failure can be. "It'll send the car out of control when it fails, unless you're real careful."

Instead of going to the movies, they'd spent the evening hunting down the proper U joint for the van and making plans to replace it the next morning as soon as there was enough light. As it turned out, light was the least of their problems. A freezing rain was whipping through Northern California, and she'd thought her hands would drop off from the cold as she worked.

That was the sound she'd heard when the Animal Control truck had pulled away from the curb. "So that's how you'll die." She began by picturing the joint she and Harper had taken out of the van. It was probably the same kind used in the Animal Control truck's front end, if she was lucky. The joint was a simple cross-shaped piece of metal no bigger than the palm of her hand, but deadly when it failed.

She stopped to think about where the Animal Control man was right then. She waited until the image was absolutely clear. The man was going down the hills. She was sure she could tell exactly where he was because of the bodies in the back of the truck, which left a psychic trail. She knew when he began to follow the narrow road into the area leading to the Animal Control offices. Funny, she thought, how they control animals by shooting them, but never thought of shooting people to control them. She'd miss the animals. She'd never miss the people.

The buildings were situated far back in the mountains where the sounds of the animals that were about to be killed wouldn't bother anyone. The road was treacherous; Fiona had driven it more than once in search of a lost cat. There was a sheer drop on one side that ended in a rocky stream. There were rough-hewn cliffs on the other side. The storm that crashed overhead would have made the streambed into a roaring torrent over the past few hours.

"The better to drown you, you bastard," Fiona whispered.

Now was the time to strike. She built a picture in her mind of the joint the drive shaft plugged into. She pictured the small pieces of metal and searched until she found the one arm of the cross that she had been looking for. She could even hear the sound the truck made as the joint rotated. They should have fixed the road long ago. The county was cheap, though. They'd have no trouble spending on bullets but not a penny for maintenance. Next time, Fiona thought, she'd vote for the candidate who promised to strip Animal Control's budget to nothing.

The shaft had worn down almost to the hole and the metal was grinding away in the old grease, wearing everything down even more.

"That's it." She began to think failure at the joint. She played with the metal, finding the crack that extended completely through the arm of the cross. It was hanging on because of the pressure of the shaft, but it was ready to let loose and cause all kinds of damage.

Fiona watched and waited until the man began to downshift into the worst of the winding road. Even in second gear he was taking it too fast for the kind of weather and the

ill-maintained surface. She waited until she saw the head-
lights flicker out over nothing and then bounce back over
the sheer wall on the other side of the road.

Then she pushed.

It was a gentle push, one that didn't even begin to strain
her capacities. She enlarged the fracture in the metal, making it widen with each movement, until the joint cracked
under the pressure.

She heard the snap and saw the drive shaft plummet underneath the truck. The metal embedded itself in the old
gummy blacktop road and scraped a few inches before the
pressure of the truck and contents wedged it firmly in place.
The broken metal gleamed as it dug deep into the surface.
The truck began to lift off the ground and the tires began to
spin free.

Fiona moved back from the damage she'd caused and
watched as the truck seemed to jump into the air in slow
motion, pivoting as it went. She could see the man inside
screaming and cursing as he tried to control the truck,
which had suddenly gone berserk. His eyes widened as the
vehicle turned toward the ravine and his mouth formed a
silent O as he realized what was going to happen to him. He
scrabbled for the door, trying to bail out, but he couldn't
unlatch the seat belt before the vehicle began the slow terri-
fying arc down into the canyon. He knew he was going to
die the same way the skunks had, seeing death coming and
no way to retreat even half a step away from the bullet. He
braced his hands against the windshield, as if that would
cushion the blow of metal against rock. The drive shaft bent
and broke; the car dropped with a sickening finality, disappearing down the side of the abyss. There was the sound of
metal tearing from the truck and the reek of hot transmis-
sion fluid mixing with the dead skunk smell as the truck
disintegrated. The first impact pushed the front of the truck
inward and the cab folded into itself. The man stopped
screaming when the engine landed heavily in his lap, fol-

lowed by part of the hood, which sliced him neatly in half at chest level.

By the time the truck ended cab down in the flash flood that filled the wash, he was dead. Fiona didn't feel even a pang of remorse.

There was a clap of thunder and the rain poured down with even greater intensity. The lights flickered on but went out again at once. The skies spilled torrential rains, inundating the parched landscape. The desperately needed water ran off into the gutters, overflowing and clogging the drains for hundreds of miles around because there wasn't time for the moisture to seep into the dried ground. The electrical storm that raged around the area started fires that were immediately smothered by the rainfall.

Fiona was so busy with her visualizations that she didn't hear Harper when he arrived home. He walked up to the door, saw the candles and Fiona with her eyes closed and knew immediately that she had not believed his warnings.

"Fiona, for God's sake, stop before you kill us all," he shouted.

Fiona whirled to confront him.

"Help me," she said simply. She held out her hand to him in supplication and the power flowed from her and touched him. "You were right. They are trying to murder Megan. They've already killed some of the animals. Whoever is out to get us won't stop just because I back away from the Old Religion. They've found some way of turning it on us. We have to fight back. If you don't help me, we're going to lose everything."

A bolt of lightning illuminated the room and Harper's face. He looked beaten and haggard. His fingers trembled from terror and he closed his eyes and began to chant in Welsh until she could feel the energy that surrounded them pulsating and building, the synergy of the two of them together increasing the power from each of them alone.

Harper finished the chant and blew toward the candles.

The flames grew and lengthened, casting eerie shadows on the wall. She could almost see figures, almost hear voices in the wind.

"Look into the flames and read our future," Harper said.

Fiona tried. Maybe it was because she didn't have the necessary mystical background, but all she saw were two flames splitting, and that was most likely caused by the shape of the wick.

"I don't like it," Harper said. He started to say something more but Megan called down from upstairs, her voice foggy with pain.

"Mom, Dad, I think you'd better do something about the backyard. It's flooding outside the cat cages. I got up to look when the lights went out. I can see the cages with the flashlight, but I can't help."

The lights glowed amber, flickered and then strengthened as the electricity came back on in the house.

"Stay up there and rest, we'll take care of it," Harper called as he and Fiona ran for the garage. They'd done this exercise before, every time the water came rushing off the mountainside. Rain in the amount that was coming down the hill now was almost guaranteed to cause trouble.

"Oh damn," Harper said as he switched on the light. The water was already making a river across the concrete. Luckily only the dirty clothes on the floor were getting soaked. The cat cages were sufficiently up off the ground that there wouldn't be any damage unless they had one of Noah's floods.

"The freezer!" Fiona said and dashed for the switch. They'd have to leave it turned off until the water was no longer a danger to the electric motor. She stepped on the rubber mat before she disconnected the appliance.

"Here," Harper said, handing her a shovel as they hurried out the back door and into the darkness. The light from the garage door shone in a feeble half circle. They'd be working in blackness because they'd never gotten the time to install the backyard floodlights Fiona had bought on sale almost two years before.

"We'd better start trenching," Harper said. "I'll start at the patio, you begin here, and we'll meet somewhere in the middle."

Fiona stepped out into the rain and gasped as the water hit her in the face. She looked up at the house above them on the hill, and shook her hand toward the building.

"I hate you, I hate you, I want you to die," she chanted toward the old man. She repeatedly visualized the heart stopping and turning blue and the old man falling lifeless to the floor of his kitchen. As she worked, she could smell the scent of the skunks that lay over everything like a haze.

She tried to take a step forward, but her tennis shoes were stuck in the mud. She wrenched one loose and then lost the other one in the swirling brown water. She'd have to go fishing for it in the bottom of a foot-deep depression that was completely filled with muck if she wanted to continue working.

Somewhere in the distance, she could hear the howl of a siren. She listened, judging where it might be. Normally the sirens stopped as the fire engines and paramedics got to the rest home six blocks away. This time, though, the sirens steadily increased. She could hear the heavy fire truck laboring up the hill. The red flashing light cut through the storm as the vehicle pulled around the corner and up into the court above the house.

Lightning forked down, cutting into the hills above the house. The strike was uncomfortably close. Fiona jumped, but nothing could tear her interest away from the lights and sounds of the firemen above her. There was no sign of fire and the men were taking in a huge red medication box.

"Please, please, let it be true," she whispered. "Please let me have killed the bastard." She'd feel no remorse at all for ending the horrible old coot's life.

The ambulance swam up the street and wheezed to a stop behind the fire truck. The men raced into the house and there was nothing more to see.

Fiona looked down again to try and find her shoe and finally spotted the heel sticking up out of the mud. She reached for it and slipped it back on, continuing with the shoveling of the drainage ditch.

She kept glancing up at the fire truck, which finally pulled away, and the ambulance, which stayed parked in front of the house. No one was going anywhere in a hurry.

Fiona had worked her way almost to the bean patch that straggled up the hillside when her shovel hit something metallic. She stopped for a second and reached down to dislodge whatever had ruined her shoveling technique by being unyieldingly hard. As she did, another lightning bolt lit the area and she saw a horseshoe and what looked like a figure made from wheat or grass woven around the iron. She reached for the metal and as she did so, felt a buzz almost like electricity that came from the horseshoe.

Where had the horseshoe come from? She'd dug this ditch at least six times before; she'd Rototilled the ground every spring and fall and she'd never seen even a hint of a horseshoe in the dirt. How could it have gotten there without her knowing about it?

She held onto the horseshoe and tried to feel its luck. No feeling came through other than the coldness of the metal and the sense that someone had not wished them well.

"Hey, Harper, come over and look at what I found!" Fiona called. The lightning flashed again, revealing her as she held up the iron shoe and wheat figures.

She couldn't hear Harper over the torrent of rain, but she saw the look of absolute terror pass over his face. He dropped the shovel into the water and began to run to her through the muck and mud. He slipped and flailed wildly until he caught his balance again and floundered on through the wetness.

"Throw it away," he yelled as soon as she could hear him. "Get rid of it!"

Fiona caught the urgency in his voice and turned to toss it toward the compost pile, where it could add a bit of necessary iron to the stuff that had been marinating for the past year and a half.

Suddenly the hair on the back of her head stood up. Her arms and legs tingled as the air buzzed with electricity. There were a crackle and thump unlike anything she'd ever heard before and the world exploded around her just as Harper reached her and grabbed her hand.

Harper took the brunt of the charge. The electricity surged and crackled around him, trying to find a way to ride up his shoes and into his flesh and muscles to fry him. Somehow he'd known that when the horseshoe touched the ground, it would make the lightning strike around them. He held Fiona upright, to keep her out of contact with the water that boiled and then steamed as the thunderbolt split the ground.

Fiona wanted to scream but her throat was constricted with pure terror. She'd turned in time to look at the flash as it vibrated around them and had seen a figure coming toward them with hands outstretched to wrap them in death.

The lightning struck again and suddenly Harper and Fiona were covered with bits and pieces of the compost pile. The stink was unbelievable. Harper started coughing and Fiona gagged as they headed for the kitchen door and safety.

"I think that's enough digging for now," Harper said in masterful understatement.

Megan was crying. They could hear her as she ran down the stairs and wrenched open the back doors to help them get inside.

"She was going to kill you. I saw her coming and she was going to murder you," she cried, hugging her parents and ignoring the awful mess they made as they dripped mud and rotten vegetables and grass on the floor.

"Darling, it's all right. What did you think you saw?" Fiona tried to comfort her daughter.

"A figure. Something coming to kill you. A woman who looked like Sally."

Fiona laughed. "Morphinemares, darling. Don't worry about it. It was just a bolt of lightning."

Harper snorted. "Maybe not. You saw what happened when that horseshoe touched down."

"How did you know it was dangerous? You had to have seen something like this before, because I didn't think it was anything except a horseshoe that had weeds around it. You were going to warn me and then the lightning hit and all hell broke loose." Her teeth were chattering.

"Let's have a quick shower and I'll tell you about it," Harper said as he walked into the downstairs bathroom, shedding clothes down to his underpants. "I haven't seen one of those since I was a small boy. It's made to get power over someone. The last time I saw it used was when the Gypsies got mad at someone who had harmed them. I figure they probably got all the revenge they needed."

Harper stripped the rest of the way and got into the shower. He was much too stinky to walk up the stairs to the bathroom he preferred.

"Gypsies? Revenge?" Fiona asked. She took off her clothes and stepped in beside him. She'd never heard that he'd even seen Gypsies, much less known them intimately enough to know about their curses.

Harper sighed. "Maybe it's time I told you about my family."

Fiona fixed him with a glare. The effect was slightly diminished because the water ran into her eyes and made her blink. "Yes, maybe it is, particularly if it has something to do with what's happening to us."

Later she discovered that she was still shaking when she tried to make some chocolate milk and couldn't manage to stop the spoon from banging on the glasses almost to the point of breaking them. She finally put the milk and chocolate into a Tupperware container and broke up the globules of cocoa by shaking the whole mixture vigorously and then pouring it into glasses.

Harper accepted the milk carefully. He was still shaking, too, and his face was white with anxiety and fear.

"Ah God, it's found me again, and all I ever wanted to do was walk away from it," he said quietly.

Fiona waited.

"I was nineteen. I'd been working in the mines for four years already, and I thought the rest of my life would always be the same. There was no way out, no money for education or travel. Our family had been tied to the village for hundreds of years. Why should I try anything different?"

So that was the reason his body had been so strong and stocky when she'd met him, she thought. He'd been used to doing hard physical work.

"The truth is, we were always set apart by being strange, my parents, my sister, my grandmum and I."

Here it was, the history of the mystery man, after more than twenty years.

"We were traveling people who had settled in the town four hundred years before and no one ever forgot our origins."

"Traveling people? You mean you moved from one place to another to live?"

"No, I mean we never had a set place to live. It's another name for Gypsies. There must not have been more than a sixteenth of pure Gypsy blood left in me, even though a good number of my ancestors had married and moved out to be with the others of our kind on the road. Still, in the village I was the half-breed, the one who was never good enough for their daughters."

"Thank heavens for that. What would I have done without you?" Fiona said.

"Thanks, love," Harper said, touching her hand. "You'd have found someone else."

"Never," Fiona said, and she meant it. "But I'm not quite sure about how you got from some village in Wales to here."

"Second sight. Witchcraft. It swallowed up everything I loved and left me alone and under threat of being killed if I didn't run. And here it is again, threatening my family, going to kill us all. They've already taken the animals, and started on Megan, and I don't know what to do to stop it, any more than I did back then." He lowered the cup to the table and wiped his hand over his eyes.

Fiona was appalled to see that Harper was actually crying.

"What made you come to the States?" she asked, hoping to steer him back onto a safe course. It worried her to see him even begin to lose control.

"Ah, the running away, you mean?" he asked, his accent getting thicker with each passing second. "That was after everyone died in the disaster. It was retribution. When we warned them, no one would listen. We all died, everyone except me, and I had to run for my life. They said they were going to get revenge by casting me into the shaft and letting me perish at the bottom with all my bones broken and my body bleeding into the water and darkness."

"What the hell are you talking about?" Fiona was shaking with anxiety now.

"I caused the disaster, don't you see? I knew it was going to happen. I had one of my dreams and my grandmum had a bad feeling. Would they listen? Hell no. Nothing but a dirty Gypsy. They'd come to my mother for the truth on love affairs, and how to win a boy or how to kill a husband and make it look like an accident or a heart attack, and she'd help them, if she could and she thought it was a just request. But we were still the outcasts. The Bible said that witches were to be punished, and we were living there on sufferance, as long as the village people could use us."

The lightning struck again in the distance and the thunder roared an accompaniment to Harper's quiet voice. "We lived in a tiny mining town. The slag from the mine had been dumped all around the village, building up mountains that leached dirt down into the streets when there was a rainstorm. Everyone knew the tailings weren't safe, but no one knew what to do about it and the mountains just kept growing."

Harper leaned forward, fixing Fiona with a stare that was frightening in its unwavering directness. "They're going to kill us all, Fiona. I had the same dream then that I had a few weeks ago. I dreamed about the mountain moving. I couldn't stop it then and I can't stop it now. It's going to happen again."

"Could you be a little more precise? Enough of this wandering around sounding like Hamlet," Fiona snapped. She was beginning to get an awful feeling in the pit of her stomach. Her husband had sustained a shock outside. Could the electricity have fried his brain a little or had he simply had so much dumped on him that he was temporarily insane?

"Oh yes, I'll tell you all of it. I went to the school where my little sister was studying. I'd already tried to keep her home for the day, but she was in a play and wouldn't have any of the sitting by the fireside routine when the other kids were having fun."

Harper stood up and began to pace. "I knew the teacher wouldn't listen to me, but I had to try. I tried to tell the parson and the police. I made a right fool of myself trying to warn the village about the disaster that was on the way. No one listened. Then one of those slag heaps that had been sitting there silent and deadly began to move. I had just left the school and was on my way home when there was the eeriest sound. It was really no sound at all. All the birds flew up in the air, and the dogs began to howl. There was a rumbling noise like when one of the mines blows up in the deepest tunnel. The hill began to creep forward an inch at a time, and then it was racing down, and there was no way to stop it or get out of the way. It swept everything with it. The school was gone, the houses behind the school, the streets, all of it, everything had disappeared and with it all the children of the village."

Harper was crying now, deep sobs that racked him from the very depths of his soul. "Everyone in my family tried to tell the village there was going to be a disaster. No one wanted to listen because saying that a catastrophe could happen was as good as saying that the mine owners weren't taking care of the town. And if they said that, why, the mine owners could pull out and leave our village behind, with no jobs and no way to stay alive. You didn't criticize the rich because they were all that kept you from starving to death. My family had been in the building when the wave of slag roared over it and I lost everyone."

"And then?"

Harper snorted. "The ones who survived came after me. James, my best friend, raced to my house to tell me to gather what I could and to leave immediately. The rumors had started that I'd somehow caused it and they were going to kill me. Never mind that none of it made sense or was the truth. Never mind that just once I'd tried to turn my devil-spawned talent to the good of the village. No, they were determined that I was going to perish in terrible pain to pay them back for their children. So I did the only thing I could. I grabbed up a few things and left town. I brought with me the fortune-telling cards and the clay tiles with Runes that linked me back to the invading conquerors from Sweden and Norway a thousand years before. The only reason I kept those things is that they were of my family. I kept two pictures bundled up in a square of the finest lace that my mother ever did crochet. I've never even opened the bundle.

"I ran away from anything ever having to do with witchcraft and the Gypsies. I never wanted to talk about it, I never wanted to think about it, and I certainly never wanted to get involved in this whole mess again. I don't like candles and spells and incantations and seeing into the future. I don't like prophetic dreams, and I don't like the powers that can overwhelm me at any time. I don't want to be psychic, and I don't want to call upon any God or Goddess to come help me.

"Don't you understand, Fiona? I ran all the way from the only home I'd ever known, all the way to America, to get away from it. The only time I've ever used it was to keep danger away from my family. I tried to keep Megan from dying. I tried to keep my job and a roof over our head, and a living, no matter how poor. If I hadn't used my powers then, we'd all have died. But it drew attention to us and troubles just kept on happening. I thought I could stop. I thought we'd be safe again. Then you bring the Old Religion right back into my house."

21

L arry looked up as the doorbell of the rented house buzzed. For just a moment, he thought wistfully of the bells he'd chosen for the house he'd shared with Gia. Sometimes he wished he hadn't gone there and messed up any chance of going home again. The fling with Kelly had only lasted a couple of weeks. By the time it was over, it was too late to go home again. His arms still ached because the cops hadn't liked him threatening Gia. To shut him up, they'd pulled back hard when they cuffed him and his wrists were still bruised from the plastic restraints. The police had been only marginally easier on him when they found out he was a lawyer. It appeared they liked lawyers only a little more than wife-beaters.

What had turned him into a wife-beater? It had never occurred to him in the twenty-some years that he and Gia had been married to actually physically harm her. She'd always been able to irritate him into a good verbal fight, but he'd never felt the need to brutalize her before and he didn't particularly like the change. He'd been overbearing, he knew that. He'd always been one to get his own way, but never by force. It almost felt as if something inside him had changed in this last year, bringing out a part of him that he hadn't known even existed.

The bell rang again.

"Leave me the shit alone!" Larry said as he pulled the door open.

"That's no way to greet me," said the woman who stood before him. "I assure you, I am not shit."

Larry stared at her. He had the feeling that he should know her, but the likelihood of his ever having met this woman before and then forgetting it approached zero. She was stunning. Her hair was white, whether bleached or real he didn't know, but she didn't look old enough to have lost all the color naturally. Her face was exquisite, small-boned and finely proportioned. He had always had a weakness for women who looked delicate, and this lady was no exception.

"Sorry about that. Don't take what I said personally." He stepped back and left room for her to come into the house if she wanted. He was glad the cleaning lady had just come and polished and vacuumed the place. "Please, come in and tell me what I can do for you."

The woman walked into the living room, studying everything about the house. She nodded approvingly at the sparsely furnished space and peered into the kitchen. "Oh, very nice," she said. "I think it shouldn't be any trouble to sell this right away." She reached into her bag and produced a card.

"Leense Nasro?" he said, saying the words carefully. "What kind of name is that?"

"Polish," Leense said. "It makes it easier for people to find me. There isn't another person with my name in the entire country, as far as I've been able to discover."

"I'll bet." He hesitated only a moment. This woman was worth trying to get friendly with. "Hey, would you like a drink? It's getting on to be cocktail time and I hate to drink alone."

"Sure, why not," Leense said. "How about a martini, if you have the fixings? I'm always game for a cocktail with a possible client."

"Sounds good." He hesitated before going into the kitchen to get another glass. His headache had suddenly flared into real pain, centered at the back of his head in one spot. It was sufficiently bad that he felt momentarily nauseated.

Leense and Larry drank and talked for most of the afternoon. He didn't get around to telling her that he didn't own the house and therefore couldn't list it for sale with Leense's company until they were both drunk and sprawled out on the master bed with no clothes on at all.

Larry was very proud of himself. He'd managed to hold back enough on the alcohol that he would be able to perform, if he managed to get her into bed.

"Oh look, it's working," Leense said, fondling him deftly to make certain he didn't deflate. She was ready for sex and then for her final act, which was to be a surprise for Larry.

Larry gave her almost what she wanted. He was thick and firm, two of her requirements. Even though he insisted on the stodgy old missionary position, he was good with his technique and he lasted for fifteen minutes, almost a record. It was going to be a shame to waste it all.

Larry began to speed up the rhythm as the pain of his headache increased with each stroke. Funny, sex shouldn't have any effect on that, he thought fuzzily.

Leense lifted her hips mechanically as she focused her mind on the place in Larry's brain where the headache had originated. It was going to be easier than she'd thought. The combination of liquor, bad eating and chronic high blood pressure had already taken their toll. He only needed a small push to blow a gasket.

Leense felt his penis beginning to swell with the final moments of passion when she pushed against the point in his brain that was already damaged. His rhythm faltered, and he looked at her with a bewildered expression as the first few drops began to squirt out in the finish of the sexual ritual.

Leense was ready. She angled out from under him as he lifted himself once more and then fell flat on the bed. His hands made a grasping motion, gathering up the sheets in his fingers, but it was obvious that it was only a reflex. He breathed in once and then out, an exhalation that never seemed to quite have an end. His back rose slightly and then was still.

Selene was sweating with the exertion of having had to cause a change in Larry's physical being with her mind. Some of the disciplines she had learned when she was young were becoming increasingly difficult as she aged and as she overlaid her original body with power she'd taken from so many others. It was rather like elastic that had been stretched too far too many times. Her special talents had lost the elasticity and freshness she needed to do some of her more complicated work.

She breathed deeply again, trying to bring herself back into focus and harmony. She couldn't afford to let any of her power go in anger. That would come later when Asron and she finally used every bit of energy they had to strike back just once, obliterating the only serious challenge they'd had in a hundred years.

"And we will win." She looked down at Larry's body. "After this, Gia will be so grateful that she'll use her own talents to help us win. It will be great fun to wipe out the opposition without them having a clue about what's happening. And Asron will be grateful to me for giving him a chance to grow young again. We'll be lovers again, and he'll be the young man I remember. Everything for Asron," she said quietly.

She put her clothes back on and made two calls, one to Gia about a body and one to Asron and the rest of the coven to let them know that she'd done all she could to remove the obstacles blocking them.

22

Gia felt as if she'd had the flu for weeks. Her head ached and every joint in her body was in open rebellion when she tried to move. It was either the worst infection or the worst asthma attack she'd ever had. In any case, she'd dosed herself with enough leftover antibiotics and antihistamines that she should have felt better days ago. She could trace it all back to the day after Larry beat her up and Elf had insisted that she put on the iron ring for protection. It was as if her body had started to war with itself then and hadn't stopped.

"I could take off the ring," she said, looking down at her hand. "But I promised I wouldn't."

She played with the magician necklace as she stared out into the darkness. The little figure's black crystal ball was smooth and cold against her fingers, no matter how long she held it. She wished she could rub it all over her body to soothe away the fevered soreness.

She'd tried writing earlier in the day, but nothing had come. She'd sat in the office and stared at the blue screen and the blinking cursor, but couldn't put down even one word of her story. The romance had disappeared behind her old writer's block the instant Larry had laid a hand on her. Now all she could do was stare past the screen and out the window and wish that the wonderful story would come alive again.

She shuffled the Tarot, hoping that this time they'd tell her something. They seemed to be sulking because she'd picked up a set of Rune stones the last time she'd gone in to the Major Arcana. Gia had been curious about them for weeks and finally bought them because she needed more guidance than she had been getting from the cards.

Gia had tried to read the cards earlier in the day, but nothing came up that made any sense when she asked questions. She'd wanted to know what the outcome would be of her affair with Asron and whether Elf would be able to settle the divorce case to her benefit. The stupid cards, though, had come up reversed ace of pentacles. Translated, that meant misused wealth, wasted money and corruption by money.

"That doesn't tell me anything new. Asron is rich, but that doesn't have anything to do with our love affair. I'm not after his money, just his body," she complained to the cards as she shuffled. The divorce brought out an even more confusing answer. Death came up three times in a row. Gia wasn't all that good with odds, but she was willing to bet that the appearance of the card that many times was unusual. When she read the book all it said was that there was a cataclysmic change about to happen, and she already knew that.

She tried again, and got the king of swords reversed. "Damn, I hate swords," she said, almost deciding not to look up the answer. She knew that whatever it was, swords were bad. "A dangerous or evil person, hidden from you" was the answer to a question she hadn't even known she was asking. She'd just been playing around, trying to see what cards came up when she cut them.

She put the cards away and began fingering the Runes to see if the stones had anything to tell her. If only Elf had been there to help her with the interpretations. She withdrew one of the Runes, the arrow pointing downward. Teiwaz, reversed, she thought. Damn, I'm getting tired of everything having the negative meanings. Danger, the book said, the life force leaks out or is spilled. The answers are within yourself.

Her spine itched.

Gia squirmed in the chair like a bear rubbing against the bark of a tree. It didn't help.

She stood up and stretched. All her muscles ached and the itch was still there. "Damn," she muttered. She'd felt like this the night Fiona was shot and burned, but had never thought anything about it.

And when Larry came home, I itched, too. She could remember thinking that if she didn't find a way to scratch her spine, which seemed to be irritated from the inside out, she wasn't going to be able to write another word of her novel.

I wonder if it's some kind of early-warning system that kicks in just before a disaster? she thought. She shifted uneasily. It was just another thing that went along with all the other warnings she'd been receiving from the Tarot and the Runes.

"Okay, what's going to happen?" Gia asked whatever was making her spine feel weird, but there was no answer.

Who could be in trouble? If it was Fiona, there was nothing Gia could do to warn her. She'd thought of calling her friend at least twenty times every day, but never carried through the impulse. She wasn't into rejection and she knew that was exactly what she'd get.

Idly she picked out another Rune, trying to get a lead on what was making her worry. She shone the reading light on the Rune and looked the sign up in the blue book. The hourglass. Transformation, maybe even death.

"Oh go away," she yelled, throwing the stone across the room. It bounced harmlessly off the wall and landed on the carpet, taunting her.

She was so glad when the phone rang that she grabbed it at the first sound.

"Gia, this is Selene. I have wonderful news for you. Can you meet me at 601 Alpine in Walnut Creek?"

"You bet," Gia said. She was glad for any chance to get out of the oppressively dark house. "I'll be there in a couple of minutes."

On the way over she wondered just why that address sounded so familiar. She knew she'd heard it or read it before, but she didn't know where.

She parked in front of the suburban ranch house set on a hill. It looked familiar but there was no flash of recognition. It was just another house.

"Gia, I'm so glad you came over promptly," Selene said as she opened the door wide. "I thought you might like to take care of the arrangements now, since you are officially a very rich widow, just as you requested." Selene extended her hand and pulled her into the house.

Gia's breath caught in her throat as she remembered her conversation with Asron after Larry's assault.

The itch in her spine increased until she wasn't sure she'd be able to stand it. Surely Asron hadn't really meant that he could do something about Larry? Not something including death!

He'd said it could be arranged and she'd never believed him.

"What do you mean, rich widow?"

"Follow me." Selene led her into the bedroom where Larry's corpse was already cooling. It was obvious from his slightly exposed penis that he'd been erect when he died. The sight made her feel ill.

"What? How?"

"Simple. Asron said you needed to be shed of your husband and you needed the divorce settled in your favor or you needed the money without being put through a legal hassle. Now, no one can really depend on what a judge is going to do in a divorce hearing, can they? Things are so unpredictable in the court system. And you did say that you'd like to have him dead. So I thought this was the best way to solve the whole thing and show you just how useful being completely tied to the coven can be."

"You killed him?" Gia's voice was so faint that she could barely hear herself.

"Oh, not so anyone would ever be able to say so. What I did was get him into bed for a round of some very physical sex play. He was already having a headache and I just followed it to the source. I simply pushed the wall of an aneurysm that was already giving him fits. Just a small push—he might have died even if I hadn't done anything to him. Besides, I don't have the kind of power that—" She stopped, and then continued. "But this way we were sure of having exactly the result that we wanted."

"And that was?" Gia couldn't believe she was having this conversation.

"You with all the money you need and a useless man out of your life. Now you can focus on helping us put the forces back into alignment. We need to have all of your concentration and talent working with us, not fragmented between your silly writing and the trouble with Larry."

Gia stiffened. "So you gave him a push, he had a stroke, and now you expect me to work with you without any thought to anything else, right?"

"I knew you'd understand," Selene said, beaming. "Sometimes it takes a little while to understand what we can all do for each other. I'm glad you're a quick learner. Now don't you think you should call the paramedics or the coroner or someone to clean up this mess?"

Gia's control shattered. She couldn't stay another moment in the same room with Larry's corpse. She couldn't even stay in the same house. She wanted out, away from these people who seemed to take death so lightly that they just gave a little nudge and it happened. No remorse, no feelings of guilt, just a tidy job that no one would ever know about.

She touched him.

The flesh was already beginning to cool. She watched his chest, hoping against hope for some shallow breath, something that would show her that he wasn't dead, he was only wounded and somehow she wouldn't be responsible for this horrible waste.

"Of course. I'll call the paramedics. But what will you do if someone finds out what you've done?"

"Who would find out? The only person who could say anything is you. What are you going to do? Go to the police and tell them that I murdered your husband while we were having sex by going into his brain and killing him? They'll have you in a padded cell so fast you'll never know what hit you."

Gia stared at her, wondering what had made her think this woman could ever be her friend.

She ran from the room.

"Come back here, Gia, you have to call." Selene was impatient.

"You do it," Gia shouted as she slammed the door behind her and headed for the car. She wasn't sure how she was going to drive; her eyes were fogged with tears, but she knew she had to get away from Selene.

"Damn you, I hated him, but I never meant for him to die, not really," she screamed as she drove toward her home. "Control freaks, that's what you are. You want to control everything in my life so you can use me, and I'm not going to let you do it. You killed him!"

She couldn't erase that final pitiful picture she had of him. The feeling of his cooling flesh and the certainty that if she'd tried to lift his arm it would already have started to stiffen with rigor mortis. What would have happened if he hadn't let Selene in? What would have happened if he'd kept his prick in his pants and hadn't left her for Kelly? What would have happened if she hadn't wished he was dead?

But all the "what if's" were over now.

She managed to drive home, but almost crashed in the last five feet of her journey because she didn't see Elf's car in her driveway. She stopped just inches short of the bumper and sat there crying until she felt Elf's arms around her shoulder, pulling her out of the car.

"What happened, love?" He held her to him, giving her the comfort of his warm, living solidity. She had never felt anything so welcome in her life.

She buried her face against his chest and sobbed like a child. It took Elf fifteen minutes to calm her enough to understand the words between the sobs.

"They killed him. Selene and Asron decided Larry needed to die because they needed me. They thought they could buy my obedience and power by killing Larry." She broke down again.

"How did they manage that?" Elf asked, his voice deadly quiet.

"I don't know. Something about an aneurysm popping in his brain. It didn't make much sense." Gia sniffled and blew her nose again, dabbing at the tears that still trickled down her cheeks.

"And do you still want to work with them?" Elf asked.

Gia shivered. "I never want to see them again as long as I live. They scare me, Elf. What if Selene was telling the truth? What if she can cause someone to die? Have you ever heard of anything like that before?"

"Oh yes, I know about such things. I'm just sorry that it had to reach this point before you could begin to believe that what you were doing wasn't just fun and games."

"It never was just fun—" Gia stopped, horrified at the

thought of what she had done. She remembered the chanting and powerful images she'd drawn of Larry shriveling up and dying. They would haunt her for the rest of her life.

Elf saw the look and shook his head. "No, you didn't do this. This was solely Asron and Selene's idea. They wanted more control over you than this gave them." Elf grabbed the magician and broke the silver chain with his massive hands.

"That has nothing to do with it!" Gia reached for the wizard. Elf moved swiftly to the back door, opened it and threw out the figurine. There was a sudden clap of thunder and lightning illuminating the figure as it sailed through the air. Halfway to the ground it shattered and the magician disappeared as if it had never been.

"That was part of their control," Elf said when he turned back to Gia. "Now they'll have to work if they want you under their power again."

He took a necklace out of his pocket and handed it to her. "Here, you have to put this on of your own free will. It will not bind you to me, nor will it influence you. It is simply for your own protection."

Gia stared at the necklace. It was a delicate chain of very good gold. There were twelve small triangles hanging from the necklace. They were made of a dark stone she didn't recognize.

"What is it?" she asked, touching one of the little triangles.

"Elf-arrow; it's a kind of flint. It's to protect you and keep you safe from harm," Elf said, his finger resting against the arrows that lay in the palm of her hand.

"Flint? Like what we used to use in Girl Scouts?"

"The same. At the very least, it'll help you start a fire if you get caught out in the woods with no matches."

Gia laughed shakily and clasped the necklace around her throat. It felt right there. The gold wasn't oppressively heavy and the arrows seemed to give off the faintest tingle of fireworks against her skin. She rather liked the sensation.

Gia stared at the point where the wizard pendant had disappeared. Already she was beginning to feel different. Some of the pain that had made her hips ache was retreating.

She put her hand to the necklace and felt the warmth cascading downward. It felt as if there were a healing force racing through her body, changing the pain to comfort, the confusion in her mind to clarity.

"Fiona's right. I did change, but I couldn't see it until just this minute."

"Of course."

She took a deep breath, testing the sensation that flowed through her. Another breath, a full one, not the constricted painful breathing that had made her so uncomfortable lately.

Nothing hurt. She raised her arms, expecting the stab of pain that had accompanied her every waking moment, but nothing happened. Even her back had stopped aching.

"Oh my God," she said quietly. Elf had been right all along and she'd been too blind to see it. Asron and Selene had been doing a number on her and she'd just let it happen. She hadn't even put up a fight.

"Thor, if you're going to be exact about it," Elf said.

Gia stared at him in confusion.

"You said God, and I presume you meant Thor, since he's the one who has helped me to win you back from the dark ones."

Gia nodded slowly. Weirder and weirder.

"Thank whoever did it, it's over now," she said, meaning every word. "If it hadn't been for you I'd still be stuck in the middle of Asron and Selene's games."

She leaned over and kissed him right on the lips.

The storm intensified outside. The crashing was becoming almost continuous, and the thunderbolts were striking so often there was no need for lights to illuminate every-thing. They ran for the house and into the living room.

"Something is not right," Elf said. "I expected to sense Asron and Selene. They won't let you go this easily. But there is something more. It's not over. We still have a battle, and I can't do this myself."

Gia didn't want to hear any more. She put her hands over her ears, trying to block out the sound of the storm. Death, destruction and terror had taken over her life. The necklace could take away the physical pain, but nothing was ever going to erase the mental anguish she'd felt at Larry's death. She started to sink back to the couch, where she could huddle in the corner and give herself time to fig-ure out what the hell had been going on in her life for the past few weeks.

"No," Elf said grimly, pulling her upright. "You can't stop now. We have to get over to Fiona's house. Together we might have a chance to win. Otherwise, we'll lose every-thing."

23

W hat would you have done if you'd known you were marrying someone who would one day turn out to have some of those talents that almost got you killed in Wales?"

"I'd—" Harper hesitated. "I was going to say I wouldn't have married you. But it isn't the truth. I couldn't live without you. We were destined to be together. That's why there wasn't any question about marrying you even when we'd only known each other two weeks. I've heard of people who went back in previous lives and found out that they had been with the same people life after life. That's the way it was for us."

Fiona nodded. He was absolutely right. "If we were fated to be together, maybe I was also fated to do this kind of thing in other lives."

"Explain 'this kind of thing,'" he said cautiously.

"I mean witchcraft and using whatever talents I have to get revenge on the murderers who killed my animals and on whoever or whatever is causing Megan's illness."

Harper closed his eyes. He had an awful feeling that

Fiona wasn't talking about an idea, she was talking about reality.

"Fiona, what have you done?" he whispered.

Fiona rubbed her hands together, wondering if she could put this off, then decided she might as well tell him.

"Maybe you'd better sit down."

He looked out into the night, hoping to catch a glimpse of whatever was gathering strength against him, but all he could see was the pounding rain that beat against the window.

"Harper," she began and then stopped.

He ran a hand over his face, as if he could brush away the worry and tiredness that were sweeping over him. "Tell away, Fiona. Maybe you'll be able to make me understand why we seem to be under siege. I haven't done anything with my craft for so long that I'm not sure I could raise a stink in a pigsty, so it's not my powers that they'd be looking to, is it?"

Fiona shook her head. "I think I'm the one with the power that someone is trying to push back into the genie bottle."

"Why? I thought you were playing around with it kind of like a Tuesday-afternoon mah-jongg meeting, only it was with witchcraft instead of little tiles."

"Not exactly. You see, I murdered two people this afternoon."

Harper closed his eyes and sagged back into the couch's cushions. "When will the police show up to take you away and did you leave prints and identification at the scene?"

"The police will never know. You've heard the term 'mind over matter'? Well, that's what this set of murders was. I was so furious that I had to do something, so I went to a place in my mind where I hadn't been for years and years."

Fiona took a deep breath, trying to keep her voice steady. "My mother told me it was a dirty bad place and never to think about it again, so I buried it all these years. But, Harper, I found a talent I could use to get revenge on people who shouldn't be alive. I discovered I could go inside someone or something and cause a disaster. I crawled right inside that old bastard's heart and made it stop beating. I made a U joint fail on the Animal Control truck and made sure the truck flipped down into a ravine and killed the man inside."

Harper relaxed. She could see the tension flow out of him as he began to smile. "Oh thank God, is that all?"

"What? I've just told you I killed two people and you say 'is that all?' "

"Honey, you're imagining things. I know it's been stressful lately with Megan so sick, and this is all a delusion that you're having in response to that."

Fiona heard echoes of the physician's "it's all in her head" speech.

"No," she said fiercely. "It is not a delusion."

"Do you know what you sound like? If someone else were listening they'd say you'd gone a few steps around the corner. You didn't kill anyone. The ambulance was sheer coincidence," Harper said.

"Do you think I want to be a freak? Do you think I'd tell you this if it weren't true?"

"No, I think you believe it. But, love, look at what you've been through lately. There's Megan's illness, and my job, and even the stress of needing to produce paintings that Big Skies will approve of. And what happened when you got stressed? You decided to play with witchcraft. Remember, I come from a family with the Old Religion in our bones and I know my mother said such powers died out long ago. They became the kind of memories that myths were made of."

"I think your mother was wrong, but just in case I'm snorting dirty bathwater, how about if I check on the Animal Control officer? His name was Barney and his last name started with a G." She dialed the phone and waited. Chances were that they'd have an answering machine on and she'd never connect with a real person, but she could hope. It took twenty rings and she'd almost given up when a voice answered at the other end.

"I'd like to find out whether Barney has returned from his afternoon shift yet?" Fiona asked.

She waited.

"No, I happened to talk to him this afternoon and I wanted to check some information."

She waited again.

"And the truck's being hauled out of the ravine now?" she asked. "I guess he won't be answering my questions, then."

Without saying another word, she hung up the phone and turned to Harper.

"If there is something evil waiting for us, it's waiting to get me. I'm not imagining devils in the dark."

Harper had gone dead white. "What do we do? How do we push this power back down into nothing so that who-ever is waiting out there, stalking us, will turn around and go away?"

"What do you want me to do? Renounce it and turn back and never use it again? Harper, Megan could die. You could have something terrible happen to you or I could be killed."

"And what happens if the talent backfires? There's this old theory in witchcraft that whatever you do to someone else comes back to you threefold. Just think what happens if you're really responsible for those men dying. The backlash from that could take us all, love. I've often wondered if the village children's dying was only a side effect of some kind of backlash against my family's witchcraft." Harper closed his eyes for a moment. "All right. If that's the way it's going to be, we need help."

"Why?" Fiona was puzzled.

"Evil is out there waiting and you've slipped the bounds and you are standing there naked, just waiting for them to hit you with everything they've got. They thought they could control you and instead you've broken free with a power and talent that are far beyond what they expected. They've tried to control you by putting spells on our house, a bottle of wine at the highest point in the rafters and dangerous amulets in our yard. We'd better have all the help we can find to get us through the next twenty-four hours. Because, Fiona, darling, if you do have all that power, they're going to try to kill you."

Fiona was so startled by his pronouncement that she didn't even ask how he'd found out about the wine. The stupid stain must have given it away.

Harper went out to the living room where Fiona's candles had long since burned to puddles of wax and spilled over the little saucers she'd used as candleholders.

Harper took two more candles out of the tin trash can where Fiona had hidden her witchcraft stuff until that very morning. He lit the candles and several strips of lavender that had been drying on the windowsill. He drew a circle, far better and faster than Fiona had thought possible.

Harper closed his eyes and turned to the four points of the compass, invoked the help of the gods and goddesses he had been intimate with in his childhood and had forsaken as an adult.

Fiona watched the transformation begin. She knew about calling down the moon. She'd taken the power of the moon into herself that one night when Sally attacked her. Now Harper was taking the same kind of energy but from a different source, one she couldn't even begin to imagine. As he talked, she heard names that appeared in some of the books she'd read. Myrddin and Lludd, keeper of the sky, Llyr and Manawyddan; then she lost the skein of thought in the language again.

When she looked back at Harper, she could barely believe that this was the same man who had sat, sad and defeated, on the couch when she'd told him about her powers. He had changed and gathered strength as he worked. If she hadn't known better, she'd have said he'd lost twenty pounds and the muscles in his torso had tightened until there was nothing extra there, only solidity and sinew. His aura was different, too. It was stronger than she'd ever seen it, gold shot through with silver and almost impenetrable. He raised his arms and she could see the energy almost crackle from his fingertips.

"Tell Megan to stay in her room. She is not to come down and respond to anything she hears. Tell her to stay there until one of us comes for her," Harper said as he lowered his arms. Then he began to undress.

Fiona was so surprised that she could barely make it up the stairs to relay the message to Megan and be sure she'd taken her latest set of pills.

Fiona heard the refrigerator open and close as she came back down the stairs. Harper walked back into the living room carrying a bowl full of various items.

Fiona stared in amazement.

Harper was naked and completely erect. The man who was usually too tired to do more than suggest that they make love and then roll over and start snoring had disappeared and left a satyr in his place.

Harper held out his hand to Fiona and brought her into the circle. He began to undress her. With an easy familiarity, he pulled her plaid blouse open and let his thumbs trail down over her breasts. He began to unhook the bra and they both laughed when his hands fumbled with the back.

"Out of practice. I should undress you more often, love," he said and leaned over and kissed her on the neck, a long sweet lingering kiss that promised more passion than they'd had in years. Fiona groaned at the touch. She hadn't realized that she'd missed this kind of lovemaking so much.

Remembering the first time they'd made love and the

fun of exploring his body and finding the points that aroused him, she began to touch all the places she knew would excite him. First on the list was a massage of his earlobes.

"Oh God and Goddess," Harper murmured and she felt him bob with sudden passion against her. It had worked twenty-one years ago and it still worked now, one of the quirks of his body that had always made her laugh.

"Oh, you think that's funny, do you?" He ran his fingers up her arm until he reached the crease inside her elbow. She gasped and pushed forward against him. He'd discovered the trick to exciting her quickly when he'd seen her rubbing a particular patch of skin inside her elbow and staring happily off into the distance.

"Now for the enjoyment, and that's what this should be, because there's a lot more energy to be gained from joy than there is from plain lust. We're going to take it slow and enjoy every second."

"Lust is good," Fiona said, licking her lips.

They lay down on the floor, laughing as the braided rug left crossed marks on their buttocks.

"Should have brought a blanket, like we did that night out at the park. Remember when the fog came in and covered everything and we made love on the grass?"

"Yes, I remember. And I remember that you'd just pulled your pants up and I'd just pulled my skirt down when a cop came by investigating the noise. I was so embarrassed."

"You'd have been more embarrassed if he'd been counting time with the strokes."

Harper reached into the bowl that he had placed on the table and brought down a can Fiona hadn't noticed before.

"Remember this? We'll use it in place of the oils. I know you haven't had your sweets for the night, and this will take care of your sugar cravings and sex desires all at the same time." He handed the can of whipped cream to Fiona.

It was just as good as she remembered. She sprayed him until his penis looked like a miniature pagoda with the barest tip of cherry protruding. She began to lick the cream off, leisurely exploring every inch between his legs. As she worked, the tension began to mount. It had been weeks since they'd made love, and both of them had been ready for days, but never at the same time.

"Enough," Harper said, pushing her away. "I'll cut the circle and you go get a warm towel." She obliged and came back in a moment with an old white cloth they'd stolen from some hotel years ago.

"First me, then you," he said. She washed the remnants of the cream off him, and took him in her mouth for one last lingering taste.

He did the honors for her, cleaning every inch between her legs with the towel; then he began to lick her as she had him. He didn't use the cream; he'd never liked the taste, insisting that her own essence was enough for him. He drew her closer and closer to orgasm, retreating when she began to climax, until she couldn't stand it any longer.

"Please, I need it so much it hurts," she whispered as she put her hands on his shoulders, urging him to come into her. She spread her legs as wide as she could. It was the ultimate surrender to the ultimate need.

She moaned as he pushed into her. It didn't matter how many times they'd done this, or how familiar his body was to her, she loved the feel of him as he thrust himself between her legs.

Slowly at first, he began to move in and out, teasing her by letting the tip of his penis play up and down in the most intimate part of her body. When she couldn't stand it any longer he filled her again.

Then, too soon, because they'd gone so long without making love, she began to climax, shaking and whimpering as he began to respond to her sounds.

She came first and he followed. She put her hands on his

hips to push him even deeper inside her and felt the goose bumps that meant he had finished.

He reached between her legs and in a swift gesture, drew his fingers through their mixed fluids and spread the liquid on his breast and then hers. "The power is ours and we bind the God and Goddess to us to help us endure."

"Now all we can do is wait," he said and kissed her. Both of them felt a final tapering pleasure, an exquisite reminder of what had just happened.

24

Fiona slept hard, as she always did after making love with Harper. Her legs felt relaxed and limp and she was so deeply satisfied that nothing should have bothered her. Even the bed's lumps felt comfortable.

But the nightmare came creeping into her dreams, displacing her satisfaction with the beginnings of horror.

In the nightmare, there were whisperings around the house. She heard the creak and crack of the beams in the attic, where she'd gone to place the talismans that should have kept them safe. In the dream she floated upward and into the top floor of the house. The wreath and other charms were swept away by winds sluicing through the unprotected attic vents. The wheat weavings shattered and spread over the insulation. The magic that had given them protective powers disappeared as the design broke apart.

In the dream, Fiona looked around. There was no wind outside. The trees that lined the street were barely moving with the nighttime breeze that usually swept the air clean around the bay. The wind blew only within the upper part of the house, and the only things that were being destroyed were the protective devices she'd put up to keep them safe. It was, Fiona decided, obvious that they were under attack again. Something or someone wanted a way cleared so that it or they could enter the house.

Someone was talking. She could barely hear the words over the roar of the wind. "Soon. The path is being cleared. The balance will be restored."

She looked around for the source of the sound, but there was no one in sight. Even the street below her, lit by new streetlamps that barely illuminated the dark, was empty. She floated downward into the bedroom and then out to the hallway. There was a glow coming from the living room. There shouldn't have been any lights left on. She drifted down the stairs toward the illumination. She rounded the corner into the living room and saw the tiny box Selene had given her glowing eerily in the dark in the living room. She moved toward the box, her hand reaching out toward it.

"Mother, don't touch the box!" Megan's voice cut through the dream, warning her to stay away. She wanted to pull back, but the illumination drew her toward it. Her feet skimmed over the braided rug where she and Harper had made love. She wanted to stop, but it was impossible.

Fiona reached the box and Megan began to scream, trying to wake Harper. Fiona had lost control over her hands. She picked up the pretty trinket, turning it in her fingers. She felt a sharp tingling pain in her hands and looked down. The flesh was falling away from the bones everywhere the box had touched. She could see her skin cracking and separating just the way tomato skins did when she dipped them in hot water. Underneath, the blood vessels were sealed shut by the heat from the box. There was no blood, just flesh and bone.

Fiona stared stupidly at her ruined hand. Radiation burns, she thought; radiation would eat away flesh like that in a matter of minutes. But how had the box developed

enough energy to burn her when all it had done for days
was sit innocently on the mantel?

A crippling burst of agony knifed through her. She
screamed and tried to drop the box, but it had fused to her
bones. There was no way short of chopping off her fingers
to break free of the box or to make the burning pain stop.

"Help me!" she shrieked, but Megan had disappeared
and Harper couldn't hear her. She screamed again as the
pain burned up her arm and doubled her over with its intensity. "Please, make it stop!" In desperation she reached
for her sacred knife, the fingers of her left hand clutching at
the plastic handle, and she began to hack at her finger
bones.

"Make it stop," she cried. The pain of the burning box
was more than she could stand, but the agony of trying to
crack her own bones was enough to make her drop the
knife and collapse.

She grabbed the Ginsu and tried again. She didn't care
that she would never paint or that she would never be able
to stitch a quilt or soothe her daughter's head. She had to
make the box stop burning her.

It hurt, it hurt, it hurt. The litany of pain threatened to
overwhelm her.

The skin had long since tattered and fallen to the floor.
All that remained was the terrible sound of the bones chipping and breaking under the onslaught of the knife. One
finger broke free, and she retched with the anguish, then
went to work on the next one, propping her hand up against
the pine of the table. She'd never get the marks out of the
wood where the knife had cut through after breaking
through the bone.

A wind roared through the house, tossing leaves and
twigs at her as it slammed into the living room. She looked
for an open door, but everything was still tightly locked. It
all seemed to come from the box, which still glowed prettily
as it burned even deeper into her hand. The gale struck vi-

ciously at her face, but she didn't stop. She had to break loose before the box killed her.

Finally, the other bones shattered and the box hung by a slender ivory-white fragment.

She lifted the remains of her right hand with her left and flung the box upward, toward the window that looked out on the street. The box was heavy enough to break glass. It would be outside, away from her and her family.

As the bone snapped completely through, Megan appeared in front of her, her hands outstretched to help her mother. Fiona watched in horror as Megan stepped directly into the path of the box.

"No!" Fiona screamed, but there was nothing she could do to slow or change the trajectory. Megan didn't even see the box coming toward her before it struck her on the head.

Fiona wailed in heartbroken terror as the box began to burn through Megan's skull.

"Mommy, help me, Mommy, please don't let me die!" Megan cried. She reached up to dislodge the terrible thing on her forehead, but nothing could stop the metal that burned deeper and deeper into her head. The skull crunched and sizzled under the assault. The bone burned with a terrible smell. Then, worse than anything else, there was a bubbling sound as the box dug through the dura and into the brain itself. Megan's voice stilled. Her eyes stared at the ceiling, but there was no movement that indicated she could see anything any longer. The blood that should have been coursing down her face from the scalp wound was burned dry by the heat of the box as it worked its way deep into her brain. The sound of the brain boiling was the only noise in the room.

"No, oh God, *no,* please," Fiona wailed, and she caught her daughter's body as it collapsed to the floor. There was nothing left but the dead flesh. The blood had ceased and the heart had stopped. Megan was gone.

Around her the cats began to wail, a high keening sound

of absolute despair. They felt the pain of Megan's death and were crying for her to return, even though it was impossible.

"I hate you," Fiona shrieked. Desperately she pulled her mangled hand across Megan's forehead, trying to soothe her daughter's ravaged head, as if her touch might still bring her back. "You've taken it all. You've taken my beautiful wonderful child and I will not rest until I have destroyed you!"

The sound of laughter answered her.

Fiona sat straight up in bed, her heart hammering wildly in her chest. Her eyes were open, staring into the darkness as she gasped for breath and tried to fight her way out of the horrible nightmare.

"Mom, Mom, help me!" As in the dream, Megan's tortured voice rang through the house.

"It was only a bad dream. An awful one but nothing that can hurt me," Fiona said as she threw the covers back and ran toward Megan's room.

Megan was sitting up in bed cradling her head in her hands as she leaned forward. "It hurts, it hurts, it hurts. It feels like there's a box in there and it's trying to cut through and come out the back. I can't stand it any longer!"

Fiona stiffened at the description. No, it wasn't possible. It had only been a dream. Maybe Megan had been linked into Fiona's dream-images and had come up with the simile from them. It wouldn't be the first time they'd shared thoughts. There was no way the little metal and gold container could actually be in her brain doing damage.

"Let me go down and get a Dr. Pepper and some ice and then I'll hold your head and see if rubbing will do any good," Fiona said. She flexed her hand to make certain the nightmare hadn't left any physical manifestation of the ruination of her fingers.

"I'll be right back, all right?" She rubbed her hand across Megan's face in a soft caress.

She didn't need the soft drink and she hated to leave Megan alone for even a few minutes, but she had to see that damned box and convince herself that it wasn't waiting to attack. If it was just sitting there, like a proper container, she was going to have Harper drop it off on the front steps of the Major Arcana in the morning when he went to work. She wanted it out of the house.

There was no eerie light downstairs. She touched the gold and glass and her fingers didn't start to melt. Even more important, the box hadn't transported itself into Megan's brain to hurt her. It was only a dream.

She laughed at herself as she hurried into the kitchen, stepping over the pileup of cats who liked to sleep in the precise middle of the doorway where they could cause the most trouble. She got herself a Dr. Pepper and ice and hurried back upstairs.

Megan was hurting so much when she came back that she didn't even bother to move the girl into the other bed. Instead, she grabbed some extra pillows and crawled up onto Megan's bed, shoving aside the usual mess of books, magazines, catalogs and stuffed toys. Fiona didn't say a word about the clutter. Who knew how long her daughter was going to be around to make such a jumble.

"Possible metastasis to the rest of the brain." The words were still there right in front of her and her stomach lurched every time she thought of it.

"Mom, it hurts," Megan said, her voice soft with weariness. "If it doesn't stop, I can't go on. I'm worn out."

Fiona shushed her, rubbing her forehead with the rose mixture and knowing that even the best salve in the world would never soothe. Gradually she began to visualize the MRI she had seen at the doctor's office that afternoon, the one that had spelled death for Megan. There was something familiar about that pattern. Something she'd seen before, if she could only remember it.

She could see the bright spots on the film. The areas of

higher intensity that meant there were small tumors spread throughout the brain and no way to treat them.

"But now I know that I might be able to help if I can find the right way," Fiona said. She touched Megan's head again, probing with her mind through the scalp, past the shunt that ran between the scalp and the bone of the skull and into the softness of the brain itself.

Where had she seen those bright spots before?

She could practically feel the pain radiating from her daughter, and for one vivid moment she visualized what it would be like when Megan died.

No pain. That would be the first wish. Megan would be gone, but she'd be out of a pain that even morphine couldn't begin to touch. Her ready wit and ability to keep on no matter what obstacles were in front of her would finally have run down, battered into the ground by the unrelenting illness.

Fiona began to list the things that would never happen to Megan, each of them enough to make a mother weep with regret and lost wishes. No wedding. The pictures of wedding dresses Fiona had been saving since Megan was a small child could be thrown away. She'd never use the lace she had crocheted for the dress if Megan wanted it.

Megan would never know the loving attention of a husband who would revel in the delights of sexual intimacy.

No grandchildren.

"I don't want to die."

She should have known that Megan would pick up her gloomy thoughts. "You're not going to, not if I can help it," Fiona said firmly. For the first time, she thought, she might actually be telling the truth.

She forced her thoughts back to the MRI. She let her mind roam, and suddenly there it was before her.

"I'll be damned!" Fiona swore softly.

"What, Mom?"

"I have to get up," Fiona said. "I just had a really weird

idea. Can you manage for a few minutes until I get back? I promise, no more than three minutes max.''

Megan nodded weakly and sat up, leaning her head forward as if it weighed a thousand pounds.

Fiona raced into her studio and snatched up her workbook, in which she had tried to draw Selene and hadn't quite managed to get the figure or the face right. She flipped through the drawings, most of which were marred with dark splotches that she hadn't been able to erase. For a while she'd blamed the new pencils and charcoal Harper had given her. She'd tested the drawing instruments out by sketching several cats and the house she'd like to own, and there were no unexpected dark patches.

Fiona stared at the last picture of Selene, which she had left as it was. The splotches were there, all around Selene's head and face, and unless she was crazy, they matched the pattern of the brighter spots on Megan's MRI.

"Son of a bitch," she whispered. That was it. That was the answer. Harper had guessed part of it, but not the whole picture. She'd known another part and her own subconscious had been trying to tell her when she drew the picture that showed Asron and Selene and the rest of them all interconnected.

Selene and Asron were the evil Harper felt outside. They weren't just playing around; they wanted to control her and control her talents. By getting involved in witchcraft, she'd changed the balance that had kept everything together for Selene and Asron. She'd started throwing back some of the trouble that they'd been sending her way, and Selene had aged and Asron was coming down with bronchitis. Silly little things, but enough to show them that they weren't as powerful as they'd thought.

Stupid, irrational, naive—how could she have been such a fool as to think they'd just leave her alone? She'd grown and matured enough in her own potential to know she would be a real threat to them. She had become far more than a housewife playing with candles and simple spells.

Now all she had to do was find a way to stop everything and defeat Selene and Asron before they sacrificed her daughter to their own needs.

She looked around, hoping for a clue, then realized it was right there on the easel. She grabbed the large drawing of Selene and hurried into the bedroom, where she propped it up on the old dresser and then ran downstairs to grab the tiny jeweled metallic container.

The box was gone.

"Damnation, cats, what have you done with it?" she demanded, expecting an answer. She started looking on the wood floor. It should have been very easy to find. The container was extraordinarily heavy and it was unlikely that the cats had been able to knock it off the mantel and onto the floor and bat it into an inaccessible hiding place for retrieval later on.

She got down on her hands and knees and looked under the hutch and the dry sink. She even looked down the air duct grating, but the box simply wasn't in the living room any longer.

Finally Fiona gave up and went back upstairs. "The picture will just have to do."

She sat back down with Megan's head on her lap.

She closed her eyes and began to concentrate. She knew now that the use of her power didn't need any ritual. All she had to do was to use the pictures in her mind and control the way they flowed and changed. Slowly she worked her way into Megan's brain again. She damped the pain because the waves of sheer agony that pulsated up from her daughter would have done nothing but distract her from her final goal.

She looked at her mental photograph of the MRI again and located the spots in Megan's brain. She compared them to the sketch she had brought in and placed beside Selene's portrait. They were the same, but reversed, like a negative.

"I'll see you in hell, bitch," Fiona said, as she gently began the work of dislodging the cancerous cells from Megan's brain and sending them back where they belonged. As she worked, the picture of Selene began to change subtly. She had drawn the woman as she had looked the first time she'd met her, without a wrinkle on her face or a bit of scraggly white old-woman's hair on her head. Fiona sent the cancer into Selene's body, letting the cells proliferate everywhere they touched. The portrait began to shift as the woman bent and bloated with the effects of the cancer.

There was a peculiar high hum in the room. Outside, the storm, which had slowed to the steady drip of the mist, began a new onslaught. Lightning and thunder roared across the valley and into the hills and the rain poured out of the sky again.

Slow. The work was so slow. She didn't think she could finish it tonight, and maybe not even at the end of the week. But surely she had been able to do some good with her powers. She had wrapped Megan in her aura and kept her safe while she worked. She knew she had felt the cancers diminish in size. She'd managed to reduce some of the pressure within the brain, and Megan finally relaxed after the torment of the day.

Fiona's hands dropped, exhausted, as she came back to the real world and the sound of someone pounding on the door downstairs.

25

"What the hell is that?" Harper woke up out of a sound sleep and called out to Fiona. The pounding continued.

Someone was beating so hard on the front door that it sounded as if the wood were splintering under the impact.

"Harper?" What if someone was coming to stop her from sending the bad luck and illness back to Selene and Asron, where it belonged? She wouldn't stop, no matter what anyone did. Let Selene deal with her own troubles instead of pushing them off on someone else as she had for years.

"What time is it?" Harper asked.

Fiona looked over at the clock.

"Three-thirty. And knowing what time it is isn't going to make whoever is downstairs quit making noise."

Megan slept, resting for the first time in days after Fiona had relieved some of the pressure within her daughter's head. Fiona sincerely hoped that Selene had the all-time biggest headache in the world as payback for what she'd tried to do to Megan.

Fiona and Harper hurried down the stairs.

"Fiona!" Gia spun into the room, pushed by the violence of the storm. Elf followed a little more slowly; the wind couldn't push his bulkier body quite so hard.

"What are you doing here?" Fiona asked.

Fiona stared at her ex-friend. She wasn't going to hold out her hands in greeting. She wasn't going to run over and embrace Gia. She'd wait until she was certain why Gia was there, as a friend or a traitor.

"Were you sent by Selene and Asron, by any chance? Because if you were, it's not going to work."

"No, Selene and Asron have nothing to do with me anymore."

Gia tried to wipe her face, but there wasn't an inch of dry clothing or flesh anywhere on her. Harper saw her predicament and handed her a kitchen towel. She accepted the cloth, but still looked worriedly toward Fiona, waiting for her to say something, anything at all, that would constitute a greeting.

Nothing was forthcoming.

Finally, uncomfortable with the lengthening silence, Gia smiled brightly and began to say the speech she had prepared on the way over in Elf's car.

"I'm sorry for what happened in the park and for the last few weeks when I got all wrapped up with Asron and Selene. I was wrong and stupid. Please forgive me."

She walked over to Fiona, who stood with her hands at her sides. Gia waited a few seconds, and then, despite her friend's obvious hesitation, reached up and hugged Fiona.

Fiona held back for just a second, then finally responded to Gia's embrace.

"I had to come over and apologize and beg you to forgive me for what I did. You have no idea what was going on with me," Gia said as she linked her arm through Fiona's. "I mean, curses and spells and such aren't just imagination, they really happen, because they did to me." She swiped at her face again and then ended by shaking her head to get rid of the water that kept dripping off her spiky hair. "Oh Fiona, I've missed you."

"I've missed you, too. But please forgive me if it takes a little while for me to warm up after all the things that have happened. I'd particularly like to know what made you and Elf come over here in the middle of a storm and in the middle of the night."

"Elf said you needed us. He also said that we had to leave the house, because it didn't feel safe. And terrible things have been happening. I'll tell you all about what Selene did to Larry when this is over. I don't think I can talk about it right now." Gia suddenly looked older.

"I'm glad for the visit, even if it is at an odd time. And I'm glad that you seem to have broken free of some bad influences. But what would make Elf say we needed him, when he's only met me once and never even seen Harper?"

Harper stepped forward and peered closely at the man who until then had been standing in the shadows.

"Oh, now I understand. You're the assistance I asked for," Harper said, suddenly smiling. "I apologize, I didn't recognize you."

"You know, we've been working together for a while, it just took us some time to link up. I knew when I first met Gia that this whole mess could end in a hell of a fight," Elf said. "We're the same kind of men, you and I. I hope it's enough."

"You are gladly received," Harper said. He shook Elf's hand. It was a formal gesture and had the look of ancient ritual.

Elf turned toward Fiona and ran his hands near Fiona's head. "A weather witch! I haven't seen one of you for ages," he said, clapping Fiona on the shoulder as if she were his long-lost friend. She staggered under the blow. It was obvious he didn't know what power he had in his hands. "You've stirred up quite a few storms this past couple of weeks. I wish you'd stop now; my house is getting water-logged."

"Weather witch?" Fiona asked faintly.

"Sure. You called the storms. Haven't you been listening to the radio, lady? There are inches of water out there; the forecasters have never seen storms just come in from out of the blue, and it's all because you sit down and get depressed or whatever you do, and you call the storms in."

"Right," Fiona said. She didn't want to embarrass the man; it was obvious he believed what he was saying, but what he was saying was a lot of nonsense. She'd never called in a storm in her life, and to think that she was responsible for single-handedly breaking California's drought was ludicrous.

"Once this is all over, you're going to show me how you do it. I've always wanted to bring rain at my command, especially here in California. But we have other stuff to do first."

Suddenly the door flew open again, pushed by the wind and aided by a faulty latch that never quite caught right the first time the door closed. Elf put all his muscle into closing the door.

"I don't like the feel of it out there. They're all around, just waiting for a chance to strike. We'd better set up our borders and protect ourselves." He reached into his pocket and took out a handful of what looked like tiny chipped rock arrowheads. He handed one to Harper and one to Fiona.

"Don't you have a daughter? She should have one of these, too. I think things are going to get rather difficult around here before they get better and this is a useful shield."

"How darling, but what are they for?" Fiona asked, turning the tiny black arrowhead in her hand. The tip was sharp enough to puncture her finger.

"Elf arrows that were made sometime in the past by

chipping flint. They're charged in a magic circle and pick up enough energy to protect the person holding the arrow against assault. The arrows have been in the family for generations, passed down through my mother's family."

"I'll take this up to Megan," Fiona said, grateful for even the help of a tiny flint arrowhead.

Megan was awake and in pain again. "It's back. For the first time in years I didn't have a headache and then it's hurting even worse than it was," she said.

Fiona whirled and looked at the picture of Selene. Sure enough, Selene had ceased to age. In fact, some of the spots that had darkened as Fiona worked to send the illness back to the older woman had begun to bleach out again until Selene's hair and head looked almost normal.

"My head hurts so bad I think I'm going to die," Megan said. "I can't stay in bed, I can't walk, I can't talk, it all hurts too much."

"Why don't you come downstairs? I think we need you with us," Fiona said.

She put her arm around her daughter's waist and was shocked at how thin she had suddenly become. She could feel Megan's ribcage even through the sweats her daughter had on. Her arms were so thin that Fiona would have broken them if she'd squeezed hard.

When had Megan lost all the weight? The changes seemed to have happened almost overnight.

Megan barely made it downstairs. She slumped in the corner of the couch, propping herself up on the pillows and staring with agony-fogged eyes at Gia and Elf. She clutched the little arrow in her hand and was comforted by the warmth of the flint.

Elf moved around the kitchen and family room, peering into corners and shaking his head.

"Focus," he muttered. He put his hand on Gia first, and shook his head. He moved on to Harper, Fiona and finally Megan.

"What do you mean, focus?" Fiona said as he touched Megan's face.

"Those bastards are focusing on something. They are determined to regain the control they had and they will stop at nothing to bring the situation back to what they consider normal. You've confused them by calling the storm and doing something else with Megan, but they're still trying to regain supremacy. Now we need to find out what they are using to try to return everything to the way it was. We need to know what they're using as a focal point, and we might be able to turn the effects back on them."

Harper moved close to his daughter. "Megan's one point, but I don't know if we can use her. She's too fragile right now to withstand much of a buffeting." Only Fiona could see the despair in his eyes as he looked down at her and saw the pallor of her skin and the way the flesh hung on her bones.

"She's going to die if they keep up what they're doing to her," Elf pointed out.

Harper closed his eyes for just a moment, as if he couldn't bring himself to acknowledge that what Elf said was true. "I guess you're right. We have male and female, Nordic and Celtic. Surely that should bring enough strength for us to win."

"Maybe," Elf said.

"Guys, could you stop for just a minute and explain to me what's going on?" Fiona asked.

Harper took pity on her. "Remember the day I stood in the shower and chanted in Welsh? You looked in and then went away, and I've always had the feeling that you saw something that scared you."

"I did. Figures in the fog," Fiona said, remembering the day vividly.

"I was calling for help because I knew you had started something that wouldn't end without a cataclysmic fight. I knew, far more than you did, that your gifts were finally beginning to unfold. There was no way to stop you, no matter how much I wished for you to go back to the woman who had never even heard of the Old Religion. I needed help to put everything back in balance, but in our favor. Elf is that help. Now that Elf is here, we need to begin to map out our plan of attack."

Elf nodded. "Even with planning and talent, we're still not certain that we can win, but we'll give it a hell of a try. First we have to find out what exactly Selene and Asron are using to dump their bad energy into this house and this family, and then we've got to negate it. And hope like hell they don't come roaring down on us because we've gone one step too far."

"We know Megan's one focal point, because they're pushing the cancer onto her to get it out of Selene," Fiona said. "And I think the other point is the portrait. I used it to push back the energy toward Selene."

"That's it!" Elf said. "Bring down the portrait and we'll work with you to put such a reverse whammy on that picture that Selene will never be able to even look at it."

The lights blinked out with the crack of thunder and a fresh deluge of rain. The house seemed to shake, moving almost imperceptibly on its foundation. There was an eerie shrieking from outside.

"Fiona, you can stop now. We're all here, we're going to help. Will you please tell the rain to back off?" Elf asked in exasperation.

"But I don't know how I'm doing it, so I don't know how to make it stop," Fiona said. "I think you're wrong, I don't think that storm is coming from me. Or at least not all from me."

Elf looked at her sharply. "Feedback. Could it be?" He had been pacing behind the couch where Megan was and running his hand down between the cushions. He gave a startled snort and grabbed something that looked like a small red crocheted piece of yarn.

"Selene again?" he asked.

"She did sit there. What is it?"

"A hex, a kind of throwing of Runes at you, something to bollix up your daily life until you can't work at all. It probably stopped you from doing anything other than the portrait."

Harper took the yarn from Elf, turned the burner under the cast-iron skillet to high and waited until the burner was deep red before throwing the yarn into the pan. The yarn flamed weakly and was almost out when it suddenly seemed to take on a life of its own. It bounced in the pan. It sizzled and then shot straight up and exploded into flames at the top of the arc. The cast-iron pan below broke neatly in half, both parts falling to the floor and narrowly missing Harper's feet. The wood underneath the pan began to scorch. Fiona, sensing disaster for her pride and joy, threw water on the pan to save the pine-plank floor.

"One down. There are a couple more," Elf said, rubbing his hands briskly.

He walked out into the living room and headed directly for the mantel. Fiona was about to tell him that there wasn't anything there to bother with when she saw that the box had reappeared where it most assuredly had not been one hour before. The beautiful container was glowing, as it had done in her nightmare.

Princess screamed and arched her back toward the mantel, and then, in one prodigious leap, elevated herself six feet to land on the wood beside the box. The container took on a life of its own and began to rock gently and to gleam with a white-hot fire.

"No you don't. We've found you now. We'll cleanse this place no matter what you've tried." Elf cast an arrow toward the container.

There was a flash as unbearably intense light and heat washed over the room. Fiona could see small fires starting all around her as the curtains and woolen carpet began to smolder and burn.

Princess yowled in pain, but stood at her post, trying to knock the box off the mantel and away from Fiona.

Elf and Harper stood their ground. They extended their hands and the box exploded, flinging shards of metal around the room.

Fiona whirled, shielding the cat, taking the brunt of the debris across her back. She could feel the fiery pieces of metal cutting into her. She heard Princess scream once in a terribly high voice, and then the cat's small body became a dead weight in her arms.

"Oh, Princess," Fiona cried and cradled the animal in her arms.

Harper and Elf were chanting something, and the fire diminished and snuffed out as their voices rolled through the room. The curtains still smoldered and the braided rug had a burned patch, but there were no more flames. Fiona straightened as Harper and Elf passed their hands over her back. The fire was gone as if it had never existed. The fragments of metal fell harmlessly from her shirt, leaving the cloth intact.

The cat in her arms stretched, yawned and jumped down. Fiona watched in amazement as Princess sauntered up the stairs into the darkness.

Harper and Elf picked up scraps of metal and threw them out the front door. Both of them together could hardly close the door against the storm.

"One more control shot to hell," Harper said in satisfaction. "Fiona, go get the portrait. It's time to do some work."

"I'm beginning to think that we might win after all," Elf said. He was obviously satisfied with what they'd just done.

26

Elf, Harper, Gia and Fiona clasped hands in the middle of the circle. The yellow candles flickered and the iron and flint Thor's hammer Elf had added to the collection on the table gleamed in the reflected light. Harper added a coin he had always carried. Fiona had never thought anything about it; now he announced that it was an old Gypsy talisman from long before Christ, probably worth a mint now and imbued with the power of generations of his people. A fist-sized piece of pink wax stood near the candles, warmed gently by the flames.

The portrait of Selene was leaning against the dry sink, and Megan sat in the circle of their arms, resting her head on the back of the small couch. The pain had been intensifying with each passing minute. She'd taken as much morphine as she could, and still there was no relief. Tears leaked from underneath her eyelashes as she tried to survive from minute to minute, with no end in sight.

"The idea is very simple," Elf said when they had finished with an invocation to the four elements and the gods and goddesses whose protection they were asking tonight.

"We need to hit them so hard and so fast as a single power that they can't defend against us. They must not have any idea that we've joined forces until the very moment when we obliterate them. Until now, they've only been dealing with Fiona and Gia on their own. I'm hoping that Harper and I are the unknown factors that will swing everything toward us. But you need to realize that if you give them any warning at all, they'll strike back fast and we might not come out alive. Sneak attack is the only way to win. Follow Fiona where she goes and help her. She's the key."

Harper looked around the circle toward Fiona and Gia. "Do you understand what you should do?" He was ready to go over everything again if necessary.

"Fiona and I push the cancer back into Selene with all our force. Megan just stays in one place and lets us work on her, and you and Elf are going to protect us while we work. Then you'll do your spell-casting against Asron."

"That's it," Harper said. "With our hands joined, start the work on the count of three. Whatever you do, don't let loose while Fiona is working on Selene."

"What if they try to stop us?"

"We'll hit them with everything we've got and drive them into the dark place. Let your mind follow me if that happens; I know the way in and back," Harper said.

Fiona didn't ask how he'd found the dark place and come back from it.

Fiona found it slightly more difficult to visualize what she was doing with other people around, but within a few seconds she had the MRI and Selene's portrait lined up in her mind. This couldn't be the delicate work she had done before. This time all she could do was grab and throw as fast as she could.

Fiona used every bit of knowledge she'd gleaned from the visits to the oncologist to strike back at Selene. First a cluster of cells to the bone marrow in her hip—that was a good place, it would spread swiftly from there. Next a whole batch to her breasts, making them lumpy and painful within a matter of seconds. The thyroid and the pancreas were the next targets. Even if everything else could have been controlled by conventional methods, Fiona knew that the pancreatic cancer would not allow Selene to last more than a few months. The death would be swift and terrible and very painful. It was exactly what Fiona wished for the woman.

Fiona barely heard the soft chanting of the people in the circle. For the most part she was almost as lost to the real world as Megan was.

Fiona slumped forward, almost breaking the circle, when she finally managed to heal the last place in her daughter's brain.

"Thirty-nine seconds," Elf said in satisfaction. "Now we have to hit Asron. We can separate now, but stay within the circle."

Elf picked up the wax from the altar and began to fashion something out of it. He rolled the wax until it was about six inches long and smooth and then added two blobs to one end and made a small bulb at the other end.

"Asron's penis!" Gia declared, when she finally got a good look at it. "And a very good replica, too."

Elf handed the wax to Gia. "Hold this and think about Asron. Are there any flaws, any particular things that we need to know about his penis to make this spell work?"

Gia picked up the pink wax and ran her hand up and down it. For a moment there seemed to be a flicker of regret. She smoothed the head and made it slightly larger and then pinched up a piece of the wax into what looked like a wart on the right side near the base. "That's as good as I can do. I think it's accurate," she said, handing it back to Elf.

Harper had already brewed some kind of infusion using several of the nastier-smelling herbs Fiona had grown over the last few years. He poured the hot tea slowly over the model and into Fiona's best copper bowl, which she had lent to the ceremony.

"Take away the prick so that it cannot penetrate, take away the thick so it cannot satisfy, take away the sensation so he may never feel another woman's substance, take away the manhood forever," Harper and Elf said and then lapsed into another language. They were working fast.

The men chanted and the smell of a new incense they had added to the burner filled the room with a sickly-sweet scent of dead roses and something else that was just slightly acrid. As Harper poured the tea over the wax the penis began to droop and drip until the replica turned to liquid and made a horrible mess in the bottom of the copper bowl. Harper, Fiona noted, looked absolutely comfortable and quite happy as he went about his work.

The men were just about finished with the last of the spell when there was an almighty crash at the front door.

"Oh, not again." Fiona started toward the door to push it closed again. Only Harper's hand on her shoulder kept her firmly inside the circle.

"What?" Fiona was stunned as the stained-glass panel in the door shattered and the hinges began to bend and then break under the force of the assault.

The whole house began to groan, protesting the attack. It moved slightly, pivoting on its corners, and there was a sinking sensation that made Fiona's stomach dive with it. Fiona screamed and grabbed Megan as the door gave one last shriek of wood and metal and burst inward, scattering debris into the room.

"You will stop now," Asron said, pushing his way through the shattered door. "You are in more danger than you know." He waved his hand and the box appeared, spinning in the air. He laughed when Fiona recoiled. With another flick of his hand, the box disappeared. Asron was grinning like a shark.

The whole world had suddenly taken on a surrealistic color. Asron in her living room, dripping all over her nice clean floor and her door smashed beyond redemption. Selene right behind him, looking older than she ever had.

"I'm here for my portrait," Selene said, almost shouting to be heard above the tumult outside. She was smiling as if nothing at all had happened. "We have to have it for the opening tomorrow. I knew you wouldn't mind if we dropped by."

Selene sounded as if she'd just come over for a cup of coffee.

"I'm afraid that's not going to be possible," Harper said. "The picture isn't quite what you'd expect."

Selene advanced into the room. Like magic, the lights flickered back on, illuminating the area and the painting on the dry sink.

"It's perfect," Selene said. "I think it's just what I want. There's nothing wrong with it at all." She reached for the painting. Fiona saw that her hands had become old and gnarled almost overnight.

"No!" Fiona said, but she moved too slowly to stop the older woman. Selene touched the charcoal-and-pencil portrait and then howled in pain. She grabbed her hand and held it against her breast as if something had bitten her.

"What have you done?" She whirled and glared at Elf and Harper. "Someone has ruined my picture!"

"Not any more than you wanted to ruin Fiona and Megan," Harper said.

"You, you did something! I knew you were dangerous when I sensed you in the house. I should have killed you long ago. What is it?" she demanded.

"I witched it. The charcoals and pencils Fiona used were made with a spell to reveal what you really were and to bind your spirit into the drawing. Every time she drew you she caught some of your soul in the painting. It didn't matter whether it was a sketch or the real portrait. Every line tied you into that painting so tightly that you'll never be completely free again. We'll always have a little control over you and Asron!"

"No, you can't do that, it wasn't supposed to work that way!"

"No, it wasn't, was it?" Fiona said. "You were going to take part of me, a part of the talent that I used to draw you and use it to restore the balance, weren't you?"

"Yes!" Selene hissed, her normally white skin suffused with red. "I will be successful in this battle. It has been promised to me."

Selene and Asron clasped hands and advanced on them. Fiona began to feel an almost physical pressure against her head. She could feel the blast as they tried to reverse all the changes the group had wrought.

"Stand fast," Elf said, his voice carrying only to the circle.

Asron laughed. "It won't do you any good. I will take everything from you, leaving nothing but ashes where your house and family have been, if you do not put things back the way they were."

"Give up now and I might even let you live!" Selene offered. She tried to touch Harper on the arm with her free hand, but drew back before she penetrated the outer ring of the circle. "You cannot win."

Harper drew back in distaste. He knew women like her, horrible old crones who feasted on souls. They left nothing, not even the bones, after they had their feast of carrion.

"Watch out," Elf said as Asron spread his hands and loosed a ball of lightning in the room. The fire raced from curtain to curtain, knocked the telephone off the wall and exploded something in the microwave. It raced through the circle and chased around the center of the altar, knocking down everything that had been so lovingly empowered to help the friends defeat Asron and Selene.

Fire began to lick again at the curtains. Fiona looked

around and saw that the cats were escaping out into the night, led by Princess. "My cats!" she cried. They'd never know what to do; they were indoor cats. They'd never survive a thunderstorm.

She tried to cross the circle, but couldn't move past the safety of the ring. Harper held her arm, keeping her from breaking away.

"Leave them. They'll be able to take care of themselves." Harper's voice was low and urgent. "We need you now."

She couldn't save her cats; she couldn't save her house from the flames that were still working their way up the curtains and had begun to eat into the ceiling. What had the firemen told her—no more than three minutes before a fire took hold and roared through a house? And no one was doing anything to stop the holocaust!

"Harper, we have to get out of here." If she couldn't save the house, she could at least save her husband and child.

"You're not going anywhere, darling," Selene said. "Not until you've been locked in a psychic straitjacket that you'll never get out of. It might take burning you like the Salem witches, but we will triumph. You'll see. I'll destroy this and you'll have nothing of me." Then she was past them, moving more quickly than Fiona had thought possible as she snatched the portrait. Selene cried out as she took the painting; it was obvious that it hurt her to touch it.

She backed up toward Fiona.

Quickly Fiona sketched a cut in the circle and slugged the woman.

Selene yelled and slid backward, landing in a heap on the floor. She grabbed at Fiona's ankles to pull her off balance.

Fiona managed to land a blow to Selene's head, leaving the older woman retching with the force of the impact. Still Selene fought. "Take it back, take it all back. I will not have cancer, do you hear me? I was promised that my afflictions would be lifted." Selene crawled toward Megan.

"Don't you dare, you malicious old monster!" Gia, true to her fondest dream of becoming a knife-wielding murderess, grabbed the magical athame, the ritual knife that was never supposed to be used for anything except the highest magic, and began slicing bits of people and clothing off if they came too near to her or to Megan. She took a divot out of Selene's arm and another one from Asron's front, altogether too close for his comfort to the part they had been cursing when they melted the wax.

Gradually the tide began to turn. Harper and Elf were more than a match for Asron, no matter how strong he was supposed to be.

Megan was still moaning in the middle of the circle, and Elf had taken up his Thor's hammer and was swinging it by the leather thong to keep Asron at bay.

"Why are you fighting like this? All you are doing is prolonging the suffering," Selene screamed at Fiona. "I will kill everything you've ever loved if you do not stop practicing magic and let everything settle back into the way it once was. No one will ever defeat me, for I am the one with the power over all others. My goddess has told me this." She hugged the portrait to her breast.

Fiona knew there wasn't another instant to lose. No one else could stop this woman. She finally knew what Selene feared—she feared being old and dying. She didn't realize she was no longer the Selene she had been a hundred years before. With every life she stole, she stole vitality and personality that mixed with her own, diluting her.

That's why I couldn't get a clear feeling for her, Fiona thought. She's all those poor suckers mixed into one body.

"Gia, Elf, together. Harper, reach for me," Fiona said. She didn't know whether Elf and Gia could hear her, but she knew her link to Harper had never been stronger. She felt his hand in hers, warm and strong.

Selene raised her hand again toward Megan, and Fiona let loose.

Holding Harper's hand, she took him with her into the place where she went to murder people.

She looked deep inside Selene, scanning her for weaknesses. The cancer was there, but it was too slow. She had to find something that would kill Selene immediately.

Selene began to squeal like a pig when she realized what Fiona was doing to her. She fought back. Fiona could feel the pressure as Selene squirmed and struggled. Fiona's head hurt and felt as if it would explode under the force. She wanted to retreat, but she knew she would die if she did withdraw. Instead, she raced through Selene's body, looking for something she could use against her. Selene pushed her back and Asron joined the struggle for survival.

Selene wasn't only Selene. Fiona's perceptions had been right. Inside that old woman, there were others who had been used in her search for eternal life. They pleaded to be let free so that they could die.

"I'll try to help," Fiona promised.

Then she found it. The one place she could attack, the one place Selene was not guarding.

She moved with absolute accuracy, weaving through the patterns of force Selene and Asron erected to try to stop her.

The fury of Selene and Asron's assault doubled and then tripled.

Fiona felt them holding her and realized they were trying to trap her and the others as they fought.

There was an ominous rumble and the house shook again for a moment before settling back on its foundation. Fiona couldn't be bothered. The rest of the world was going to have to go on without her until she managed to defeat her enemy.

She gave one last lunge through the mists and battlements and began to press against the carotid artery. She could feel the blood fighting to reach the brain, but she kept up the pressure. It wasn't hard; the vessels were already damaged and once the arterial walls came together, they stuck fast, the fat acting like glue. The thin tissue stretched to the limit of its tolerance and then the vein began to split. Selene choked and her eyes rolled back in her head.

Asron screamed when he realized he'd missed his chance to get out. He was forever trapped inside Selene's body.

"But she promised we would win!" he cried, before even his voice faded and died.

There was the faintest sound of laughter above the wind and rain, as a tantalizingly familiar voice cried out, "I lied again!"

27

The house began to shake and a deep rumbling roar of destruction headed directly toward the living room. Elf and Gia scrambled to their feet. Harper and Fiona turned to Megan, shielding her from whatever was coming.

The roar increased, thundering toward them. The sound—it was the way Harper had described the mountain moving.

"Harper, Megan, get outside, quick," Fiona screamed, pulling at her husband and daughter. She knew what was happening. It was no earthquake. The hillside behind them, sodden with rains, had begun to move.

The house began to groan as beams were torn from beams and the stucco and two-by-four fir strips shattered under the massive weight of the mountain. The glass in the back door exploded and Fiona heard the slither of the mountain as it pressed inward, taking everything with it. The wall of the living room began to screech as the plasterboard ripped away from the wall and fell toward them.

"Harper, Megan—" The house was shaking so hard she

couldn't get to her feet. All she could do was hold on to her husband and child.

Then, suddenly, Fiona was engulfed in utter darkness. Harper and Megan were ripped out of her hands. There was a sliding sensation and cold wet mud pressed in on her, making it impossible to breathe. The muck surged into her nose. She knew if she opened her mouth to scream, she'd fill her lungs with mud. The pressure against her chest was more than she could bear and she fought against the weight of the mountain sitting on top of her. There was one last heave and the mud coughed her out onto the sidewalk in front of the house. The river of silt separated around her old van and roared on down the hillside toward the houses across the street.

"Well, well, look what the mud brought out. Damn shame you survived. And a damn shame Carl's such a lousy shot. It would have been so much easier if you'd just died in the fire. Hell, it would have been easier if you'd stayed at the ceremony and let Asron and Selene bind you to them. But no, you had to run, and Carl had to shoot you in front of the whole neighborhood. Bad for our reputations. We'd have paid a little something to Harper and Megan, and they'd have gone on without you, and no one would have been the wiser."

Fiona looked up, digging the mud out of her eyes to see who was talking. "Sally?"

Sally, dressed in her best tight jeans and Neiman Marcus cowboy shirt, stood above her, tossing a green and gold box into the air. It gleamed malevolently as it reached the top of its arc and came back down, landing neatly in Sally's outstretched hand. She smiled and pushed back a strand of her perfectly cut blond hair. Four huge stones gleamed on various fingers, competing with the glow from the box. Even in the middle of a disaster she looked cool and collected.

"Sally, what do you mean?"

"You're so stupid. We lost Asron and Selene in the battle, but that's all right. They were getting old and losing their powers anyway. You didn't think they were the brains behind this, did you?" Sally snickered.

"What are you talking about?" Fiona repeated stupidly.

"Oh, I know what it is, all right," Sally said. "I told you to leave it alone. I stopped you when you began to flex your infant powers on the Ouija board. Then when you started playing around a few weeks ago I tried to stop you again. When Selene was diagnosed with cancer, I thought what marvelous luck, we can send it to Megan and you'll be so wrapped up in her you won't even think of rituals and ceremonies again. Every time you took a step forward in learning what you could do I sent you more trouble. But no, you decided to be stubborn. You had to keep going until someone died."

Sally pointed a languid hand toward the rubble of the house. "You provided the water, all I had to do was provide the push. I had it planned for weeks, just in case you got completely out of hand. Don't you understand? I've been trying to keep you from finding out what you could do. In the beginning, when you were a child, it was easy. A few spankings, your mother getting upset, a teacher who called you a pagan—you forgot all about your powers until years later."

Of course it couldn't be, Fiona thought. But the face of the teacher who had accused her was etched clearly in her mind. With a different hairdo and a different dress, the woman was Sally.

"And now?"

"I thought brute force would work. If Megan and killing the skunks didn't stop you from learning how to use your talents, I figure killing your family would. I almost got you and Harper both with the lightning, but he knew how to protect you, damn it. But I finished the job anyway, didn't I?"

"You couldn't have. You're just a woman, just like me."

"Hardly," Sally snorted. "Now I'm warning you. You've lost your family, you've lost everything you love, all for the sake of power. If you persist, it will cost you your life."

Sally turned and walked away. As she reached the entrance to her house, she simply disappeared.

"You've lost everything you love." The words rang in Fiona's mind as she shook her head, and finally, still dazed and terrified, she turned back to look at the house.

A thin wail whistled out of her throat. There was nothing where the house should be. At one end, she could see a few sticks and the remnants of the huge pine that had shaded her studio from the fierce summer sun. There were scraps of stucco and metal, but nothing else. It looked as if the mountain of mud had been squatting there forever.

Fiona's heart constricted, the pain making her cry out. Sally couldn't be right. She couldn't have lost everything.

"Harper, Megan, where are you?" She struggled upward, making her legs work whether they wanted to or not.

"You have to be alive!" she cried. She headed toward where the front door and the living room would have been. She clawed at the mud, finding a brick here and there from the fireplace, broken studs and stucco, but there was nothing to tell her what had happened to the people in her house.

What you send out will come back threefold. Be prepared for the consequences. Harper's words came back to haunt her.

"Fiona?" Gia approached her from down the street where she'd escaped.

Fiona turned and grabbed her friend fiercely. "Have you seen Harper? Is Megan all right? You were closer to them than I was. Where are they?" She was feverish in her intensity, almost forcing Gia to give her the answer she craved.

"No, Fiona," Gia said, her voice breaking. "No, they

aren't down there. Only Elf and I survived. We were caught under the pine table."

"My family!" Fiona screamed again, her heartbreak echoing down through the neighborhood, melding with the sound of the sirens that were coming closer and closer.

She grabbed a piece of shingle and attacked the mess, searching for a clue to where Harper and her daughter were.

"Oh God, Harper's hand." Fiona grabbed it, praying that it would be warm. It was cold and lifeless. There was no pulse and no feeling of life around him.

"Help me," she pleaded. Gia and Elf began to scoop up handfuls of the viscous mud until they'd removed enough to be able to lift his body. There was a thick ugly sucking sound as the mud gave up Harper's corpse.

Underneath him, they saw something move.

"Mom? What happened?" Megan whimpered as she reached up for her mother.

"Megan, oh my darling baby!" Fiona cried. Her daughter was alive for at least a few more minutes, a few more days. Sally was wrong; she hadn't taken away everything, not quite yet.

"What happened to Dad? Is he dead?"

"I don't know. Let me go to him. Gia will stay with you," Fiona lied. She did know. She knew Harper was dead, but she couldn't accept it.

"No, don't go over there." Elf tried to stop her, holding her back from the sodden mass of skin and bones that lay on the sidewalk. "You don't want to see him."

"Don't tell me I don't want to see him," Fiona said fiercely. "He is my husband, and I'll stay with him until I've had time to say goodbye, do you understand?" She pushed by him and knelt beside Harper's body.

Gently she cleaned the dirt from his face, looking down at the features she had loved for all the past years of this life and, it seemed, for lifetimes beyond that. It couldn't be over. It couldn't have ended this way. She loved him too much. He'd been alive a few short minutes ago; surely it couldn't all be taken away from her, could it?

His eyes were closed. She touched the fair eyebrows and lashes, which were much too long for any self-respecting man. She wiped the dirt out of his nose and mouth and then sat down and cradled his head and shoulders in her lap, just as she'd done when he wanted to rest on the couch and still be close to her while they watched television.

Her tears washed down over her face and onto his. What was left of the mud washed away in rivulets as she rocked back and forth, wishing him alive again.

She went into him, trying to find her beloved, but there was nothing there. He was cold and lifeless. The Harper she had known was gone. A soundless cry of absolute anguish tore through her. She couldn't bear it. She was left with only half of what she'd been an hour before. She had been split and tortured and half of her life had been snatched from her.

She held him close to her breast and began to sing the healing song she'd used on Megan so many times before. It wouldn't work; she knew in her rational self that he was gone; but she had to try.

If only she could have him back for just a moment out of time to tell him she was sorry and she'd never have hurt him, not for anything in the world. She'd never meant for something like this to happen.

Harper had known. He had realized that she was playing with everyone's life and he'd still tried to help her because it might have saved Megan. And in the end, it was his poor battered body that had saved their daughter's life. How could she bear the guilt?

"Harper, please, my love, come back," she crooned. She took his hand in hers and rubbed it against her face. She felt the calluses on his fingertips and wept that he would never touch her face again.

"Please, Harper, I can't live without you. I'll use all of

my power, I'll burn myself out with whatever is needed, if you can just come back for a moment with me."

She pushed into Harper, following his essence with every bit of energy she had. She went out into the universe and tried to bring back the power of a sun to heal him. She reached into the darkness and cried for his soul to come home again, where they could be together.

She found him.

It was just a whisper of Harper. He had gone away so far from her that he was almost lost. He had almost moved from one life to the next. A few more seconds and he would have been engulfed in the light that was waiting for him and she would have been forever bereft of her heart's love.

"Come back with me." She pulled at him, using every ounce of her strength to coax him back.

Now she knew why she'd found her gift of being able to leave her body and go hunting for other people. It wasn't to murder Animal Control people or the neighbor up the hill. It wasn't even to stop Selene and Asron or Sally and Carl. Everything she had done had been training for this purpose—she was to save Harper and bring him back to life.

They began to journey down the eons of past and future that awaited them. Some of the paths were what lay ahead for her if she came back alone; others were for them as a couple. As they traveled, Harper became stronger, his voice more sure, until finally she could touch him and knew that he was as he had always been. She had forced him back to life.

Harper chuckled. "I wanted to come back. I just needed help to do it, so I prompted you into saving me. You've never had an original thought in your life," he thought as he moved his cold hand against her face. She could feel the warmth return to his fingertips as the life blood began flowing through them again.

28

E lf and Gia slowed as they came to the fork in the road. The late-Thursday-afternoon traffic in Angels Camp allowed them to come almost to a complete stop before they had to decide on where they were going. It was a small town, and Fiona's place was in an even smaller town.

"I guess primitive is all right, now that Megan's finished with her therapy and on the road to recovery, but I'd hate to be this far away from the amenities of life," Gia said. "Like they say, once a city girl, always a city girl."

"Do they say that?" Elf asked.

"They do about me." She peered at the road ahead of them.

"Where do we turn?" Elf asked. "There's a Y up ahead and I don't want to take the wrong side."

"Turn left at the frog statue." Gia read the directions again to make certain she hadn't made a mistake. "There, that has to be it, right beside the Strawberry Patch ice cream store."

She pointed to a bronze statue of a goldminer and a frog

sharing the same pedestal. "Nine miles ahead turn right at Murphy's and come down Main Street until you see Granger Road, then left to the end of the road." Gia believed in giving directions long before they were needed.

She looked around as Elf drove up the winding road. She could see why this area appealed so much to Fiona; her friend had always wanted to live the bucolic existence that she painted. Gia, on the other hand, still loved the city, and more and more she was realizing how much she loved Elf. She wondered how Harper liked the life of a country gentleman. Fiona had said he was looking better than he ever had and that with the settlements on the accident in which Fiona's van had been rear-ended and the insurance on the house, as well as her artwork, they'd never have to worry about money again, even if Megan came out of remission and needed treatment again. Harper was making quite a nice living doing small coal carvings for galleries in San Francisco. It was a skill he'd learned as a child and it served him well now as he made intricate birdcages and boxes.

"Wouldn't you like to live up here?" Elf asked, catching at least part of Gia's thoughts.

"Nope. You've got the perfect place and I thank you for sharing it with me but I don't want to live in the mountains. Give me the clang of the cable cars and the fog rolling over good old city streets any time. I don't even want to be in the suburbs any longer, it's too weird there."

"You really don't miss the house at all?"

"Not a bit. I was so glad when I sold that house. Do you know, every time I walked in, it was like I expected Larry to be there. I'm sorry he died the way he did, but at least I don't have to deal with him any longer."

"You might have to deal with me. I was hoping that this weekend would be the one where you agree to marry me. The Runes came up Dagaz, for transformation day. I presume that means either we get married or I find myself someone else."

Gia was silent. He was pushing again. She'd asked him six months ago to just let her get over the changes in her life and he'd agreed. She'd spent the time learning to be around a man who didn't psychically or physically batter her. A man who was as kind and gentle as it was possible to be. A man who was in love with her.

So what's the hangup? Her conversations with herself always ended like this. She knew she needed to commit, and her huge mistake with Asron still hung over her.

But Elf still wants me, even after I made such a fool of myself, she told herself. And she'd just read the Tarot cards for the first time in six months right before they left, and the cards had told her that changes were coming and she'd better prepare herself.

They were just nosing into the front yard of Fiona's house when Gia made up her mind.

"All right," she said suddenly. "If Fiona can find a place that will marry us and if you can get the license tomorrow, we'll do it. Otherwise we'll get married in the city next week."

Elf almost wrecked the plush new Mercedes when he realized what Gia had said, then pulled to the side of Fiona's van and turned off the key to make certain he hadn't misheard over the purr of the engine.

"Do you mean it?" His voice was hushed, as if making too loud a sound would scare away the very thing he'd been wishing for. He turned toward her with a look of such stark hope in his eyes that Gia almost blushed.

That any man could look at her like that! What heaven, she thought. She'd be a fool to let this one get away. She kissed him and then pulled back as she heard a chorus of cheers from the front porch of Fiona's house.

"Welcome! Come in, tell us the news. You'd never be-

lieve how much I've missed you." Fiona hurried down the
wide wooden stairs of her Victorian house, past the white
rose in the old copper kettle and quite a few cats, and em-
braced Gia. "You've got to see what just came in the mail."
She ushered her friend inside to the long pine table in the
middle of the kitchen.

There in shining splendor was Fiona's own calendar.
Madge Lorenz had promised that the first copy to roll off
the Big Skies presses would be sent to Fiona, and she had
lived up to her word. Madge wasn't about to alienate her
hottest new artist by not doing everything she could to
make her happy.

Fiona had opened the calendar to her favorite picture,
the one of the house she now owned, with room enough in
the basement for the loom and spinning wheel, and plenty
of land for her cats and herself to wander in. Secluded, iso-
lated, protected, safe. Those had been the things she looked
for when Harper had finally recovered from his injuries
enough to go house hunting. They'd both agreed that
before they moved in they'd put new iron nails and rings all
around the house to keep it safe. There were special plants
at the north, south, east and west corners.

The front and back doors sported wheat wreaths hung
on iron nails. Harper had buried his old coin at the corner
of the house, and there had never been a speck of trouble in
the year they'd lived there.

Part of the house's good feeling came from their cats, all
of whom had been found after the slide, along with eight
new ones. Fiona had always suspected that the neighborhood kids who had been so diligent in rounding up the animals she'd advertised for might have accepted any cat
whose owners had tired of it. That was fine with her. There
was plenty of room, and the more animals the better. They
still guarded the house just as they had in the suburbs.

"What are these?" Gia picked up one of several small

cast-stone Siamese cats decorated with a fine gold necklace and sparkly gems.

"That's the Princess line. Madge Lorenz started developing it just as soon as she realized we were going to have a real winner on our hands with the Princess calendar. You wouldn't believe the amount of money they're paying me for preliminary design and I don't even have to do the hard work. Someone else makes the statues and does all the production chores. I made certain that Madge sent two of everything, so if you want a set, you can have one."

"Of course I want one of each." Gia hugged her friend again.

"God, I've missed talking to you every day,' Fiona said. "How are we going to live a hundred miles apart? Can't you move up here where we can run over for coffee every afternoon?"

"Wouldn't it be nice! But it's never going to happen. I just told Elf that I don't want to leave the city. I feel safe there, especially with him."

"Good. You deserve a nice man for a change."

"Oh, I have a present for you, too," Gia said, digging in her capacious bag. She pulled out a small wrapped rectangle and handed it to Fiona.

"Open it now?" Fiona asked.

"I'll die if you don't," Gia said.

Fiona slid the paper off the package to reveal a new romance, *Mountainside Mists,* by Gia Michaels.

"It's out? It's on the racks? Oh Gia, I'm so glad for you. The writer's block finally disappeared for good?"

"Not only that, I just signed another three-book contract, and everyone is happy that I'm back in business. I guess it was time we had some good luck."

"Come on, let the men talk while we have cocoa and doughnuts. I just made some this morning, knowing that you were coming." Fiona led her friend to the other end of

the table, where she'd already set out two of the mugs
Madge Lorenz had sent her. There was a pitcher of cocoa
and a mound of every kind of doughnut she'd been able to
think of. She knew that if Gia didn't eat everything, the men
certainly would.

"So how do you like it up here?" Gia asked. "Are you
far enough away from the Bay Area to make you feel safe?"

Fiona sat on the old pine chair she'd found at an auction
almost a year ago. The table had been made to replace the
one lost in the mudslide. She'd managed to pull the old rose
and kettle from the muck, but nothing else could be sal-
vaged.

"It's better. I still keep looking over my shoulder, and I
hear the name Sally and still feel like I'm going to go into
heart failure, but it's getting better. How about you?"

"I'm doing all right, too. Living with Elf helps. We do
our protection rites every morning and every night and it
seems to be working. But I don't go shopping at Neiman
Marcus, or even any place on Union Square, for fear that I
might run into Sally, and I turn and walk away when I see a
rich-looking blond."

"I know what you mean. Harper and I do our monthly
big-time rituals to keep everything safe. It's not bad,
though, since they include lots of sex and that's better than
we've ever had before. He's not tired and neither am I. It's
amazing what sleeping through the night can do to your li-
bido."

Fiona was silent for a few minutes as they munched
their way through several more doughnuts.

"I wish I knew for certain," Fiona said, looking out the
window at the two men who were enthralled with Harper's
newest toy, a riding lawn mower that was guaranteed to
take care of the greenery all the way back to their ten acres
of woods at the rear of the property. He'd been trying to
convince her to let him ride it in among the trees, but she

had told him sternly that woods were meant to be natural, not trimmed, and he'd finally given in.

"Knew what?" Gia asked.

"If it's really over."

There. She'd said it. She'd never dared say it to Harper, or to Megan. They'd simply been happy that their lives had finally taken a turn for the better. But Fiona had lain awake late at night. She'd waited for the nightmares that didn't come. She still expected them, though there had been no sign of Sally or Carl since the night of the disaster. She'd gone back to look at Sally and Carl's house, but the place was empty, stripped of everything that might have helped Fiona finally confront her enemy just to make sure that Sally couldn't hurt her family again. There had been no forwarding address and no way to trace them.

"Don't worry about it. Even if they come back, this time we know how to protect ourselves. But we ought to be putting together some kind of coven with a full complement of witches just to make sure we have enough energy surrounding us all the time. Five people really aren't enough."

"Oh, speaking of protection—Elf wants to learn about your weather witching. How about if you and he and Megan plan on a vacation in the city and he can work with you for a while to learn how you do what you do?"

Fiona shook her head. "No, we'd have to get someone to come in and take care of the cats. Instead, why don't you come up here for a vacation and we'll work through the weather things then?"

"I'll see if he can get a couple of weeks clear on the calendar. Do you really think you'd like to have me around for that long?" There was a certain note of wistfulness in Gia's voice.

A pounding on the door interrupted them.

Fiona opened the kitchen door. "Norma! What a nice

surprise," she said, ushering the other woman into the kitchen.

"Gia, this is my next-door neighbor from two miles down the road, Norma Blum." Fiona passed the doughnuts to Norma. Since the woman was even bigger than Fiona and since they shared the same enjoyment of good food, especially chocolate, Fiona knew she'd like the crispy dough circles.

"Do you have a plumber's snake?" Norma said as she licked the sugar off her lips. "My toilet backed up and then the electricity flickered and went off, and there's a smell of burned insulation. I'm going to have a hell of a time getting it fixed. And on top of that, I had to walk over because my tire's flat on the Jeep."

Gia and Fiona looked at each other, their eyes widening.

"Norma, does it seem that you've had an extraordinary run of bad luck lately?" Fiona asked.

"Have you been feeling desperate because killer budgets and prayers aren't working?" Gia asked.

They both leaned forward, waiting for the answer.

Norma's round face turned to one and then the other.

"Well . . ." She drew the word out. "It sure seems like I'm getting kind of desperate. Every time I think I'm going to come out ahead something bad happens. I've been looking everywhere for something that will help me keep my head above water, because I'm sinking fast right now. I've even been looking at those ads in the tabloids for answers. You know, tell me your problems and let the stars give you advice. Then I picked up a book on something called the Old Religion the last time I was in Stockton, and it really made sense, this worship of the gods and goddesses that are part of the earth. Hell, it's better than nothing."

Fiona and Gia stared at each other again and then turned back to Norma.

"Here, Norma, have another doughnut," Fiona said, passing the plate again. "We'd like to talk to you about a little group we're thinking of forming. It might be just the thing to help you through some of these problems you're having. Now, do you know what a coven is and do you have an unused Ginsu knife somewhere in your kitchen?"